A low chuck

Eyes widening, she drew her second sword and turned in a slow circle. "Damn it! Show yourself!"

"Well, since you asked so nicely," a deep voice laced with a French accent purred

Gasping, she spun

Once more, he cau

was gentle, carrying n

Krysta stared.

His touch sent elec

flesh was warm, his long fingers free of calluses.

Her heart slammed against her ribs as butterflies erupted in her stomach.

She should be furious. Frightened. Instead, she felt as excited as she would on a first date.

Crap.

Stepping back, she withdrew her arm from his grasp.

Dropping his hand, he tilted his head and studied her with those entrancing amber eyes.

Yeah, he was hot all right.

Short, midnight hair glinted in the moonlight. Faint stubble shadowed a strong jaw. Straight nose. Broad shoulders. What was clearly a well-developed, muscular build beneath a black T-shirt that clung to him courtesy of the vampire blood that saturated its front. Slim waist. Slim hips. All revealed by the gap in the long, black coat he wore.

She didn't let her gaze stray farther. The last thing she wanted to do while facing him was blush like a schoolgirl if he had a nice package.

His tempting lips stretched in a slow smile.

Also by Dianne Duvall

DARKNESS DAWNS

NIGHT REIGNS

PHANTOM SHADOWS

PREDATORY
(with Alexandra Ivy, Nina Bangs, and Hannah Jayne)

Published by Kensington Publishing Corporation

DARKNESS RISES

IMMORTAL GUARDIANS

Dianne Duvall

ZEBRA BOOKS
KENSINGTON PUBLISHING CORP.
http://www.kensingtonbooks.com

ZEBRA BOOKS are published by

Kensington Publishing Corp.
119 West 40th Street
New York, NY 10018

All Kensington titles, imprints, and distributed lines are available at special quantity discounts for bulk purchases for sales promotion, premiums, fund-raising, educational, or institutional use.

Special book excerpts or customized printings can also be created to fit specific needs. For details, write or phone the office of the Kensington Special Sales Manager: Attn. Special Sales Department. Kensington Publishing Corp., 119 West 40th Street, New York, NY 10018. Phone: 1-800-221-2647.

Zebra and the Z logo Reg. U.S. Pat. & TM Off.

ISBN-13: 978-1-4201-2978-6
ISBN-10: 1-4201-2978-3
First Printing: October 2013

eISBN-13: 978-1-4201-2979-3
eISBN-10: 1-4201-2979-1
First Electronic Edition: October 2013

10 9 8 7 6 5 4 3 2 1

Printed in the United States of America

For Dad

Chapter 1

Étienne stared down at the house across the street and watched shadows writhe and dance on the closed curtains. The music and drunken laughter that swelled every time the front door opened didn't surprise him. But those curtains did.

Hard to imagine a bunch of frat boys out shopping for them. Choosing the right decorative curtain rods. Finding fabric of a pleasing look and texture. Damned if it didn't look like it was floral. He would've thought bent, dusty blinds would be more their style.

A faint breeze ruffled his hair.

If he concentrated, he could read the thoughts of everyone partying within. Not much there really. Just sex and a determination to get blitzed. And one poor guy who thought he had flunked his biology final. A quick scan of his memories confirmed that he had.

Étienne sighed. Things had been slow of late. Dare he say boring?

For a while there, vampires had roamed in such large packs that he and his sister, Lisette, had had to hunt together just to ensure they would survive the battles. But now . . .

The frat house door burst open as a woman stumbled out. Booming bass swelled and pulsed through the night as a tall, broad-shouldered figure stepped into the doorway behind her and held the door open. "Come on. Are you sure I can't talk you into staying?" the man—twenty-one or twenty-two years of age—asked.

The woman staggered to the edge of the porch and tripped down the steps. Low, sultry, feminine laughter wafted up to Étienne.

Nice. If the woman weren't sloppy drunk he might find her appealing.

"You know me," she slurred. "Places to see and people to go."

Her friend laughed.

Odd. It was late May. Nighttime temperatures in North Carolina had been mild, in the sixties perhaps. Yet the woman wore a long, black coat not unlike the one he sported himself.

His own concealed a small arsenal of weapons: katanas, daggers, throwing stars, and autoinjectors Dr. Lipton had prepared that bore the only sedative that worked on vampires and immortals.

Hers was pretty formfitting. And fit a lovely form. She was slender, perhaps five foot five, with long, black hair that concealed her face as she fought to keep her balance.

The college boy grinned. "Hey, maybe I should walk you home."

Again she laughed. "Who says I'm going home?"

She wasn't a Goth. The style of the coat was wrong and her hair was naturally black. Or perhaps a dark brown. While he could see as clearly as a cat in dim or even no light, he sometimes had difficulty discerning color in those conditions.

The woman finally succeeded in planting both boots firmly on the pavement and straightened. Combing a hand through her hair, she drew the tangled locks back and gazed up at the moon.

Étienne's breath caught. She was beautiful, with porcelain skin, her features pert perfection.

And she seemed to be looking right at him.

She even froze for a moment.

Impossible. There were no lights up here and he stood in the shadow of a chimney where the moon's beams wouldn't touch him.

"Hey, Krysta!" someone called.

She looked to her left.

Three more college boys, who clearly had already been celebrating the end of the spring semester, approached the frat house, trampling grass strewn with the occasional empty beer can.

"You aren't leaving, are you?" a jovial blond asked.

She smiled. "Yep."

"But we're just getting here!"

She shrugged, swayed a bit, then pointed at them. "Your loss, knuckleheads."

All laughed.

"Couldn't you just stay for one game of beer pong?" the blond asked hopefully. "Or maybe to shoot some pool? I need to win my twenty bucks back."

"Already spent it," she called merrily. "See ya!" She waved, nearly losing her balance again. Stumbling to one side, she threw her arms out as though she were on the deck of a rocking ship, listing one way then the other. When she didn't fall, she grinned big and threw her hands up in the air like an Olympic gymnast finishing a routine.

The men all clapped, whistled, and cheered.

Laughing in delight, she staggered down the sidewalk, turned, and headed up the street.

"You think we should walk her home?" the blond asked softly.

The brunet beside him leered after Krysta. "I'll walk her home. I'll walk her alllllll the way home."

The blond shoved him. "Cut the shit. She isn't like that."

Étienne decided he liked the blond.

The brunet scowled. "Whatever." Loping up the steps, he entered the house.

The blond frowned after Krysta, then—urged on by his other buddy—joined the party.

Étienne watched Krysta pause under a streetlight, part her coat, and reach into an inner pocket.

Beneath, she wore tight, black pants that showed every shapely curve of her long legs and a black T-shirt that hugged small, firm breasts.

Étienne had always been a sucker for women with athletic builds.

Out came an iPod touch. She conquered her inebriation long enough to tuck earbuds into her ears, but the battery must have run down because she swore and tucked everything back into her pocket.

Étienne rose.

That pause had cost her.

Dark figures slithered from the shadows on either side of the frat house and followed her as she resumed her trek uphill.

Étienne leapt nimbly to the next roof, careful not to make any sound that would alert the vampires to his presence.

He counted four and monitored their progress as they slunk from shadow to shadow, dogging the woman's wobbly footsteps.

Krysta began to sing, utterly oblivious to the creatures who stalked her.

Unfamiliar with the song, Étienne assumed it was one of the latest pop hits. His lips twitched as he leapt to the next roof. She was having a hell of a time remembering the lyrics. *Or* the right notes. Krysta couldn't carry a tune. And he was pretty sure it wasn't the alcohol.

She came to a corner and halted. A look of confusion flitted across her pretty features as she squinted up at the street sign.

Étienne froze, careful to ensure no light touched him.

Had her gaze flitted from the sign up to him?

No. She was looking all around like she either didn't know where she was or couldn't remember where she intended to go.

The vampires slunk farther into the shadows mere moments before she glanced in their direction.

"Hmm," she mumbled. "I think . . ." She spun in a circle. "Right."

She crossed the deserted street, passed Bastien's building, and . . . entered a dark alley. *Really?* Had she *no* sense of self-preservation?

Étienne drew his katanas as the vampires flowed into the alley behind her like a black tide. Their thoughts—a writhing mass of madness, violence, and anticipation—struck him like poisoned arrows.

Being telepathic could really suck sometimes.

He frowned, only then realizing he hadn't heard any of Krysta's thoughts. As he watched her stumble toward the end of the alley, not yet noticing that her path would soon be blocked by a tall chain-link fence, he focused on her tipsy head and . . . heard nothing.

Very unusual. He could count on one hand the number of humans he had encountered in his two centuries of existence who could block, intentionally or not, his entrance into their minds.

She halted.

The vamps spread out across the alley, facing her. Light from the street distended and distorted the shadows at their feet, making it seem almost as though they reached for her ankles.

Étienne stepped to the edge of the roof, preparing to drop down and save Krysta's attractive, but flighty ass, then . . .

She ceased swaying. Her shoulders straightened.

Spinning around, she offered the menacing foursome a cool, measuring stare.

Étienne frowned.

The vampires boasted no weapons. Yet. But their eyes glowed and their lips parted to expose long, glinting fangs. She should be screaming her head off. Instead . . .

"Finally," she pronounced with a healthy dose of exasperation. "It took you guys long enough. I mean, did you really have to make me walk up that damned hill?"

What. The. Hell?

Krysta shifted, balancing her weight lightly on the balls of her feet as the vampires exchanged puzzled looks. There were four of them. Four would be a challenge. Okay, more than a challenge. *Way* more. She had had her ass handed to her more than once in the past couple of years when trying to combat such numbers on her own. But, until they actually closed in, she was often unable to tell just how many had taken the bait and followed her.

Sneakers shuffled on dirty asphalt.

These seemed to be typical examples of the vampires' ilk. Young. Twenties or thereabouts. Could blend in easily on a college campus if you disregarded the brilliantly glowing eyes and fangs. Hopefully they hadn't been vampires for very long. The older they were, the more insane they were. At least that was how she *thought* it worked. And the deeper they descended into madness, the harder they were to defeat. Krysta didn't have their speed. Or strength. Or size and weight. But she did have two things they didn't.

The first was skill. She had spent years training in tae kwon do, karate, and jiujitsu, and had trained with weapons long enough to kick ass. Most *vampires* had spent a majority of the time, prior to their transformation, sitting on their asses and either texting, yakking on the phone, surfing the Internet, or playing video games. That didn't lend them much skill with knives and swords, so she didn't really understand why they carried them. They were vampires. They could disarm a human easily and, if they didn't, could survive a bullet wound, so what was the deal with that? As far as Krysta knew, she was the only vampire hunter in existence. She seriously doubted her reputation preceded her.

The orange glow around the vampires moved and shifted as the not-very-bright predators tried to figure out why she wasn't fleeing in terror.

And that was her second advantage. She could see auras. Until she had begun to hunt vampires, she had never thought much of the ability. It warned her of people's moods, so she could turn and walk the other way if someone was pissed about something and she didn't want to hear it. Big whoop.

Then her life had changed dramatically, and she had actually found a use for her talent.

Vampires were incredibly fast. Like as fast as The Flash. Their movements became blurry and indistinct when they moved at top speeds. But their auras behaved very differently than those of humans. Vampires' auras moved and shifted before *they* did, telling her exactly where they intended to go before they even took a step.

Krysta eyed the vamps before her, waiting for the telltale shift in auras that would precede their attack.

"Aren't you afraid of us?" one asked.

"No. Should I be?"

Looks were exchanged.

"Yeah, ya dumb bitch," another proclaimed. "We're vampires!"

So polite. She slid a hand into her coat and grasped the handle of one of the shoto swords she carried, ready to teach him some manners. "Yeah, and?"

"What, are you a second?"

She fought a frown. He wasn't the first vampire who had asked her that. What the hell was a second? A second what?

"Fuck this. Let's kick her ass!" a third cried.

The aura of the one closest to her shifted. Krysta drew her sword and swung it, the blade sinking into flesh as the vampire blurred and caught up with the orange glow.

Krysta drew her other sword.

The three remaining vampires gaped as the severed head of their companion hit the ground and rolled several feet away from the body that tumbled after it.

The first kill was always the easiest.

The vampires' faces contorted with fury. Growls and snarls erupted. Eyes glowed brighter.

Crap. Here we go.

Orange auras deepened in color and shot forward just before the vampires' forms all blurred.

Krysta swung both swords with as much speed and strength as she possessed. Her heart raced. Adrenaline surged through her veins. Her blades sank into her opponents.

When warm blood slapped her in the face, she clamped her lips shut. No way did she want any of that getting into her mouth. She didn't know exactly how one became a vampire, but figured it probably had something to do with the blood.

One of the vamps landed a blow to her back that sent pain careening through her as she flew forward and hit the ground.

Rolling, she came up swinging as the vamps converged on her. The momentum of one came to her aid and made a hit that normally would have just cut him instead sever his arm. Vamps tended to not recover from such severe wounds, bleeding out faster than they could heal. As this one did, stumbling backward and falling to the ground while he fought to staunch the crimson river flowing onto the pavement around him.

The vampires divided, attacking from opposite sides.

Krysta continued to wield her deadly shotos, creating a barrier as formidable as a rotary fan's blades. Cuts opened on the vampires, who became manic in their fury, slavering like rabid dogs.

Fear a constant companion, she delivered a round-house kick to the vamp behind her. Agony shot up her leg. It was like kicking a damned boulder. But at least it had kept him from diving low and biting her leg as his aura had warned her he intended.

She landed several more slashes before silver glinted in their hands.

Hell.

Needlelike pain erupted in her arms, sides, and back as they cut her.

Time to take a huge risk.

Ignoring the vampire behind her, she focused all of her attention on the one in front of her. The next time his aura shifted, she swung with all of her might.

The vampire's eyes widened. Stumbling back, he raised both hands to the throat her sword had laid open. The gray shirt he wore turned red as blood spilled down his chest and saturated it.

Spinning around, she raised her weapons. The last vamp, who should have been all over her after the opening she'd given him, stared at her stupidly and stumbled back a step.

She frowned.

He grunted. And grunted again. Blood spilled from his lips.

What the hell?

Groaning, he sank to his knees and clumsily tried to reach behind him with both hands.

Was this a trick?

Swords at the ready, she limped forward and began to edge around him to see what the hell he was reaching for.

Krysta stopped and stared. Half a dozen daggers protruded from his back. And, judging by their positions, they had pierced his heart and probably sliced through at least one major artery.

A whole new fear invaded her as she backed away, her

gaze darting all around her and seeking the source of those weapons.

A sound drew her attention to the entrance of the alley.

Ice skittered through her.

Seven vampires. Eyes glowing various shades of blue, green, silver, and amber.

I'm dead. The panicked thought barreled through her brain at light speed. *There's no way I'll survive this.*

"She's a second!" one snarled.

What the hell is a second?

Their glowing orange auras zipped toward her.

Kysta swung and thrust as she backed away toward the chain-link fence. But, even as she scored hits, the vampires flew past to circle around and cut her off.

A thud sounded behind her. The vamps in front of her paused to look over her shoulder. Something bumped her back.

Krysta spun around and swung.

A large hand clamped around her wrist, stopping her with infuriating ease.

Her gaze rose, taking in the tall figure garbed all in black who towered over her. His luminescent amber eyes, as bright as the moon, met hers. His lips parted, exposing deadly fangs.

But his aura . . .

It wasn't orange like the other vampires'. It was bright white and purple, the two colors swirling together without ever mixing. She had never seen anything like it.

Or had she?

Hadn't she seen it up on the roof earlier and dismissed it as a trick of the eye?

"You," she breathed, and waited for him to strike a death blow.

* * *

Étienne frowned.

She knew him?

He released her arm, ready to catch it again if she should try to skewer him.

The vamps behind her decided to take advantage of her inattention and zipped forward.

Quick as lightning, Étienne drew four throwing stars and threw them. Two struck carotid arteries.

Krysta's eyes widened as blood splattered her back.

"You started this," he said. As soon as this was over, he intended to reprimand the hell out of her for stepping outside the bounds of her duties. She must be a new Second. Reordon usually made it clear that the human guards who aided immortals were *not* to strike out and hunt vampires on their own unless they suspected their immortal had been captured and, for some reason, couldn't reach anyone at the network for help. "Now let's finish it together. I'll watch your back."

Turning his own back, he drew his katanas and tore into the four vamps who had circled around to attack her from the rear.

Bloody bastards had no honor. Attacking a woman—a *human* woman at that—from behind.

Battle sounds erupted over his shoulder. Étienne listened closely for any sound that might indicate Krysta wasn't holding her own, still astonished by the skill she had displayed thus far.

The last of the four vampires he fought fell.

Étienne swung around. Three still remained. Krysta had managed to keep them at bay, but had struck no more killing blows. She was tiring. Fending off blows backed by supernatural strength tended to do that to a human.

Étienne stepped up beside her, careful to avoid her swords, and dove into the fight.

The vamps immediately turned away from her to defend

themselves, but didn't succeed. Étienne opened the arteries of two, who fell to the ground. The last vampire opted to abandon his dying comrades, some of whom had already begun to shrivel up like mummies as the virus that infected them devoured them from the inside out in a desperate bid to live. The vamp's crimson-stained form blurred as he darted toward the street.

Étienne caught him easily at the mouth of the alley, yanked him back into the shadows, and swiftly dispatched him.

When he turned around, Krysta had sheathed one of her swords and was texting away on a cell phone.

He strolled toward her.

Head jerking up, she pocketed the phone and drew her other sword.

He frowned. She watched him as though she expected him to attack her.

"How badly are you hurt?" he asked. Surely she could tell friend from foe. Even Sheldon, his brother Richart's notoriously green Second, could do that much.

"I'm fine," she lied, chin rising. Her clothing sported a dozen or more cuts and tears. She also rested most of her weight on one leg and limped when she moved. Like now, as she inched backward at his approach.

Étienne stopped several feet away from her.

She feared him. He could both smell it and see it in the dilation of her warm, brown eyes.

"You *are* a Second, aren't you?" he asked.

"*What* is a Second?" she practically shouted.

Ah, hell. This was a problem. She was a civilian?

He should call Chris Reordon, the head of the East Coast division of the human network that aided immortals. But Étienne couldn't bring himself to do so. This mortal woman had just hunted and defeated four vampires on her own. And she hadn't broken down when facing almost certain death. He found that damned appealing and worried over what Chris might do to her to ensure her silence and cooperation. He hadn't had much hands-on contact with the human network until recently, but had heard Chris could be ruthless when it came to protecting the identities and ensuring the safety of the Immortal Guardians.

"What are you?" she demanded and began to edge around him, giving him a wide berth.

"You don't know?"

"Would I ask if I did?" she countered. "You're different from them." She motioned to the deceased vampires, a couple of whom were only piles of empty clothing now.

Étienne studied her closely. "Because I didn't kill you?"

She shook her head, her eyes roving him as if she could *see* a difference.

"You seemed to know me, when I joined the battle. Do you?"

She inched toward the entrance of the alley.

Étienne didn't follow. He could catch her easily if she should decide to run and he didn't want to frighten her any more than he already had.

"I saw you," she said. "On the roof of the building across from the frat house. Were you following me?"

"Actually I was hunting the vampires you lured away and had no knowledge of your existence until that time."

"I'm supposed to believe you hunt vampires?" She snorted. "You *are* a vampire."

"You yourself said I'm different."

"Different but the same." Her gaze went to his fangs.

Étienne breathed deeply and forced his fangs to retract.

Her eyes widened.

The rumble of an approaching engine reached Étienne's ears. Fortunately most drivers were so busy chatting or texting that they wouldn't notice anything peculiar taking place in the alleyways they passed.

"Put your swords away and let us discuss this," he suggested reasonably. He needed to keep her talking while he decided what to do about this, whether to call Reordon or . . .

Well, he didn't know what else.

"No," she responded. "I don't think so."

"You've nothing to fear from me. I just saved your life."

"So you could take it yourself?"

"No," he said with the same exasperation he had heard in her voice earlier.

"So you could turn me?"

"Hell, no."

Her frown deepened. Perhaps she had finally identified the sincerity in his voice.

A somewhat battered economy car screeched to a halt behind her. The driver leaned over and thrust open the passenger door.

Krysta backed into it, never taking her eyes from him. Sitting down with swords still at the ready, she swung her feet into the car. "Don't follow me."

As soon as she lowered her blades, the car shot forward out of sight, her door slamming shut from the momentum.

Merde. He hadn't expected that.

Gritting her teeth, Krysta turned around and stared through the back window.

"Who the hell was that?" her brother demanded, barely tapping the breaks as he turned the corner and began a round-about, wild-ass ride in the general direction of their home.

"I don't know."

"His eyes glowed. He was a vampire?"

"I don't know what he was. Is. He looks like a vampire, but . . ."

"But what?"

She grabbed the door handle and hung on as Sean skidded around another corner. He had all of the talents of a freaking stunt driver. And that had come in handy. Not once had a vampire managed to follow them all the way home.

"His aura is different," she told him. "*Way* different. And . . ."

"And what?"

"He saved me."

"Oh, shit. He didn't bite you, did he?"

"No." She faced forward and slumped back in her seat, wounds throbbing. "There were four vampires this time."

"Damn it! I told you to stick to one or two!"

"I didn't know there were going to be that many!" she defended herself. "It's not like I can stop, look back, and take a head count. That would kinda spoil the whole *Victim Here* deception."

He shook his head. "Four? How did you even—?"

"I took out three." She began to shake as reaction set in. "But I had to leave myself wide open for the fourth in order to take out the third and, when I turned around, there were half a dozen daggers sticking out of his back."

Sean shot her a disbelieving look. "Are you saying the vampire in the alley who was dressed like Johnny Cash killed him?"

"Him and the seven vampires who showed up next."

Epithets filled the little car, full of force and fear and determination. "That's it. No more. This is over. You're done."

"It—"

"When it was one or two, that was one thing. You could handle it. But for the past couple of years it's been insane. You've nearly died too many times to count and I'm not ready to lose you."

"I'll just have to be more careful—"

"You've been singing that bullshit song for months now. No more."

"If I don't do it, who will?"

"Let that crazy-ass vamp from the alley do it if that's his madness."

"He didn't seem mad," she murmured, still puzzling over it. She had never met a vampire who was *nice*, for lack of a better word.

"All the more reason to let him hunt his fellow bloodsuckers. If they slice *him* up, he'll heal."

"You always manage to patch me up."

Not without cost on his part. That had always filled her with guilt and regret, but she didn't see any way around it. She couldn't do this without him.

"There are some things I can't do, Krysta. I have limits. When I reach those and you have to bury me, will it have been worth it?"

She couldn't bear the thought of it. "We'll just have to find another way."

He shook his head, alerting her to the huge argument ahead of them, and glanced in the rearview mirror. "Is it clear?"

She turned around and peered through the back window once more. The rest of the car may be coated in dirt and look like crap, but the windows were always sparklingly clean. Their lives depended upon it.

No bright orange glows streaked toward them in the street, so no vampires tailed them. Or no *regular* vampires tailed them. She didn't see any purple either. She thought she saw a glint of white, but it was so fleeting she decided it was the moonlight shining on a storefront window.

Turning around, she studied the scenery that whipped past through the passenger window. "It's clear."

"Good." His meandering path ended as he headed straight for the small frame house they rented on the outskirts of Carrboro, North Carolina. "How badly are you hurt?"

"I don't think my leg is broken, but it hurts like hell. And I'm bleeding from a lot of cuts."

"No major arteries hit?"

"No."

"No ribs broken?"

"Not this time. That vamp really saved my ass."

He shook his head again and took his foot off the gas.

Krysta checked behind them as the car slowed, just to be doubly sure, then nodded.

Sean guided the car onto a drive that was supposed to be gravel, but was about eighty percent dirt and weeds instead.

Krysta's sore, aching body wobbled from side to side as he navigated the pothole-riddled path about fifty yards to the little, brown frame house hidden among the trees.

They had tried to find a place in Chapel Hill, so they would be closer to the colleges (prime hunting grounds for vampires), but hadn't been able to afford it. This had ended up being ideal in terms of isolation anyway. No neighbors. No one to see her blood-painted face and clothing when they returned home. No one to call the police if they glimpsed her weapons.

Sean parked and, unfolding his large form, circled around to help Krysta.

He was a lot taller than she was, taking after their father, who towered over their tiny mother. Krysta stood at only five foot five and boasted a slender build with enough muscle to lend her strength without bulking her up like a man. Sean was six foot two or thereabouts and packed about two hundred pounds of muscle that made many a woman drool. He also possessed the same fighting skills Krysta did. Had he been able to anticipate the vampires' moves the way she could, they would have made a formidable team.

Unfortunately, he couldn't. And the few times he had joined her on the hunt, he had ended up so battered and bloody she had almost had to take him to the hospital.

Krysta kept her swords in hand as he opened the car door, reached in, and practically lifted her out. "I can walk," she insisted, though her leg was *really* hurting. Maybe the bastard *had* fractured it. Could one walk on a fractured leg?

Sean mumbled something about stubbornness bordering on stupidity and wrapped a supportive arm around her to help her to the door.

Krysta let the slur slide. She knew he was just worried about her and terrified of losing her. His mood always turned sour when she was wounded, which happened pretty much every time she hunted. She'd avoid it if she could. She sure as hell didn't enjoy it. But, how?

There was no need to flip through keys to open the front door. They always left it unlocked. The house was hidden from the road by trees and drew no notice of passersby. Even the mailman didn't deliver. All of their correspondence went to a post office box.

And if someone *did* choose to wander down their drive and found the frame house, nothing about its appearance would entice a burglar. It was over a century old and built on uneven ground that left it slanting to one side. (She and Sean had had a hell of a time leveling the furniture when they had moved in.) The roof sagged, as did the porch and back deck. The paint was old and worn and peeling.

Who would even bother to look inside?

"You need to mow the lawn," she huffed, gritting her teeth against the pain as they trudged over uneven ground, up the steps, and through the door.

They also left it unlocked for expediency's sake. There had been nights when time had been of the essence.

"Ground's still too wet." He flicked a switch, and bright light flooded the small living room.

Krysta limped over to the futon and slumped down on the waterproof tarp they always placed over it on nights she hunted. That bright idea had come to them too late to save their first from bloodstains.

"Do you need help getting your coat off?" he asked, sitting in front of her on their dented and scarred coffee table.

She nodded. Pulling cloth away from the wounds it stuck to always made the pain worse.

Sean, tight-lipped and silent, removed her coat as gently as possible.

Krysta tugged her shirt over her head. Underneath, she wore a heavy-duty sports bra that covered *everything*. Not one hint of cleavage could be found, not that she had much. And, beneath the pants she removed, she wore bike shorts.

Sean scowled as he examined her wounds. "The leg isn't broken. It's sprained. I don't like how these two cuts"—he motioned to one on her shoulder and one on her thigh— "are bleeding, so I'll heal them first."

"Thank you."

He closed his eyes and rested his hands on his splayed knees. Krysta remained quiet while he breathed in through his nose, held it, then released it several times. Opening his eyes, he covered the wound on her thigh with his hands.

Warmth flooded her skin. The cut began to tingle as if a numbing agent had been applied. Blood ceased oozing from beneath his fingers. The pain eased.

When Sean withdrew his hands, the cut had been replaced by a faint scar. "Turn to the side a bit."

She did so, giving him greater access to the wound scoring her shoulder.

He cupped a hand over it. Again a soothing warmth suffused her wound as it healed beneath his touch. Sean had borne this gift all of his life. Just as she had borne hers. And he had been healing her for as long as she could remember. Though she was two years older than Sean, she couldn't count the number of times he had stopped her crying in their youth by covering a scraped knee or cut elbow with his little hands and making the wounds disappear.

Of course, they didn't actually disappear. Neither of them

were sure how exactly it worked, but he seemed to transfer the wound to his own body, which healed at an accelerated rate. Even now, a red stain appeared on the shoulder of his shirt.

"I'll heal the leg now before I heal the others."

"The others aren't bad," she insisted. "I can just use some butterfly closures on them."

He shook his head. With careful hands, he lifted her foot and propped it next to him on the coffee table. "Do we really have to do this every time?" He settled his hands on her shin where it hurt the most. A muscle in his jaw jumped as he clenched his teeth.

She hated causing him pain. That was the worst part of all of this. Not the vampires trying to kill her. Or having to hide what she did from everyone so they wouldn't think she was crazy and commit her. But the pain Sean experienced when he healed her time and time again, saving her ass so she could go out and do the same thing again tomorrow.

The pain in her leg vanished. And she knew Sean would limp if he were to stand and try to walk now. But he didn't. He stubbornly healed every cut and bruise on her arms and legs and back.

She hugged him gingerly when he finished, knowing he now ached in all of the places she had. "Thank you."

He patted her back, then shifted over to slump down on the futon.

Healing her didn't just open wounds on him. It also exhausted him.

"Can I get you anything?" she asked.

He shook his head. "How long are we going to do this, Krys?"

She slumped back beside him. "I don't know. As long as it takes, I guess."

"Takes to do what? For a while there, it seemed like we were making a difference. The vampires' numbers decreased. You'd go weeks sometimes without running into one. But eleven in one night?"

"Twelve, if you count the . . ."

"What? The good one?"

She sighed. "I don't know."

"It's turning into a never-ending battle. We can't win this."

"How can we stop?"

Another deep sigh soughed from him. Raising a hand, he rubbed his eyes and shook his head.

She understood his weariness. Some may have counted tonight a victory. But she and Sean could see it only as defeat, as proof that they would never succeed in ridding the world of every bloodsucker on the planet.

It was a war they couldn't win.

And sooner or later it would kill them.

Étienne stood in the small frame home, staring down at Krysta. Darkness surrounded them, broken only by the glowing red digits on her alarm clock.

She slept the sleep of the utterly exhausted, curled on her side with a faded, striped sheet tucked beneath her chin. Sean slumbered in the only other bedroom in the house. Both were blissfully unaware that he had invaded the safety of their home. Étienne had gone to great lengths to avoid detection while he had followed them from UNC.

Taking his time, he inspected the interior of the house. It reminded him a bit of the one Sarah had been renting when Roland had met her. Small. Old. Tidy. He guessed, by the pictures displayed on the wall, that the two were siblings. Why that was a relief puzzled him. Though he didn't know them, he hadn't wanted the two of them to be lovers. It made no sense.

He returned silently to Krysta's bedroom, a task made more difficult by the many squeaky floorboards.

The conversation he had overheard earlier led him to believe that hunting vampires was not a new endeavor for her. How the hell had she gone undetected? There were over a dozen immortals in the area. Seth, their leader and the most powerful among them, had been dropping in regularly. Seconds and cleaners abounded. And the network headquarters was stationed in Greensboro. Yet *none* of them had ever encountered Krysta? It seemed rather remarkable.

Rustling sounded in the next room. Étienne melted back into the darkest corner as Sean shuffled past the doorway in boxer shorts and a T-shirt. Moments later the door to the bathroom closed and Étienne returned his attention to the warrior woman slumbering so peacefully a few feet away.

She would have to be dealt with.

Both of them would.

When Sean next passed by his sister's bedroom, Étienne was gone.

Chapter 2

Sebastien slipped through the front door of David's home. The amount of time he spent here was ironic, considering how eager he had been to leave this place a couple of months earlier.

Of course, he hadn't left under the circumstances he had assumed he would. He had thought he would tell the Immortal Guardians to kiss his ass and either leave and never see them again or fight them to the death. Most likely the latter.

Instead he had fallen in love with a mortal doctor (who was now immortal), gotten her into all kinds of trouble, then married her and moved into a quaint home in the country.

Life could be strange as hell sometimes. Who could've foreseen *that* fate for him?

Well, maybe Seth. That bastard seemed to know almost everything. Very annoying.

No one called a welcome when Bastien closed the door behind himself. The French immortals—Étienne, Richart, and Lisette—lounged on a couple of sofas along with Richart's wife, Jenna, watching some movie with a lot of explosions while they snacked on pita chips.

Lisette barely spared him a glance. Richart nodded. Jenna sent him a tentative smile. Étienne didn't even seem to notice his presence. Tracy, Lisette's Second, was on the other side of the living room flirting with a human Bastien thought might be Ethan's Second. Bastien knew neither the American immortal nor his Second well. Sheldon, Richart's Second, entered from the kitchen, carrying a pizza the size of a fucking big rig wheel.

When he caught sight of Bastien, he reverse-nodded. "'Sup?" He stopped short. "Dude. What's the deal with your coat? It's moving."

"Is David here?" Bastien asked, offering no explanation.

His eyes fastened on Bastien's coat pockets, Sheldon said, "Yeah, he's in his study."

Bastien strode toward the darkened hallway. "Thank you."

As he reached the entrance to David's study, he heard Sheldon murmur to Richart, "I think something's wrong with Bastien. He just thanked me."

A sigh escaped him. That was Melanie's influence.

Seated at his massive desk, David perused what Bastien assumed was another medical text. As usual, his long dread-locks were pulled back with a leather tie.

"Got a minute?" Bastien asked.

The elder immortal raised his head—and his eyebrows—at the polite query and motioned for him to enter.

Bastien stepped inside and closed the door behind him, not that it did much good. Unless they were closeted in one of the quiet rooms, any immortal in the house could hear their conversation.

David was the second eldest immortal in the world and wielded incredible strength and power. Unlike younger immortals, who had only one or two gifts, David possessed several. He was such a powerful healer that he could reattach severed limbs. He could shape-shift, something most of them hadn't realized until the last big battle they had engaged in with Emrys's mercenaries. He could also hurl Bastien across the room with a thought. So, though he was perhaps the most even-tempered immortal, it was nevertheless wise not to cross or anger him.

Bastien had never felt comfortable around David. Melanie didn't understand why, but it was the same reason she puzzled him herself. David had always been kind to Bastien, welcoming him into his home and defending him when the other immortals had all called for his execution. He had behaved casually and almost like a brother toward Bastien since the moment the two had met.

Bastien didn't understand it.

"Those had better not be for me," David warned as Bastien approached his desk.

"Actually, they are."

"Are you off your nut?"

Bastien laughed. "No. Read my mind so we can talk without the others listening."

"All right."

Can you hear me? Bastien asked mentally. He wasn't telepathic himself and could only hear the elder's thoughts if David spoke them in Bastien's head.

One moment. Lisette?

There was a pause. *Yes?*

Close your mind to us.

Bastien hadn't thought of that. He still wasn't used to being around the telepaths.

Done, she responded grudgingly.

Étienne?

Nothing.

Étienne, close your mind to us.

Still nothing.

Étienne!

What? Why'd you elbow me?

Because David is speaking to you, Lisette said. *And I only knew that, David, because you were projecting it. I'm out.*

Who did what now? Étienne asked.

Never mind, David told him, then met Bastien's gaze. *He's distracted and won't hear us. Go ahead.*

Reaching into his pockets, Bastien began to withdraw the motherless kittens he had found earlier. They were tiny, eyes barely open, and clumsily scrambled toward each other on David's desk, forming a squirming, furry pile. *I thought these would buy us some time.*

David frowned, but couldn't resist picking up one of the kittens and stroking it. The white and orange fur stood out starkly next to the elder immortal's black as midnight skin.

Buy *us time or* consume *our time?* he queried. *These need frequent feeding. Where is their mother?*

Hit by a car. And, yes, they need feeding. Every two hours, I think, which will be a pain in the ass. But . . . listen.

The kittens began to mew as they vied for position in the pile. Beneath those sounds . . .

Heartbeats, David said as understanding dawned.

Until you decide what to tell the others about Ami's pregnancy, this will help conceal it from them. With these little guys roaming the house, anyone who hears the baby's heartbeat will assume it's a kitten's. Hell, who here has spent enough time around a pregnant woman since transforming to tell the difference?

True. David set the kitten down next to its brothers and sisters, then picked up a black and white one. *Smart thinking.* He smiled when the kitten clumsily walked up his arm and sank its claws into one of his long dreadlocks. He caught it before it became too entangled and held it up before his face. *He's cute, isn't he?*

Bastien smiled. *Yeah. I dropped by the pet store and bought cat milk, bottles, and everything else we'll need. It's in my car.*

Get it and meet me in the living room.

Bastien went to the car and retrieved a large bag of essentials, some of which he was pretty sure weren't essentials, but the saleslady had been nice and hadn't shied away from him the way so many humans did. When he returned to the house, David was just entering the living room with all six kittens cradled in his large hands.

The television shut off.

"Hey!" several protested and turned toward him.

"What the hell is that?" Sheldon asked, staring at the kittens.

"Your new assignments."

Krysta's nerves jangled as she strolled through the quiet college campus, adding a stagger here and there for show.

She had hunted every night for the past two weeks with nothing to show for it. No vampire attacks. No vampire deaths. No glimpses of the mysterious . . . other. The vampire who had saved her ass.

Why was his aura so different? He clearly was a vampire. Same fangs. Same glowing eyes. Same incredible speed and strength. Just no orange aura.

An owl hooted.

Why had he helped her?

What was his agenda?

And why hadn't she seen him again?

A nice breeze blew her hair back from her face.

She was beginning to suspect he had been following her each night as she hunted.

Not just following her. Protecting her.

The notion was insane. As insane as the vampires she loathed so much. And yet, there had been moments when she would have sworn she had drawn out some vampires, just as she had the night she had met Mr. Tall, Dark, and Hot.

He isn't hot.

Yes, he is.

Damn it, he is.

Some nights, she had heard faint footsteps behind her and caught glimpses of shadows stalking her. Shadows with flowing orange auras. She had continued her helpless, drunken student act until she was sure, then had turned down this street, into that alley, and . . .

Found herself alone. Safe. Unassailed.

It made no sense.

Last night, she had heard a muffled thump, followed by a metallic clatter as she drew her weapons and spun around to face the vampires she had thought were pursuing her. Once more faced with an empty alleyway, she had hurried forward, rounded the corner, and found a flashy bowie knife—typical vamp weaponry—lying on the sidewalk.

She hadn't mentioned it to her brother. If Sean thought the new vampire was stalking her or playing some weird game with her, he would argue like hell to get her to stop hunting.

And it did seem like a game. She just couldn't figure out the rules or the why's of it.

Her favorite frat house again boomed music. Shadows danced on the curtains.

Sighing, Krysta headed down the hill toward it.

She really didn't feel like being around people right now. Especially drunk, gropey people. But she had a job to do.

As she approached the sidewalk that led to the porch steps, the shadows on this side of the house shifted minutely. A dark figure with an orange aura slipped around the corner. Another joined it.

Perfect. She had no interest in making small talk. And being around drunk people was a lot more fun when she was drunk, too.

Krysta continued past, faking a stumble, and dropped her purse. Mumbling to herself, she scooped it up and staggered to one side. A shake of her head at herself and she headed farther down the hill, where she paused at an intersection.

Pretending to look both ways allowed her to catch a glimpse of wisps of bright orange behind her.

Score!

Finally. A fight. She needed one to clear the cobwebs. To get rid of this frustrated, pent-up energy. To feed her need for vengeance.

Adrenaline flooded her veins as she crossed the street and turned down a dark, narrow side street. She couldn't see well in the dark like vampires could, but the vamps' glowing auras tended to light the field of battle for her.

A scuffing sound behind her halted her footsteps. Swinging around, she drew her swords with a triumphant smile, and . . .

"Damn it!"

No vampires faced her with leering, evil intent. No vampires faced her at all.

She was alone. Again.

More rustling sounded.

Racing back to the street, she flew around the corner and skidded to a halt.

Nothing. Just an empty road glowing green from the streetlight at the corner.

The unmistakable *shick*, *ting*, and *clang* of metal striking metal split the air several blocks away.

"Oh, no you don't," she growled and took off running. She didn't care that she raced down a sharply sloped hill that would make it damned near impossible to stop once she got going. She didn't care that she ran with an unsheathed sword in each hand. (Her mother and father's frequent admonitions not to run with scissors chose that moment to dance through her head.) She didn't even care that anyone who saw her would likely call the police and report a madwoman fleeing through Chapel Hill, waving deadly weapons, and get her arrested.

She had only one goal in mind: Get to those damned

vampires before Mystery Man did whatever the hell he'd been doing for the past two weeks and disappeared.

Her heart pounding in her chest, she honed in on the battle's location and managed to put on the brakes enough to zip around the corner at a speed that would keep her from rolling ass over elbows downhill.

She jerked to a halt and stared.

The darkened alley was deserted except for a Dumpster about twenty-five yards away and—she released a growl of fury—a pair of jeans, a bloody blue sweatshirt, and a pair of bright red Chucks spread out on the pavement as if they had been laid out by some kid's mother.

Krysta sheathed one of her swords, stomped over the place a vampire had clearly fallen, and grabbed the sweatshirt. "Oh, come on!" she shouted, her voice echoing on the somnolent night. She shook the sticky clothing at the sky. "Where are you?" she demanded. Turning in a circle, she examined every nook and cranny at street level, then peered up at the rooftops.

She could see no sign of Mystery Man's unique purple and white aura. Had he already left?

Krysta tossed the shirt down in disgust. "This is bullshit."

A low chuckle wafted on the night.

Eyes widening, she drew her second sword and turned in a slow circle. "Damn it! Show yourself!"

"Well, since you asked so nicely," a deep voice laced with a French accent purred behind her.

Gasping, she spun around and swung a shoto.

Once more, he caught her wrist. "Careful." The warning was gentle, carrying neither malice nor anger.

Krysta stared.

His touch sent electricity tickling its way up her arm. His flesh was warm, his long fingers free of calluses.

Her heart slammed against her ribs as butterflies erupted in her stomach.

She should be furious. Frightened. Instead, she felt as excited as she would on a first date.

Crap.

Stepping back, she withdrew her arm from his grasp.

Dropping his hand, he tilted his head and studied her with those entrancing amber eyes.

Yeah, he was hot all right.

Short, midnight hair glinted in the moonlight. Faint stubble shadowed a strong jaw. Straight nose. Broad shoulders. What was clearly a well-developed, muscular build beneath a black T-shirt that clung to him courtesy of the vampire blood that saturated its front. Slim waist. Slim hips. All revealed by the gap in the long, black coat he wore.

She didn't let her gaze stray farther. The last thing she wanted to do while facing him was blush like a schoolgirl if he had a nice package.

His tempting lips stretched in a slow smile.

Usually, the minds of mortals were revoltingly easy for Étienne to read. Krysta's thoughts, for some reason, were proving rather elusive, although he *had* caught something about his package.

He grinned.

Her pretty brown eyes narrowed. "Who *are* you?"

He performed a gallant bow and offered his hand. "Étienne d'Alençon."

She raised one eyebrow. "If you think I'm going to put away my weapons, think again."

He had expected no less from this bewitching warrior. "As you wish."

She motioned to the clothes of the vampire he hadn't had time to discard. "What happened here?"

"Exactly what you think happened." He had taken out

the vampires who had fallen for her ruse, damn her and her insistence on putting herself in danger.

"You killed a vampire?"

"Three actually."

"Where are the other two?"

"Deteriorating on the roof."

Her gaze darted to the building beside them, up to the edge of the roof, then returned to him. "You fought them up there?"

"No. Down here."

"And you—what—carried them up there?"

"Threw them. Two of them, anyway. I didn't have time to toss the last one before you arrived." Again, he smiled. "You're very fast for a mortal."

As she stared up at him, he tried again to read her thoughts and couldn't. Was she a *gifted one* like her brother? If so, what was her gift? Neither had referenced it the night he had followed them home. And he hadn't seen her demonstrate one.

"Why did you kill them?" she asked. "Are you guys engaged in some kind of turf war or something? Are they *encroaching* upon your *territory?*" Such derision and scorn. It didn't belong in that melodic voice.

"I have no territory—not here in the States, at least— unless you count the small parcel of land upon which my current abode resides."

"You sleep in a crypt or something?"

He laughed. "No. I like my creature comforts. And, no, I am not engaged in a turf war as you called it. I killed the vampires to protect you."

Anger flared in her gaze. "First of all, I don't *need* protecting."

"The events that transpired the night we met suggest otherwise."

"That was a unique situation. Vampires don't usually travel in packs."

"A comment that makes me wonder just how long you've been hunting them." The fact that she still lived led him to believe this was a fairly new endeavor for her.

"Years," she responded defiantly.

He may not be able to read her thoughts clearly, but he could glean enough to know she told the truth. Even so, doubt plagued him. "How *many* years? You can't have seen more than twenty-five in your lifetime."

"Twenty-seven, not that it's any of your business. And I've hunted vampires for six of those."

Astonishment gripped him. This fragile, mortal woman had hunted and fought vampires for six years and survived to tell the tale? With no help from the network?

So much had been happening in North Carolina in recent years: The uprisings. The battles. And she had hunted vampires through it all?

"That's impossible."

"Apparently not or I wouldn't be standing here." She frowned. "Wait. You said *them*."

"What?"

"You said *them*, that I had been hunting *them*, not *us*."

He swore silently.

"What *are* you?"

"I have fangs. My eyes glow. I heal at an accelerated rate. And I have preternatural speed and strength. What do you think I am?" he retorted. Until he was sure she and her brother were operating independently and weren't part of some new threat—especially not members of the mercenary group he and the others had recently defeated—he was reluctant to tell her that he was an immortal.

He had actually once been like her brother: a *gifted one*, or mortal born with special abilities stemming from advanced DNA, before he had been infected with the vampiric virus. Vampires were human before they were infected and, lacking the advanced DNA, were driven insane by the brain damage it caused.

She shook her head. "You're different. You're not like the others."

He arched a brow. "Because I didn't try to kill you?"

Her head continued to wag back and forth as her gaze skipped over him. "You're different."

He frowned. She didn't seem to be checking him out. She seemed to be studying him.

Did she see something that set him apart from the others?

"*How* am I different?"

"You tell *me.*"

Not bloody likely.

She mimicked his frown and took another step back. "Why have you been following me?"

She'd caught that, had she?

Well, curiosity had driven him to watch her. And she *did* prove to be a very good vampire lure. He hadn't killed this many vamps on a daily basis in quite some time.

He should have turned her name and address over to Chris Reordon. But there was something about her. He couldn't get her out of his head.

Not that he would admit it.

"You make good bait," he stated just to rile her.

Her face flushed with fury. "I *what?*"

Damn, she was beautiful. "You make good bait. Hunting vampires has never been so easy. I just follow you and take out the dullards who can't resist you and slink after you."

"You . . . I . . . Is that an insult? Are you saying only dullards would be attracted to me?" she sputtered.

If that's true, you're standing before a big-ass dullard, he wanted to say. "Of course not. Only dullards would want to *kill* you."

"Oh. Well, you can't do that. You can't just follow me and take out any vampires who fall for my trap."

He shrugged. "You can't really stop me, can you?"

"The hell I can't."

"Well, you could if you ceased hunting and left the slaying of vampires to me," he suggested.

She stared at him. "Seriously, what *are* you?"

"What are *you?*"

"What do you mean? I'm human."

"Your brother isn't."

The tip of one of her swords nicked him as she pressed it to his throat. "What do you know about my brother?"

"That he's a healer, a *gifted one.*"

"I don't know what a *gifted one* is, but you leave him the hell out of this," she snarled.

"As long as he aids you in your quest, I'm afraid I can't do that."

"I'm not kidding." Her expression fierce, she pressed forward. "Stay. The hell. Away from him."

"If you fear for his safety, you have only yourself to blame. *You* led me to him."

Alarm and self-condemnation flitted across her pretty face.

"It's only a matter of time before you lead vampires to him as well," he pointed out, "if you haven't already."

"I haven't. I've been careful."

"Are you sure? Did you know *I* followed you?"

Fear suffused Krysta.

Stupid. Stupid. Stupid.

She'd been so stupid! She'd been so confident! She'd been so sure that she had gotten away clean after each hunt.

And she had led this vampire straight to Sean?

Worse than that, she wouldn't have even known it if he hadn't told her.

Her hand began to tremble.

How many times had Sean begged her to stop? Told her it

was too risky? Admitted he feared losing her? And now *she* could lose *him* because of her own hubris and carelessness.

She lowered her sword. "Don't hurt him. If you're going to kill one of us, kill me."

"Why not kill the both of you?" he posed.

"Because I'm the one with the quest."

"And what quest might that be?"

"To kill every bloodsucking vampire in existence."

He pursed his lips. "That's quite a quest. I've been killing vampires for two hundred years and have barely made a dent."

Shock struck her speechless.

Two hundred years? She didn't know what stunned her more. That Étienne was *that* old—he didn't look a day over thirty!—or that there were really that many vampires on the planet.

"Are you serious?"

"Quite."

"I had hoped . . ."

"That vampires were a regional thing?" he finished for her.

She nodded dumbly. How had he guessed so accurately?

"They aren't," he said, and there was kindness in his voice. Sympathy. From a vampire.

One who had, if she could believe him, spent the past two centuries—*two centuries*—killing other vampires.

Abruptly, the song "Squirrels in My Pants" from *Phineas and Ferb* filled the air.

Étienne fumbled in his pocket and withdrew a cell phone.

She hadn't even noticed until then that his weapons were all sheathed. Not once, in this entire conversation, had he threatened her.

He glanced at the caller ID. "One moment, please." Turning away slightly, he answered. *"Oui?"* He glanced at her from the corner of his eye. *"Maintenant? . . . Je suis dans le milieu de quelque chose . . ."* He groaned. *"Bien. Bien. Deux minutes."*

He pocketed the phone.

"Squirrels in My Pants?" she couldn't resist asking.

His handsome face lit with a faint smile. "Inside joke. I'm afraid I must leave."

"Places to go, vampires to party with?"

He shook his head and backed away. "Go home, Krysta."

How the hell did he know her name?

And why did hearing him say it induce shivers of pleasure?

"No more hunting," he ordered. Or implored.

She just couldn't read this guy. She was attracted to him, damn it, and it was warping her judgement. So she said nothing.

"Promise me," he insisted.

"I promise," she said. "No more hunting."

His handsome face relaxed into an easy grin.

"Tonight," she added. "No more hunting tonight." She needed to take a step back and try to absorb everything she had learned.

His scowl returned. "Stubborn wench. Until we meet again then." He bowed. *"Bonne nuit."*

His form blurred and dashed around the corner, moving so swiftly ordinary humans wouldn't be able to follow him with their eyes. He could run past some and all they would feel or notice was the breeze his passing created.

But Krysta could follow his aura. It lit up the night.

Hurrying to the corner, she peered around the building's edge.

Étienne was a distant, dark figure surrounded by phosphorescent, constantly shifting white and purple near the frat house.

In the blink of an eye, a second dark figure with an identical aura joined him.

She gasped. The other's aura hadn't approached from any direction. It—*he*—had just appeared out of thin air.

The stranger touched Étienne's shoulder. Both vanished.

Her knees weakening, Krysta leaned against the rough bricks of the building beside her.

There were two of them. Two vampires with that fascinating aura she had never before beheld.

And one of them could teleport.

Or could both of them? She hadn't heard or seen Étienne's approach tonight. One second she had been demanding he show himself. The next he had spoken behind her.

After talking with him, she had assumed he had just jumped down from the roof. Had he instead teleported?

Was that even what it was called? Teleporting? It sounded so sci-fi. Not vampirish at all.

Sighing, she took out her cell phone and called Sean.

A moment later, their battered Dodge Shadow halted before her and the passenger door sprang open.

Her brother's curious gaze pierced her as she sank into the bucket seat and slammed the door.

"No luck tonight?" he asked.

Kinda hard to miss the lack of blood splatter.

She shook her head.

He sent her an encouraging smile. "Maybe you killed them all."

She laughed. "I wish."

He began the journey home. "You must have scared them off. You haven't gone this long without fighting one in a few years."

She made some noncommittal sound as guilt consumed her. She should tell him about Étienne. She actually opened her mouth to do so three or four times as the engine stuttered and struggled to get them home. But what could she say? *I'm being stalked by that gorgeous vampire you saw me with two weeks ago. No, he doesn't fight me. He claims he's protecting me. Yes, the vampire. Yes, by all appearances, he is protecting me. He keeps killing all of the vampires I hunt. No, I don't know what his game is. And, yes, I'm attracted to him. That's right—attracted. As in I would love to see him naked. It's sick. I get it. He's a bloodsucking vampire. But I can't help it. My freaking heart pounds every time he comes near me and it isn't from fear that he'll kill me.*

She gazed into the blackness beyond the passenger window.

There was just something about him. Something mesmerizing.

Her reflection's brow furrowed.

Was she losing it? Was the strain of six years of battling vampire after insane vampire beginning to get to her? Or . . .

A chill skittered through her.

Was the vampires' madness rubbing off on her? Was it contagious?

She *had* been bitten that one time seven years ago. She had assumed, because she hadn't turned into a vampire overnight, that there had been no long-term damage. What if she were wrong? What if the madness that crippled vampires had slowly but surely been finding and securing a home in *her?*

Fear cut through her veins like diamonds.

Could it be true? Could that be it?

Even if one bite couldn't do it, she had been exposed to their blood countless times over the years in battle. How many times did it take?

"You okay?" her brother asked.

"Just tired," she lied.

"Are you sure?" He took his eyes off the road momentarily to study her. "Are you worried about the vampire who helped you?"

She sent him a sharp glance. "What do you mean?"

He shrugged. "It's just weird that he helped you. You've never encountered a vampire who didn't try to kill or turn you. I've been worried that he might . . . I don't know . . . come back and finish what he didn't have a chance to start."

"If he had wanted to kill me, he had ample opportunity to do so."

A scowl creased his brow. "How can you be so sure? Maybe he's screwing with you? He didn't get into your head, did he?"

Relief and anger overwhelmed her as she realized her brother might have just hit the proverbial nail on the head.

A slew of silent epithets drowned out whatever Sean said next.

That's it! It has to be! Étienne has literally gotten into my head. I mean, if he can freaking teleport, a little mind control really isn't that hard to believe.

Other vampires could do it. The reason no one knew vampires existed was because victims of vampire attacks who lived could never recall having been bitten or give any description of their attacker. They even laughed outright at the notion that Krysta had saved them from a vampire who had been eagerly draining their blood.

Not one vampire victim with whom she had spoken had retained any memory of being attacked. If that wasn't mind control, what was?

Anger simmered within her. "I am *so* going to kick his ass," she growled.

Sean's eyebrows rose. "The purple and white vamp?"

She had told him about Étienne's aura. "Yes."

"What makes you think you'll see him again?"

"Oh, I'll see him again. He left me alive for a reason. And I'm going to kick his ass until he tells me what it is."

His frown returned. "Just don't go looking for him, Krys. Seriously. I have a bad feeling about this."

"I won't," she was able to say with complete honesty.

If he stayed true to his recent pattern, Étienne would come looking for her. And when he did . . .

She smiled grimly.

He was going to regret messing with her head.

Chapter 3

Étienne glanced at his twin as they arrived in David's large living room. "Are you the smart-ass who changed my ringtone?"

"Someone changed your ringtone?" Richart asked. "To what?"

"Never mind."

Darnell approached, a tiny kitten in each hand. "Okay, which one do you want?"

Étienne reached for the little gray and white one. "We're really doing this?"

"Yes."

A faint, high-pitched scream came from Étienne's pocket, accompanied by a drumbeat. "There are squirrels in my pants!" a girl cried as *Phineas and Ferb's* "Squirrels in My Pants" song began blaring from his phone.

Every immortal in the room turned to look at him.

Étienne scowled at his brother.

Laughing, Richart closed his cell phone and put it away. "I didn't change it. I just wanted to know what it was."

"Asshole." He took the ridiculously small bottle of milk Darnell handed him. "As I was saying, we're really doing this?"

"Every two hours."

He groaned. He could still be chatting up Krysta if he didn't have to play feline nursemaid.

"How much has David done for you over the centuries?" Darnell retorted, his shaved, brown head gleaming in the overhead light.

"A hell of a lot," Étienne answered without hesitation. David was like Seth. He gave everything he had to the Immortal Guardians and those who aided them.

"And what has he asked in return?" Darnell continued.

"Not a damned thing."

"Exactly. So feed the kitten."

Étienne cuddled the mewling little bundle of fur to his chest. "Done."

Richart took the orange and white kitten and did the same.

"Every two hours, guys," Darnell reminded them again as they crossed the room and sank down beside Lisette on one of the sofas.

Roland and Sarah fed two kittens on another sofa.

Roland was quite possibly the most aggravating, antisocial immortal on the planet. Seeing him cuddle and nurture a black and white kitten that could fit in the palm of his hand was nothing short of bizarre.

Grunts and thumps floated up from downstairs, where Seconds sparred in the training room.

Ami entered, carrying Slim. *That* scrawny little feline didn't look fully grown either, though it had long since reached adulthood. It also bore several bare patches, scars, and cuts from its most recent fights with whatever woodland creature it had felt ventured too close to Slim's new territory: David's property.

"Hi, Ami," Sarah called with a smile.

"Hi."

The men all echoed the greeting.

Every male Immortal Guardian in North Carolina adored the two women. They loved Sarah for being the first *gifted one* in history to ask to be infected so she could spend eternity with Roland's antisocial ass. They loved Ami for . . . well . . . being Ami.

She was so sweet and shy. And fucking ferocious on the battlefield. A mere week after being named Marcus's Second, she had helped him stand against and defeat thirty-four vampires. *Thirty-four*. No mortal had ever attempted such a feat. Hell, no immortal had either until then. Except, perhaps, for Seth or David. Those two had lived thousands of years. Étienne didn't know half of what they had done.

"Where's Marcus?" Sarah asked.

"Out hunting."

"How did he get out of kitten duty?" Roland asked dourly, even though everyone here could clearly see he had a soft spot for animals.

Ami stroked Slim's fur. "Slim doesn't like smelling other cats on him."

Étienne suspected there was more to it than that, but didn't say anything. Marcus had been giving off all kinds of stress vibes lately.

"In fact, I'm going to take Slim out for a jaunt until you're finished in here. I think he needs a break."

Slim chose that moment to emit a peculiar howl.

Chuckles circled the room as she passed through the kitchen, then exited through the back door.

Stepping out into the brisk wind, Ami set Slim down on the back deck and gave his skinny little butt a pat. "All right, you crazy kitty. Have fun."

Perking up, he meowed and trotted down the steps into the darkened yard.

Ami stood still for a moment, enjoying the night.

Quiet engulfed her. Since she didn't have the superior hearing of immortals, the conversations of those within couldn't reach her out here. Only the rustling of leaves that fluttered in the breeze broke the silence.

Retrieving the lightweight aluminum ladder kept on the deck, she descended the porch steps and walked around to the side of the house. The ladder was just tall enough to reach the roof. Ami leaned it up against the gutters and gave it a shake to ensure it was steady before she placed her foot on the first rung and began to climb.

At the top, she peered over the edge of the roof, already knowing whom she would find seated upon it.

As usual, he wore black leather pants and nothing else. A pair of beautiful wings, as tan as his skin at their base and darkening to black at their tips, were folded against his back. His shoulder-length, wavy, black hair danced in the wind.

Hi, she greeted him mentally.

He shook his head. *How do you always know I'm here?* Rising, he strode silently across the roof, took her hand, and helped her the rest of the way up.

I know your energy signature now.

His brow furrowed. *I'm glad Seth can't detect me so easily. I doubt he'd respond well to learning I've been . . . visiting.*

She thought he might be right on that one. Her husband Marcus wouldn't either, if he knew.

Seating herself, Ami waited for Zach to reclaim his spot, then withdrew two lollipops from her jacket.

His lips tilted up in a faint smile. *Which one do I want tonight?*

She offered him a green one. *Apple.*

The smell of fresh fruit—Granny Smith apples and ripe strawberries—filled the air as they unwrapped their treats and let the flavors coat their tongues.

This was the sixth or seventh time she had met him up here. She alone seemed capable of detecting his presence.

She still didn't know who he was, but sensed he posed no threat to her.

He rarely spoke. That didn't bother her though. She hadn't been much of a talker either after Seth and David had rescued her from her torturers. And the first time she had met Zach he had been riddled with wounds and trembling with pain.

Ami understood pain.

She also understood a reluctance to trust.

Wind buffeted her, rocking her on her perch.

Zach unfurled his wings to shield her from the breeze.

So, he drawled, surprising her, *how are you?*

She turned her head and found him studying her intently. *You know?* she asked.

About your pregnancy? Yes.

Only a handful of people had been told, so either he had overheard it or he had detected the baby's heartbeat and, unlike the others, knew it didn't belong to one of the kittens.

Dr. Lipton said the baby has a strong, healthy heartbeat.

I didn't ask about the baby. I asked about you. How are you *doing?*

Shrugging, she lowered her gaze to the lollipop wrapper and began to fold and unfold it. *The nausea is pretty bad. Lollipops are the only sweet things I can stand to smell or eat. Anything else makes me throw up.* As did most foods. Marcus was worried that she wasn't getting enough nutrition, because almost everything she put in her stomach came right back up again.

Are you afraid? he asked softly.

Ami's throat thickened. Her vision grew hazy as tears welled in her eyes. Raising her head, she met his gentle gaze. *Terrified.*

Zach's chest constricted when tears spilled over her lashes and trailed down her cheeks. Ami was the kindest, gentlest mortal he had encountered in his long existence. Ironically, she was also one of the fiercest, most determined fighters. To see her so vulnerable made his heart hurt.

And Zach hadn't even realized he *had* a heart.

I wish I could see the future, he said, *so I could tell you how this will turn out.*

She smiled and brushed at her cheeks. *At least you didn't tell me everything will be all right.*

Is that what your husband does? he asked curiously.

She shook her head. *Marcus never lies to me.* A sad smile tilted her lips. *So he says very little. He asks how I feel and does everything he can to make me happy, help me feel better, keep me from stressing over what might happen, all the things that could go wrong.* More tears welled. *And tries to carry all of the burden himself.*

Zach swallowed. There really wasn't anything he could say to ease her mind and steal away her despair. It surprised him that he even wished to try.

Did you know, she asked, sniffling, *that before I came here I had never seen a pregnant woman?*

No. He couldn't imagine it, and sometimes forgot that she was from another planet.

She smiled. *The first one I saw had a belly so huge I thought something was seriously wrong with her.*

She must have wondered what the hell was *in* that belly. *How is that possible?* he asked. *Don't people on your planet reproduce the same way we do?*

She nodded. *Visitors came to us from another solar system under the guise of friendship and used a virus as a bioweapon against us. No one died from it, so we thought it was an accident, that they hadn't known they were carriers, and didn't think much of it until we realized that almost every woman on our planet had been rendered infertile by it. Those who weren't usually miscarried. Successful pregnancies that go to term are practically nonexistent now. And female children are just as likely to be infertile. It's one of the reasons I came here.*

I hoped to find some Earth women who might like to either serve as surrogate mothers or marry our men and help us repopulate.

And the other?

She shook her head. *To warn you that the beings who tried to eradicate* us *are on their way to eradicate* you.

Lovely. And for that you were ruthlessly tortured for six months.

Yes. She was quiet for a long moment. *I never thought I would be a mother.* Another minute passed. *Marcus never thought he would be a father.*

The odds of either were . . .

Well, hell, he would have thought it impossible even *without* knowing her people's history.

Congratulations.

She stared at him. Moisture once more welled in her eyes.

Again Zach's chest tightened. He cupped his knees in his palms, slid his hands over the soft leather anxiously. *Should I not have—?*

She shook her head, lips curling into a trembling smile, and brushed the tears from her cheeks. *I'm sorry. It's just . . . you're the first person who has congratulated me. Everyone else . . .*

Is concerned.

She nodded.

He looked at her stomach, hidden beneath one of Marcus's large sweatshirts. *May I?*

She nodded.

Zach leaned close. Placing a hand on her stomach, which was rounder than he had expected beneath the soft material, he concentrated on the life it sheltered. *The babe seems healthy. Maybe a little large.*

She smiled, her face lighting a bit. *That's what Seth said. Marcus is large, too, though, so that's the one thing that* doesn't *concern me.*

He hoped that was the explanation. A mixture of *gifted one* and alien DNA with the vampiric virus thrown in . . .

No one knew what the hell to expect.

And all feared the worst. Those who knew, anyway.

You know what I think you should do? he said, drawing back.

What?

Enjoy the moment. Live like there is no tomorrow. You have a healthy babe in your belly and a husband who loves you. Let the others worry about the what-ifs. Stressing over what might happen isn't good for the baby.

She nodded. *I'll try.*

The front door opened and closed below them.

"Bon soir!" Lisette called, stepping into view as she donned a motorcycle helmet.

"Good night," Sarah responded cheerfully.

"Good hunting," Roland added.

A moment later, the French immortal sped away on the back of her motorcycle.

"Want to run home?" Roland asked as he and his wife strolled into view.

"Do you mean *literally* run?"

He nodded and wrapped his arms around her, drawing her body against his. "I know how exhilarating you find it. And I love anything that lights your beautiful eyes with excitement." He kissed her.

Her eyes began to glow as she sank into him. "We'll be all sweaty when we get home."

He kissed her again. "We're going to get sweaty once we're home anyway."

She emitted a throaty laugh. "Shall we make it interesting then and race?"

"How about we race naked? If I catch you, we make love wherever I tackle you."

"And risk having vampires catch us *in flagrante delicto?* I don't think so."

He laughed. "Perhaps another night then."

She stepped back. "On three?"

"On three."

"Okay. One. Two." She took off, her slender form blurring as she sped off into the night. "Three!" she called from half a mile away, laughter trailing after her.

Roland's usually dour face broke into a wide grin as he took off after her.

Zack looked at Ami and found her smiling.

What's it like? he asked, curious.

What?

He started to say love. Affection. Friendship. *Nothing. Never mind.*

She grimaced. *Ech. My stomach is starting to churn again. I'd better go. I doubt David would appreciate it if I vomited all over his solar panels.*

Zach thought David wouldn't care if Ami puked all over his dreadlocks. The elder immortal just wanted her to be happy and healthy and safe.

Rising, he walked with her over to the ladder and steadied her as she found the rungs with her feet. She didn't need his aid. She was as sure-footed as a cat. Her condition just made him feel protective.

He frowned.

Would you like to come with me? she asked.

No, thank you.

She smiled and descended the ladder.

Zach retook his position in the center of the roof. Tucking his wings in close, he listened as she returned the ladder to its hangers and went inside.

Quiet enfolded him, broken only by the occasional conversation filtering up from the house.

What the hell are you doing, Zach? he asked himself. Why

was he so drawn to this place? To these people? What had changed?

Was Seth right? Had *he* changed?

He heard Darnell greet Ami inside as he collected kittens from immortals and returned them to whatever basket or box they kept them in. "I'm heading downstairs to challenge the Seconds that are training tonight. How much you wanna bet I beat them?"

Had Ami been the one to make the challenge, Zach knew every dollar would be placed on her. But she hadn't sparred with the others since she'd learned she was pregnant.

"All at once?" Richart asked before Ami could respond.

"Nah. One or two at a time."

"I'll bet a thousand on you," the Frenchman declared.

"No way," Étienne said. "There are too many. They'll tire him out. A thousand on the other Seconds."

"You're on."

"Can I get in on this?" another asked.

"Me, too."

"Where are *you* going to get a thousand dollars?"

"Bite me."

They all moved down to the basement, where loud cheering and taunting erupted as the first match began.

They really did seem like one big family. How had Seth accomplished that?

Something stung Zach's neck. Reaching up, he felt around and found three darts sticking out of it.

Yanking them out, he stared down at them. These weren't mercenary darts. They were the darts Dr. Lipton had fashioned for the immortals to use against vampires.

He scanned the dark scenery around him, looking for the culprit, and belatedly heard the heartbeat behind him that his thoughts had drowned out.

Casually, he turned. His own heart gave a weird little skip.

Lisette, the French immortal, crouched there, her lovely face expressionless.

And her face truly was lovely. He had never been this close to her before. Her skin was pale perfection, her raven hair pulled back from her face in a braid that fell to her waist. Her slender body was clad in a formfitting T-shirt and cargo pants accentuated with holstered Glock 18s. The handles of two sheathed shoto swords peeked at him over her shoulders.

She reminded him of that woman in the *Tomb Raider* games he had seen Darnell and Ami playing.

And her scent . . .

He drew in a deep breath. She smelled even better than Ami. And Ami smelled better than the lollipops she brought him.

A long minute passed during which Lisette stared at him, waiting for the tranquilizer to take effect. Little did she know the drug would have no more effect on him than it would on Seth.

Zach raised an eyebrow.

Her forehead crinkled in a frown. Quick as lightning, she drew three more darts from her pocket and stuck them in his neck.

With slow, deliberate movements, Zach reached up and removed them.

She bit her lip.

"That hurts, you know," he said softly enough that he hoped those down in the house wouldn't hear it over the sparring noises and boisterous cheers.

A thin wire slipped over his head from behind and jerked across his neck, shutting off air.

"Not as much as this will, asshole," a male voice growled in his ear.

It carried a British accent, so it wasn't one of her brothers.

What exactly was going on here?

Before Zach could ponder further, a figure appeared on the roof beside him. Sarah met Zach's gaze, took in the piano wire choking him, glanced at Lisette—who looked guilty as hell—then turned her attention to the man behind Zach.

"Hi," Sarah said.

"You followed me?" that one growled.

Ah. Roland.

"Yes, I did."

"Why?"

"Curiosity. You wouldn't say why you were coming back and told me not to follow you, which left me no choice but to do so."

Both spoke as softly as Zach had.

Roland grunted.

"So," she said.

"So?" Roland parroted.

"Watcha doin'?"

"Lisette has some questions for this one."

"Uh-huh. And . . . you thought this was the best way to elicit answers?"

"Yes."

"Uh-huh. Uh-huh. You don't think . . . maybe . . . this sort of thing might be why everyone calls you antisocial?"

"Considering the questions, I thought he would likely be uncooperative."

"Oh." She studied Zach, then looked at Lisette. "Ohhhhhh." Her brows drew together. "Is this a lover's quarrel kind of thing? Did he do something to piss you off?"

Lisette looked uncomfortable.

"He didn't cheat on you, did he?" Sarah asked, all concern. "I didn't realize you were seeing anyone."

Zach watched Lisette, ignoring the pain in his throat and the burn beginning to fill his lungs.

Lisette visually consulted Roland over Zach's shoulder. "It isn't about me."

"Then who is it about?" Sarah asked.

Roland must have mouthed a name, because—though Zach

heard nothing—Sarah's eyes blazed a bright luminescent green, very rare amongst immortals. "Really." She moved, silently circling around to stand with her husband at Zach's back. "Let me give you a little help with that, sweetie."

In all of his thousands of years of existence, Zach didn't think anything so peculiar had ever happened to him.

Or so intriguing.

Or entertaining.

As the husband-and-wife team slowly choked him toward unconsciousness, he pondered what to do. He could make enough noise to draw David's attention. But David wouldn't appreciate his presence here any more than Seth would.

He could teleport away. But anyone touching him would go with him. So he would only escape Lisette, and she was the most interesting person here. *She* was the reason he hadn't yet attempted to secure his freedom.

Roland planted a boot in Zach's back and pulled harder.

Roland had said Lisette wanted to talk to him. That she had some questions for Zach.

What kind of questions?

How did she even know about him?

How had she detected his presence when Seth and David hadn't?

His heartbeat sounded loudly in his ears as his lungs hungered for oxygen.

Zach couldn't seem to find the will to fight them. He wanted to know what Lisette wanted from him. Had Roland and Sarah stopped trying to suffocate him and stepped back, he didn't think he would have left.

Hmm. He could just go with it.

The idea appealed to him far more than it should. He wasn't supposed to care about this. Any of it. Or these people.

But his damned curiosity wouldn't leave him be.

And Seth hadn't been far from the truth when they had spoken in South Korea. The numbness *was* wearing off.

Boredom *had* set in. Zach was drowning in it. And he would do just about anything, including allow the odd couple behind him to force him into unconsciousness, to swim his way back to the surface and leave it behind him.

A very dangerous mind-set that had already gotten him into trouble once.

His eyes locked on Lisette's face.

Fuck it. He wanted to know.

The smile he gave her as darkness enfolded him must have puzzled the hell out of her.

Lisette stared down at the unconscious male Roland dumped onto the floor of the safe house they had claimed for the day.

He was incredibly handsome. Dark, wavy hair fell below his shoulders. A muscled chest devoid of hair tapered to a narrow waist and slim hips encased in black leather.

Her gaze went to his wings.

They were beautiful. The same tan as his skin at their base, the nearly translucent wings darkened to black at their tips and would span twelve or fourteen feet when fully extended.

The man himself was taller than Seth, who stood a good six foot eight or thereabouts.

"Do you know him?" she asked Roland as he left the room.

"No." He returned, carrying titanium chains thicker than her biceps that humans would probably have to use a forklift to move. Dumping the lot on the floor, he crouched next to their prisoner.

"Is he an immortal?" Sarah asked as she took a position beside her husband, weapons drawn.

"He must be," Roland mumbled, taking the man by the throat and dragging him upright. "Vampires don't have wings."

"Wait." Lisette halted him before he could start wrapping the man in chains. Hurrying to the only bedroom in the small house, she yanked the covers off the bed and took them into the living room.

"What's that for?" Roland asked with a scowl.

She knelt beside him. "If he's immortal, Seth won't respond well to him being damaged." Dropping the bedding, she leaned forward and tentatively touched one of his wings.

So soft. Like the delicate strands of hair on a newborn baby's head.

Her heart began to pound as she gently took both wings and folded them in close to his back. Holding them in place with one hand, she wrapped the sheet and blanket around him.

"What's wrong?" Roland asked with a scowl. "Your heart is beating faster."

That part of being an Immortal Guardian sucked. There really were very few secrets among their ranks because of their damned heightened senses. "Are you sure he's an immortal? I can't smell the virus on him."

"Can you smell it on me?"

"Barely."

"What about David and Seth?"

"No."

"Then there's your answer. He's an immortal. He just must be old as hell." Once she finished and sat back, he started wrapping the chains around and around the stranger.

"If he's that old," Sarah murmured, "wouldn't you know him, honey?"

Lisette snorted. "As antisocial as Roland is, he wouldn't even know *me* if I hadn't made myself a nuisance."

The dour immortal's face actually lightened with a smile. "You weren't the nuisance. Your brothers were."

She grinned. He may be curt and surly with the others, but he had always been kind to her.

Soon the winged mystery immortal was swathed tightly in chains from his neck to his feet. Why did seeing him like that bother her so? She didn't know him. Had never met him. And had good reason to dislike him.

"What now?" she asked as the three of them stood in a semicircle and stared down at him.

"We wait until he wakes up, then extract information."

She glanced at the window. "Dawn is approaching."

Roland followed her gaze. "Go home. We'll take first watch."

"I want to be here when you question him."

"If he wakes before sunset, we'll await your return."

She nodded, strangely reluctant to leave. Giving their prisoner one last look, she said her good-byes, then headed out into the night.

Étienne paced outside Krysta's home, listening to her shoot the breeze with her brother while they prepared for the night's hunt.

This was ridiculous. He had awoken this afternoon, full of anticipation, eager to see Krysta again, and hadn't wasted a second getting here once the sun had set. Even Cameron, his Second, had noticed something was amiss. He hadn't said anything, but Étienne had caught the *What's up with you?* looks Cam had shot him while doling out weapons.

A slender shadow crossed the curtains. Étienne glimpsed Krysta in the living room. She was arming herself with more weapons than he had realized she carried. Damned near as many as *he* carried.

Why did that turn him on?

He sighed.

Was this what he had come to? Stalking her like one of those freaks on the Internet you heard about on the news?

Yes, he imagined Cam telling him.

Had he really sunk so low?

He had even been tempted to circle around to the other side of the house, peer through her bedroom window, and watch her dress, but that had just seemed too sleazy. Besides, if he ever saw Krysta naked, he wanted it to be on *her* terms with—

Wait. What the hell was he thinking? He wasn't going to see Krysta naked. He *couldn't* see Krysta naked. She bore what was obviously a deep-seated hatred for vampires, from which she didn't differentiate him, and would destroy him in an instant if given the opportunity.

Even if he managed to lessen her desire to decapitate him, there was still the whole mortal-immortal thing. He wasn't sure she was a *gifted one.* If her brother was her half brother, she may not possess the advanced DNA needed to transform without becoming vampire. Not that she would want to anyway because of the whole *I hate vampires* roadblock.

Étienne straightened.

Was he really trying to think his way into a relationship with a woman who wanted him dead? Was he *that* lonely?

Or was she just that irresistible?

Don't answer that, he warned himself and blamed all of the happy pappy lovestruck crap that had surrounded him of late for his current confusion. First Roland had fallen in love with Sarah, who clearly was delusional for thinking him sweet.

Then Marcus had found Ami. The jury was still out on whether or not their relationship was going to have a happy ending because Ami had not yet asked Marcus to transform her.

Richart had fallen hard for Jenna, who—Étienne was very pleased to note—made his brother *very* happy.

Even that bastard Bastien had fallen in love with and married Dr. Lipton.

The jangling of keys shook Étienne from his musings. He ducked out of sight as the front door swung open.

Krysta exited first, her shoto swords clutched in one hand, her coat in the other.

Étienne silently cursed as his pulse picked up its pace.

Sean exited next, carrying a pile of heavy books, and tromped down the stairs.

Étienne had learned from his shameless eavesdropping sessions (there had been more of those than he cared to admit in the two weeks he had been following her) that Sean was in medical school and usually studied in the car while she hunted.

Krysta's eyes scanned the area as they crossed the yard to their crappy car.

Both doors groaned when pried open. And the damned engine barely turned over.

Though Krysta worked days and Sean weekends, freeing up the nights for hunting, they barely made ends meet.

Étienne had been tempted to call in the network to make all the repairs the car needed, but that would bring the sibling vampire hunters to Chris Reordon's attention.

Not a good idea.

Étienne raced through the countryside, following the shabby vehicle and making sure forest, field, or structures always hid him from view.

Looked like they were heading for Duke tonight.

The hunt was on.

That's right, dullards, Krysta thought, mentally smiling as she used Étienne's term, *come along, follow the poor, unsuspecting undergrad who doesn't know you're there because she's busy drunk dialing her ex.*

That one was always popular. There were times, in fact, when she could actually hear some of the vampires laugh over the crazy-ass things she said or shouted into the phone while staggering up the path. Perhaps, in another life, she could have been an actress.

There had been no vamp action around the frat houses tonight. Rather she had found them lingering in Research Park, waiting for an egghead to stumble out after working on whatever it was he or she researched until the wee hours.

Along the sidewalk, Krysta led them between two buildings, and into a darker area near the loading dock. She thought there had been lights back here the last time she had passed by. The vamps must have broken them, intending to feed on their victim where none would see.

Perfect.

Her heart began to pound, not with fear as she prepared to spin around and fight, but with anticipation. Étienne was nearby. She knew it. She could feel it. And she wasn't going to let him snatch away her prize this time. She was going to confront the vamps before he had the chance.

Drawing her shoto swords, she spun around at the same moment Étienne appeared behind the vamps.

Ooh. *Six* vampires. Good thing he *had* come.

Étienne's brows drew down in a frown as he met her gaze. "Damn it! You're early!"

She grinned. "Nope. You're late."

The vampires' faces went blank with surprise. Their gazes zigzagged between the two of them.

"Oh shit," one said, his face filling with fear as he stared at Étienne. "An Immortal Guardian."

Gasps from his vampire cohorts.

A what?

Another vampire looked at Krysta. "She's human. She must be his Second."

"*Bastien* has a mortal Second," another said.

Who had a what now?

Krysta was given no time to ask.

Their faces contorted with fury. "Bastien the Deceiver!"

"Death to Bastien!"

"Kick their fucking asses!"

The vampires drew weapons and attacked.

Krysta inched backward and swung her swords as multiple orange auras shot toward her.

The vampires must think they would have an easier time killing *her* than they would Étienne.

Smart vamps.

Sucked for her, though.

Even as she struck lethal blows with her blades, slicing the throat of the first vampire to reach her, pain streaked through her thigh as another vamp's blade cut into her flesh.

Krysta gritted her teeth and swung at the orange aura leaping away from her.

Score! Tit for tat. She'd cut his femoral artery, the bastard!

Limping backward, she kept her swords in constant motion. Glowing orange auras swirled around her, so numerous that fear threatened to paralyze her.

She struck more blows, aiming at auras and hitting the flesh they preceded.

The vampires struck blows as well. Cuts stung her arms, back, legs. Just as she was silently celebrating a particularly good blow, one of the vamps circled around behind her and hit her in the head, landing a simple punch with his fist, backed by preternatural strength, that felt like a freaking anvil.

The world around her lit up with sparkly things that had nothing to do with auras. All strength left her limbs as agony pounded her head.

Krysta staggered. Her thoughts scattered.

Somewhere a lion roared.

The glowing orange auras surrounding her fell away as

shining purple and white rolled through them like a bowling ball felling pins.

Krysta's weapons clattered to the ground, her fingers unable to grasp anything but her aching head.

She sank to her knees.

"Krysta!"

Chapter 4

Étienne wasn't usually one to panic. Even as a mortal, when fighting, he had always kept his cool.

But seeing Krysta felled by a vampire's fist . . .

"Krysta!" he called again, after severing that fist and leaving the vampire to bleed out.

His swords swung like the blades of a propeller, cutting through the vampires as though they were no more than air.

Had it been more than a glancing blow, wouldn't she be down on the ground and either unconscious or dying from a fractured skull? Sarah had nearly died when Bastien had fractured *her* skull. Her ears had even bled.

Étienne tried to see if Krysta bled from her ears, but couldn't take his eyes off the damned vampires.

Finally, the last vamp succumbed to Étienne's swords.

Racing to Krysta's side, he knelt before her and dropped his weapons. "Are you okay?" He clasped her shoulder with one hand and gently raised her chin with the other.

Her lovely face was pinched with pain. "I'm okay," she gritted. "My head just hurts like a bitch. I think I might have a concussion. My vision is all fuzzy."

Her pupils were a little dilated, too.

"What about you?" she murmured. "Are you okay?"

Shock, pleasure, and all kinds of things he refused to examine too closely flowed through him. "I'm fine. Hardly a scratch on me."

"Must be nice. Help me up, will you?"

"Of course." He helped her to her feet, wrapping an arm around her when she swayed.

"The bastards all came after *me*," she complained, leaning into him.

Did she realize the trust she was placing in him?

He cleared his throat, trying to ignore how good it felt to have her tucked up against his side. "Vampires are often cowards and seek the weaker target."

"Gee, thanks."

"I just meant—"

"I get it. I just don't like it."

"That I'm stronger than you are?"

"Yes. What's an Immortal Guardian?"

Étienne swore silently. He had hoped she hadn't caught that.

"A what?" he stalled, not knowing how to answer.

"You heard me. An Immortal Guardian." Stepping away, she clung to his arm until she was steady, then released him and met his gaze. "The vampires called you an Immortal Guardian."

His cursed mind went blank.

"They also called me a Second. What's a Second?"

Still nothing. What had Roland told Sarah when faced with such questions?

"Who is Bastien the Deceiver?"

He swore aloud then. "Aren't you supposed to have a concussion? How are you remembering all of this?"

"You're stalling."

Yes, he was.

Étienne paced away several steps. "I can't tell you."

"Can't or won't?"

"Can't."

"Why?"

"I can't tell you secrets that are not solely my own to share," he tried to explain.

"So there are more like you."

Étienne stared at her, wanting to trust her.

A sharp pain pierced his neck.

Wincing, he reached up, felt something protruding from the skin, and removed it.

"What's that?" Krysta asked.

His blood went cold as he stared down at the tiny object his fingers clutched.

"Is that a tranquilizer dart?" she asked, voice full of confusion.

Yes, it was. *Merde*.

"Run," he ordered as weakness began to infiltrate him.

This wasn't supposed to happen. This shouldn't be possible.

"What?" She started to approach him.

Étienne shook his head. "Run!" He closed the distance between them, retrieved her weapons from the ground, and urged her toward the corner of the nearest building. "Call your brother. Choose a safe place for him to meet you a few blocks from here and run there. Don't stop. Don't look back. And don't let anyone follow you home."

"I don't understand. What's going on? Why is your accent getting thicker? What—?"

Another sting. Étienne yanked another dart from the back of his neck and swore foully. The shooters were definitely behind them.

His knees weakened. He didn't carry the autoinjector containing the antidote anymore. He hadn't thought there was a reason to. The human threat had been extinguished.

Hadn't it?

"Please, Krysta. Just trust me on this. Go! *Maintenant!*"

As his strength waned, he shoved her hard and turned to face his attackers.

Still dizzy, Krysta stumbled and fell to her hands and knees behind the building. The weapons Étienne had thrust into her arms hit the ground a moment before gravel abraded her palms.

What the hell?

Cursing, she dusted off her stinging hands, grabbed the weapons, and spun around, ready to blister his ears.

Étienne staggered, as if he had lost his balance. Turning back to face the way they had come, he gave her his profile. His eyes flashed a brilliant amber.

Bullets slammed into his chest, the guns firing them barely making a sound. His body jerked again and again as blood sprayed from too many wounds to count.

Krysta stared in horror. "Étienne!"

The first wave ended.

He turned his head, met her gaze. "Run, damn you!" he growled. Blood poured from his mouth and down his chin. Drawing his swords, he roared and leapt forward, out of sight.

Krysta's feet glued themselves to the ground. She couldn't move. Couldn't breathe.

He had pushed her out of the way to save her. If Étienne hadn't shoved her behind the building, she would have been shot to death beside him.

Her body began to shake uncontrollably.

He could have run. He could have left her there for whoever the hell it was to kill her.

Screams lit the night. The gunfire resumed.

Krysta transferred one of her swords to her left hand, drew out her cell phone, and dialed with shaking fingers.

"Yeah," her brother answered on the first ring.

"I need you," she hissed. "Now. Behind . . . Shit!" It took

her a moment to get her bearings. "We're in Research Park behind . . . or on the side of that Environmental Whatever Building. Just find me. Come quiet and stay low. Someone's shooting at us."

"What?"

"Just come now! Please! And hurry!"

Pocketing the phone, she drew in a deep breath (which wasn't nearly as calming as she had hoped it would be), gripped her weapons, and headed for the edge of the building.

Crouching down, she peered around it.

Soldiers?

Men garbed in black camo and armed to the teeth with silencer-equipped automatic weapons were doing their damnedest to kill Étienne. Only they didn't seem to actually want to *kill* him. They seemed to want to slow him down or weaken him with blood loss and whatever was in those darts.

And it was working.

Another dart hit Étienne in the throat even as he broke two soldiers' necks.

He staggered, grabbed another soldier and sank his teeth into his throat.

Krysta's mouth went dry.

She'd known all along he was a vampire, but seeing him drink blood . . .

The other soldiers evidently viewed their associate as expendable, because they continued to shoot.

Étienne used him as a shield while he drank and fired the man's automatic weapon at the same time.

His victim sank to the ground, sightless eyes staring up at the sky.

Another dart struck Étienne in the arm.

He lurched sideways. Shook his head drunkenly.

Oh shit.

There were still three soldiers left.

Two moved in for the kill or to capture him or whatever the hell the plan was.

Krysta dropped her swords and drew two daggers. Without giving herself time to think, she stepped into the open and let them fly. One dagger struck a soldier in the throat. The second sank into another soldier's heart. The third soldier turned his gun on her and fired. She ducked behind the building and hit the ground. Brick and mortar showered down on her as the high-caliber bullets passed right through the building.

A yelp split the night.

The bullets stopped.

"Krysta!"

Relief poured through her at the raspy call, bringing tears to her eyes. "Étienne!"

Scrambling to her feet, she peered around the corner of the building.

Every soldier was down.

Étienne still stood. Barely. Blood saturated his clothing. Dozens of holes perforated his shirt and coat and pants.

He stumbled forward a step and dropped to his knees.

As Krysta limped toward him, she looked around, praying no more soldiers would leap out of the darkness and start shooting.

"C-call your brother," he wheezed. Fumbling in his pocket, he muttered something in French.

Just as she reached him, he collapsed backward onto the pavement.

Something clunked to the ground by his hip. A cell phone.

"He's on his way," she said, kneeling beside him. "Can I call someone for you?"

She picked up his phone and heard the telltale squeak of their car's brakes, though her brother approached as quietly as he could.

Étienne closed his eyes and mumbled something else in French.

"I don't understand." Damn it. Why hadn't she studied French in high school?

"Krysta?" Sean whispered.

"Over here!" she hissed as loudly as she dared, terrified that more men might be lurking nearby.

Nearly silent footsteps approached. "Oh shit," her brother swore. "What the hell?"

"Come help me," she ordered. Tucking Étienne's phone in his coat pocket, she scooted around to cup his broad shoulders.

"Those don't look like vampires," Sean said as he joined her, his eyes on the fallen soldiers.

"They aren't. They're humans, and they tried to kill us."

"Us?" He looked down at Étienne. "Is that . . . ?"

"Yes. Grab his feet."

"No way. He's a vampire."

"And he saved my ass. Again. Come on. Grab his legs. We need to get the hell out of here before more of *those* guys come along."

Étienne's head lolled as they hefted his heavy form and began carting him to the car parked behind the building.

"Is he dead?" Sean huffed.

Étienne wasn't disintegrating, so . . . "No. They drugged him with something."

"And shot him all to shit?"

"Yes."

"Who the hell are they?"

"I don't know. But *he* does. As soon as he saw the tranquilizer dart . . ." She shook her head. "He knew what was coming." Crap, he was heavy. "I didn't hear anything or see anything. All of a sudden he just shoved me behind the building. Then they opened fire and he fought them."

"Why didn't he just run? They're human. They'd never catch him. And they can't shoot what they can't follow."

She met his gaze and said nothing.

"What? You're saying—"

"He fought them to buy me time to get away. They would have killed me, Sean. They would've shot me, too. They *tried* to shoot me."

He looked as confused as she felt.

Together they managed to cram Étienne's long, muscled body into the backseat.

Sean slammed the door. "Okay, let's go."

"Wait." Running back to the soldiers, she paused and swallowed hard. Creeping forward, she leaned down, grasped the bloodied handle of one of her daggers, and yanked it out of the dead soldier's throat. The other's lifeless eyes seemed full of accusation as she pulled her dagger out of his chest.

When she turned around, she found Sean staring at her somberly.

"Krysta, did you . . . ?"

She couldn't meet his gaze. Limping forward, she circled the car. "Just get us out of here."

The silence that filled the car as they drove away hurt more than her throbbing head did.

Tonight she had done something she never would've thought she could do. Something she didn't know how she could justify.

Tonight she had killed humans to protect a vampire.

"He's too long for the futon. Put him on my bed." Krysta raced for the bathroom while Sean carried Étienne into her bedroom. Grabbing the vinyl shower curtain, she yanked it down and hurried after him.

"Wait." She jerked the top covers back, spread the curtain over the bed to protect the mattress from bloodstains, covered it with a sheet, then stood back. "Okay."

Sean dumped Étienne on the bed.

Étienne didn't move.

"Are you sure he's still alive?" Sean asked.

Biting her lip, Krysta leaned down and pressed two fingers to Étienne's blood-slick throat. A long moment passed in which her heart slammed against her ribs and Étienne's didn't appear to do anything at all. "I don't feel anything." Throat thickening, she feared she might burst into tears.

Had he died protecting her?

Sean said nothing. Face impassive, he moved to the opposite side of the bed, bent over, and felt for a pulse himself.

Minutes passed. Krysta didn't know how many. But with each, she felt shakier inside and more ready to scream with panic and regret and everything else building inside her.

"He's alive," Sean pronounced. "His pulse is so slow he would be declared dead in a hospital, but it's there."

Despite her attempts to stop them, a few tears spilled over her lashes. Krysta sank onto the side of the bed, all of her aches and pains making themselves known in a big way now that she wasn't completely distracted.

"Before we get into what happened tonight," Sean said as he strolled around to stand before her, "tell me where you're hurt."

She scrubbed her hands down her face and hoped he hadn't noticed the tears. "My head is the worst. I think I might have a concussion."

Sean closed his eyes a moment, then cupped his large hands around the back of her head. Seconds later, they heated and the pain slowly disappeared. "What else?" he asked, teeth clenched against the pain that now bombarded him.

"Nothing that can't be patched up with Band-Aids, butterfly closures, and a few stitches." Healing the head wound would have taken enough out of him that any cuts or gashes he healed on her now would open on his own body. She wouldn't let that happen. After the mess she had just brought down on their heads, she wouldn't make him bleed, too.

"Go shower. I'll stitch you up when you get out."

Nodding, she grabbed some clean clothes from her dresser.

"Do you want to lie down for a while?" His head must be killing him.

He gave her a grim smile. "I can't. Someone needs to watch our *guest*."

Krysta said nothing.

What *could* she say? She had just welcomed one of the vampires she had sworn to kill into their home and placed them both in danger.

Heading into the bathroom, she closed the door.

The hot water stung her open cuts like salt, making her want to scream as she hurried through her shower. The most she would permit herself, however, was a grunt or two.

Damn, it hurt!

And rushing things didn't help. She couldn't be careful with wounds when she was dragging a rough, soapy wash-cloth across them as quickly as possible because she feared what her brother might do to Étienne if she took too long.

Or what Étienne might do to Sean, if she weren't there when he awoke.

If he awoke.

She barely took the time to dry off before hurriedly donning a sports bra, tank top, panties, and shorts. Leaving her hair to air-dry in whatever tangled mess it had acquired, she grabbed a smaller towel, held it to the thigh that still bled sluggishly, and hobbled back to her bedroom.

Sean had dragged one of their sagging director's chairs into the room and sprawled in it, his gaze shifting from the television to Étienne and back.

He didn't look up when she entered. "Nothing on the news yet."

Jeeze. She hadn't even thought of that. But how could what had happened tonight *not* make the news? A dozen or more soldiers killed in what would be deemed a firefight on an elite college campus?

Just what kind of soldiers had those men been? Military? SWAT?

Crap. What if surveillance cameras had caught it all on tape? She knew where most of the cameras on the various college campuses were positioned and lured vampires *away* from them so she could destroy them without witnesses. But cameras could have caught her going into the loading area just before the fight broke out. They could have caught her and Sean loading Étienne into the car and fleeing the scene.

What had she done?

"You need to tell me what happened tonight," Sean said in a low, don't-fuck-with-me voice. "All of it. And you need to tell me everything else that has been going on." His gaze went to Étienne, then rose to meet hers. "Because you've clearly been holding out on me."

And he deserved more than that. After all he did for her, all he sacrificed for her . . .

Nodding, Krysta started to sit on the side of the bed.

"No. Sit here. I need to see to your other wounds."

She hadn't even noticed the first-aid bag on the floor beside him.

Krysta crossed to him and turned her back to show him the wound in her thigh as he rose.

"What is it with vampires and hamstrings?" he muttered as he knelt behind her and went to work.

It seemed to be one of their favorite places to strike.

"I don't know." She gritted her teeth as he began to stitch the wound.

"So?" he prodded.

"He's been following me."

"The vamp on the bed?"

"Yes. Ever since the first night I encountered him, he's been following me and taking out the vampires I lure away before I can engage them."

"That's why you haven't come home battered and bloodied lately?"

She nodded. "He kills the vamps before I can even draw my weapons."

A pause. "You should have told me."

"I didn't know. Not for sure. Not until last night. I knew vampires were following me, I was sure they had taken the bait. But when I spun around to confront them, they were gone just like on the other nights. I heard the sounds of a struggle a few blocks away and ran like hell to see what was happening."

"You *what?*"

"By the time I caught up, there was nothing but a pile of clothes. He had already killed them."

Quiet enfolded them as Sean stitched. It must have been a longer and deeper cut than she had supposed.

"I confronted him. Goaded him into showing himself."

"Brilliant," he groused.

She'd let that slide, knowing worry spawned it.

"Did he say *why* he killed them?"

"He said he was protecting me."

"That doesn't make any sense."

"I know."

"He's a vampire and you're a vampire hunter."

"I know."

He finished torturing her with the needle and applied a bandage.

Exhaling a deep sigh of relief, Krysta turned around and sank gingerly into the chair. "He wanted me to stop hunting. He said it was too dangerous and couldn't believe I've been doing it for so long without getting myself killed."

"*I* can't believe you've been doing it so long without getting yourself killed."

"Smart-ass."

He grunted.

"He said he's been hunting vampires himself for two hundred years, Sean."

He glanced up at her as he retrieved some butterfly closures. "Two hundred years?"

"Yes."

"Why would a vampire hunt other vampires? Is it a territorial thing or something?"

"He said it wasn't, but wouldn't go into it. And tonight . . ." She didn't want to think about it.

"What the hell happened, Krysta?"

"I played my usual *Victim Here* role, lured some vampires behind the building where you found us, and confronted them before Étienne could snatch them away."

He nodded at their guest. "I assume he's Étienne?"

"Yes. They called him an immortal guardian, and thought I was something called a second."

"What the hell is that?"

"I don't know. But they were afraid of him and pissed at him all at the same time. And I can see why. There were six vampires and he took out most of them with no help from me and *again* saved my ass. Then, all of a sudden, someone shot him in the neck with a tranquilizer dart."

"Vampires can be sedated? Shit. I didn't even think of that."

"I didn't either. As soon as he saw the dart, Étienne told me to run and shoved me behind the building. Then the soldiers you saw appeared and shot him all to hell. They would have killed me, Sean, if he hadn't saved me. If he had run, they would have come after *me*. But he stayed and fought and took those bullets so I would have time to get away."

He sat back. "I don't understand. Why would a bunch of human soldiers want to kill *you*, another human? I mean, if they're vampire hunters like you, wouldn't they want to protect you?"

"I think they believed I was a second—whatever that is—

like the vampires did. Either that or they wanted *him* and thought I was expendable. Hell, maybe they thought I was his Renfield."

"Shit."

"I know."

"If he wanted to save you, why didn't he just toss you over his shoulder and run?"

"Maybe he was already too weak. Or maybe he was afraid they'd shoot me before he could get us out of range. Or maybe he just wasn't thinking straight because of the drug."

He went back to work. "And your daggers?"

How had they ended up in the throat and heart of two human men?

"I couldn't let them kill him or capture him after he sacrificed himself to protect me."

Sean sighed. "Were they military?"

"I don't know. They didn't identify themselves. Didn't shout, *Halt! Don't move! Police! Army! SWAT!* Nothing. They just opened fire."

Zipping his bag closed, Sean sat back on the floor. "What a mess." He dragged his hands down his face. "I can't think straight. My head is fucking killing me."

Guilt suffused her, as it always did when he suffered physical pain after healing her wounds.

"So what's the plan?" he asked wearily. "What are we going to do with Count Chocula over there?"

"I don't know."

Rising, Sean stared down at the unconscious vampire. "Immortal guardian," he muttered.

"That's what they called him."

"His wounds aren't healing. He probably needs blood."

"Well, I'd kinda like to keep mine where it is, particularly since I lost some tonight."

He loosed a tired laugh. "Yeah. Me, too. I guess I should patch him up since he saved your stubborn, reckless ass."

"I was hoping you would."

Krysta helped him remove Étienne's coat, weapons, and shirt.

Both swore when they saw just how many bullet holes he sported.

Krysta didn't know how he could still live. The vampires she usually hunted often died from blood loss. And Étienne had lost a *lot* of blood.

They moved on to his shoes and pants.

Sean's lips twitched.

"What?" she asked as she tugged off a heavy boot.

"Did you know your boy here's ringtone is "I Feel Pretty"?

She frowned and smiled at the same time. "What?"

"His phone rang while you were in the shower."

As if on cue, a female voice filled the air, singing, "I feel pretty! Oh so pretty! I feel pretty and witty and gaaaaaay!"

Laughing, Krysta retrieved Étienne's phone from his pocket and opened it just as it stopped ringing.

"It must have gone to voice mail," Sean said, peering at it. "If it rings again should I answer?"

"And bring another vampire down on our heads? I don't think so. At least not yet."

They stripped Étienne down to a pair of black, silk boxer shorts.

Although he had a beautiful body, trim and rippling with muscle, Krysta had a hard time admiring it. Blood coated nearly every inch of him, having poured from *so* many bullet holes. Even his legs were littered with them.

Sean swore.

Krysta nodded.

None of the wounds still bled. Neither did they heal. Some

of the holes even appeared to still contain the lead that had carved them.

"We need soapy water and some towels," Sean said, staring down at his patient. "A butt-load of them."

Krysta nodded. It was going to be a long night.

Lisette nibbled her thumbnail as she stared at the uncon-scious immortal male wrapped in titanium chains. Apparently he hadn't yet awoken, so Roland and Sarah were off hunting while Lisette took second watch.

Lisette didn't know who the mysterious immortal was, but he fascinated her.

He lay on the floor where Roland had dumped him, his wavy, raven hair shielding much of his face. A face she had not minded staring at in the least these past few weeks as she had spied upon him.

He was strikingly handsome. And so somber. Sad almost. Or maybe lonely? Ami always managed to lure a smile from him, even if only a small one.

Her eyes strayed to his wings. Those beautiful wings.

Only a few feathers peeked out from the blankets and chains.

Was he an immortal? Or was he something else? Some-thing a little more . . . angelic?

She hadn't posed the question to the others, knowing how ruthlessly Roland would have mocked the notion. But the idea just wouldn't leave her.

Easing closer to the male, she cautiously leaned in and sniffed his neck.

His scent was . . .

She sighed.

So good. He smelled like she remembered her father's country estate used to when she was a girl. Like spring rain. Fresh and clean and new.

She smiled. With a hint of the fruity lollipops Ami had given him last night.

What she *didn't* smell on him was the virus. Which didn't necessarily mean anything. As Roland had pointed out, she couldn't smell it on Seth either. Or David. Or some of the other elder immortals who had lived a great deal longer than she had.

Her gaze returned to his wings.

Still . . .

Her cell phone chirped.

Jumping, she shook her head at herself and stepped back from the captive as she retrieved the phone.

"*Oui?*" she answered when she saw it was Richart.

"Have you heard from Étienne tonight?"

"No. Why?"

"He was wounded earlier, judging by the pain I felt, and I haven't been able to reach him."

The twins had always referred to the unique bond they shared in much the same way the fictional character Adrian Monk described his own ability: It was a gift . . . and a curse.

It sucked that they felt each other's pain. And only pain. They never felt each other's pleasure, which—now that she thought of it—would be awkward now that Richart had wed and made frequent love to his wife.

The bond *did* come in handy, however, in times like this when one might be injured and require aid.

"Did you try Cam?" Surely Étienne's Second would know something.

"Cameron hasn't heard from him and is making discreet inquiries."

"Why discreet?"

"I don't know. Something's been going on with Étienne, something he's been keeping from us. You've noticed how distracted he's been."

"Yes. I assumed it was a woman, but could glean nothing from his thoughts. He has kept them from me of late."

And usually did so when he took a lover. Not that such had happened often over the past two centuries. Immortal/human love affairs never ended well.

"Should I call Seth?" he asked, that question telling her more than anything else how concerned he was.

"Would you have wanted Seth to hunt you down when you were with Jenna, recovering from your wounds the time you were tranqed?"

"No."

"Then there's your answer. Give it a little more time. If Étienne was wounded badly enough, he may simply be sleeping too deeply for the phone to awaken him."

"You're right, of course."

"Call me when you hear something. And tell Jenna hello for me."

"I will," he said, a smile entering his voice.

Lisette had only recently met her new sister-in-law and had never seen her brother as content and quick to smile as he had been with the former single mother. Not since his transformation anyway.

Guilt, an ever-present companion, stirred.

Lisette ended the call and returned her cell phone to her pocket.

Sighing, she focused her attention once more on the prisoner.

And found him staring up at her with piercing brown eyes.

Chapter 5

"I feel pretty! Oh so pretty!"

Krysta jerked awake.

"I feel pretty and witty and gaaaaaaay!"

Sitting up in the director's chair, she winced and rubbed her aching neck. She must have fallen asleep.

Her gaze went to Étienne.

He lay as he had ever since she and Sean had finished cleaning and bandaging his wounds. Still as death. The rise and fall of his chest so faint it seemed an illusion.

She reached for the cell phone she had dropped on the battered table beside her. Sean shuffled into the room, eyes puffy from sleep, boxers and T-shirt as rumpled as his short, black hair.

"How's your head?" she asked.

"Better."

She glanced at the phone. "It's someone named Richart."

"Are you going to answer it or let it go to voice mail?"

Glancing at Étienne, she answered the call.

Before she could say one word, a slew of French poured over the line. Biting her lip, she waited for it to end.

An expectant pause ensued.

Diving in, Krysta asked, "Do you speak English?"

"Yes," the man replied in a voice and accent very similar to Étienne's. "Who is this? Where did you find this phone?"

"In the owner's pocket. Who is this?" she countered.

"Where is he?"

She looked at Sean, who watched her with furrowed brow. "You didn't answer my question."

"I'm his brother."

Not what she had been expecting. "Vampires have brothers?" she asked, realizing the moment she said it what a stupid question it was. Of course they did. They had all been human once. It was just hard to remember that once they turned monstrous.

Sean's eyebrows flew up as he mouthed, "His brother?"

She nodded.

A tense silence followed.

"Hello?" she asked at length.

"If you have harmed him in any way," the man began, his deep voice so full of menace that she felt a twinge of fear.

"I haven't." She thought she heard a sigh of relief. "But someone else has. And I'm a little worried that they might come after us."

Sean nodded, sharing her concern.

They still had seen nothing about it on the news and didn't know whether that was a good thing or a bad thing. Both feared it was bad.

"How sorely is he wounded?"

"I'm pretty sure he needs blood."

"Did you give him any?"

"Um . . . no."

"Yet you know what he is."

"If you mean, do I know he's a vampire, then yes."

Another long pause. "Tell me where you are located."

Covering the phone, she whispered, "He wants to know where we are."

Sean looked as uneasy as she felt. "I don't know . . ."

"Who is there with you?" Richart demanded.

"My brother."

"Who else?"

She bit her lip. If Étienne was a two-hundred-year-old vampire and Richart was his brother, then Richart must be a vampire, too. What if Richart planned to bring a few of his bloodsucking friends? What if they didn't share Étienne's rare desire to protect humans?

"You hesitate," he pointed out.

"Look, I'm just not used to trusting vampires, okay? How do I know you won't bring a horde of others along with you and kill us both?"

"I wouldn't need a horde of others to kill you," he responded simply.

Crap.

"Honey," she heard a woman say in the background with an American accent, "if you're trying to reassure her that you won't hurt them, saying things like that won't help."

Krysta raised her eyebrows.

Sean mouthed, "What?"

"I think he has a girlfriend," she whispered.

"Étienne?"

"No." He'd better not. "His brother."

Wait. Why should it matter to her if Étienne had a girlfriend?

"I shall come alone," Richart tried again. "Unarmed. You may arm yourself however you will."

She looked at Étienne, so still and pale.

Hoping she wasn't making a huge mistake, she gave Richart their address.

Sean left the room, then returned in jeans with two holstered 9mms, socks, and sneakers.

Krysta rose and reached for a shoto sword.

Richart repeated her address. Krysta heard typing in the background.

"Here it is," the woman with Richart said.

"Is there a satellite image of it? Or a street view?"

"The closest street view," the woman said, "is this. A gas station a couple of miles away."

"Thank you, my love."

Krysta could have sworn she heard them kiss.

"Be careful," the woman cautioned.

"Always," he murmured. Then louder to Krysta, "One moment, please."

"Okay."

"What?" Sean asked, tying his laces.

"This is so weird." She had never really thought of vampires as anything other than monsters.

A laugh came over the line. "It worked," Richart said, with a great deal of surprise in his voice.

"What did?"

"Open your front door."

Frowning, Krysta strode past Sean into the den and crossed to the front door.

Her hand tightening on her sword, she glanced back.

Sean stood in the doorway of her bedroom, one Ruger aimed at the door, one aimed at Étienne.

Krysta turned the lock with the hand holding the phone and opened the door. Tilting her head back, she eyed the figure standing on the front porch.

A mirror image of Étienne stared back.

"Holy crap," she whispered. "Richart?"

The vampire's gaze moved past her to take in her brother and the rest of their tiny abode. He drew in a deep breath, nostrils flaring, then nodded. "May I come in?"

Swallowing, she stepped back.

Richart nodded to Sean, who nodded back, but didn't lower his weapons.

Krysta closed the door. "Étienne is in there."

Richart's boots thudded loudly on the worn wood floor as he strode toward the bedroom.

Sean eased back into the room, never shifting his aim from the two vampires.

"Sean."

"It's all right," Richart said, surprising her. "I understand." Once in the room, he leaned down over his brother and drew back the sheet. "His wounds are not healing?" All were covered by bandages.

"No."

"Étienne, *mon frère?*"

No response.

"How deep are the cuts?"

"Not cuts," she corrected. "Bullet wounds."

He looked at her sharply, then glanced at Sean. "Your weapons have not been fired tonight."

"It wasn't us," Sean confirmed. "I removed the bullets, but didn't stitch the wounds because they weren't bleeding. I just bandaged them instead."

"You have my gratitude," Richart uttered with a bow. Turning back to his brother, he peeled one of the bandages back and muttered something in French.

Krysta fervently wished she knew French.

Richart took his brother's forearm in his hands and raised Étienne's wrist to his lips. As he parted his own, fangs descended.

"Wait!" Krysta protested.

He met her gaze. "What?"

"He's lost enough blood, don't you think?"

Richart considered her for a moment, then seemed to come to some decision. "Our fangs are like needles. They siphon the blood of anyone we bite directly into our veins and, if necessary, can infuse others with *our* blood."

Sean lowered his aim slightly, medical curiosity brightening his face. "Really? So you can transfuse him just by biting him?"

"Yes." Richart bent his head and sank his fangs into his brother's wrist.

Krysta shared a *Holy Crap!* look with Sean.

It didn't take long at all, which was actually frightening. If he could infuse his brother with blood that swiftly, then he could drain a human that quickly, too.

As could Étienne.

Lowering his brother's arm, Richart systematically removed all of Étienne's dressings. "Thank you," he said, "for caring for him and bandaging his wounds."

The mortal siblings nodded.

The male even holstered his weapons.

"Why did you do it?" Richart couldn't resist asking. They clearly weren't Seconds or other members of the human network or they would have known Étienne wasn't a vampire.

"He saved my life," the woman said. "I would have died tonight if it weren't for him."

Ah. "A vampire attacked you?"

She shared a look with her brother. "Sssssssort of. But they weren't—"

"More than one vampire?"

"Yes. There were six. But we took care of them."

Tossing the bandages in a nearby rubbish bin, Richart stared at her. "You fought alongside him?"

"Yes."

"Both of you?"

"No. Just me. My brother came later and got us out of there."

Richart stared down at Étienne. Odd that there were so many bullet holes. Vampires usually stuck to blades like the immortals, knowing—even in their madness—that attracting too much mortal attention would likely lead to their demise.

Étienne's wounds slowly began to close and heal. Neither human expressed the amazement Richart would have expected upon seeing such.

Hmm.

Étienne looked much better, but it took longer for his wounds to close than it should have. And he wasn't rousing.

Richart nudged him. "Étienne."

Nothing.

The healing sleep *could* be deep.

Richart shoved him hard. Hard enough to wake him even from a healing sleep. "Étienne! *Réveiller!*"

Still nothing.

"Something is wrong," he muttered, his concern mounting.

"I think it's the drug," the woman said.

Richart's head snapped up. "What?"

"The drug."

"You drugged him?" Fury rushed through him. Only one drug existed that could knock out an immortal like this. And, if these two possessed it, it meant they were the enemy.

An enemy who should have been destroyed months ago.

Both mortals took a cautious step back as his eyes began to glow.

The male raised his weapons.

"No," the woman blurted. "We didn't drug him. That's what I was trying to tell you. The vampires weren't the biggest threat tonight. It was the soldiers who arrived *after* we defeated the vampires."

He swore. "Soldiers?"

"Yes."

"Describe them."

She did, and told him everything that had happened

from the time the vampires had been defeated to Étienne being felled.

"C'est impossible," he whispered. They had eradicated the mercenary threat. Completely. Darnell had erased all of the computer files and cyber files. Seth and David had wiped the memories of those they had allowed to live. The rest of the mercenaries had been killed.

It just wasn't possible. They had left no dangling threads.

Immortals didn't even carry the tranquilizer antidote with them anymore because *no one* was supposed to have that drug. No one but the researchers at the network, and none of them would use it against one of the immortals they aided.

The woman shifted, easing her weight off one leg. "Who were they?" She had limped when she had followed him into the room. She must have been injured, too.

"I didn't ask your name," he said, still reeling.

"Krysta Linz. This is my brother Sean."

Richart performed an abbreviated bow. "Richart d'Alençon." There was only one way to confirm that this drug was the same one the mercenaries had used against them. "Please excuse me for a moment. I will return shortly."

Too shaken to worry about their reaction, he teleported to his home. "Sheldon!"

"Yeah?" His young Second entered Richart's bedroom, holding a sandwich in one hand. As soon as he caught Richart's expression, he sobered. "Oh shit. What happened?"

"Do we have any of the tranquilizer antidote left?" Richart asked as he gathered a change of clothes for Étienne.

Nodding, Sheldon set the sandwich down and left the room. Richart followed him to the bathroom in which Sheldon kept much of their first-aid paraphernalia.

A solitary autoinjector was stashed in one of the drawers.

Jenna appeared in the doorway as Sheldon grabbed it and handed it over without a word.

Richart didn't think he had ever seen the young man look so worried. "Thank you." He met Jenna's gaze.

"Is it Étienne?" she asked.

He nodded. Knowing she would understand if he explained later, he teleported. Returning to his brother's side, Richart dropped the clothing on the bed.

Krysta and Sean jumped at his reappearance.

Removing the cap, Richart pressed the autoinjector to Étienne's neck.

"Is that an EpiPen?" Sean asked.

Richart shook his head. An EpiPen wouldn't do squat to an immortal. They were unaffected by all but two drugs: The mercenaries' tranquilizer and the antidote Dr. Lipton had developed to counter it.

Turning the used autoinjector over and over in his hand, he waited.

Étienne opened his eyes.

The first thing he noticed was his brother looming over the lumpy bed that supported him. The second was Krysta and her brother.

As the lethargy induced by the tranquilizer rapidly faded, Étienne sat up and took stock of the situation. They were in the mortals' home, in Krysta's bedroom. Étienne wore only his boxer shorts, a bedspread covering him from the waist down. Instead of being riddled with wounds and stained red with blood, his body was clean, healed, and carried the pleasant citrus scent he associated with Krysta.

"Are you okay?" she asked, the words leaping from her lips as if she could no longer contain them.

He nodded. His gaze went to the autoinjector Richart held. "How did you find me?" Étienne asked him.

"Krysta answered your phone."

"Does anyone else know you're here?"

"Jenna and Sheldon know I'm with you, but not where."

Étienne turned to Krysta and her brother. "I assume you got me out of there. Thank you. Both of you."

"You saved my life," Krysta said. "Again. Thank *you*."

Sean nodded. "Thank you."

Richart held up the autoinjector and drew Étienne's gaze. "We have a problem."

A colossal understatement.

Étienne's eyes widened as a thought occurred. *Oh shit. We have to call for a cleanup,* he told Richart mentally. *If humans haven't already found the bodies we left lying around, it will be a miracle.*

Richart swore and tucked the autoinjector away. *I'll go to Chris now.* He glanced out the window. *The sun will rise soon. Are you coming with me? Or are you going to stay and handle this?* He glanced at their audience.

I'll stay. And do not *give Chris this address. Or their names.*

Étienne, they've seen too much.

And Jenna didn't get an eyeful when she was still mortal?

A muscle in his jaw twitched. *Jenna could be trusted.*

I believe Krysta and Sean can be, too. They saved my life. If that isn't an endorsement, what is?

"Um," Krysta broached, "what's going on? You guys are looking kind of intense."

Just do what you can to appease Chris when you tell him what happened.

As you wish, brother. Call me if you need me.

Richart nodded at Krysta and Sean, then vanished.

"That is *so* cool," Krysta professed.

Étienne smiled. "Yes, it is. I've always envied him that talent." Rising, he reached for the black cargo pants Richart had brought him and tugged them on.

Krysta, he noticed, didn't even pretend not to watch him, her gaze roving him like fingers and making him wish her brother weren't in the room with them.

"You can't do it?" she asked. Had *she* been the one who had undressed and bathed him?

"Teleport? No."

"Why is he the only vampire who can do that?"

"I feel pretty! Oh so pretty! I feel pretty and witty and gaaaaaay!"

Étienne raised his eyebrows. What the hell was that?

"Oh." Krysta grabbed something off a nearby table and held it out to him. "Sorry. Here's your phone."

That was coming from *his* phone?

Sean's lips twitched.

Étienne frowned. "Damn it. Who keeps changing my ringtone?" He took the cell. "Hello?"

"Finally!" Cam said. "Where the hell have you been? Sheldon called and said you'd been injured and tranqed. Or that he *thought* you had been tranqued."

"I was, but I'm all right."

"Where are you? Do you need me to come and get you?"

"No, I'm safe."

"Are you sure? Because Richart called, too, and he didn't sound too confident about that."

"I'm sure."

"He didn't go into details. What's the situation? What do you need me to do?"

"Nothing. Just sit tight. I'll fill you in when I return home at sunset," Étienne ordered, knowing his friend would chafe at having his hands tied.

"Fine. You're the boss," Cam griped. "And, Étienne?"

"Yes?"

"Richart told me to tell you Chris knows about the woman."

Click.

Merde.

Mind racing, Étienne tucked the phone into the back pocket of the pants Richart had brought him, then reached for and donned the T-shirt.

"Who was that?" Krysta asked.

"A friend."

Sean frowned. "Why didn't what happened at Duke tonight make the news?"

"We kept waiting for someone to come after us or track us down," Krysta added.

Little did she know they would if Richart didn't succeed in cooling Chris's temper.

Sean swore.

"What?" Krysta asked with a frown.

"I have to get ready for work."

"Call in sick. Your head must still be hurting."

"I can't. We need the money and I can't afford to lose this job if Ed gets a bug up his butt again." Sean crossed the room, pausing in the doorway to look back at Étienne. "Harm my sister in any way and I will hunt you down and destroy you. Not a threat. A promise. And I won't play nice like she does. I'll do it during the day when you're vulnerable."

Étienne didn't mention that he wasn't physically weaker during the day as vampire folklore suggested. He may have to avoid sunlight, but he could still kick ass. Instead, he said. "I've no wish to harm her. Or you."

Sean delivered a jerky nod, then left to prepare for work.

For several long moments, Étienne and Krysta stared at each other.

"Are you really okay?" she asked.

He nodded. "And you? You were injured."

"I'm okay. Sean patched me up."

And healed the worst of her wounds with his hands, Étienne assumed.

Her gaze slid to the digital clock on her bedside table. "Sean is running late. Let's put this on hold for a minute while I fix him some breakfast. I don't want him to go to work on an empty stomach after last night."

And Étienne had heard enough about their financial struggles to know Sean couldn't afford to pick something up in the drive-through on the way there.

He followed Krysta into the tiny kitchen and kept her company while she whipped up a breakfast of scrambled eggs, toast, and orange juice.

Sean demolished that in about a minute, then rushed out the door with a last warning look at Étienne.

"I'm surprised he left," Étienne admitted.

Krysta shrugged. "Money has been tight. School limits the number of hours he can work and vampire hunting limits the number of hours *I* can work. But we're making it." She put Sean's dish and glass in the sink and filled it with soapy water. "You're worried."

He watched her with some surprise. How had she known that?

"You were worried before the phone call, but afterward . . ." She trailed off.

"We have a problem," he admitted. Chris knew about her. Even if Richart managed to stall him, Chris and his henchmen would come looking for her. And it would be best if Étienne were by her side when they found her.

"We?"

"You and I," he clarified.

"Let me guess. The soldiers we killed tonight have friends who are now out for our blood."

"Yes." He'd have to explain all of that, too. "But that's a whole different problem."

She frowned. "Someone *else* is out for our blood?"

"No. Just yours. Figuratively speaking."

"Your vampire friends?"

"My human friends."

Her eyebrows rose. "What?"

"Perhaps it would be best if I started from the beginning."

"I was hoping you would."

"I have a question I would like to ask you first."

"Okay." Crossing her arms, she leaned back against the counter and stared up at him. Her hair was a little mussed, finger-combed into submission rather than brushed. Her face was free of makeup, and bore a couple of faint abrasions, one on her jaw and one on her cheekbone, both on the left side of her entrancing face.

Her slender frame was garbed in a tank top and shorts that left her arms and shapely legs bare. Without her coat and assorted weaponry, she appeared so fragile. He still found it hard to reconcile this lovely, delicate mortal with the vampire hunter he had been observing for the past two weeks.

"Why didn't you go?" he asked, needing to know.

She tilted her head. "You mean when Sean left? Why didn't I leave with him?"

"No. At Duke. Why didn't you run when you had the chance?"

"After you threw me behind the building?"

"Yes. I stayed and fought so you would have time to get away."

"That's why," she said, her gaze never leaving his. "You could have escaped. Even tranquilized, you probably could have gotten away fast enough to elude them."

"They would've killed you had I left. And the drug had already weakened me and slowed me enough that I couldn't toss you over my shoulder and run without risking you being shot. Or tranqed. I couldn't let either happen."

"And I couldn't let them kill you. Or capture you. Or

whatever the hell they planned to do to you. I couldn't let you sacrifice yourself for me."

And that meant far more than it should have.

He eased closer to her. "Why?"

She lowered her arms and shook her head. "I don't know."

He cupped her face in his large hands, heard her breath catch, her heartbeat pick up its pace just as his own did. Heat rushed through him at the simple touch. "You saved my life tonight," he whispered.

Reaching up, she curled her small, soft hands around his wrists.

Étienne held his breath, waiting for her to pull his hands away. When she didn't . . .

"Thank you," he said.

As she nodded, he dipped his head and pressed his lips to hers.

Fire licked its way through Krysta's veins at the soft contact. Étienne caressed her cheeks as his silky smooth, surprisingly warm lips brushed hers.

What am I doing?

His tongue stroked her lips, tempting her into parting them.

What the hell am I doing? she repeated just before he deepened the kiss and she stopped thinking.

Her heart pounded in her chest, thudding against her ribs so determinedly she thought Étienne must feel it.

If he didn't before, he did then as he moved forward, crowding her against the counter and pressing his large, muscular body into hers.

It felt so good. *He* felt so good. Tasted good. He even smelled good. Familiar. Bathed as he had been in the soap she used every day, the citrus aroma blending exquisitely with his own masculine scent.

As Étienne leaned into her, every muscle tightened, pleasure dancing through her everywhere they touched.

He slid his arms around her. Heat simmered inside her, preventing Krysta from pulling away. Her breasts pressed against his hard, muscled chest. His rippling abs melded to hers. Her hips settled against his arousal.

I have to stop, the voice of reason intruded. *He's a vampire.*

His arms tightened as he continued to tease and tempt her with his tongue.

I don't sleep with vampires. I hunt them. I destroy them. I loathe them. Damn, *he can kiss. I want to tear his freaking clothes off.*

Krysta almost moaned a protest when Étienne drew back. Peeling heavy lids open, she stared up at him and caught her breath.

His eyes glowed a brilliant amber. Sharp fangs peeked from between parted lips. And both totally turned her on because he looked like he wanted to devour every inch of her.

Damn.

A growl rumbled forth from deep in his throat as he lowered his head and stole another brief, hard kiss.

Oh, yeah.

Then he ruined it (*and* did her a favor, she would later grudgingly admit) by again withdrawing and taking three determined steps backward.

Her heart continued to pound. She noted with some chagrin that she was practically panting. And her body tingled *everywhere*.

That would bother her a lot more if she hadn't noticed the large bulge straining against the front of his pants that told her more than words that he had been as affected as she had.

He cleared his throat. "I'm not a vampire."

She blinked. "What?"

"I'm not a vampire."

"Said the man with the glowing eyes and glinting fangs. Not to mention the super speed and strength."

"Vampires are not the only preternatural beings who boast such characteristics."

Oh, shit. There were other preternatural creatures out there?

He shook his head and motioned to the futon. "Will you sit with me so I might explain?"

Krysta nodded, a bit dazed, and followed him over to the futon.

They sat simultaneously and turned toward each other, knees touching.

She liked that their knees touched. Liked the casual contact as much as she had liked the kiss. And wondered where exactly along the way she had lost her damned mind.

Vampire. Vampire hunter. Remember? she mentally chided herself.

"I'm not vampire," he repeated, stretching an arm along the back of the futon. "I'm immortal."

Krysta stared at him. Weren't *all* vampires mostly immortal? Unless slain, that is? They didn't age or get sick, after all, and could withstand a lot of damage that would kill humans. "What's the difference?"

"The difference is that vampires are human before their transformation. I and my immortal colleagues, on the other hand, were like you."

Her heart, already misbehaving from their recent make-out session, began to beat a little faster. "I don't know what you mean. I'm human."

"No, you aren't. Or rather I assume you aren't because your brother isn't. Is he your full brother or your half brother?"

"My full brother. And he's human. We both are."

"No, you aren't. You're different."

How did he *know* that? She hadn't said or done anything

to reveal her peculiar gift. And tonight was the first night he'd had any direct contact with Sean.

Wasn't it?

A gentle smile curled his lips. "Don't look so panicked, Krysta. If with anyone, your secret is safe with me. I'm just like you. Or I was once. Born with special talents and abilities ordinary humans don't posses. In centuries past, we called ourselves *gifted ones.*"

"*Gifted ones*," she parroted. Other than her brother and her parents, she had never met another *gifted one* before.

"My brother," Étienne continued, "was born with the ability to teleport. Yours was born with the ability to heal with his hands."

"How do you know that?"

"I followed you home that first night and watched him heal the worst of your wounds with a touch."

"What, like through the window?" she demanded. What the hell else had he watched, the perve.

His face creased with a disgruntled frown. "Yes, but I'm not a perv. I didn't watch you shower or anything. I just needed to know who you were. You tried to kill me, remember, and thought me one of the vampires you hunt."

She frowned. He had kind of nailed the *perv* thing right on the head. How had he known what she was thinking? Her face wasn't *that* expressive, was it?

"My sister and I were both born with the ability to read others' thoughts," he admitted.

Her mind went blank, then filled with a maelstrom of reactions and concerns and freak-outs.

He could read her thoughts? He had been reading them all along?

Fury, alarm, and a ridiculous feeling of betrayal barreled through her. "You read my thoughts?" she came close to yelling. He must know, then, that he had intrigued her from the first night they had met. That she thought about him all the time. That she had, not five minutes ago, wanted nothing more than to strip him naked and roll around in bed with him.

The snake!

He held up both hands in a placating gesture. "Not all of them. Not even most of them. Just a few here and there."

Her face must be turning as red as a raspberry because he seemed quite desperate to assuage her anger.

"Some *gifted ones*, like yourself, have a natural defense and are difficult to read," he claimed.

"*How* difficult," she snarled, ready to kick his ass if he gave the wrong answer.

"*Very* difficult," he hurried to reassure her. "Extremely difficult. Sometimes I can't read you at all. Other times I only catch a word or two."

A word or two. That could be less incriminating, she supposed. Maybe her mind was closed enough that he didn't know she was attracted to him.

"Well, no. I knew that," he said.

Mouth falling open, she stared at him in dismay. Hell. Did she have *no* secrets from him?

"You have *many* secrets from me."

"Stop reading my thoughts!"

"I'm sorry. It's just . . . you're broadcasting them rather loudly at the moment and . . . There is no reason to feel embarrassed, Krysta."

"Easy for you to say! You weren't caught mentally checking out my package!"

A startled laugh escaped him before he hastily quelled it. "You're attracted to me. I know that. But I'm attracted to you, too. I have been ever since the first night I saw you when you stumbled out of that damned frat house, pretending to be drunk, turned your face up to the sky, and seemed to look right at me."

Her mind quieted. "Really?"

"Yes. And now I can't read what you're thinking at all, so if that offends you . . . Well, I won't apologize for it. You're a strong, beautiful woman who knows her way around a blade. I find that"—he drew in a deep breath as his eyes traveled over her with a heat that scorched her—"incredibly appealing. But I *will* apologize for whatever discomfort it causes you."

How the hell was she supposed to respond to that?

Best to just change the subject and try not to *broadcast her thoughts,* whatever the hell that meant. "Tell me again how immortals differ from vampires."

He did, beginning with *gifted ones* and blowing her mind. She and her brother and parents had always known they were different. But they hadn't known *why*. They hadn't realized they possessed advanced DNA.

And she hadn't known that vampirism was caused by a virus.

"So the virus causes brain damage and madness in humans, but not in *gifted ones?* "

"Correct. Our advanced DNA protects us."

"Where does the DNA come from?"

"We don't know."

Recalling all of the times she had been splattered with vampire blood, the time one had bitten her, and the long, wet kiss she had just shared with Étienne, she asked uneasily, "How contagious is this virus?"

He smiled. "Fleeting contact with it won't transform you. A few drops of vampire blood mingling with yours in a wound won't infect you. And you can't get it from a kiss. *Or* from sex."

That was nice to know for future reference.

"You can only be transformed in two ways: By having most of your blood drained, then being infused with the blood of a vampire or immortal. Or by being fed from and exposed to the virus in small amounts repeatedly." He frowned. "Have you ever been bitten by the vampires you hunt?" The idea seemed to upset him.

"Only once." And it hadn't been a vamp she had been hunting.

Darkness swept his visage as his brown eyes flashed bright amber once more. "Describe the vampire who bit you."

Why should it thrill her that he wanted to hunt down the vamp who had sunk his filthy fangs into her?

"No need," she assured him. "I killed him myself."

A slow smile lit his face as he wagged his head back and forth.

"What?" she asked.

"I like you more with every tidbit I learn about you."

She smiled. "You're pretty likable yourself."

"Now that you know I'm not a vampire?"

"You were likable even as a vampire. It was very annoying."

He laughed, flashing those pearly fangs.

If he was infected with the same virus that vampires were, then he must need blood. She had even seen his brother bite his wrist and *infuse* him with her own eyes. "If you hunt vampires who prey upon humans, does that mean you don't . . ."

"Kill humans myself?"

"Yes." She hadn't wanted to ask, in part because she wasn't sure she would like his answer.

"I don't feed from humans *or* prey upon them as vampires do. But, as you saw tonight, I *will* kill any human who threatens me or mine."

Which had it been tonight, she wondered, me or mine? Then called herself a fool. "But, you do need blood?"

"Yes. I assume Richart gave me blood while I was unconscious?"

She nodded. "He, ah, bit your wrist and fed you or whatever."

"Normally we receive sustenance from blood bags. The

humans who work with us also donate blood regularly, so we don't feed directly from humans unless extreme circumstances drive us to do so."

Drinking blood. Gross.

"We don't drink the blood," he said. "Our fangs carry it straight to our veins."

Right. That's what Richart had said. "Are you reading my thoughts again?"

"No. Your face sort of scrunched up with disgust."

"Oh. Sorry about that." It wasn't *his* fault he needed blood.

He smiled.

Damn, he was handsome when he smiled.

Hell, he was handsome when he didn't.

Étienne leaned forward a bit. "Listen, about the humans who aid us . . ."

It was so weird, hearing that there were other humans out there who knew about all of this. "Yes?"

"Their top priority is to protect us, to protect immortals, or Immortal Guardians as they call us."

Wasn't that sort of backward? The weaker mortals protecting the powerful immortals? "*They* protect *you?*"

"Yes. They have a vested interest in doing so. After all, we're the only thing keeping vampires from slaughtering humans unchecked. And we've been fighting to protect humans for millennia. So, the network—"

"The network?"

"That's what we call the organization of humans who aid us. The network not only provides us with blood, it protects our identities and keeps the general public from finding out that vampires, immortals, and *gifted ones* exist. Our ability to hunt and destroy vampires would be severely inhibited, if not halted altogether, if mankind learned about us and began to hunt us."

"But wouldn't they *help* you if they knew? Why would you

think they would . . . ?" A sickening dread soured her stomach as she recalled the way those soldiers had gone after Étienne earlier. "Is that what happened at Duke? Humans found out about you?"

He nodded. "We dealt with another such threat recently, but quashed it. I'm *certain* we quashed it. The attack tonight should not have happened. Should not even be possible. No mortals outside of the network should know about us."

"Except, those solders did. And . . ." Oh, crap. "I do."

"Precisely." He shifted the arm resting on the back of the futon and cupped her shoulder in his large hand. The warmth of it still caught her off guard. She had assumed vampires—and immortals now that she knew about them—would be cold to the touch.

"The network is going to want to talk to you," he told her somberly. And the concern on his face made her nervous. She had thought vampires were the biggest threat to her. His face said something different.

"You say talk," she voiced. "I hear *interrogate* and *make disappear*."

"It won't be like that."

"Are you sure? Because you look worried."

"I'm not worried." He looked away, muttered something in French, then turned back to her. "All right. I won't lie to you. I *am* worried. The head of the East Coast division of the human network can be ruthless when it comes to protecting us from perceived mortal threats."

Alarm rose. "You aren't reassuring me. Are you saying I should run? That *we* should run? Because Sean knows about this, too."

"No, don't run. It wouldn't do you any good. Chris could find a white dove in a blizzard."

"Who is Chris?"

"Head of the network."

"Great."

"I don't mean to scare you, Krysta. As long as you don't view *us*, Immortal Guardians, as the bad guys and start hunting us, then everything should be fine. In fact, once Chris finds out you're both *gifted ones* and that you can successfully hunt vampires, he will likely want to recruit you."

That was a lot to take in. And could potentially be a good thing. How cool would it be to have other people working with her to eradicate the vampire menace? And to maybe even get paid for it?

Paid. Awesome.

"That sounds pretty good, actually."

"Yes, it does," he agreed. "You and Sean would fare much better if you worked for the network and had their support."

"Then why don't you look happy about it?"

"Because until he assures himself that you and your brother pose no threat to us, Chris will be a hard-nosed bastard and I don't want him to upset you."

Étienne was upset because he didn't want *her* to be upset?

That was so sweet. It made her feel all mushy inside. And made her wonder . . . "Why?" she asked. "Why would it bother you so much if I were upset?"

"Honestly?"

"Yes."

He shook his head and fingered a strand of her hair. "Because I like you far more than I should."

Her heart began to pound once more. "You say that like it's a bad thing."

And she thought it wasn't? She had spent the past six years hunting down and destroying men infected with the same virus that infected Étienne. She was pretty much going on faith here that he wasn't like them, though his words and actions were pretty damned convincing. Plus . . .

He was immortal.

She was mortal.

Liking each other *too* much could have some serious consequences.

He gave her a faint smile. "You mimicked my thoughts so closely I may as well have spoken them aloud."

"Stop reading my thoughts," she murmured without heat or anger.

"Stop broadcasting them," he said, equally hushed. "You haven't told me your gift, Krysta."

She did *not* want to go there. "Could we maybe save that for another time?" Everyone she had ever told (outside of her family—and there had been precious few) had thought her a nutcase.

"If you wish. But you will receive no mockery or condemnation from me when you do. I've dealt with the surreal and paranormal all of my life. Very little surprises me anymore."

"Fine." Hoping he would be the one person who *wouldn't* think she either needed a straitjacket or was bullshitting, she drew in a deep breath, ordered herself not to feel hurt if he laughed, and said, "I can see auras."

"Auras. The glowing colors some say surround people? Those are real?"

She breathed a little easier. He sounded curious, not doubtful. "Yes."

"How does that help you hunt?"

"What do you mean?"

"The only mortals who can hold their own in battles with vampires are *gifted ones* whose particular talents give them some kind of edge. How does reading auras help you?"

She hesitated, wanting to tell him, but . . .

He smiled. "Not quite ready to trust?"

"This is all a lot to take in. I just don't want to—"

"Don't worry," he said, touching her shoulder again. "I

understand and can wait for you to tell me in your own time."
He winked. "No need to share all of our secrets at once."

Which implied he thought they would be spending more
time with each other and could share secrets later.

The notion pleased Krysta far more than it should.

Chapter 6

"Who are you and why are you sniffing after Ami?"

Zach raised an eyebrow at the question and fought back a smile when Roland's wife grimaced.

"Really, sweetie? You couldn't have worded that a little less . . ."

"Offensively?" Lisette suggested.

"Thank you."

"No," Roland grumbled, scowling. "Answer the question. What do you want from Ami?"

Zach arched a brow. "Lollipops?"

Sarah grabbed Roland's arm and stopped him as he drew back a foot to level a powerful kick Zach's way. "Honey, you know Seth doesn't like fighting amongst the ranks. What's he going to do if this one shows up bloodied?"

Roland glared at Zach. "He's immortal. As long as I don't remove a limb, he'll heal before Seth sees him."

Zach felt Lisette's gaze. She had been quiet since he had awakened. The second time. He had awoken this morning, but, upon realizing she had gone, had feigned unconsciousness all day until sheer boredom had coaxed him into sleeping for real. When he had opened his eyes the second time, she had been standing nearby, talking to her brother on the phone.

Her pulse had picked up a bit when she had noticed he was awake. Unfortunately, the only words she had spoken before her friends' arrival had been into the phone to Roland, alerting him to Zach's return to consciousness. The rest of the time she had merely studied Zach silently with those piercing, light brown eyes.

And, much to his confusion, Zach had found studying *her* as entertaining as engaging in conversation.

"Are you immortal?" she asked, finally speaking to him directly.

"Yes." It was an honest answer, he told himself.

"I can't smell the virus on you," she stated.

He shrugged, rattling the heavy chains. "Can you smell it on Seth?"

"No."

"You don't have to answer his questions, Lisette," Roland uttered. "This isn't a free exchange of information. It's a demand for it."

Lisette's brow furrowed.

Sarah tilted her head. "How old are you?"

Zach looked at Roland. "Old enough to make *him* seem young."

"What's your name?" Roland demanded.

Zach was curious to learn the source of that one's hostility. Lisette seemed curious. Sarah seemed worried. Roland seemed as furious as though he had caught Zach trying to catch a glimpse of Sarah naked.

"Zach." May as well tell him the truth. If Seth read their minds and thought one of the Others had been snooping around, all hell would break loose. Best to let him know who it was, though Zach doubted Seth would be pleased. "If you're worried that I'm pursuing Ami romantically—"

"She's married, asshole!" Roland shouted.

"I know, *asshole.*"

Roland's face mottled with anger a second before he slammed his fist into Zach's temple. And Roland didn't pull the punch since he knew Zach was immortal.

Ouch. Despite the pain, this was actually turning out to be very entertaining.

"Stay away from her," Roland warned as the women looked on anxiously. They seemed more inclined to reason with Zach and coax him rather than take Roland's hot-tempered—

Wait. Wasn't there an infidelity in Roland's past?

Zach sneaked into Roland's mind and gave his past a quick look.

Yes. His first wife had cheated on him with his brother. That clarified things a bit. Roland loved Marcus like a brother and didn't want to see him go through the same pain of being cuckolded. Roland didn't want to believe Ami would deceive Marcus like that, but had learned the hard way not to trust his instincts.

"First, don't do that again," Zach warned. He'd give the guy one shot, but that was it. Any more and all bets would be off. "Second, Ami is a friend," Zach said. And damned if something didn't shift inside him at the admission.

Had he ever had a friend before?

"We know you've been meeting her regularly. If you're hoping she'll be a friend with benefits," Roland warned, "think again."

"I don't know what that is."

Sarah's eyebrows rose.

Lisette continued to study him somberly.

"What kind of benefits?" Did they think he thought rubbing elbows with Ami would help him score points with Seth? That was a joke.

"Sexual," Roland snapped.

Zach scowled. Sex had never even occurred to him. "A

friend you sleep with isn't a friend. It's a lover. I told you, Ami is a friend."

Sarah stepped in and asked in her soft, lilting voice, "Then why do you meet with her in secret? Why not talk with her inside?"

"What makes you think we talk? Have you ever heard us?"

Lisette shook her head. "I'm telepathic. I know the signs of unspoken conversation."

"Could you *hear* a conversation?" he asked curiously. How powerful was this young immortal?

"No," she admitted.

"Can you read my thoughts?" That would be an impressive feat.

He felt her probing, trying to enter his mind. He had thought it would annoy him. It sure as hell annoyed him when Seth tried to read his thoughts. Yet, for some reason, it didn't. He actually found himself rooting for her to succeed, which made no sense at all. He really didn't want her to see what was in there.

"No," she blurted, her lovely features dark with frustration.

"Then perhaps we were merely sharing lollipops as you no doubt observed." Which raised the question . . . "How did you learn of our meetings?" Even Seth and David had not noticed his comings and goings.

"I followed Ami outside and saw the two of you together," Lisette answered.

"Is Ami aware you're surveilling her?"

"No."

"Why are you doing it?"

Had she guessed what Ami is and didn't trust her? Did she fear Ami? Did she wish her ill?

"I worry about her," Lisette answered hesitantly.

"You barely know each other," he pointed out. An intense fear of strangers had been instilled in Ami by her torturers, making it difficult for her to get to know others. So, while she cared about *all* of her immortal family, she was only personally close to a handful of them.

And Lisette was not one of them.

Roland and Sarah eyed Lisette curiously.

Lisette looked increasingly uneasy. "All right. What I say does not leave this room."

Both immortals nodded, then looked at him.

"You trust my word?" he asked with some surprise.

"If you repeat whatever Lisette tells us, next time we won't drug you while you aren't paying attention, we'll decapitate you," Roland warned.

Zach shrugged. "All right." He didn't mention that there wouldn't *be* a next time. They wouldn't be able to sneak up on him again. He was shocked that they had done it *this* time.

Lisette shifted. Clearly she didn't want to talk about whatever it was that had driven her to follow Ami. "Ever since we found out that Ami was the primary target of Emrys's mercenaries, Richart, Étienne, and I have been spending more time at David's place. As have you two."

Roland nodded. "Bastien breeched my home and took Sarah. I learned from that mistake and, despite my solitary nature, wanted to be there in case the mercenaries breeched David's defenses and tried to take Ami."

Lisette nodded. "Exactly. And often I would spend the day there, as would you two."

They nodded expectantly.

She sighed. "My gift isn't like Seth's and David's. Or rather it is, but I don't have the control over it they do. Seth and David only hear other people's thoughts when they wish to. Étienne and I, on the other hand, *always* hear other people's thoughts unless we consciously block them."

"That sucks," Roland said.

"Yes, it does. And, when I sleep, I lose the ability to block others' thoughts. So, their dreams often become mine."

Zach began to dread where this was going.

"In all these years, I've come to understand that there are three kinds of dreams. The first kind is a whimsical collection or rehashing of things that happened to us or things we thought about during recent days. If you watch the movie *The Birds*, for instance, you might dream about birds. If you're a student, you might dream about school. The second kind is like yours, Sarah. The dreams foretell the future or tell us something about the present that we may not know. And the third kind . . . In those dreams, we revisit the past."

That's what he had been afraid of. And what Seth probably hadn't realized or he would've found a way to convince the telepaths they didn't need to sleep at David's.

"Dreams that revisit the past usually don't reflect it precisely. There will be elements of the past there, but whatever the event was won't just replay itself exactly as it happened. Ami's . . ." She looked away. "Ami's reflect her past exactly. They don't deviate at all."

Roland frowned. "How do you know? I thought you didn't meet Ami until Seth brought her to North Carolina."

"She has the same dreams over and over again and they are more detailed than any dreams I have ever been in. Only pure memory could spawn those."

Sarah frowned. "What did you see?"

Lisette swallowed hard. Moisture welled in her eyes. "They tortured her," she choked out. "I mean they really tortured her. They . . . dissected her . . . and experimented on her over and over again while she was conscious. She felt every incision. Every burn. Every electrical shock. And, because she heals even more swiftly than Roland, she didn't die."

Sarah touched a hand to her mouth, horror filling her features.

Roland's face tightened with fury.

"Why?" Sarah whispered. "Why would they do that?"

Zach held his breath.

Lisette shook her head. "They must have found out she was a *gifted one*."

Relief rushed through him.

"Seth was right to protect us all this time," she continued. "If you saw the things they did to her . . ." She wiped her tears away impatiently. "After only two or three days, I began to fear falling asleep."

Zach had the oddest urge to comfort her.

"I had to start sleeping at home every few days just so I could get some rest without being locked into those nightmares." She turned her attention to Zach. "There was no way in hell I was going to let mercenaries get their hands on her again. I guess I became a little obsessed with her safety. And, even though Emrys is dead and rotting in hell, his colleagues Donald and Nelson are not. I know they should pose no further threat because Seth and David wiped their memories, but"—she shrugged and offered them all a sad smile—"I can't seem to shake my fear for her. So I followed Ami when she would go out alone at night and saw *you* with her."

"Has Étienne seen her dreams, too?" Zach asked.

Her eyes narrowed. "How do you know my brother?"

"I know all of you." Not really. He knew their names and some of their backstories. Bits and pieces he had overheard during his visits and while listening to the Others grumble.

"Étienne has seen the same dreams I have," she answered finally and looked at Roland. "That's why he has softened toward Bastien, by the way. Something else the dreams revealed to us is how gentle Bastien was with Ami right after her rescue. How much he helped her overcome the paralyzing fear those monsters instilled in her."

"He killed Ewen," Roland reminded her.

"I know. But, if you could see how he is with her when no one else is around . . ."

"That's all?" Zach persisted. "You saw nothing else in her dreams?"

She shrugged. "They weren't all memory-based. Some were the usual whimsical variety in which she looked up at the night sky and saw three moons instead of one. That sort of thing."

Which were likely just as memory-based as the others. Fortunately, neither Lisette nor her brother seemed to have figured that out.

"Anyway, when I saw you with her, I asked Roland who you were."

"And I didn't know," Roland said, "so I began watching over Ami, too."

"Me, too," Sarah added.

"Does her husband know you're spying on her?"

"No," Roland admitted, "and we want to keep it that way."

"Why?" Zach couldn't resist asking, "because you're afraid Marcus might think *you* are sniffing after her?"

Roland lashed out with his fist again, the force of the blow snapping Zach's head back.

And there went the fun.

His own ire rising, Zach used a combination of telekinesis and brute strength increased by adrenaline to burst from his restraints. Restraints no one else in this room could have broken.

The others ducked as broken lengths of chain went flying.

The women's eyes widened as he spread his wings, the tips brushing the walls on either side of the room.

Roland drew swords and stepped in front of the women.

"I've indulged you enough," Zach said. "Hit me again and you will not survive my retaliation."

"Who *are* you?" Lisette asked, her eyes straying to his wings as they had so often.

Did he have *her* to thank for the bedding that had protected them from the damaging chain links? He would peek into her thoughts, but generally disliked doing so. Most people were unaware of the ugly things that could reside in the darkest corners of their minds and he always seemed to find it.

"Call Marcus," Roland ordered Sarah over his shoulder.

When she reached for her cell phone, Zach raised a hand to stop her. "Don't. Marcus has enough on his plate. He doesn't need the added worry of this, and it truly isn't necessary. I mean Ami no harm."

She hesitated.

As did Roland. He even straightened from his fighting stance and lowered his weapons. "Added worry? What's going on with Marcus?"

Sarah nodded, brow furrowed. "What do you mean he has a lot on his plate? Is he worried about Ami, too?"

That was an understatement. And not his story to tell.

"If Marcus wants you to know what's going on with them, he'll tell you."

That didn't improve Roland's mood. "You expect me to believe he told *you?*"

"No. Because he didn't." Zach shrugged. "I hear things."

Sarah bit her lip. "Has Ami refused to let Marcus transform her?"

All those in the Immortal Guardian community who weren't in the loop thought Ami was a *gifted one.*

He shook his head. "It isn't my place to say." Before anyone could speak again, he turned to Lisette. "Don't pry into their thoughts, seeking answers. I know the temptation is great but—as I said—if Marcus and Ami want you to know, they will tell you."

"I wasn't going to," she said, face troubled.

All *three* of them looked troubled. More troubled now than they had when he had escaped his bonds.

Zach folded his wings in and tucked them against his back. His curiosity had been appeased. He'd been entertained. Now it was over. "I believe we've said all there is to say." He headed for the front door.

No one moved to stop him.

He paused, one hand on the knob. "I wouldn't mention this to Seth, if I were you. He has a lot on his plate, too, and this will just piss him off."

Opening the door, he stepped outside and leaped into the sky.

Krysta started to konk out around noon. Étienne watched her yawn, then released a jaw-cracking yawn himself.

She gave him a sleepy grin. "Made you yawn."

He laughed. "Yes, you did. Why don't you go ahead and get some rest? You can't have actually slept in that chair while watching over me."

"I think I may have dozed off once or twice."

"That's not enough. You need rest. You were wounded tonight." He frowned. His own wounds had healed for the most part. Only a deep sleep or more blood would finish the job at this point. But hers . . . "How *are* your wounds?"

"They hurt like hell, but I'm used to it. What about you?" She glanced at the bright sunlight outlining the faded window curtains. "You're kind of stranded here, aren't you, until sunset? Or will Richart be coming back for you?"

"If I haven't worn out my welcome, I'd like to stay. I trust Richart not to give away your identity or location. But Chris is like a bloodhound. Once he has the scent . . ." He shrugged. "I want to be here to run interference should his men find you."

She frowned. "Are you sure Sean is safe?"

"Yes. The first thing Chris will do once he learns your name is track down your home address." And race to her doorstep. *Hmm.* "Perhaps I should have Richart teleport us to . . ." He thought for a moment. "Where would Chris not think to look? Our home in France?"

"You want to teleport me to France?"

"Yes."

"Right now?"

"Yes."

"So, one minute I would be here and the next I would be across the ocean in France?"

"It's just a thought."

A long pause ensued. "You know, I just don't think I'm up for that right now."

He smiled and touched her hair. "It *has* been a long night."

"Do you really think your human friends will burst in here and threaten me?"

"They might burst in, if you don't answer the door. But, with me here, they won't have the balls to threaten you."

"Why don't you get some rest, too, then?"

He nodded, but didn't think he would succeed even if he tried. The futon that barely kept their asses from hitting the floor was old and lumpy and badly needed to be replaced. "I'll stretch out here on the futon, if you really don't mind."

"Do you want to take Sean's bed?"

He shook his head. "Sean doesn't want me in the house. I doubt he would appreciate my confiscating his bed."

"You're probably right on that, but he'll get over it."

Étienne smiled. "No, thank you." He stood when she did.

"Okay." She started to stretch, then winced and dropped her arms.

If he knew Roland better, Étienne would call him and ask him to heal her. Unfortunately, Roland had kept him—and everyone else, save Sarah and Marcus—at a distance. And *really* didn't trust humans.

Krysta headed for her bedroom. "You should know I'm a very light sleeper, so . . ."

He raised an eyebrow. "Don't try to drink your blood while you sleep?"

Her cheeks flushed guiltily. "Yes."

"I would never do so, with or without your permission, unless both of our lives depended upon it. I wouldn't want to risk infecting you."

She stared at him as if she truly wanted to believe him.

And he hoped she did. Or *would*. In time.

He bowed as she turned and entered her bedroom. He expected her to close and lock her door, not that it could keep him out.

Instead, she drew back the covers and climbed into bed.

Étienne turned off the overhead light and attempted to stretch out on the futon. His feet and most of his calves hung over the arm. One of the metal bars beneath the cushions dug into his back.

He sighed. He could always wait until Krysta drifted off, then sleep on the floor. That would probably be the more comfortable solution.

He heard bedding rustle and closed his eyes, trying not to picture Krysta sprawled across the covers under other, less appropriate circumstances.

She laughed.

Opening his eyes, he glanced at the doorway.

She was leaning over in bed, peeking at him. "Comfortable?"

"Yes, thank you."

She shook her head. "You're lying."

"With good intentions."

Still grinning, she waved him toward her. "Go ahead and come sleep in here with me."

His body went rock hard at the notion even though he knew damned well she didn't mean it the way he wanted her to mean it.

"I . . ." *want to rip your clothes off with my teeth, so I don't think it would be a good idea.* "That's very kind of you, but . . ." *I really* do *want to rip your clothes off with my teeth and explore every inch of your beautiful body.* "I'm fine."

"Your legs are hanging off the end by a good foot and a half and I can't even sleep on that lumpy piece of crap when I'm drunk."

He smiled. "I've slept on worse surfaces."

"Have you ever slept in a coffin?"

"Yes, but only as a practical joke."

"What about in a crypt?"

"More than once when it took me longer than expected to track down a nasty vampire and I couldn't find any other shelter before the sun rose."

"Was the crypt more comfortable than my futon?"

He grinned. "Hands down."

Again she laughed. "Then get in here. We're adults. We can do this."

He couldn't find the strength to refuse. "*Merci.*" Rising, he strode into her room and circled the bed. "I'm surprised you trust me enough to sleep beside me."

"To be honest, I am, too. You really aren't going to bite me?"

"No." He settled beside her on top of the covers.

"Any plans to cop a feel?"

Her scent enveloped him as he turned his head to stare at her. "Would you mind if I did?"

"I'm still considering that one."

Yes. This was definitely a bad idea.

"What is it about you that makes me want to forget what you are," she asked softly, "that makes me *believe* you are what you are and not one of the vampires I hate so much?"

"I don't know. Perhaps the same thing about you that makes me want to believe you won't drive a stake through my heart or chop off my head as soon as I doze off."

Curling onto her side to face him, she raised one hand and drew delicate fingers down his cheek as her gaze roved his face. "Truce?"

"Truce."

"Good night, Étienne."

Heart racing, he clasped her fingers and brought them to his lips. "Good night, Krysta."

She fell asleep holding his hand.

He wanted to stay awake and savor that. The sweetness of it. But the healing sleep swiftly claimed him.

Étienne dreamed vampires hunted him.

No. The vampires hunted Krysta. And the dream was hers. He could always tell when someone else's dream became his because he first saw them from that person's perspective. And he wasn't a slender, significantly shorter woman.

Usually, he could separate himself from the dreamer and participate as he would in his own dreams. He had never been able to do that when Ami's dreams had seized him. He had been as much a victim of the atrocities committed against her as *she* had in those dreams and often dreaded sleeping when he stayed the day at David's.

As Krysta confronted the vampires and began to swing her shoto swords, Étienne left her form and joined in the fight as himself.

She grinned when she saw him. "About time!" she quipped.

Étienne laughed and engaged the vamps, who were much more organized and swung their weapons with greater control and accuracy in the dream.

A dozen vampires fell. Two dozen replaced them.

Then Sean arrived and was somehow thrust into the middle of everything.

Krysta's brother had skills. But—without whatever edge Krysta's ability to see auras gave her—he fared badly, accumulating wound after wound as Krysta fought to get to his side.

The more panicked she became, the more wounds she suffered and the weaker she grew.

Étienne couldn't reach her. Every time he cut down one vampire a second took his place.

One vamp disarmed and captured Sean. Pulling him back against his chest, the vampire sent Krysta a cruel smile.

"Kill him!" the others cried.

"No!" Krysta screamed.

"Remember, the male is the one we're after," another voice said softly, strangely calm amidst the slaverings of the vampires. "We want the immortal alive. The human female is expendable."

What?

"Don't hurt him!" Krysta begged, her eyes still on her brother. "Please!"

"Rendezvous with target in one mile," the same calm voice announced.

Étienne stopped fighting. Something was wrong.

The vampires converged upon Krysta, yelling and taunting. None spoke with the voice Étienne had heard.

The vampire holding Sean began to sing in a falsetto voice, "I feel pretty! Oh, so pretty! I feel pretty and witty and gaaaaaay!"

What the hell was with that song?

Krysta vanished.

Frowning, Étienne spun in a circle. "Krysta?"

"Étienne?"

"Where are you?" He resumed fighting, doing his damnedest to reach her brother while the vamp who held him continued to sing in that weird high voice.

"Étienne!"

He looked around, but still couldn't find her. "Krysta?"

"Étienne! Wake up!"

He jerked awake.

Krysta knelt beside him on the bed, shaking the hell out of him. "Jeeze. It's a good thing I *didn't* want to stake you. You would have slept right through it!"

Groaning, he sat up. "I sleep deeper when I'm healing. What's wrong?"

"Your cell phone has been ringing like crazy and that damned song is making me mental."

When the singing started up again, he yanked his phone out of his pocket and answered.

"Yes?"

"We have a serious problem," Chris Reordon said without preamble.

Damn it. "No, we don't. I—"

"Richart told me you left quite a mess at Duke tonight."

Étienne frowned. "Yes."

"So we have a problem. I sent my cleaning crew over there ASAP and they didn't find dick."

Étienne stood, alarm striking. "What?"

"There was nothing. No bodies. No blood. No vampire clothing or bling. No dental fillings or caps. No humans freaking out. Nada."

"That's not possible. There should have been a couple dozen bodies—"

"There weren't. There *was*, however, a large area of wet pavement where no sprinklers could reach. And the surveillance tapes for the security cameras in that area of the campus are all gone."

Étienne swore.

"Exactly. Where are you? Are you still with the woman?"

"Yes, but—"

"Hang up, call Richart, and have him teleport you to safety."

"That isn't—"

"You aren't getting it. The group that attacked you now has the surveillance tapes. They also have connections or they wouldn't have been able to clean that mess up so quickly. They can use the tapes to trace the license plate on her car.

They probably already know where you are. Get the hell out of there. Now."

Étienne looked to Krysta, who watched him with concern. "We have to go."

"Now?"

"Yes."

"Where? Why?"

Someone shouted something in the background on Chris's end of the conversation as engine noise flowed over the line. "Where are you?" Étienne asked.

"At the network, getting into a Black Hawk with reinforcements. More will follow on the ground in a Humvee."

A twig snapped outside. Then another.

Étienne looked toward the window. "Too late. They're here."

"Call Richart!"

Chapter 7

Krysta stared at Étienne with wide eyes. Something was wrong. Really, really wrong.

He grabbed her arm and, practically lifting her off the bed, urged her into the den.

"What's going on?" she asked.

"Richart," he spoke into his phone. "I need you . . . Yes." He pocketed the phone. "Does this place have a basement?"

"No. I mean, not really. There's a crawl space under the house that you can access from outside, but—"

Étienne stopped short and looked toward the bedroom, then the kitchen, his head tilted as though he were listening to something.

Krysta remained quiet, but heard nothing save her heart slamming against her ribs.

Kneeling, Étienne dragged her down with him. While she fought for balance, he drew back his arm and punched through the floor as though it were cardboard. Half a dozen times. Knuckles splitting. Bones cracking.

Krysta gaped at the hole he created, an absurd thought rearing its head: No way were she and Sean going to get their security deposit back.

Without warning, Étienne picked her up and dropped her through the jagged hole.

She grunted as she hit the hard-packed dirt floor. It was only a four or five foot drop, but she didn't have time to twist around and use her hands to break the fall.

Then, as though they were in a Warner Brothers cartoon, Étienne landed on top of her, flattening her and stealing her breath.

Holy crap, he was heavy!

"Sorry," he murmured in her ear as he rolled off her and sat up.

"What—?"

Bullets tore through the house overhead. *Large* bullets, judging by the debris flying around the den and the narrow rays of sunshine beginning to brighten the room.

Her mouth fell open.

Étienne rose into a crouch, eyes staring intently through the hole.

Richart appeared above them. His body jerked as bullets slammed into him.

Étienne lunged up and yanked his brother down into the crawl space with them.

Richart landed hard, too.

Étienne spoke urgently to him in French.

"No," Krysta protested shrilly. "No way! You can't do that! You can't talk in French while I'm sitting here freaking out because I don't know what the hell is going on!"

Richart rolled onto his stomach and managed to get to his hands and knees.

She swallowed.

His head hung low. Blood dribbled from between parted lips as ragged breath wheezed in and out through them. The front of his shirt bore several holes, as did the back, and began to glisten as blood saturated it.

"Are you okay?" she asked.

He nodded, but didn't raise his head.

Étienne rested a hand on his brother's back. "What took you so long?"

"I was . . . making love to my wife . . . not that it's . . . any of your . . . business. Did you . . . want me to show up here naked?"

Étienne's gaze went to Krysta. "No."

She had a feeling he would have said *Hell, yes* if she weren't there.

"Take my wrist," Étienne ordered.

Richart grabbed Étienne's wrist and sank his teeth into it.

A muscle leapt in Étienne's jaw.

Krysta knew from experience that being bitten didn't produce the ecstatic pleasure in real life that it did in movies that romanticized vampires. Rather, it hurt like hell, feeling as though someone had just stuck you with a couple of large needles.

Richart retracted his fangs and released his brother's wrist.

Bullets continued to fly back and forth overhead like psychotic bees, tearing her rented home apart.

She glanced again at Richart. A couple of misshapen lumps of metal fell out of his shirt and hit the ground as his wounds began to heal.

"Can you teleport?" Étienne asked.

Richart nodded and sat back on his heels.

"Get her out of here," Étienne said.

"What?" Krysta looked to Étienne as Richart reached out and gripped her shoulder.

The world darkened. Dizziness assailed her. She grabbed Richart's shirt.

Light burst into being, illuminating a lovely living room with modern furniture.

Krysta gasped. "Did you just teleport me?"

"*Oui.*"

A pretty, petite woman with red hair and dark brown

roots appeared before them, a white and purple aura swirling around her. Her face clouded with concern when her gaze landed on Richart. "Honey . . ." She took a step toward him.

He raised a hand to hold her at bay and vanished.

She looked up at Krysta. "What happened?"

Krysta shook her head. "I'm not sure. Someone was shooting the place all to hell and—"

"Sheldon!" the woman called over her shoulder. "John!" She wore black cargo pants and a black T-shirt that hugged a narrow waist and full breasts Krysta would kill to have. Her hair was mussed and her face flushed, leading Krysta to believe this was the American wife with whom Richart had been making love.

Two men strode up a nearby hallway, coming from the back of the house. Both looked to be around twenty years old. One was roughly five eleven with bright red hair. The other was at least six feet with short, dark brown hair.

Krysta took a wary step backward, then another. She didn't know these people. She barely knew Étienne.

"What's up, Mom?" the brunet asked.

The other man's eyebrows flew up when he noticed Krysta. "Well, hello," he said in a deep, flirtatious tone.

She scowled. "You're *hitting* on me? Really?"

Richart appeared with Étienne, who was pretty much holding his brother upright.

Krysta damned near sank to the floor with relief.

"Sheldon," Étienne said as the woman hurried forward, "get the protective suits we wear in daylight. John, get Richart some blood. And bring some for me, too."

The redhead took off toward the back of the house. The brunet raced into a large adjoining kitchen.

"Here, honey," the woman said, looping Richart's arm over her shoulder and taking his weight from Étienne, "let me help you to the sofa."

He smiled and nuzzled her ear. "It's not as bad as it looks. I'm already healing."

"Good, because you look like shit."

He chuckled, then winced.

In all the years Krysta had been hunting vampires, she had never thought of one having a wife.

But they weren't vampires. They were immortals. Their every movement wasn't dictated by evil and insanity. The two actually seemed . . . loving. Warm. Affectionate.

Étienne stepped in front of her, blocking her view, and gently clasped her arm with his left hand. "Are you all right?"

She looked up at him, touched by the concern in his handsome face. "Yes. Just shaken, I guess."

He nodded and pulled her into a hug.

Krysta leaned into him, letting her racing heart calm, her body stop trembling.

John returned from the kitchen. "Here you go."

Étienne released her and took a bag of blood with his left hand.

Krysta frowned. He wasn't using his right arm. Or, more specifically, his right hand.

He gave her an uneasy look. "I'm sorry. I have to do this."

"Do what?"

He parted his lips.

She swallowed as fangs descended from his gums. Fangs he sank into the bag of blood.

Oh. Right. Gross.

I'm not drinking it, he spoke directly into her head.

She jumped. "Are you reading my thoughts again?"

No. Your face said it all.

"Oh. Sorry."

While he continued to syphon the blood into his veins or whatever, she took his right arm and carefully raised it so she could get a look at his hand.

It was a mess of cuts and bruises and who knew how many

broken bones. Her little house may be all wood and look like crap on the outside but it had been built to last. Étienne had punched through flooring and heavy support beams alike.

She looked up at him and found him watching her. "Does it hurt?"

He lowered the now-empty blood bag and gave her a wry smile. "Like a bitch."

She grinned at his use of her words and shook her head. "You saved my life. Again."

"After endangering it. Those men weren't after you. They were after me."

"And I'm expendable."

"Apparently."

"Who were they?" she asked.

"That's what I intend to find out."

Sheldon entered, his arms full of . . .

Krysta frowned. What the hell was that?

Stepping back, Étienne tossed the empty bag to John, then blurred.

Her eyebrows flew up when he stilled a second later, wearing only a T-shirt and boxers. The rest of his clothes formed a pile on the floor at his feet. "Wow." She unabashedly ogled his powerful biceps and strong, muscled thighs dusted with dark hair.

Richart's wife laughed.

Grinning, Étienne reached for the suit Sheldon held out to him. It reminded Krysta of a diving suit, except it appeared to have a rough texture, almost like that of a car tire.

Sheldon took another one to Richart, who rose. Both immortals blurred and donned the suits in only a second or two.

Sheldon himself donned a bulletproof vest and tugged on a helmet with a glass shield.

"Where the hell do you think *you're* going?" Richart demanded.

"With you."

"The hell you are."

"I'm your Second. Quit bitching and let me do my job."

Étienne zipped from the room and returned with a mass of weapons. "Do you have any of the antidote?"

Sheldon shook his head, holstering a couple of Glock 18s with long-ass clips, then picking up an M16. "No. The threat was supposed to be over, so I didn't reorder any when we started running low."

The two brothers armed themselves in a blink.

"Where's *my* suit," Richart's wife asked.

"You don't have one," Richart responded.

"She could use Lisette's," Sheldon suggested.

"No, she can't," Richart snapped, glaring at his Second.

"No, she can't," Sheldon parroted. "Because Lisette, uh, didn't bring it back after the last time she—"

"This is still too new to you," Richart told her. "You haven't completed your training. I don't want you to get hurt." Leaning down, he pressed a kiss to her lips. "*Je t'aime.*"

"I love you, too."

Crossing to Étienne, he clapped a hand on his shoulder. "Ready?"

Étienne nodded.

"Be careful!" Krysta blurted.

Étienne grinned as the two teleported away.

A second later, Richart reappeared, grabbed Sheldon's shoulder, then they vanished.

Silence fell.

Krysta looked at John, then Richart's wife. "I don't know what's happening."

Richart's wife smiled, though worry shadowed her eyes. "We don't know much more than you do." Rising, she approached Krysta and held out her hand. "I'm Jenna. Richart is my husband. And John, here, is my son."

Krysta shook her hand. "Krysta." She looked back and

forth between John and Jenna, who looked as though they were about the same age. "I'm sorry. Did you say he was your son?"

Jenna laughed. "Yes. When I transformed, the virus healed all of the damage age had done to my body." She pointed to the dark roots that stood out against her red hair. "See? No more gray. I look like a kid again."

John shook his head and sent Krysta a wry smile. "It's weird, right? I'm still trying to get used to it."

Jenna motioned for Krysta to sit with her on the sofa. "Something tells me you're the reason Étienne has been so distracted lately."

"He's been distracted?"

Jenna nodded. "*Very*."

Good to know Krysta wasn't the only one. Étienne had been a major player in her thoughts since that first night she'd encountered him. *And* her dreams. She hadn't had many sex dreams in her life, but *wow*. She had had a couple of doozies since meeting Étienne.

"Oh, wait." Jenna looked over her shoulder at her son. "John, toss me my phone."

Krysta turned around in time to see John pick a cell phone up off the bar and sling it Jenna's way.

Jenna caught it easily. "I'm sorry. I need to make a quick call." She dialed and held the phone to her ear. "Darnell? Hi. It's Jenna. Richart and Étienne are—" She tilted her head. "Oh, he did? . . . No, they made it here safely." She looked at Krysta. "She made it safely, too . . . Our place . . . No, they put on protective suits and headed back with Sheldon . . ." She lowered the phone slightly and addressed Krysta. "Are you injured?"

"No."

"She's fine," she said into the phone. "Okay. Bye." She set the phone on the coffee table. "I'm sorry. I didn't think to ask you earlier. I'm still pretty new to this."

"I'm *totally* new to this. New to the immortal thing, anyway."

"Well, Darnell said Chris is on his way to your home with a small army. So Richart and Étienne will have help fighting whomever they're fighting."

Krysta nodded.

"John," Jenna said with a smile, "you can go back to studying. They might be gone for a while."

He nodded. "Nice to meet you, Krysta."

"Nice to meet you, too," she murmured, then turned back to Jenna.

Jenna smiled with pride. "He's pre-med at UNC."

"Oh. Great. My brother's in med school there." Alarm shot through her at the thought of Sean. "Oh, shit. My brother."

Jenna leaned forward. "What about him?"

"We live together. Those men were looking for Étienne, but they found him at *our* house. Do you think they'll go after Sean? Is Sean in danger?"

Brow furrowing, Jenna reached for her phone again and dialed. "Darnell? It's Jenna again. Krysta has a brother and is worried he might be in danger . . . Oh. He did? . . . Okay, good. Thanks."

She set her phone down again. "Chris took care of it."

"Chris?" The same Chris Étienne expected to threaten her?

"Chris Reordon. Head of the East Coast division of the human network that aids immortals."

Yep. Same one.

"He sent men over to guard your brother at work. No one will get near him."

Krysta stared at her. Guard or interrogate? "Could I borrow your phone, please?"

"Of course."

Krysta dialed Sean's cell.

"Krys?" he answered almost immediately.

"Yeah. You okay?"

"Yeah." He lowered his voice. "What the hell is going on? A bunch of Secret Service–looking guys showed up, pulled me aside, and said they're friends of Étienne and are here to protect me."

"They are." She sure as hell *hoped* they were, anyway.

"Well, they're freaking out my boss. They told Ed I'm in a witness relocation program and that there may have been a leak. What the hell? Did something happen? Or is this about last night?"

"Something happened. Étienne and I were sleeping and—"

"Oh, shit. Not together, right?"

"What?"

"You didn't sleep with him, did you?"

She looked at Jenna and turned away, lowering her own voice. "Yes," she whispered, "but all we did was sleep in the literal sense."

"Are you *crazy?*"

"I said we didn't do anything!"

"You let your guard down with a vampire in the house!"

"He isn't a vampire. He's an immortal."

"A what?"

"Never mind. Some guys with guns showed up."

Sean swore again.

"I didn't see them, but assume from the way Étienne and Richart were acting that they were like the soldiers or whatever last night."

"Are you okay?" he asked again.

"Yes. But the house is all shot to hell."

"*What?*"

"And Étienne punched a big-ass hole in the floor."

"Great. There goes our security deposit."

Jenna laughed.

Krysta turned back around.

"I'm sorry," Jenna said. "I didn't mean to listen. I'm still getting used to the acute hearing thing and haven't learned how to tune things out yet."

"Who was that?" Sean asked.

"Richart's wife."

"Vampires marry?"

"He isn't . . . Forget it. Listen, the bottom line is if the soldiers could trace us to our house, they could trace you to your job. So I guess Étienne sent his friends over there to keep you safe."

"Where are *you?*"

"At Richart's house."

"And you're sure you're okay? You haven't been fed on or brainwashed or anything?"

"I'm fine, Sean. Just a little shaken up."

Someone spoke in the background. "That was Ed. I have to go. But keep me posted. Okay?"

"Okay."

"Can you believe this shit is happening, Krys?"

"No."

"Me either. Be safe."

"You, too."

She ended the call.

Bastien stirred, smiling as the dream faded. He and Melanie had been riding through the countryside near the home in which he had been raised. The horses beneath them had been those he had cherished so much as a young man. The air had been sweet and unclouded by pollution. The land quiet, free of the noise of man and machine that assaulted his sensitive ears on a nightly basis now.

Little had changed on the estate since he was a mortal. He had made sure of that.

Bastien had not lived the pristine life the other Immortal Guardians had after being transformed. Seth had not come to him and trained him, found a Second to help him conceal his nature, or paid him a wage. Bastien had had to fend for himself.

He didn't resent it. How could one miss what one had never had?

He had simply done what he had to do to survive, which had included using his ability to feel other people's emotions and his newfound strength and speed to acquire the money needed to buy his family's ancestral estate and ensure it remained how he remembered it from happier times.

In the dream, he had been taking Melanie around to all of his favorite places. His favorite fishing spot as a boy. His favorite thinking spot as an adolescent. His favorite trysting spot as a young man.

As he stretched and woke fully, he decided he would have to take her there for real. Get away from everything.

If Seth would let him.

He grimaced. Going from leader to subordinate had not been easy and still chafed at times. But, if that was what it took to stay with Melanie, he would do it without complaint.

Or with *little* complaint.

Rolling onto his side, he reached for Melanie and found cold sheets.

Frowning, he lifted his head and followed the light to the corner of their bedroom.

Melanie sat at her desk, garbed only in one of his large T-shirts. Bathed in the light of a small lamp, she peered down at another of her thick medical books. Several more rested in piles at each elbow and clogged the floor-to-ceiling shelves beside the desk.

She leaned forward, one elbow resting on the wooden surface, while she scoured the text at preternatural speeds. Brow furrowed, she turned the page, read, turned the page, read, careful not to make a sound.

Bastien sat up, the sheet tangling around his waist. "What's wrong, sweetheart?"

Jumping, she spun around. "I'm sorry. Did I wake you?"

He shook his head. "No. What's wrong?" He knew her well and didn't have to touch her to know her shoulders were knotted with tension.

She looked down, toyed with the corners of the book's pages.

"Melanie? Talk to me, love. Tell me what's troubling you."

She sighed. "I'm flying blind, Bastien." When she raised her head, her hazel eyes glistened with tears.

Swearing silently, he leapt from the bed and crossed to kneel at her side, unconcerned with his nudity. (She knew every inch of his body.) Reaching up, he cupped her face and caught the tear that spilled over her lashes.

"Everyone is counting on me to carry Ami safely through this pregnancy," she said, "and I'm flying blind."

"Tell me what you need and I'll get it for you. Tell me how I can help you and I will."

She shook her head. "Chris and Seth have already seen to it that I have all the books and equipment I need."

"Then I'll get you what you need *beyond* that."

"You can't. That's just it."

Bullshit. He could feel the worry and fear coursing through her. She was stressed as hell and he would do whatever it took to help her.

"All right. Tell me your top three concerns and we'll see how to alleviate them."

"Let's start with the fact that I've never been pregnant myself and have never spent any time around pregnant women, so I don't know what's normal. The books only say so much. They say it isn't uncommon for some women to experience cramping during pregnancy, but I'm not clear on how much. Is it constant or sporadic? Do they mean super mild, I'm ovulating cramping? Or moderate, I'm about to get my period cramping? Or full blown, where the hell are the painkillers cramping? How much is too much? How often is too often? When should I be concerned? How do I know what's normal and what might be a result of difficulties that could arise from Ami's being an alien, Marcus being an immortal, and the baby possibly being infected with the virus? Or from the difficulty women on her planet have carrying babies to term?"

Bastien thought furiously. They needed someone with experience to be their guide. "The network employs thousands of humans. Surely *one* of them must be a . . . woman . . . female . . . I don't know what you call them . . . vagina doctor."

Melanie laughed. "Vagina doctor?"

He smiled, relieved to have lightened her mood a bit. "I've had very little contact with doctors in my lifetime. You know what I mean."

"They're called OB/GYNs."

"Thank you."

"You know Seth wants Ami's being an alien to be kept secret, especially from the mortal employees. If any of them were captured and tortured—"

"Seth took care of that. The men who were hunting her are dead. And Seth wiped the memories of those with whom they sought to join forces."

"So you think he's going to let down his guard? Him *or* Marcus?"

"No. You're right." There must be something else. "Wait." He grinned. "I have the answer."

"You do?"

"We'll bring Jenna into the loop."

"Richart's wife?"

"Yes. She has a son. She's been through pregnancy and can help you get a better idea of what's normal and what isn't."

"If we brought her into the loop, we'd have to ask her to keep secrets from the man she loves. I wouldn't feel right about doing that."

"Then we'll bring Richart into the loop, too. We don't necessarily have to tell them Ami's from another world. We can just tell them she's pregnant. That alone, they'll know, is cause for concern because we have no idea what the virus will do to a baby."

She looked thoughtful.

"We're going to have to bring all of the local Immortal Guardians into the loop soon anyway. The cats and kittens will help conceal the baby's heartbeat, but how long do you think we'll be able to hide Ami's growing belly? She's tiny, like you, and weighs less than a hundred pounds. A thirty-pound weight gain is not going to go unnoticed."

"That's true. They'll all think our concern revolves around the virus. They won't know we're worried about alien and *gifted one* DNA mixing unless we tell them." She nodded. "Jenna would be a huge help. She could tell me all of the little things the books don't. Things that, in the human world, would be considered insignificant. The more information I have, the better I can monitor Ami and know normal from abnormal."

He dropped his hand to her knee and squeezed it. "Great. So, what's your next concern? We can solve it, too."

Her frown returned. "I don't think there's a solution for this one."

"You didn't think there was a solution for the other one either, but we came up with one. Come on. Let's hear it."

"It's Ami's regenerative capabilities. Her body heals as fast as yours does when you're at full strength."

Ami's regenerative capabilities actually *exceeded* that of most Immortal Guardians. When Ami had been tortured and the butchers had removed two fingers and two toes, the digits had grown back on their own. The most an immortal could do in that situation was hope that David or Seth could reattach them.

"Isn't her swift healing a plus in health matters?"

"Not if something goes wrong with the delivery and I have to perform a C-section."

"Oh, shit."

"Exactly. How will I keep her body from healing the incision while I operate?"

"Shit." He thought furiously. "When Seth and David rescued Ami, the fuckers had cracked her chest open and were shocking her heart. How did *they* keep her from healing too quickly for them to work?"

"The drug."

"Then why don't you—?"

"I have no idea what effect it might have on the baby. In strong enough doses, it will knock *you* out cold and slow your healing. Once you're given blood, your wounds heal, but you remain unconscious. And, while all encounters seem to suggest immortals can't overdose on it, vampires can. When given too strong a dose, they die. Any human given the drug dies instantly."

"And we don't know what the baby is or will be: alien, immortal, *gifted one*, vampire, or a combination thereof."

"So there's no way to predict what will happen if the baby is exposed to it. It's too risky to use."

There had to be something. If not something medical, then some power Seth or David could use. "Wait. When he was so pissed at me for putting Ami in danger, Seth must have used telekinesis or—I don't know—a reversal of his healing abilities, because it felt like a fist was squeezing my heart. Maybe he and David could prevent her body from healing if it came to that."

Another thoughtful pause. "You may be right. I'll ask them."

He smiled. "You see? We'll figure it out." Rising, he took her hand and drew her up to stand before him. "We can do anything as long as we're together."

She smiled up at him. "I believe we can." Sliding her arms around his waist, she leaned into him for a hug.

Bastien held her for many long moments, so fucking glad they were together. He would do anything for her. *Anything.* And hoped she knew it.

"Let's go to bed," he murmured into her hair. "We'll tackle number three tomorrow."

Nodding, she let him guide her back to their king-sized bed.

Chapter 8

Richart, Étienne, and Sheldon crouched in the crawl space beneath Krysta's house. Bullets still whizzed past overhead, and damned if it didn't look like a grenade had exploded in the small kitchen. *Something* had blown a hole in the floor over there.

Sheldon gaped at the chaos above them.

"Can you believe this shit?" Étienne muttered.

Richart shook his head. "How much damage do they think we can take?"

"A hell of a lot, apparently, but they must know Krysta can't." Fury ignited within him.

The ground beneath the house was uneven, so the crawl space was about five and a half feet high on one side of the house and only about a foot high on the other.

Richart stuck close to the ground and crept over to the vertical wood slats that enclosed them. "Come here."

Étienne crawled over to him, Sheldon at his side.

"See? There in the trees just off the yard. There. And there. They have the house surrounded."

"Stupid bastards are risking shooting each other through the house."

Richart chuckled. "That would be convenient."

"There's a farmhouse in the distance there, beyond the trees. If you teleport us there, we can come up behind them and take them out instead of bursting out of this place and giving them instant targets."

"Sounds good." Richart looked at him a moment. "Is Krysta the reason you've been so distracted lately?"

"Yes."

"I know you're pissed that they put her in danger, but don't follow Bastien's example. Try to leave a couple alive for questioning and read the mind of every man you can before you kill the rest."

"If I must."

The brothers reluctantly donned the head coverings, which looked like rubber ski masks, then added shades and gloves.

"I hate this shit."

Richart nodded. "Makes me feel like I'm suffocating."

"Let's do this fast, then."

"Wait," Sheldon said. "What do you want *me* to do?"

Étienne and Richart looked at each other and said, "Stay here and keep them busy."

Sheldon frowned. "Kinda boring, but I'll make it work."

Shaking his head, Richart touched Étienne's shoulder.

Sunlight bathed them as they appeared beside the farmhouse. In unison, they stepped back into the shade.

As younger immortals, they could not tolerate full sunlight without wearing the protective suits the network had designed. They wouldn't burst into flames or explode the way movie vampires did. They would instead quickly begin to sunburn, and things would go downhill from there.

Older immortals, at full strength, could withstand several minutes before they would begin to suffer consequences. David could endure several hours. Seth was completely unaffected by daylight.

Étienne envied him as he shifted in the uncomfortable suit.

Damn thing chafed. "You take the west and north. I'll come up behind them on the east and sweep around to the south."

"Be careful." Richart vanished.

Étienne raced eastward, entered the trees, and circled around to head back toward Krysta's house. Whoever this new group hunting immortals and vampires was, they were well funded and large. There were at least two dozen soldiers on this side of the house, arcing around to the south.

Someone on the other side cried out.

Étienne smiled. Richart had already gone to work. And few could compete with him in combat. How could you shoot or stab what kept disappearing?

Étienne swooped down on five soldiers who seemed intent on filling this side of the house with enough holes to make the damned walls collapse. Their thoughts focused on shooting blindly into the house, wondering if anyone was actually in the house, if this was just a bullshit mission, and if the guy who had just cried out had been hit by friendly fire.

The fact that the latter didn't seem to bother them much spoke volumes about their character.

Knowing the immortals needed information, Étienne tamped down his desire to make these pricks pay for trying to kill Krysta and knocked the first two unconscious. The other three spun around.

He caught a fleeting *Holy shit! Vampires are real!* thought before he accidentally hit the third one too hard and killed him.

The last two turned their weapons on him. Blood spurted from their chests as they jerked and danced like marionettes on strings and dropped their aim. One squeezed and held the trigger. A couple of mercenaries to the south cried out as they were hit.

Étienne heard Sheldon whoop and credited him with the hits. *Don't get cocky,* he spoke into Sheldon's mind. *Stay low and stay mobile.*

"Dude," Sheldon said over the racket, "stay out of my head. You startled me so badly I nearly shot myself in the foot."

In the distance, Richart laughed.

Smiling, Étienne shook his head.

A quick scan of the mercenaries' minds as they fell and breathed their last told him nothing of their employers.

Determined to come out of this with *something*, he made his way to the south, taking out soldiers as he went. Thanks to the jackass who had shot his colleagues, several of the soldiers were looking his way as Étienne swept toward them. A few got in lucky shots. One managed to tranq him. But the antidote he had taken earlier, once injected, not only countered the effects of the drug already in his system, it had a prophylactic effect, protecting him from reaction to *further* exposure for several hours.

Fortunately for him, it still worked.

Étienne wasn't used to taking prisoners and kept instinctively striking killing blows.

Sheldon apparently hadn't mastered the shoot-to-wound mind-set either, killing as many as Étienne did. The boy may not be the brightest bulb, but he was damned proficient with a weapon.

Are you helping Richart at all? Étienne risked asking. His brother had not been dosed with the antidote. If he were hit with a tranquilizer dart, he would lose a lot of speed and strength. If he were hit with enough, he would go down.

"Richart doesn't need help. He keeps popping up between two groups and the stupid bastards are panicking and shooting each other."

Nevertheless, keep checking on him. He doesn't have the antidote.

Sheldon laughed. "One of them just tranqed himself. Dumbass."

Shaking his head, Étienne ignored the wounds opening on his body as bullets tore through flesh.

Wagner's "Ride of the Valkyrie" rose in the distance, the music swelling as the *whup-whup-whup* of a helicopter approached.

"What the hell is that?" one of the mercenaries demanded, firing his weapon at Étienne as he looked up into the trees.

Étienne smiled. "The cavalry." He knocked the firearm from the distracted man's hand and punched him hard enough to give him a concussion.

The man dropped like a stone. As did two of his comrades.

The branches above Étienne began to thrash and sway as a Black Hawk helicopter slowed and hovered overhead. Ropes fell to the ground. Soldiers in green camouflage tumbled from the open doors and slid down the lines to land fluidly on their feet.

A blond—just under six feet tall—issued orders with hand signals, sending half the troops to Richart's side of the house, then leading the rest to Étienne.

And still the music roared.

Bodies in a ready-for-anything crouch, tranquilizer guns loaded with the human dose of the tranquilizer aimed and ready to fire, network soldiers nodded to Étienne as they flowed past him.

Mercenaries dropped like flies as tranquilizer darts found vulnerable throats.

Shaded by the trees, Étienne tugged off his protective shades, head covering, and gloves, and smiled as the blond strolled toward him. "You *do* like to make an entrance, don't you?"

Chris Reordon grinned. "May as well have fun with it. Besides, it will help me with the coverup. Any calls the neighbors make to nine-one-one will be intercepted and they'll be told we're filming a movie."

"That won't attract spectators?"

He shrugged. "If it does, my guys will steer them away."

The walkie-talkie on his shoulder squawked. "Location secure," a tinny voice declared. "Targets down."

Chris reached up and pressed a button. "Set up a perimeter and stay sharp. If they repeat last night's performance, they'll have a second team sweep in shortly."

"Yes, sir."

The network guards began to check the downed men and call out their conditions.

"Dead."

"Dead."

"Dead."

"Dead."

Chris frowned at Étienne.

Étienne pursed his lips. He *thought* he had left some alive.

"Dead."

"Alive. Pulse thready. Pupils blown."

"Same with this one."

Chris sighed heavily.

"What?" Étienne asked, beginning to feel defensive. "What does that mean?"

"It means you hit them too hard."

"Well, I'm not used to fighting humans."

"You spar with Cameron all the time."

"No, I don't. I spar with immortals. Cam spars with other Seconds."

"But you've fought humans in the past. Hell, we just fought a minor war with them."

"And we fought to kill. Vampires can take a punch. I can fight to wound them, crack their skulls, and they'll recover. How the hell would I know how hard I can hit a human?"

Chris was silent for a moment. "Okay, I see this is going to be a problem."

"Dead," another guard called.

"Dead. Sheesh. What the hell did you do to *this* guy?"

Étienne winced.

Richart approached—tugging off his own shades, head covering, and gloves—and stood next to Étienne. He was pretty blood-splattered. Had he run into the same problem?

"Did you get anything from their thoughts?" Richart asked.

Étienne shook his head, frowning as Richart weaved on his feet. "Are you wounded?"

"Huh?" He glanced down. "I don't think so. Maybe. A couple of gunshots. Why?"

Sheldon walked up, looking as though he had rolled in a puddle of mud. Reaching up, he yanked a tranquilizer dart from Richart's upper back. "Dude, are you okay?"

Chris reached into one of the pockets on his thigh and drew out an autoinjector full of the antidote. Flicking off the lid, he jabbed it into Richart's neck.

Étienne took his brother's arm and steadied him until it kicked in. He gave Sheldon a once-over. "What the hell happened to you?"

"Some asshole shot the hot water tank. The water spilled down into the crawl space and muddied the shallow end. I had to take cover there after they figured out someone was shooting from the house."

Richart straightened.

"Better?" Étienne asked.

He nodded.

"Did you leave any men alive?" Chris asked.

Richart sent him a sheepish look. "Yes, but your men seem to think I scrambled their brains."

Grumbling, Chris took out his cell phone and dialed. "Seth? Chris. You have a minute?"

The leader of the Immortal Guardians appeared beside Étienne, pocketing his cell phone. "What's . . . up?" He glanced around and swore. "Mercenaries?"

"Yes," Étienne, Richart, Sheldon, and Chris responded.

Seth studied the house, the grounds, the bodies. He

returned his attention to the younger immortals. "Go home. Rest. And be at David's an hour after sunset tonight."

Étienne looked at his brother. "Don't you want us to stay and tell you—?"

"I know what happened. Go home. And, Étienne, when you come to the meeting tonight, bring the woman."

Merde. Had he read Étienne's thoughts and seen Krysta? Seth was so powerful that he could do so without Étienne even knowing it.

"What about the brother?" Chris asked. "What do you want us to do with him?"

Seth eyed Étienne. "Will you be going home or staying with Richart today?"

Étienne consulted Richart. "Can you teleport us to my place?"

"Yes."

He turned back to Seth. "Home."

Seth nodded and told Chris, "When her brother gets off work, provided no one comes looking for him before then, take him to Étienne's home. Ensure you aren't followed and can't be tracked. Station guards outside the home and around the property's perimeter."

"Is that really necessary?" Étienne asked.

"Which part?"

"The guards."

"Yes."

He didn't like it, but said nothing. One didn't argue with Seth.

Frowning, Seth looked up at the helicopter, made a brief motion with his hand, and stopped the music. "Show's over."

Chris motioned for the helo to land.

"Go home," Seth instructed the d'Alençons.

"Should I bring the brother to the meeting?" Étienne asked.

"Yes," Chris answered, monitoring the cleanup.

Étienne looked to Seth.

Seth nodded.

Richart touched Étienne's shoulder.

Krysta listened with amazement as Jenna described her recent courtship with Richart, which had been a bizarre combination of conventional and unconventional.

The tale helped calm Krysta's nerves. As well as her fears. Jenna seemed so human. So normal. She'd been a single mom, struggling to put a son she'd had way too young through college, when she had met Richart. Her concerns seemed so *not* paranormal. And her love for Richart so sweet. Still fresh and new.

Krysta actually found herself envying the woman.

Very unsettling.

Richart and Étienne suddenly appeared a few feet away.

Heart slamming against her ribs—and not just because it startled her—Krysta leapt to her feet.

Jenna did, too. Hurrying over to her husband, she hugged him hard despite the blood that stained him. "Are you okay?"

"I'm fine, sweetheart. I just need some blood."

Krysta had the odd impulse to do the same to Étienne, to run to him and hug him tight and tell him how glad she was to see he was okay. Or mostly okay. She couldn't tell if any of the blood staining his weird suit was his.

She settled for crossing to stand in front of him. "Are you okay?"

He nodded.

Two more men suddenly materialized before the brothers. Krysta noticed absently that Sheldon looked as though he had been wallowing in mud. The other man . . .

She gawked. *Damn*. He was *hot*. As hot as Étienne and Richart, but several inches taller with wavy, black hair that fell past his waist. He positively oozed power. And his aura . . .

She had never seen anything like it. It was an almost

blindingly bright white with none of the swirling purple that flowed through Étienne, Richart, and Jenna's auras.

"Thanks," Sheldon said.

The man nodded and disappeared.

Krysta returned her gaze to Étienne, whose face had darkened with a scowl. "Who was that?"

"Seth, the leader of the Immortal Guardians. The eldest and most powerful among us."

"What *is* he?"

"As I said, he's our leader."

"No, I mean, he isn't a vampire or an immortal. So what is he?"

"He's an immortal."

Krysta eyed Étienne's aura. "He is?"

"Yes."

"I don't understand any of this."

"I know. I'll explain everything when we get home."

"My home?"

"Nnnnnno. Your home is . . ."

"Shot to shit," Sheldon supplied for him.

Richart popped the young man on the back of the head.

"Dude, I'm wearing a helmet. I didn't even—"

Richart popped him on the head again with enough force to send him stumbling several steps away.

"Okay. That I felt."

Étienne consulted his brother. "Can you take us both at once?"

"Let me get some blood first."

Richart headed into the kitchen, Jenna at his side, clinging to his hand and leaning into him.

Sheldon gave Krysta a sheepish look. "Sorry about your house."

She nodded, not knowing what else to do.

Sheldon unfastened the chin strap of his helmet and tugged it off. "See you guys at the meeting tonight. I'm gonna go take a shower." Spinning on his heels, he trudged down the hallway and out of sight.

"What meeting?" Krysta asked.

"Seth has called a meeting to discuss what has happened and how to identify and deal with the new threat."

"I can't go home, can I?"

"No."

"Great. I guess I could stay in a hotel." It would have to be the cheapest one she could find.

"You can stay with me," Étienne suggested. "You'll be accompanying me to the meeting tonight anyway."

She raised her eyebrows. "I will?"

He grimaced. "I'm afraid so. Seth has asked that you be there. And no one gainsays Seth."

"Is he that much more powerful than the rest of you?"

"Absolutely. I'm a babe compared to him."

Yes, he *was* a babe. A total babe. But not the way he meant it.

He grinned.

Krysta frowned. "Damn it! Stop reading my thoughts!"

Étienne shrugged. "I was just peeking to see how you were taking all of this."

"Not well," she admitted.

"Would you take it better if I told you I think you're a total babe, too?"

"A little bit."

He laughed and, wrapping an arm around her, drew her close for a hug.

Krysta looped her arms around his waist, surprised by how natural it felt despite the rubber suit.

"Every day you amaze me more," he murmured. And she could have sworn he brushed a kiss across the top of her head.

"Every day you *confuse* me more," she countered.

"It will all become clear soon."

His earlier words squeezed past the confusion and concern

for her brother, as well as the worry over where the hell they were going to live and how they would pay for everything. "Wait. Who is going to be at this meeting?"

"Most likely all of the Immortal Guardians in the area, as well as their Seconds."

"What's a Second again?"

"The human guard or assistant of an immortal. We all have one."

"Like a Renfield?"

"I suppose so."

"And how many Immortal Guardians are we talking?"

"Fourteen or fifteen."

Krysta inadvertently tightened her grip on him as fear returned.

"We won't hurt you, Krysta. I know it seems like we've been doing a piss-poor job of it, but we're here to help you and protect you."

She nodded. She supposed she would just have to trust them. Go with gut instinct. Blind hope. Because what other choice did she have?

Richart and Jenna returned.

Rather than leap away from her as Krysta expected, Étienne kept one arm around her and shifted her to his side. As if they were a couple.

"Ready?" Richart asked. "I'd like to go and get back so I can rest for a few hours before the meeting."

Étienne nodded. "See that he *does* rest," he implored Jenna. "He was tranqed earlier."

Jenna frowned up at her husband. "You didn't tell me that."

"I didn't want to worry you. Besides, Chris gave me the antidote."

She nodded at Étienne. "He'll rest."

"Thank you."

Richart stepped away from his wife and touched Étienne's shoulder.

Blackness engulfed them. A second later, the room brightened. Only it was a different room.

Krysta glanced around.

In a different house.

"See you at the meeting tonight," Richart said.

"I'm serious about you getting some rest," Étienne said.

Richart's lips quirked. "As soon as I finish what you so rudely interrupted earlier."

An instant later he vanished.

"Seriously?" Krysta said. "After being shot and hunting whoever the hell that was at my house and being tranqed, he's going to go home and make love to his wife?"

"They're newlyweds," Étienne said with a shrug. "That's actually why I wanted to spend the day here instead of there. Their relationship is still new enough that they haven't had a chance to soundproof the walls of their bedroom, so spending the day there can be awkward."

"I would think so. With *your* ears, you can probably hear *everything*."

He nodded. He and Lisette had learned very quickly that, although they were always welcome at Richart's home (the three of them had always been close and routinely slept at each others' houses to stave off loneliness), Richart wasn't going to let their presence dampen his amorous pursuits of his wife.

Actually, Richart was so besotted that Étienne wasn't sure it had even occurred to him that his brother and sister could hear him making love with Jenna. This situation was new to them. Lisette was the only one of them who had ever been married, and that had been before her transformation.

Cam entered, his hair mussed from sleep. He wore his usual sleeping garb: a T-shirt and sweatpants. When he had first been named Étienne's Second, he had slept in the buff, which Étienne had nixed when he had arrived home one night battered enough to require immediate aid. Then had come boxers, which had been replaced by the sweats and a T-shirt after Lisette and Richart had made several surprise visits.

The pants were for Lisette's benefit. Cam couldn't care less about either of the men catching him in his drawers.

"Came home after all?" Cam said, eyeing Krysta curiously.

"Yes. Cam, this is Krysta. She saved my life tonight and lost her home as a result. Krysta, this is Cameron, my Second."

Cam strode forward and offered his hand. "Good to meet you. Sorry about your house."

Krysta shook his hand. "Thanks. Étienne seems to think it would be best if I bunk here for the day. I hope you don't mind."

"As long as you're on *our* side, you're welcome."

"She is," Étienne stated.

Cam nodded. "First things first. Are you wounded?" he asked Étienne.

"Yes."

"Let me get you some blood." He left, then returned with two bags of blood Étienne swiftly drew into his parched veins. "The men you fought were mercenaries?"

"Yes."

Cam slid a glance Krysta's way. "You're sure she isn't one of them?"

Krysta answered before Étienne could. "Would they have tried to kill me if I were?"

"Yes. The mercenaries we fought in the past considered each other expendable."

"Cam," Étienne warned, "don't press her. She isn't one of them."

"You've read her thoughts?"

Étienne shifted. "Some of them. I can't read her at will the way I can you and most other mortals."

Cam stared at Krysta. "Damn. Lucky you."

Much to Étienne's relief, Krysta sent his protective Second a wry smile. "Not when the thoughts he *can* read are the inappropriate ones."

Cam laughed. "I'm guessing you're the reason he's been so distracted these last few weeks."

Krysta smiled as she met Étienne's gaze.

He sighed. Was *everyone* he knew going to say that when they met her? "This is getting embarrassing."

She laughed.

"You could have told me it was a woman," Cam continued. "I've given you an earful about Laura."

"Do we really have to talk about this now? In front of Krysta?"

"Yes. I'm pissed about you keeping me out of the fight. And, instead of pouting, I've decided to irritate you."

Étienne shook his head. "You've been spending too much time with Sheldon."

"Not by choice. Do you two want something to eat before you turn in?"

"No, thank you," Krysta said.

Étienne agreed. "Seth has called for a meeting at David's tonight, an hour after sunset. I want to get some rest before I face the inquisition."

Cam nodded. "I'll keep a sharp eye out in case any of the mercenaries show up on our doorstep."

Krysta raised her eyebrows. "I don't see how they could. Richart teleported us." Her face scrunched up. "It feels so weird to say that."

Cam laughed. "Like in a B-movie, right?"

She grinned. "Yes. But he did. So I don't see how anyone could track us here."

Cam held up a finger. "I'll be back in a minute."

Étienne watched him head up the hallway to the room they affectionately called the armory.

A moment later he returned, carrying a handheld metal detector. "Disarm."

Étienne removed his weapons one by one and set them on the scarred coffee table nearby. *That's new,* he spoke in Cam's mind. *A metal detector?*

Yes. Chris sent it over when we were dealing with Emrys.

Krysta examined the blades piling up on the table.

Cam crossed to stand in front of Étienne. "Now. Let's see if you've got any shrapnel I need to dig out."

Shrapnel, my ass, Étienne drawled.

If you've got shrapnel in your ass, it's going to stay there, Cam responded with twitching lips. *I'm looking for tracking devices the mercenaries may have tagged you with and didn't want your girlfriend to know.*

She isn't my girlfriend.

Yet.

"Is that a metal detector?" she asked, abandoning the weapons to watch Cam and Étienne.

"Yes," Cam said, sweeping it up and down Étienne's limbs. "Usually, the bullets will be pushed out during the healing process, but little pieces that break off can take longer. He'll heal faster if I dig them out."

Her brow furrowed with concern. "Oh."

You could have told her the truth, Étienne said, uncomfortable with the lie.

No, I couldn't. Not until we're one hundred percent sure she's on our side. I assumed you wouldn't want to lie to her yourself, so I did it for you.

Thank you, Étienne said grudgingly.

Cam shook his head. *You really have it bad for her, don't you?*

Yes, damn it. But keep that to yourself.

Will do. "All clear," Cam announced.

Krysta sighed with relief.

"Can I do anything for the two of you before you turn in?"

"No, thank you," Krysta said again.

"Reordon is going to have some men escort Krysta's brother Sean here when he gets off work," Étienne informed him. "They're well trained and shouldn't be followed, but that's when it will happen if it does."

Cam nodded. "Is the brother on our side?"

Étienne glanced at Krysta. "That's yet to be decided."

"He will be," Krysta said, uncertainty in her voice. "Once he understands that Étienne isn't a vampire, I'm sure Sean will come around."

Cam frowned. "He thinks you're a vampire?"

"Yes."

"Then why is he being brought here?"

"To be with Krysta. He'll be won over faster if he sees firsthand that I've no wish to harm her. Don't worry, though. Chris is sending a contingent of guards to watch the house and grounds. Seth's orders."

The rumble of approaching vehicles swelled outside, accompanied by the muffled conversations of network guards.

"That's them now."

Cam nodded. "I'll take care of everything. You say the meeting is scheduled for an hour after sunset?"

"Yes."

"I'll be ready. You two see if you can't get some sleep." Cam placed the metal detector on the coffee table beside Étienne's weapons and strode over to the front door. Opening

it, he called a greeting and stepped outside to deal with their
new security detail.

Silence fell. Krysta stared up at Étienne.

Awkward.

He smiled. "Not really."

"You're doing it again."

"You projected that one."

"I don't know how that works and am too tired to try to
figure it out." Fatigue clawed at her, leaving her weary enough
not to put up any more of a fight if he read her thoughts.

Étienne closed the distance between them. "Let's try to get
some sleep." Resting a hand on her lower back, he guided her
into a hallway. "You can have my sister Lisette's room. I never
know when she'll drop in, so I always keep it ready for her."

She nodded, full of ambivalence.

On the one hand, she was relieved that he hadn't asked
her to sleep with him. She may have known him, in a manner
of speaking, for a couple of weeks, but she didn't *know* him.
Not really.

Nor did she fully trust him yet.

On the other hand, it *had* been nice, falling asleep beside
him earlier. And this had been a hell of a day. Or night. Or
whatever. Not only had her beliefs concerning the paranormal
world and its inhabitants been rocked off of its foundations,
she had killed two men. And she had nearly been killed herself by a whole host of others. *Men* not vampires.

And she had lost everything. From the sounds of things,
the little house she and Sean rented had been completely
trashed. The contents destroyed along with it. How were they
going to bounce back from this? They lived paycheck to
paycheck.

And what would happen to her when she went before all

those immortals at the big meeting ahead of them? What would they do to her?

Étienne paused before an open door that led down into a basement. "After you."

"This is so surreal," she muttered as she tromped down the stairs.

It wasn't what she expected. She had thought it would be cold and dark and damp. Instead, the basement looked remarkably like the first floor, just without windows.

Again, Étienne placed a hand at her back and guided her to the first door on the right. "You and Lisette are of a similar size, so please feel free to delve into her closet and borrow whatever you will."

"Thank you." When he reached in and turned on the light, she studied the room.

It was pretty. Expensive hotel room pretty. She would have thought anyone two hundred years old would furnish their home with big, bulky antiques. But this room, and the rest of the house, was quite modern. Clean. Almost minimalist, with none of the froufrou stuff that professionally designed rooms featured in magazines all seemed to boast.

"Is it to your liking?" Étienne asked, brow furrowed. He actually seemed worried that it may not appeal to her.

"It's the nicest place I've ever stayed," she admitted.

He smiled. "I hope you'll be comfortable. I'll be across the hall if you should need anything."

She nodded, suddenly feeling lost. "Thank you."

Étienne took her hand and drew her into a hug, one she very much needed in that moment. "Don't lie awake all day, trying to figure everything out. There will be time enough for that tonight."

Easier said than done, but she'd try.

He drew back. Reaching up, he curled his hand into a loose fist and stroked her face with the backs of his fingers.

"Are you messing with my head, Étienne?" she asked.

"No."

"You aren't brainwashing me and tricking me into believing you're a good guy?"

"I'm not powerful enough to brainwash you. I can search others' thoughts. I can catch yours every once in awhile. But I can't alter them. The elders can, but not I."

"Then why do I feel like I've known you for a lot longer than I have?"

He shook his head. "I don't know. But I feel the same way." Lowering his head, he touched his lips to hers.

Her heartbeat picked up, surely drawing his notice. It really sucked that he knew how much he affected her while *she* was left in the dark.

He captured one of her hands and pressed it to his chest.

Beneath the rubber and all of that hard muscle, his heart raced as swiftly as her own.

When he raised his head, his brown eyes bore a faint amber glow. "This has all been as much of a surprise to me as it has been to you."

She nodded, incapable of doing anything else.

"No one has ever tempted me more."

She swallowed.

"Right across the hall," he murmured, backing away from her.

"Good night," she said, surprised she could sound so normal when such upheaval teemed within her. "Or rather day."

"Sleep well."

Passing through the darkened doorway across the hall, he flicked on the light and closed the door.

Chapter 9

Though he needed a good healing sleep, Étienne found rest elusive.

Chris hadn't skimped on the security detail. A dozen men stood sentry along the house's exterior. Three dozen more patrolled the grounds and manned the perimeter.

Étienne had made sure his home rested on enough private land that he wouldn't be able to hear his neighbors' thoughts and *they* wouldn't be able to see him return home covered with bloodstains, so it was a rather large perimeter.

All the guards were very focused and spoke little, but Étienne's sharp ears still picked up their movements, murmured comments, and periodic radio checks.

And then there was Krysta.

He hadn't lied when he had told her no one had ever tempted him more.

He had once told Sarah that he loved strong women.

Krysta was *very* strong.

Krysta was amazing. Krysta hunted vampires and had killed two men to protect him.

Krysta set his body on fire.

It had been hard as hell to back away from her and leave her to seek sleep in Lisette's room. But she didn't trust him fully. Asking him if he had brainwashed her had been ample proof of that. And she had been through hell during the past twenty-four hours.

Étienne regretted that the mercenaries, whoever the hell they were, had destroyed her home, and fully intended to make them pay. But he was very happy to have her here in *his* home and to have this chance to win her trust.

Was this how Richart had felt about Jenna? Why he had pursued her even when he thought a happy ending impossible for the two of them?

The door across the hallway opened.

Étienne's heart ceased beating for several long moments, then began to slam against his ribs.

Was Krysta coming to him?

He'd be lying if he said he hadn't hoped she would.

Alas, no. Nearly silent footsteps took her down the hallway and up the stairs.

Tossing back the covers, he rose and donned the sweatpants he'd laid out in case Krysta needed him for anything. (Somehow he didn't think creeping up behind her naked would send the right message.) Then he opened his door and went in search of her.

He found her in the living room.

Why was it, he wondered as he paused in the doorway to admire her, that pajamas made men look geeky, yet made women look incredibly alluring?

The pajamas Krysta wore were made of some silky burgundy material. Having been raised in far different times, Lisette sometimes complained about constantly having to *dress like a man*. To compensate, she wore feminine things like this when she wasn't hunting.

Her back to him, Krysta leaned forward over a chair to peer through the window, out into bright sunlight.

Étienne, too, had been born in a different time. He wasn't like men today. He didn't need to see a woman's breasts shoved up to her neck in a push-up bra and spilling out of her blouse to take notice. He didn't need skirts so short the women who wore them couldn't bend over without showing their underwear or exposing their vaginas. He didn't need pants cut so low that thongs and butt cracks peeked out at him.

If it was out there, it was out there. No surprises. No anticipation. No fun.

Étienne was more titillated by what he *couldn't* see. He liked being kept guessing. He liked imagining what that silky material might conceal, how it would feel to peel each layer back and reveal what no one else could see. What no one else had even glimpsed.

The pajama pants covered Krysta from hips to ankles. Her feet, smaller than he had imagined, were bare. The long sleeves of the top had been rolled back almost to her elbows. Her hair was loose and rumpled.

Utterly delicious.

"What are you looking at?" he asked softly.

Gasping, she spun around. "You startled me."

"Forgive me. I didn't intend to."

"I was just looking at the guards. They seem very formidable."

"They take their job very seriously and will give their lives to protect us, should such become necessary."

"They're that devoted to you?"

He strolled into the room, uncomfortable with the question. It made the guards seem subservient. "I wouldn't put it that way. It's more that we're brothers in arms. Soldiers all fighting a common enemy. It bonds us, even if we don't know each other."

She glanced back at the window. "You don't know those guys?"

He stopped beside her and, avoiding the golden rays of sunshine that poured through the filmy curtains, peered outside.

"Careful," she said, touching his arm and nudging him farther away from the light.

He smiled, warmed by her concern. "It's all right. I won't burst into flames. I'll just sunburn in record time."

"Will sunlight kill vampires?"

"Yes. Vampires can't tolerate any level of sunlight. Immortals have greater tolerance to it because of our advanced DNA, but younger ones like me are still vulnerable."

"Oh."

He studied the faces of as many guards as he could see from this perspective. "I believe I've seen one or two of these men before, but have never spoken with them."

"And yet they would die for you."

He nodded. "It isn't a one-way street. They know we risk our lives every night, hunting and destroying vampires who would prey upon them. There was a night not long ago when Richart, Lisette, and I, along with the other immortals you will meet later, risked our lives battling not vampires, but humans who would have killed or tortured every man you see out there." He drew back from the window. "Couldn't you sleep?"

She shook her head. "I always have trouble sleeping in a new place."

"And the past few hours have been difficult."

"Yes. So much has happened." She shrugged. "I'm still having trouble processing it all. My mind is racing. And I keep obsessing over the stupidest things. Like how Sean and I are going to explain the crater in the living room floor and the bullet holes Sheldon said riddled every wall to our landlord."

"Don't worry about that. We'll take care of it. We're very good at cleaning up our messes." He touched her shoulder, the silky material cool beneath his fingers, and guided her toward the sofa. "What you need right now is something that will take your mind off of everything so you can relax." She sat down at his urging, the V-neck of her shirt giving him the briefest glimpse of shadowy cleavage. "And what *I* need is something to take my mind off of you in those pajamas."

She smiled and fingered the neckline. "They really aren't my style. I'm more of a sleep-shirt kind of girl."

He groaned and sank onto his haunches to examine the DVDs lining the shelves beneath the large flat-screen TV. "Don't put that image in my head."

Krysta stared at his broad, muscled back and narrow waist, bare and totally drool-worthy, as was his chest when he faced her. "Tit for tat. I lost my ability to concentrate as soon as I turned and saw you wearing nothing but those sweatpants."

Surely, he had heard her heart's crazy antics.

He laughed.

She liked his laugh. Smooth and deep.

He chose a DVD and slipped it into the player. Rising, he grabbed the remote and joined her on the sofa.

And he didn't leave any space between them. His hip pressed against hers as he draped his arm across the back cushion. "I keep telling myself to keep my distance, but . . ."

She nodded, leaning into his side. "I'm too tired to worry about it right now." She smiled at the television. *Monk*?

He nodded. "It's smart. It's funny. And it advocates true love."

"It's a tragic love, though. His wife is dead."

"Don't most love affairs end tragically?" he asked, frowning at the screen.

"I don't know. Your brother seems pretty happy."

His face lightened. "Yes, he does. I didn't see that coming."

"If you tell me you're psychic, too—"

He laughed. "I'm not." Still smiling, he glanced down at her. "I didn't see you coming either."

Manic butterflies invaded her stomach as she licked lips suddenly gone dry.

The amber glow returned to his eyes as he followed the motion with his gaze.

The TV brightened with the menu for *Monk*.

He looked toward it.

Krysta sighed. She had been sure he was going to kiss her.

"I thought I would be pushing my luck if I did," he murmured.

"Oh." She didn't even care that he was reading her thoughts again.

"I also thought you might need a little distance."

She fought the urge to laugh. Their sides were glued together and his arm now rested across her shoulders, his fingers toying with her hair.

His lips twitched as he glanced at her from the corner of his eye. "Note I said I thought *you* needed some distance. Tonight I find myself needing the opposite, so this was my compromise."

She smiled. "I'll take it."

The show began.

"You didn't say why *you* were up," she mentioned. "Couldn't you sleep?"

"No. Too many bodies nearby, moving and murmuring. I'm used to it only being Cam and I and sometimes my siblings."

"Ah."

A moment passed.

"And," he continued, "I found myself obsessing over a thought."

"What thought?"

"That, had I not arrived when I did last night, you likely would have died."

"At Duke?"

"Yes."

She didn't refute it. He was right. Even had the mercenaries not shown up with guns blazing, she couldn't have defeated that many vampires on her own.

"Doesn't it bother you?" he asked.

"That I could have died?" she countered. "Of course. A *lot*. But I know every time I go out hunting that my death is a possible outcome."

"Then why the hell do you do it?"

She thought a moment. "Because it needs to be done. Because it's worth the risk. Because I promised myself a long time ago that I would kill every vampire on the planet or die trying."

"It's personal."

"Yes."

He said nothing, just returned his gaze to the screen.

"You aren't going to call me a fool or demand I stop?"

"You aren't a fool. I understand a need for vengeance."

"And the other?" she asked.

"I believe I already tried to convince you to stop hunting. I don't have the energy tonight to bang my head against a brick wall."

She laughed. "To be continued, then?"

He smiled. "To be continued."

She tore her gaze away from his handsome profile and stared at the screen. "Have you seen this episode?"

He nodded. "It's one of my favorites."

"I saw it once a few years ago, but can't remember how the husband did it. Don't tell me."

He curled his hand over her shoulder and drew her a little closer. "I won't."

Resting her head in the crook of his shoulder, she drew her legs up onto the sofa and relaxed against him.

Étienne heard the front door open and close and didn't bother to open his eyes. Cam had been coming and going throughout the afternoon, as quietly as a mortal could, so as not to disturb the duo slumbering on the sofa.

Krysta would have to watch the *Monk* episode they had begun another time. She had fallen asleep only fifteen minutes into it.

Unwinding at last himself, Étienne had lain back on the sofa, drawn his legs up, and managed to spoon his body around her without landing them both on the floor.

Damn, it felt good. Even better than holding her hand had as they had slept beside each other at her house.

He had really needed this. The more he thought about what had happened at Duke, the more panicked he felt. That many vampires would have defeated her and ended her reign as North Carolina's—if not the world's—most successful mortal vampire hunter. And, if by some miracle they hadn't, the mercenaries who had come later would have likely thought her an immortal and tranqed her with a dose that would've been lethal to her.

Either way, she would have died.

Tightening his hold, he buried his face in her hair and breathed in her scent.

Something sharp pricked his neck just beneath his chin.

He stilled, opened his eyes.

Sean stood over them, his face set in stone, with one of Étienne's own daggers in his hand, angled to slit Étienne's throat.

Easy, Étienne spoke into his mind.

Sean's eyes widened. "How did you do that?"

I'm telepathic. Speak softly so you won't wake her. She had difficulty falling asleep.

"And you thought feeling her up would help?"

He sighed. *If we're going to do the keep-your-hands-off-my-sister thing, let me put her to bed first.* Her *bed*, he stressed before Sean could suggest otherwise.

Sean withdrew the blade.

In one fluid motion, Etienne rose with Krysta in his arms. She stirred, but didn't awaken.

Sean frowned. "What did you do to her? She's usually a light sleeper."

"Nothing. She's just exhausted. Too little sleep and too many adrenaline rushes."

Frowning, Sean followed him down to Lisette's room, where Étienne laid Krysta on the bed and drew the covers up to her chin.

He turned to her brother and abandoned all hopes of getting any sleep today. "Let's return to the living room, and I'll bring you up to speed."

Krysta was a nervous wreck on the ride to the meeting.

Cam drove while Sean sat in the passenger seat, scowling out the window.

Her brother wasn't taking this very well. He was worried about her, afraid Étienne was screwing with her head (even more so now that he knew Étienne was a telepath), afraid the whole immortal versus vampire thing was bullshit, even though the concept of both being caused by a virus intrigued the medicine lover in him.

Krysta didn't blame him. He had only had twenty-four hours to try to figure this out while she had known, or suspected, for two weeks now that Étienne was different.

And there was also the whole attraction thing that softened her toward Étienne.

Or blinded her to the truth, as Sean feared.

But Krysta didn't think so. Vampires were insane. They were mentally off, and anyone who spent two minutes in their company knew it. Not once, all day, had any of the immortals she had met done anything to suggest they weren't completely lucid. Not once had she felt threatened by them.

Nervous? Yes. Confused? Yes. In danger of being harmed by them? No.

"Who is David?" she asked as dark arboreal shadows in monstrous proportions whizzed past outside the window. The meeting to which they had all been summoned would be held at the home of someone named David, who seemed to live way out in the middle of nowhere.

Seated beside her, Étienne said, "David is the second eldest, most powerful immortal in existence."

"How old is he?"

"I don't know exactly and suspect he ceased counting centuries ago. Suffice it to say, he is old enough to have witnessed biblical events."

Her neck popped as her head snapped in his direction. "What?"

Sean turned to look at them over his shoulder. "Are you saying he's thousands of years old?"

"Yes."

"Do vampires live that long?" Sean asked, mimicking her own thoughts.

"No. Vampires rarely live a century because of the madness that claims them. Either they kill each other in fits of rage, are hunted and killed by immortals, or grow careless and inadvertently bring about their own destruction."

Krysta couldn't even imagine living that long. She had suspected vampires didn't live as long as movies and books often claimed they did. But immortals . . .

Living thousands of years? What was that like?

"You said second eldest," she murmured. "Is the tall one I met earlier older?"

"Yes. And he's only about an inch taller than David."

Sean frowned at her. "You met another one?"

She nodded. "He must have been six foot seven or eight, and he positively oozed power."

Sean shifted his gaze to Étienne. "Just what are these elders' gifts?"

"Don't answer that," Cam said, catching Étienne's gaze in the rearview mirror.

Krysta waited for Étienne to respond.

He remained silent, disappointing her, but she couldn't fault him for it. Sean wasn't exactly cooperating. Or he was, but had put up quite the verbal fight in an attempt to avoid this meeting. The idea of being sequestered in a home with over a dozen immortals was very unnerving.

So Krysta could see why Étienne might be reluctant to share more secrets without first securing Sean's favor.

"We're here," Cam announced, turning onto a secluded drive and following it to a tall security gate. Heavy silence filled the car as he rolled down his window, reached out, and entered a security code she couldn't see from her vantage point.

The majestic gates swung open on well-oiled hinges.

Dark trees towered over them, blocking out the moon, as the car crawled forward along a winding road that ended in a circular drive full of . . . hybrids and electric cars?

Sean peered through the window as Cam parked behind a shiny black Prius. "Are you guys, like, environmentalists or something?"

"*All* of our senses are heightened," Étienne said, "not just our vision. Our sense of smell is more acute than a polar bear's or an arctic fox's. The pollution you barely notice that makes the air smell a little stale to you makes it smell to us as though we're living downwind of a garbage dump on a hot summer's day."

Krysta grimaced. "That sucks."

He nodded. "Particularly since most of us have lived long enough to remember what the world smelled like before the industrial revolution."

Cam exited the car and pocketed the keys.

Étienne opened his door, stepped out, and circled around to open Krysta's before she could reach for the handle.

She took the hand he gallantly offered and let him help her from the car.

Did she *need* the help?

Of course not.

Did she leap at the excuse to touch him?

Absolutely.

Sean joined them and slammed his door shut out of habit.

Étienne motioned toward the house. "Shall we?"

The door swung open at their approach.

Étienne nodded to Darnell, who greeted them all with a smile.

"Hi. You must be Krysta and Sean. It's nice to meet you. I'm Darnell, David's Second."

Krysta and Sean each shook his hand.

"So you're human?" Sean asked.

"Actually, I'm a *gifted one* like you two."

That was news to Étienne. He had thought Darnell human.

"I'm afraid I'm going to have to ask you to let me hold on to your cell phones while you're here."

Is that really necessary? Étienne asked him.

Darnell met Étienne's gaze. *Yes. We can't risk them recording anything they see or hear. Chris also wants me to go over them with a metal detector.*

Hell. Isn't the fact that the mercenaries didn't attack us at my place or at Sean's job proof enough that they aren't being tracked?

Not in Chris's mind.

Paranoid bastard.

That paranoid bastard brought you reinforcements today.

I know, damn it. I'm just tired.

Darnell's lips twitched as he stepped outside with them and held out his hand.

Krysta and Sean dropped their phones into it, their irritation obvious.

Darnell checked the phones to ensure they were turned off, then pocketed them. "I'll return them to you when you leave." He reached behind him and pulled a handheld metal detector from his back pocket.

Étienne sighed. "I apologize for this."

Krysta did not look pleased. "So you expect *me* to trust *you*, even though *you* clearly don't trust *me*?"

"I trust you," Étienne assured her. He really did.

"If Étienne weren't attracted to you, the rest of us would, too," Darnell said, earning Étienne's wrath. "But smitten immortals have trusted the wrong humans often enough in the past to make us wary under such circumstances."

A frown creasing her brow, she held out her arms. "Smitten, huh?"

Étienne didn't deny it.

Sean eyed the two with disapproval.

Darnell passed the wand over Krysta's head and chest, then down one arm. It beeped.

Pursing her lips, Krysta rolled back the sleeve of the black shirt she had borrowed from Lisette and revealed a small, sheathed dagger she had strapped to her wrist.

Darnell moved on to the other arm without removing the weapon. Another beep. A dagger graced her other wrist as well. Two more beeps revealed more tucked into the waist of her pants.

Étienne raised a brow.

"Well," she declared defensively, "what did you expect? Total trust? I haven't known you for that long and am going on faith that you all are what you say you are and aren't vampires."

More beeps on her ankles. More weapons.

Darnell found the same on Sean. Étienne wasn't sure why that surprised him. Krysta had said Sean had skills and Étienne had witnessed as much in her dream.

Darnell pocketed the wand. "Okay. We're good."

Krysta stared at him. "What?"

Sean looked at Étienne, then Darnell. "Aren't you going to confiscate our weapons?"

"No," they said simultaneously.

Étienne wanted them to feel safe and knew the weapons would lend them a sense of security.

The siblings shared a glance.

"Why not?" Krysta asked.

Darnell shrugged. "Immortals are stronger and faster than vampires. Your weapons are useless against the men and women here tonight."

And there went the sense of security.

Really? Étienne asked him. *You couldn't have said you were letting them keep them as a gesture of faith or friendship?*

No. I appreciated honesty when I stumbled into this world and assumed they would, too.

Étienne grunted, knowing he was right, but not wanting to admit it.

Krysta swallowed. "If you don't care that we're carrying weapons, what were you looking for with the metal detector?"

She was sharp. Étienne loved that.

Darnell shrugged. "More cell phones. Voice or video recorders. Anything you might use to capture the meeting digitally."

And tracking devices. An overlooked tracking device had

cost them lives in the past. They wouldn't make the same mistake again.

Darnell entered the house and gestured for them to follow. "Welcome. And thank you for your cooperation."

David's home was large and spacious and tastefully decorated with modern furniture. Étienne had always felt at home here.

"Wow," Krysta whispered to Sean. "This place is huge. Our whole house wouldn't even fill this living room."

David maintained an open-door policy, inviting all immortals, Seconds, and other members of the network to come and go as they pleased. Like Seth, he worked hard to create a family atmosphere. So his home saw a lot of traffic and needed to be big enough to handle it.

Several sofas graced the living room on the right, which bled into a dining room on the left. Étienne turned his attention there and saw that everyone else had already arrived. Everyone save Seth and David.

He guided Krysta toward a table that now seated twenty-eight. A leaf had been added to extend the table and accommodate the Immortal Guardians' growing numbers.

Conversation ceased as all eyes watched their approach.

The chairs at the head and foot of the table were vacant, reserved for the eldest immortals. At the far end, Ami sat beside her eight-century-old husband Marcus. Ami looked rather pallid tonight. She must have heard about the mercenary attack and, having been the primary target of the last one, was understandably distressed by the news that the threat had resumed.

Roland, the notoriously antisocial, nine-hundred-plus-year-old immortal, sat beside Marcus. The two Brits had known each other for eight centuries and were like brothers. Roland's wife Sarah, transformed only a couple of years earlier, occupied the seat beside him and leaned into his side.

Next came Yuri and Stanislov and their Seconds. They

were fairly new to the area, and Étienne hadn't had a chance to get to know them very well. Ethan, an American and formerly the youngest immortal in their midst at a hundred years, lounged beside the Russians. Then Edward, another Brit. Their Seconds.

A scowling Chris Reordon occupied the chair across from Ami. Beside him were Dr. Melanie Lipton, only recently transformed, and her husband Bastien, the black sheep of the immortal family who was still pretty widely hated. Next was Bastien's Second, Tanner. Sheldon, who actually seemed to like Bastien now. Richart. Jenna. Tracy, who was Lisette's Second. Lisette, who studied Krysta intently.

I like her, Lisette declared in his head.

You don't even know her, he countered.

She's a mortal who strode into a house full of immortals with her head held high and her body loaded down with weapons. And she's smart enough to be attracted to you.

Can you read her mind? he asked curiously. He didn't like the idea of his sister intruding upon Krysta's thoughts, but wanted to see if he were the only one who couldn't (most of the time).

She frowned. *No, I can't. Can you?*

No. Not really. Not at will.

A sly smile slid across her pretty features. *Perfect.*

He didn't dispute it. It was hard to pursue a relationship with someone when you could hear her every thought, including the ugly ones that slipped through when she was cranky or the occasional dark one that made even *her* think, *Where the hell did* that *come from?*

The soft sound of boots hitting bamboo drew his attention to the hallway that led from the living room to the back of the house and basement.

David entered, garbed in the black hunting clothes everyone else wore. His dreadlocks had been pulled back from his face and framed his hips as he strode toward them.

Étienne glanced at Krysta and saw her mouth fall open.

Wow.

He frowned. That thought had come through loud and clear.

She gazed up at the elder immortal as though he were the most gorgeous thing she had ever beheld. He knew women found David's hair, height, muscles, and dark-as-midnight skin attractive, but Krysta looked as though she were about to begin drooling.

Don't get your shorts in a bunch, Lisette admonished. *She isn't drooling. Your jealousy is making her response seem more than it is.*

David stopped before them and smiled. "Krysta, Sean, welcome to my home. I'm David." Taking Krysta's hand, he raised it to his lips.

Étienne listened carefully to Krysta's heartbeat and relaxed a little when it didn't speed up at the attention.

"Nice to meet you," Krysta offered.

He shook Sean's hand. "I'm glad you're both safe and have decided to join us tonight. The events of the past twenty-four hours have caught us off guard. You, too, I understand. But we'll sort it all out together."

The sister and brother shared a look.

"Okay," Krysta said.

David turned to Sean. "No, we aren't vampires. Étienne told you the truth. We're immortals and I'm sure Dr. Lipton would be happy to discuss all of the medical intricacies of our differences with you." He looked at Krysta. "Yes, I'm reading your thoughts. The safety of everyone under my roof is my responsibility and I wish to ensure you mean them no harm. And, no, Étienne was not lying when he said he couldn't read your mind. You have very strong natural defenses, but I'm older and more powerful, so they proved minor obstacles for me."

Is she attracted to me? Étienne asked before he could stop himself. It was odd, not being able to freely access her thoughts and he was eager to confirm what the little glimpses he had managed thus far had told him.

"Yes," David answered aloud, "she's attracted to you."

Krysta frowned at Étienne and popped him on the arm. "That's not fair."

David turned to Sean. "No, Étienne isn't brainwashing her. And this isn't a total clusterfuck. Chris Reordon has already taken steps to purchase the home you rent so the two of you won't have to worry about the landlord giving you grief. Our cleanup crews are salvaging all of your possessions that they can and are packing them up for you so you can move into a new place—a safe house of your choice—once we've squelched this latest threat. I know it will take some time to earn your trust, but whether you wish it to be true or not, you're one of us. We were all *gifted ones* like you before we were transformed. And we take care of our own."

"They're *gifted ones?*" Lisette exclaimed with glee.

"Yes," David said, then addressed Krysta. "And no, Étienne isn't messing with your head. You have totally captivated him."

"Damn," Sheldon said. "This is better than a soap opera. Maybe we should start an Immortal Guardians reality show and air it on theimmortalguardians.com."

David ignored him. "Won't you please join us in the dining room?"

Darnell and Cam had already seated themselves, Darnell taking the seat closest to this end and Cam the one next to him. Sean sat next to Cam. Étienne held the chair next to his for Krysta until she was seated, then claimed the one between her and Lisette.

David took the seat catty-corner to Darnell at this end of the table.

Darnell retrieved his cell phone and dialed. Étienne heard Seth answer.

"Yes?"

"All set."

Darnell ended the call and put away his phone.

Seth appeared at the opposite end of the table.

Sean and Krysta jumped, startled by his sudden appearance.

"Thank you all for coming. Krysta and Sean, we appreciate your joining us. I'm Seth, the leader of the Immortal Guardians."

"Nice to meet you," they murmured.

He took his seat. "Étienne, would you formally introduce our guests?"

Chapter 10

Krysta listened carefully and tried to memorize every name and face as Étienne introduced her and Sean to the group. It was a relief to see other humans present. Or *gifted ones*. She wasn't sure how to tell those apart. But she could tell by their auras that there were almost as many mortals present as there were immortals.

Her gaze slid to Seth, whose aura glowed that brilliant white, then to David, whose aura did the same, but had a tiny sliver of purple mixed in. The other immortals had a pretty equal mix of white and purple.

She looked at the small redhead—Ami?—who sat beside Seth. Her aura was unlike anyone else's. It contained the same color variations of humans and *gifted ones*, but had little sparkly things in it, as if the stars in the night sky were peeking through a rainbow. It was beautiful and very peculiar. What was she?

Seth and David's auras were different because . . .

Actually, she wasn't sure. Was it because they were so old? Or were there other supernatural beings? Étienne seemed sure they were immortals, yet . . .

Those auras.

"Let's begin," Seth said when the roll call of names ended.

Chris cleared his throat. "Before we get started, there's an issue we need to discuss."

Seth motioned for Chris to continue. "What's on your mind, Chris?"

Chris's gaze circled the table. "My goal is the same as the network's: To protect you. It's why I scrutinize so carefully every member of the network before hiring him or her. It's why every Second is handpicked. If even *one* person leaks the truth to the media, in this information age in particular, it is hell to clean up and counter. Every year, with every new gadget and fucking cell phone with apps that can realign the damned planets, it gets harder. We can't afford to make a single mistake."

"What's your point?" Ethan asked.

"My point is I can't protect you if you keep hiding your girlfriends from me."

Every eye swung toward Krysta.

She glanced around. "Why is everyone looking at me?"

Silence.

"Oh. Oh, no. I'm not Étienne's girlfriend. We just . . . hunt together . . . sort of. It's not like we're dating or . . . We haven't slept together or anything . . . I mean we *slept* together . . . twice, actually . . . but we didn't—"

"You aren't helping," Étienne murmured.

She clamped her lips shut. What a time to find out she babbled when she was nervous.

"He has a point," Roland spoke. "Étienne hid this woman from us—"

"The woman has a name," Krysta interjected.

"—and Richart hid both Jenna and her son from us. Every mortal is a potential threat."

Chris frowned. "Says the immortal who threatened to kill me if I went anywhere near Sarah when you two got together."

"That was different."

"How?"

"You've all said it a thousand times. I'm an untrusting, antisocial bastard."

"No, you aren't," Sarah protested and glared at the others. "Stop saying that."

Roland continued. "Anyone who can win *my* trust deserves it. Besides, she saved my ass. Twice."

"Technically," Krysta said, "I saved Étienne's ass."

"After I risked it to save you."

"That's true. I thanked you for that, right?"

Chris waved his hands. "It doesn't matter who saved whose ass. The point is every mortal poses a threat. Especially now. If you don't let me interro—ah, interview these women, you place everyone in danger, because sooner or later someone always trusts the wrong person."

"True," Seth murmured.

"Ah *hah!*" Richart blurted at the same time. "You were going to say interrogate! I knew it! That's why I kept Jenna a secret!"

Chris swore beneath his breath as Roland and Étienne both nodded. "Okay, *maybe*, in the past, I *might* have been a tad harsh when ensuring that an immortal's lover could be trusted. But can you blame me? Look what happened to Mattheus."

"Who the hell is Mattheus?" Roland grumbled.

"Mattheus got screwed?" Tracy said. "That sucks. He's so hot."

"Who's Mattheus?" Sheldon seconded.

"He's an immortal from Brazil," Chris said. "His mortal lover, whom he thought was completely trustworthy, video-taped them having sex—"

"Awesome!" Sheldon interjected with a grin.

Everyone looked at him.

"What? I like porn."

Still they stared.

He frowned. "I have to give up booze, parties, *and* porn? Can't a Second have *any* vices?"

Chris sighed. "Anyway. She videotaped them having sex and intended to auction it off to news outlets once it had been authenticated by an expert who would swear the glowing eyes, fangs, and . . . ah . . . unusual speed and other things demonstrated were not special effects produced by a post-production house."

"Maybe they were," Sheldon suggested somberly. "Maybe she was out to discredit him. I think we should all watch it and—"

"The tape has been destroyed," Seth cut in.

"Damn." Sheldon slumped down in his seat.

Chris met Richart's gaze. "Anytime you want me to get rid of him . . ."

Richart shook his head. "He amuses me."

"Chris does have a point," Seth said, returning to the subject at hand.

At the opposite end of the table, David nodded. "We have seen it countless times. This is a lonely existence that can sometimes drive us to trust where we should not."

"Chris," Seth continued, "perhaps if you allowed the immortal to be present when you met with his lover, he would no longer feel wary of your possible treatment of her."

"Or him," Lisette tossed in.

Étienne raised his eyebrows.

"What? I can't date?"

"Fine," Chris said. "If any of you acquire a lover with whom you wish to share the truth, you can be present when I meet with her. But I *do* need to meet with her. Or him. If you'd consent to a telepath being present or listening in from the next room, all the better."

When no one spoke, Seth spoke for them. "They'll take it

into consideration." The casual words carried the weight of an order. "Is that all, Chris?"

"For now, yes."

Seth turned to Étienne. "So?"

"So?" he repeated.

David leaned forward and braced his elbows on the table. "Tell us what happened last night."

Étienne hesitated. He wasn't sure how to tell them without explaining Krysta's role in it. And he thought it best to minimize that as much as possible.

No one seemed to have caught her reference to their hunting together. They had all been too titillated by the idea that he had been hiding away a girlfriend.

Which, as she had pointed out, was not to say that Krysta was his girlfriend.

You're rambling, David spoke in his head.

Étienne shot him a glance. Much to his surprise, the elder immortal seemed amused. *No, I'm not.*

Yes, you are, Seth said.

Is everyone *listening to my thoughts?* he demanded with exasperation. His barriers were usually stronger than that.

No, just us, David answered.

Go ahead and tell them what happened, Seth advised. *We've already gleaned it.*

Étienne leaned forward and braced his elbows on the table. "I was out hunting with Krysta—"

"Wait," Chris interrupted. "You two really *do* hunt together?"

Étienne looked at Krysta, who shrugged. "In a manner of speaking."

Chris threw up his hands. "Okay. Another point of business. Most of the immortals at this table are at least a hundred years old, so I didn't think I had to remind any of you of this, but you *cannot* recruit your own Seconds. *All* Seconds must be assigned by the network, which thoroughly vets and trains them. What the hell, Étienne?"

Now Krysta leaned forward. "I'm not a Second."

Before everyone could start bitching at once, Étienne held up a hand. "Krysta came to my attention a couple of weeks ago. I was out hunting and saw several vampires tracking her with the clear intention of preying upon her. Much to my surprise, however, the *vampires* turned out to be the prey. Krysta is a vampire hunter."

"No way!" Sheldon blurted.

Étienne scowled at him. "As soon as I realized this, I began to follow her." As swiftly as possible, he caught them up on his adventures with Krysta.

"No wonder you've been so distracted," Lisette said, studying Krysta curiously.

Marcus frowned. "By vampire hunter you mean . . . ?"

"She hunts vampires. She lures them into traps, then dispatches them."

"That's impossible," Ethan said.

Krysta stiffened. "Then I've been doing the impossible for six years."

Disbelieving stares.

"Mortals can't defeat vampires in battle," Edward said.

"This one can," Krysta insisted.

"Ami can," Sheldon pointed out.

"Melanie could, when she was mortal," Bastien added with a proud smile.

"But Ami and Melanie didn't take them on alone," Ethan said. "They fought by Marcus's and Bastien's sides."

Marcus leaned forward and caught Ethan's eye. "Ami wasn't fighting by my side when she kicked your ass in that sparring session. And you're faster than a vampire."

Sheldon laughed. "Burn!"

Seth sighed. "We're getting off topic here. I've examined

Krysta's thoughts. She has indeed been hunting vampires for the past six years with the help of her brother. And, before you ask, neither of them are members of the mercenary groups who keep troubling us. Her gift gives her an edge"—he held up a hand to stay him when Ethan opened his mouth again—"which I will not disclose. If Krysta wants you to know, she'll tell you herself."

Ethan stared at Krysta. A teasing gleam entered his eyes, making Étienne narrow his own as his hackles rose. Offering Krysta a flirtatious grin, Ethan said, "I'll show you mine if you'll show me yours."

In a heartbeat, Étienne drew a dagger and threw it.

The hilt struck Ethan right in the center of his forehead, snapping his head back. "Ow! Shhhhit! What the hell, man?"

Krysta gaped up at Étienne, who squirmed as everyone at the table stared at him.

He cleared his throat, but didn't know what to say. He hadn't really meant to do that. He had just reacted.

"*Oh* yeah," Sheldon said. "He has fallen and he has fallen hard."

Snickers and head shakes all around.

"*Merde*."

David held up a hand and called for quiet. "Please continue, Étienne."

Eager to change the subject (Why did it seem to return so often to his being smitten with Krysta?), he told them about defeating the vampires, then being set upon by mercenaries.

No one reprimanded him for not getting the hell out of there as soon as he saw that first tranquilizer dart. That's what they were supposed to do to avoid capture, but all understood his desire to protect Krysta.

Cam leaned forward and braced his elbows on the table, his attention on Krysta and Sean. "Thank you. You don't know what they would have done to him if they had gotten their hands on him. If these are the same people we dealt with before—"

"I don't see how they can be," Melanie interrupted. "That threat was neutralized."

Étienne shook his head. "These soldiers were very reminiscent of the others." He related the events that followed at Krysta and Sean's home.

A steady stream of curses and exclamations of disbelief accompanied him.

Marcus looked ready to snap, his fury fairly heating the room. "How the hell is this possible?"

Chris shook his head. "It must be a different group."

"They have the fucking tranquilizer!" he shouted.

Ami placed a hand on his arm.

Étienne understood Marcus's rage. The last mercenary group had included some of the monsters who had tortured Ami. And they had been eager as hell to get their hands on her again.

Cam shook his head. "We must have missed something."

Seth shook his head. "We didn't. Every mercenary who knew of our existence was either killed or had their memories wiped. And David and I saw to the latter ourselves."

David nodded. "Darnell worked tirelessly with the network's techno-geeks to expunge all mention of us, of vampires, and of Ami from their computers and servers."

"And replaced it with malware," Darnell added. "There's no way they could recover those files. *I* couldn't even recover those files."

"And yet," Roland said, "Étienne was tranqed and attacked by humans garbed as soldiers."

"Could they be military?" Sarah asked, brow furrowed. "Could Emrys have gone to the military without our knowledge?"

Seth shook his head. "I would have seen it in his thoughts."

"Donald and Nelson didn't either," David mentioned before anyone could ask.

Donald was the leader of the elite Private Military Company Emrys had drawn into his war with the immortals near the end. Nelson was Donald's second in command or yes-man. Because their company was widely known by the public, killing the two men would have raised too many questions, so their memories had been erased instead and a story concocted—something about a couple of transport planes colliding in a freak accident—to explain the deaths of the soldiers slain by the immortals.

"So where does that leave us?" Cam asked.

Seth shook his head. "Without an explanation."

Krysta studied the men and women seated around the table in the grim hush that followed.

She glanced at Sean to see how he was taking all of this.

Suspicion had fled his face and been replaced by the same fascination she suspected lit her own. This was amazing. She didn't know what she had expected, but it hadn't been this.

They were like a big family. They teased. They bantered. They got snippy with each other, like when Étienne had tossed his dagger at Ethan.

That had been too funny. *And* rather revealing. Étienne's eyes had actually glowed with jealousy. How cool was that?

Sean shifted slightly. "How did the mercenaries find out about you before?" he asked, surprising her. She had sensed he was relaxing into the situation, but hadn't thought he had relaxed enough to participate in the conversation.

David answered. "The brother of a vampire we slew told them, enlisting their aid in his quest for vengeance."

"Could something similar have happened this time?"

Seth shook his head. "It was the first time in history that such had occurred. Because of the madness that plagues them, vampires tend to either kill or transform relatives they bring into the loop. And most vampires think the only thing that differentiates us is immortals' unwillingness to kill innocents, or to let *them* do it. Because we don't fraternize, vampires often don't realize how much longer immortals live or know that we differ genetically. This human male was in a unique position to learn this information."

Everyone shifted their gaze to a man at the opposite end of the table who sat with his arm around a pretty brunet. Krysta thought his name was Bastien, but was having trouble keeping up.

As her own attention was drawn that way, she noticed for the third or fourth time that the forbidding immortal across from Sheldon was staring at her.

Roland? Was that his name?

Krysta didn't know what it was about him, but he unnerved her more than anyone else present. He just seemed menacing. Like he could slit your throat, then sit down, prop his feet on your corpse, and eat a sandwich.

Uneasy, she looked up at Étienne. "Who else could be in a unique position to share this information?"

He shook his head. "No one."

"Bullshit," Roland growled.

Étienne frowned. "No one at this table would betray us."

"I wasn't thinking of someone at this table," he intoned. "We all know the mercenaries' goal. At least the goal of those we fought before. They know vampires swiftly lose their mental faculties and immortals don't. They need to capture one of *us* so they can torture and dissect us and figure out why. Once they do, they intend to use the virus and whatever information they can glean from us to create an army of supersoldiers they can hire out to the highest bidder."

"Oh, shit," Sean breathed. "They could make billions."

David nodded. "And wreak havoc upon the world. No

human army could stand against an army of immortals. Or a more expendable army of vampires."

"Why expendable?" Sean questioned.

"Any human soldiers they intentionally infected with the virus would have to be slain a year later to ensure their leaders could maintain control."

One year? "The madness kicks in that fast?" Krysta asked. No wonder she had never encountered a sane or non-murderous vampire.

"It varies from human to human and can be accelerated by things like poor living conditions or torture," David explained. "Sometimes vampires begin to lose impulse control and experience psychotic breaks six months after infection. Sometimes, if they are extraordinarily strong, they can have three or four years before lucidity abandons them. Since the change can be insidious and difficult to detect in the beginning, the mercenary leaders would have to limit the lifespan of their soldiers in order to prevent chaos and collateral damage."

Damn. Krysta wondered how that would work. Would the soldiers volunteer to be infected? Would they even understand what they would be infected with? Would they know, going in, that they would be killed a year later? Or would that caveat be kept from them?

"I think we all know what happened," Roland spoke again, "why mercenaries have risen against us once more."

"Not really," Étienne said.

Several others nodded. They truly seemed baffled.

Roland shook his head. "Isn't it obvious? Someone at the network betrayed us."

Chris slammed a hand down on the table. "Bullshit!"

Krysta jumped.

Unperturbed, Roland returned his irate stare. "One of your mortal pets decided a billion dollars in his bank account sounded pretty damned good and sold us out. Probably one of your techno-geeks."

"Geeks," his wife murmured, chewing her lower lip.

"Fuck you, Roland! My people are handpicked and loyal to the core. You have no reason to doubt them beyond your massive paranoia and I'm sick of you trying to dump that shit on my doorstep!"

Roland's eyes flashed amber.

Krysta's heartbeat picked up nervously.

Étienne reached across her lap and rested a hand on the thigh farthest from him as though readying himself to sweep her behind him if all hell broke loose.

From the corner of her eye, she saw Sean palm a dagger under the table.

Oh, crap.

Roland leaned forward. "I doubt *everyone* because of what you call my massive paranoia. Experience has taught me that even those I trust the most could stab me in the back. And have. However, I doubt *your* people and think *them* responsible for this new threat because it is the only plausible explanation. No one else knew. No one else could gain access to the tranquilizer, of which you keep a substantial supply at network headquarters. A network employee or employees, therefore, must be responsible."

Judging by the looks of things, Roland wasn't the only one present who thought so now that he had suggested it.

Chris was furious. "That *isn't* the only explanation. Maybe one of the memory wipes didn't work."

"The memory wipes worked," Seth said. "Had Étienne or Lisette handled the memories, then I would be concerned."

Krysta looked at Étienne, who shrugged. *I told you there were limits to my telepathic abilities. I am only a couple hundred years old.*

Uh-huh. Just a couple, she thought back to him. *A veritable infant.*

His lips twitched. But he kept his hand on her thigh and didn't relax.

"However, David and I handled it," Seth continued. "Any memories *we* bury never see the light of day again."

Jenna slowly raised a hand.

Seth smiled. "Yes, Jenna?"

"I'm confused. Do you *erase* the memories or bury them?"

"We bury them. Truly wiping them or erasing them can cause brain damage and scarring."

"Oh."

Roland leaned back. "And thus my point is proven."

"Well," Chris said, "we must have missed something on the technical side. A laptop or a DVD or an exterior hard drive one of the mercenaries took home."

David shook his head. "We searched their minds before we buried the pertinent memories. If someone so much as wrote themselves a note on a napkin and took it home with them, we found it and destroyed it."

Even though Étienne thought Chris wanted to interrogate her, Krysta actually found herself feeling sorry for him. The blond looked both furious and crushed at the idea that one of his own people may have strayed from the fold.

"Look into it," Seth told him. "It's the most logical hypothesis. Someone at the network must have taken information to another mercenary group and sold them the tranquilizer. Narrow down the possibilities."

Stone-faced, Chris nodded.

"Seconds," David said, "make sure your immortals have an ample supply of the antidote and don't let them leave the house without it."

The mortals around the table nodded.

Seth leaned back. "Immortals, start carrying your infrared goggles and scopes again and check periodically for heat signatures in shadows even your acute vision cannot penetrate. If you are struck with a dart, get the hell out of there and call your Second. The younger immortals among us should consider returning to hunting in pairs. For now, I leave the decision up to you. That will change if another mercenary attack ensues."

Bastien cleared his throat. "We should also step up our attempts to recruit vampires."

"What?" Krysta blurted, then flushed when everyone looked at her.

"The ones who have not yet entirely lost their sanity," he clarified. "We can't risk the mercenaries getting their hands on the virus by capturing a vampire, so we must convince the vampires we're the lesser of two evils and see if we can't bring them over to our side."

"Why don't you just kill them all?" she asked. No way in hell would she partner with a freaking vampire.

Marcus smiled. "I like this woman."

Roland nodded.

Bastien shook his head. "The point is to have them spread the word to the other vampires that they should do everything they can to stay out of the hands of the human mercenaries. We *can't* let the soldiers get their hands on the virus."

Seth nodded. "Do it. I know you don't like it, but vampires outnumber us and could be a valuable tool we could use to thwart our new enemies. Recruit those you can. Kill the rest. David, have you anything you wish to add?"

The other elder looked to Chris. "Only that I will make myself available anytime you wish me to examine the thoughts of network employees you think may be involved in this."

Chris gave an abrupt nod.

"All right" Seth said. "Meeting adjourned. Safe hunting, everyone."

Several mumbled a response.

Étienne's hand on Krysta's thigh relaxed.

"Étienne," David said as they rose, "would you, Krysta, Sean, and Cameron join Seth, Chris, and I in my study?"

Krysta cursed inwardly. They had been *that* close to getting away unscathed.

"Of course," Étienne responded.

Seth strode around the table, Chris on his heels, and joined David as he walked through the throng and crossed the living room.

Trying to ignore the stares she drew, Krysta peered through the black-clad bodies and glimpsed a wicker basket on the floor near one of the sofas.

Kittens?

The multicolored fur pile shifted, revealing a little triangle-shaped face.

Yes, kittens. In a house full of incredibly powerful men and women who instantly seemed less intimidating.

Well, everyone except Roland and the two elders.

She returned her gaze to Seth and David's broad backs.

Following them to the study, she felt a bit like a child being called to the principal's office. To distract herself she studied the elders' auras.

So bright and beautiful. Almost mesmerizing.

You're drooling, Étienne spoke in her mind.

Krysta detected a bit of rancor in his tone. *What?*

You can't take your eyes off them.

It isn't what you think. Their auras are different.

He rested a hand on her lower back. *Different from what?*

Different from yours. From mine. From vampires'. From humans'. I've never seen anything like it.

The two elders shared a look as they entered a darkened hallway.

Were they listening?

David and Seth paused before an open doorway and motioned for them to enter.

Étienne and Krysta proceeded inside, followed by Chris,

Cameron, and Sean, then the elders. As Seth started to close the door, Darnell slipped inside.

Smiling, Seth closed the door.

Nice study. Books lined floor-to-ceiling shelves on every wall, and the room had ten- or twelve-foot ceilings. The little home she and Sean rented had ceilings that ranged from eight feet to a mere six and a half. These men wouldn't even be able to stand upright in her kitchen, so she imagined they appreciated the extra headroom here.

Potted plants abounded, filling the room with color. A massive desk had been planted close enough to the large windows to allow anyone seated in the chair behind it to benefit from the natural light without sitting directly in it. Five chairs faced the desk. Two looked as though they had been there for years. Three more appeared to be new additions, probably added for this little get-together.

Some distance away, a smaller desk resided, something vaguely feminine in its appearance.

As they all congregated near the large desk, she waited anxiously to see what would happen. Would the interrogation Étienne feared begin now? Would they threaten her? Threaten Sean? Bury their memories of all of this?

Did they think her in league with the mercenaries? She had killed two of them. Didn't that count for anything and show where her loyalties lay?

Wait. Was she saying she was loyal to the immortals?

She thought about everything she had learned at the meeting and from her time with Étienne.

Hell. Why not? They seemed like good guys.

Seth and David smiled.

Seth held out his hand. "It's a pleasure to meet you, Krysta."

"Oh." She took it. And, wow, was it large. Her own hand looked like a child's in his. "Thank you. It's nice to meet you, too."

He covered their clasped hands with his other hand. Her

own heated with a tingling warmth that swept up her arm and rippled through her body.

She gasped. "What just happened?"

He patted her hand, then released her and shook Sean's hand. "I healed your injuries," he said as he stepped back.

She looked at Sean, whose eyes widened.

"Just like that?" Sean asked.

Seth nodded. "The older the immortal, the stronger his or her gifts."

Beside him, David smiled. "The two of us have lived so long and seen so much that very little surprises us."

"You two surprised us," Seth admitted. "We are very impressed with your successes and all that you have accomplished."

"Really?" She had been more impressed herself before she had found out that they hadn't even made a dent in the vampire population.

"Mortal vampire hunters, particularly those who hunt alone or in small numbers, have traditionally had very short careers. The fact that you have been doing what you do for six years now and still possess all of your limbs is nothing short of extraordinary."

"Please," David said, "have a seat."

Krysta and Sean took the two chairs in the middle. Étienne sat beside Krysta with Cam on his other side. Chris sat beside Sean. Darnell carried another chair from the corner over and placed it beside David, who took the chair behind the desk. Seth sat beside him.

Darnell stood beside David.

"As I said earlier," Seth began, "I am the leader of the Immortal Guardians. David is my Second in Command. We are the highest authorities in the Immortal Guardian world. We know you are both *gifted ones*. All immortals were *gifted ones* before being infected with the virus, so we hope you will consider us your brethren."

David nodded. "It is how we think of you. As one of us. As family."

That was not what she had expected. What were they saying exactly?

Seth smiled. "We would like you to join us."

Sean looked at Krysta. "Are you saying you want to infect us with the virus?"

"Not necessarily. Because you are *gifted ones*, you can safely transform without suffering brain damage and losing your sanity. But it is not a requirement. Many mortals, both humans and *gifted ones*, work with us and aid us in our desire to eliminate the vampire threat."

Krysta stared at them. "I'm sorry. I thought you were going to interrogate us or threaten us or castigate us for whatever wrong this one here"—she hooked a thumb in Chris's direction—"imagines we've committed."

Darnell laughed.

Chris sighed. "Had I met with you earlier today, I would have *interviewed* you."

Darnell coughed. "Interrogated."

Chris scowled. "But since Seth and David have cleared you and determined you aren't a threat, that won't be necessary and I would welcome you on our side."

Krysta slid a look in Étienne's direction. *You're being awfully quiet.*

He arched a brow. *This is* your *decision. I thought you wouldn't appreciate my weighing in on it.*

Do you think I should join you?

Hell, yes.

She returned her attention to the elders. "In what capacity?"

Seth looked to Reordon. "Chris?"

"Sean, since you're a healer and are already studying medicine—"

"Do I even want to know how you know that?" he asked.

Chris shrugged. "Once I had your name, I traced you to

Duke. And Seth told me you were a healer. Anyway, we could use someone with your gifts and knowledge in our medical department. Should you decide to join us, we will pay off all of the student loan debt you've accumulated." Which was considerable. "And pay all future tuition. I'm sure Dr. Lipton, the immortal woman who sat beside me at the table, would be happy to mentor you and appreciate your aid in her pursuit of a cure or treatment for the virus."

Krysta met her brother's gaze and knew he was thinking the same thing she was.

It sounded incredibly good. Too good. What's-the-catch good.

"We also," Chris continued, "would immediately put you on the payroll, so you could quit your current job as early as tomorrow. I recommend that you do that anyway to ensure the mercenaries can't trace you there as we did. Krysta, we'd like you to train as a Second. Your fighting skills already exceed the needs of the position, so we would—"

"Wait," she interrupted. "A Second? Do they hunt vampires?"

"Not actively, no. They guard and assist the immortals who *do* and back them up whenever necessary."

"I'm not giving up hunting."

Étienne swore. "You would be accomplishing the same goal without subjecting yourself to so much risk."

"I don't care. I'm not giving up hunting," she insisted stubbornly.

"Not even for a six-figure salary?" Chris asked.

Six figures? Really?

No. Despite the temptation, she couldn't do it.

Sean shook his head. "Krys, don't be stupid. This is perfect."

"Perfect!" she exclaimed. "You still thought these people were our enemies and in league with the vampires an hour ago!"

"Well, clearly they aren't," he snapped. "And you can't go on the way you have been. How many times have you nearly died in the past six years? In the past one or two? You've been coming up against larger and larger numbers and even admitted yourself that you would have been killed twice in the past month if Étienne hadn't saved your ass!"

"Those were exceptions," she protested, anger and panic rising. She couldn't stop hunting vampires and just sit on the sidelines. Hunting was what she did. It was who she was.

Sean snorted. "Those exceptions nearly killed you."

"I can't stop hunting," she insisted.

"You would still be contributing to the destruction of vampires," he insisted. "You'd still be making a difference."

"Not the way I want to."

He clamped his lips shut, his face tightening in anger. "And when you're mortally injured and I die healing you?" It had been her biggest fear all along. "It's an even greater possibility now than ever before because you're battling vampires *and* being hunted by mercenaries who are *shooting* at you," he pressed.

She swallowed hard. "If I suffer a fatal injury, you'll just have to let me go."

"You know I won't do that."

She did. And it killed her to think that he would die for her.

Her eyes began to burn as her throat thickened. She had promised herself she wouldn't stop hunting until the vampire threat had been eliminated. Not hunting would feel like giving up. She didn't want to give up. She wasn't *ready* to give up.

Étienne clear his throat. "She can hunt with me."

The silence that followed was deafening.

Chapter 11

While Étienne inwardly cursed himself in every language he knew, Krysta swung around to gape up at him in disbelief.

"What?" Chris, Cam, and Sean spoke at the same time.

He gritted his teeth. "I said, she can hunt with me."

It wasn't what he wanted. He wanted Krysta safe, damn it. But when her brother had slapped her in the face with reality, the barriers of her mind had crumbled. He had heard every panicked thought and hadn't been able to bear her unhappiness and dismay.

Seth and David glanced at each other, then examined Krysta and Étienne for several long moments, during which he suspected they were communicating telepathically.

If Seth and David nixed the idea . . .

Seth met Étienne's gaze. "She'll be a liability."

Krysta did *not* like hearing that. A dozen denials immediately flooded her mind, overriding the panicked despair.

But Étienne couldn't contradict it.

David drew Krysta's gaze. "Though they don't like it, immortals' orders are very clear. If they are tranqed, they are to immediately flee the battle in order to avoid being captured and call their Seconds before they lose consciousness. When the two of you were attacked by mercenaries, Étienne put himself in a position where he would likely be captured in order to keep them from killing you."

She lost some of her fight. "But I kept them from taking him."

Seth acknowledged her words with a slight nod. "Had he been hunting alone, however, he would not have lingered once he saw that first dart. He would have gotten away without further injury."

Quiet descended upon them, heavy and uncomfortable.

"Krysta," Chris said, "you have to understand that, if you and Sean join us, your actions will affect us all. If you had been shot despite Étienne's efforts to keep you safe, he would have been captured, tortured, and killed before we could even identify whoever the hell our new enemy is. The mercenaries would have then obtained both the virus and the DNA evidence they need to build their research and their army."

"The fault was not entirely Krysta's," Étienne mentioned. "I thought the mercenary threat over. Had I not been so caught off guard by their reappearance, I would have reacted faster and likely could have gotten us both out of there before they could hit me with a second dart."

Cam shook his head. "I could just as easily argue that you may have noticed the mercenaries' approach and not *been* so caught off guard if Krysta hadn't been distracting you."

"I won't make the same mistake twice," Étienne insisted.

Another long moment passed.

Krysta fidgeted.

Sean said nothing.

Étienne didn't have as much difficulty reading Sean as he did Krysta. The younger man was hoping the elders would forbid Krysta from hunting. Not because he feared he might die healing her, but because he feared she might be so badly injured one night that she would die before he could reach her.

He didn't want to lose his sister.

Don't make me regret this, Seth spoke in Étienne's head. "I will allow it for now," he decreed.

Much to Étienne's surprise, Krysta didn't smile with relief.

"Until we have eliminated the mercenary threat," he continued. "I would like the two of you to either stay here at David's home . . ."

"You are both welcome for as long as you wish," David said.

". . . or remain with Étienne at his," Seth continued. "You have both now become targets of the mercenaries and will fare better with an immortal's protection."

The rest of the meeting comprised logistics. The siblings opted to stay with Étienne, who couldn't be more pleased with the decision. Sean would have to refrain from attending classes until this was resolved, but would spend time at network headquarters working with Dr. Lipton and gaining a greater understanding of the virus in the meantime. Krysta would hunt with Étienne at night and train with him during the day.

Étienne was happier than he would've thought about that. Was he already so drawn to her that he would use *any* excuse to spend time with her? Even if it put her in danger?

Which it wouldn't. He would keep her safe and ensure no harm befell her.

The ride home was quiet.

When Cam and Sean headed into the house, Étienne held Krysta back.

Guards still walked the perimeter, he noted, but those near the house had been dismissed.

She crossed her arms under her breasts and avoided his gaze.

Once the door closed behind the others, Étienne tilted her chin up. "What troubles you?"

For a moment, he thought she wouldn't respond.

"Am I really a liability?" she asked, voice low.

He didn't know how to answer that, whether he should be

honest or sugarcoat it. Since he would've preferred to hear the truth if *he* were in her position, he opted for that. "Yes."

"Then why did you agree to hunt with me?"

"Because I know how much hunting means to you. And, though the thought of you continuing to hunt terrifies me, I want you to be happy."

At last, she met his gaze. "Why?"

"Because I care about you."

"You barely know me."

"I've been following you and learning everything I can about you since the night we met. I've listened to your conversations with your brother. I've caught occasional glimpses of your thoughts. I've fought beside you, both when you were awake and while you dreamed."

"That was you in my dream?"

He nodded and tucked her hair behind one ear to expose her troubled features to the moonlight. "I know you," he said simply.

She chewed her lower lip. "I don't want to endanger you, Étienne."

"You won't."

"I already have. I don't want you to sacrifice yourself for me again."

"At the risk of angering you, in this instance I don't care what you want. If hunting endangers your life, I will do whatever it takes to protect you." He rested a hand on her lower back and urged her toward the door.

He loved touching her. Even casually. And he loved that she let him.

"Now," he said while she pondered his words, "you've already donned hunting clothes. *And* filched some of the weapons my sister left in her room. Before we embark on the night's hunt, you may have your pick of the weapons in my armory."

"We're hunting tonight?"

"If you're up to it."

At last he won a faint smile from her. "I don't know. What if you don't have all of the weapons I need?"

He grinned. "I'm sure we can find something."

A minute later his smile broadened as Krysta surveyed, with wide eyes and gaping mouth, the vast array of weaponry in his armory.

"Ho-ly crap!" she breathed.

Étienne laughed. "Think you can make do?"

"Uh . . . yeah. But it may take me several hours to choose."

It *was* quite a selection. He usually kept on hand enough swords of varying lengths and styles, daggers, throwing stars, and more to outfit himself, his brother, his sister, *and* their three Seconds on any given night. With some left over for immortal visitors.

She strolled around the room, studying the blades displayed on the walls. "Could I just say holy crap again?"

Again he laughed. "This is only the portion of my collection that I keep in *this* home."

She looked at him curiously. "You have others?"

He nodded. "In various countries. Many immortals own multiple homes. When we've been stationed in one place for long periods of time, it's sometimes hard to move on and abandon what we've built there."

She stopped before a pair of red-handled shoto swords. "May I?"

He smiled. "Be my guest."

She drew one down and slid it from its gleaming sheath. "It's beautiful."

"My sister's weapon of choice. Though, since the vampire population in this area has swelled, she has also begun to carry a couple of Glocks." He closed the distance between them. "Here." He reached for the sword. "Let me serve as your Second tonight."

While she stood patiently before him, her eyes never leaving his face, he armed her with all of the weapons he knew she preferred to carry. Shoto swords in sheaths she could conceal beneath a coat. Daggers, in case she was disarmed.

His heartbeat picked up as he knelt and fastened sheaths to her slender thighs. Rising, he moved even closer to her (just because) and unfastened the belt that rode low on her hips and fell beneath her belly button.

Her pulse picked up, mirroring his own.

Slowly, he drew the belt from the first couple of loops on her cargo pants. Once the end was free, he slipped a gun holster onto it, then began threading the belt back through the loops. As he refastened it, he drew in a deep breath and savored her scent.

"I'm not really a gun kind of girl," she whispered, leaning forward to nuzzle his throat.

His body hardened.

"Tonight you will be," he murmured gruffly, fingers fumbling with the narrow buckle. "I want you to carry a tranquilizer pistol."

She leaned back. "You want me to *tranq* the vampires?"

"Those I deem salvageable. I don't suppose I could talk you into carrying a Glock as well, could I? In case we come up against more mercenaries?"

She frowned. "I'm afraid the extra holsters and weight of the ammo will restrict my movements."

"I'll carry it for you and toss it to you should the need arise," he offered.

"Okay."

He gave the belt one last tug, then hesitantly withdrew his hands. "You do know how to use it, don't you?"

She snorted. "Of course."

Even her confidence turned him on. "I do so love strong women."

"Your eyes are glowing," she commented softly.

"I want you."

"You do?"

He nodded. Dipping his head, Étienne captured her lips with his own, pouring all of the passion he felt for her into the contact. As it had before, the brush of her lips struck him like lightning, firing his desire like no other ever had. He wrapped his arms around her and drew her up against him.

Breath catching, she rose onto her toes and slid her arms around his neck, pressing her breasts to his chest, her hips to his arousal.

He swore silently when she tore her lips from his.

"I want you, too," she admitted.

He groaned and kissed her again, teasing her lips apart and sliding his tongue within to stroke and dance with hers.

"Whoa!" Cam blurted.

Étienne had been so distracted, he hadn't even heard his Second approach.

"Ah, hell," Sean said. "I knew it! I *knew* she was falling for him!"

Krysta dropped onto her heels, her lips abruptly leaving his.

He tightened his hold momentarily before letting her go with a sigh.

Cam stared at him as Krysta took a couple of steps back and sheepishly met her brother's unsettled gaze.

"What?" Étienne demanded irritably.

"Nothing," Cam responded. "Just . . . I didn't think you had it in you."

Krysta frowned. "We were just kissing. It's not like you walked in on us having sex."

Étienne fought back another groan. *Don't put that image in my head. I'll be hard all night.*

She tossed him a startled look, then grinned. *Nice.*

He shook his head. *Not when we're fighting vampires, it isn't.*

She laughed.

"Hey, don't knock it," Cam told Krysta, pointing at Étienne.

"Kissing is big for this guy. He hasn't been on a single date since I started serving as his Second."

"Really? How long have you been his Second?"

"About as long as you've been hunting vampires."

She winked at Étienne. "Cool."

Damned if that didn't make him want her even more.

Shaking his head, he motioned for the door. "Let's get out of here before I do something that will embarrass you in front of your brother."

Sean held up a hand, alarm crossing his features. "Wait. You're just going hunting, right?"

Krysta rolled her eyes. "No, we're going to park in Lovers' Lane and spend the next several hours making out. Of *course*, we're going hunting." She headed past the duo and out into the hallway.

Cam raised his eyebrows as Étienne approached. "You have everything you need?"

"Yes."

"We'll be here if you need us."

Étienne followed Krysta down the hallway and out the front door. "Relax," he heard Cam say inside. "Étienne is a good guy. You can trust him."

Cam was a good guy, too. Steady. Somber. Reliable. (Unlike Sheldon, who was still learning and could be a handful.)

Étienne's last Second had been killed in a car accident. Étienne hadn't been able to believe it at the time. The man had survived twenty-five years of backing up an immortal who hunted vampires for a living, then had died because some dumbass had been too busy texting to stop for a red light.

"So," Krysta said, skipping down the front steps, "how are we going to do this? Do *you* pick the campus we investigate or do I and how will we get there?"

"I thought I would pick the place—I'm thinking Duke again—and drive us there."

"Duke sounds great and, for some reason, you driving a car seems weird."

He laughed and led the way to the Tesla Model S Cam had backed out of the garage for him while he and Krysta were in the armory. "Why? Because I can run as fast as one?"

"Yes. And that is totally cool."

It really was.

"Speaking of cool," she said, admiring the shiny black sedan, "this is *nice*. Very sleek."

"Thank you. It's electric."

Her eyebrows flew up. "Are you serious? I thought all electric cars looked like a toddler's shoe. This . . . looks like money."

He opened the passenger door for her. "I like it, too. There are zero emissions, so my sensitive nose gets a break from exhaust fumes, and I can go up to three hundred miles on a charge."

"Daaaaaamn. I—and my bank account—really need one of these. The price of gas has been kicking my ass."

He smiled down at her as she sank into the comfortable seat and fastened her seat belt. "You'll get one if you come to work for us. Every job working for the Immortal Guardians comes with a low or no emission, fuel efficient car of your choice."

"No way!"

He nodded. "Sean will get one, too."

"Wait. We'll each have our own car?"

"Absolutely." He closed the door, zipped around to the driver's side, and sank into the seat Cam had pushed all the way back from the steering wheel.

The engine started as he buckled his seat belt.

Krysta's eyes widened, then fastened on the touch screen.

Hell, if a cool car would entice her to join them, he'd see that she got two of them. He really didn't want her to continue hunting. She was mortal. Vulnerable. Fragile. It was only a matter of time before tragedy struck.

And he didn't want to think about that.

* * *

Krysta strolled through Duke's campus, Étienne at her side. Her mind raced with everything she had learned earlier. Her heart raced at his nearness.

Oddly, it almost felt as if they were out on a date.

Maybe he was just naturally gallant, opening the car door for her, often guiding her with a hand on her lower back. Even his speech sometimes seemed old worldish.

He *was* from another era.

"This is so weird," she said.

"What is?" he asked, his sharp eyes searching every shadow.

He had said he loved strong women. Well, apparently she *adored* strong men, because in his warrior mode he was breath-stealingly, heart-racingly appealing.

Tearing her gaze away from her gorgeous companion, Krysta kept an eye out for glowing orange auras. "Me walking and talking with a man born in the nineteenth century."

"Actually, I was born in the eighteenth century. Seventeen eighty three, to be exact."

Unreal. She was lusting after a man born over two hundred years before *she* had been born. "So, you lived through the French Revolution?"

He nodded. "The Reign of Terror."

Honestly she had forgotten almost everything she had learned about the French Revolution and knew only the dates (roundabout) and that thousands had died under the guillotine. She wanted to ask if *he* had lost anyone to Madame Guillotine, but thought it too morbid. "That must have been . . ."

"Bad," he said, his face clouding.

She shouldn't have said anything.

Then she realized . . . "You lived during Napoleon's reign?"

He nodded. Glancing at her from the corner of his eye, he smiled faintly. "Your mouth is hanging open again."

"I'll bet it is." This was so crazy. "Was Napoleon really short like everyone says?"

"*Oui.*"

"How many languages do you speak?"

"Not many. I'm fluent in half a dozen or so and know a phrase here or there in half a dozen more."

"That many?"

"Older immortals know far more. Seth knows them all. David, too, most likely."

"All?"

"Even those that have long since been forgotten."

Krysta wished *she* were fluent in more than one language. She had learned Spanish in high school, but had forgotten most of it. And her college career had been cut short by a vampire attack and her resulting obsession with hunting vamps.

"Say something else in French," she requested.

A series of lilting indecipherable words flowed smoothly from his tongue.

"What did you say?" she asked curiously.

"Something I can't repeat without you either blushing furiously or striking me."

"Was it naughty?" she asked with a smile.

His smile turned wicked. "Very naughty."

Now she *really* wanted to know what he had said.

"Does it trouble you?" he asked hesitantly.

"What? You talking dirty to me in French?"

He chuckled and shook his head. "No, that I've lived so long."

"No." And she wasn't sure why. "Maybe because you don't look your age."

He grimaced. "I should hope not."

Quiet fell.

A breeze ruffled their hair. His, she knew from burying her fingers in it, was thick and as soft as silk.

"This isn't working," he pronounced.

Crap. She shouldn't have brought up his age. "Why? Is it because you think I'm too young for you?"

"What?" He stopped walking and faced her. "No. I was talking about our . . . outing." *Hunt,* he added in her head, in case someone out of sight was listening.

"Oh. Right."

"You aren't too young for me."

"Of course I'm not."

He frowned. "Do *you* think you're too young for me?"

"No."

"We're both adults."

"Yes, we are."

"There will be cultural differences, of course."

"Could make things more interesting."

He looked around, eyes sharp. Returning his attention to her, he tilted his head to one side. Moonlight filtered down through the trees and highlighted his handsome face. "What do you say we do this your way?"

Krysta wasn't sure how to answer that. Were they talking about pursuing their attraction to each other or hunting? Or both? "What exactly are we talking about?" she asked, just to be sure.

His lips twitched. "I was talking about our outing. Why? What were *you* talking about?"

Smiling, she hit him in the shoulder. "Stop teasing me."

He grinned. "Absolutely not. I'm enjoying it too much." Again, he surveyed the campus around them. "As much as I love your delightful company, I think I should leave now. I've work to do and the night is passing quickly."

"Really?"

He nodded and smiled again. "Go do your thing."

Was he actually giving her the go-ahead to act as bait? She had assumed he intended to do all the hunting himself and was pretty much just letting her tag along.

"Okay." Though she regretted having to give up his company.

I'll monitor you from the rooftops, he added telepathically. *Anytime you wish to speak to me, just direct your thoughts toward me as though I were standing before you and you were speaking them aloud and I should hear them.*

Okay. Did you hear that?

He smiled. *Yes.*

Can you hear everything else I'm thinking?

He was silent a moment. *No. Your barriers are still in place, so I can only hear what you wish me to hear.*

Good.

He pursed his lips. *Any naughty thoughts about me floating around up there?*

Many many *naughty thoughts.*

He stepped closer to her. *In case anyone is looking . . .* Resting his hands on her waist, he drew her up against him and proceeded to kiss the stuffing out of her.

Fire licked through Krysta's veins as she locked her arms around his neck. Her heart pounded a rapid beat as he slid his hands up her rib cage, his thumbs nearing her tingling breasts.

He murmured something in French in her mind.

Say it in English, she reminded him.

How you tempt me.

Good, because he tempted the hell out of her.

When he dragged his lips away, she was happy to discover his breathing was as ragged as hers.

"Good night," he said, voice low and hoarse.

"Good night."

Taking her hand, he raised it to his lips.

Krysta didn't have to fake a stumble as she turned to walk away from him. Her knees were weak. All this time she had thought that was just corny crap found in chick flicks. She hadn't realized passion really *could* weaken your knees.

She shook her head at herself. She was twenty-seven years old and no virgin. She should already know that, shouldn't she?

As she walked up the sidewalk, exploring the quadrangles that hosted her favorite frat houses, she caught periodic glimpses of Étienne's pretty white and purple aura leaping from roof to roof.

She wished *she* could do that. That would be so much fun. *Testing. Testing. Can you hear me?* she asked.

He laughed. *Yes.*

When you said we'd be hunting together, I didn't think you meant as we have been.

I may not like it, but you do make good bait.

She was getting used to hearing his warm, deep voice in her head. *Can I drunk dial you?* Her fictional drunken phone calls worked well to distract any vamps tailing her.

Anytime we aren't hunting.

She smiled. *I'm not a big drinker.*

Nor am I. Alcohol has no effect on us, so there isn't much point.

Oh. Well, I was just going to fake it anyway.

As you have before. I admit I found your rants both credible and entertaining.

That gave her a warm feeling.

But, he went on, *if you were to call me, the vampires would hear your conversation both down there* and *through my phone up here, alerting them to my presence.*

Oh. Your ears really are *sensitive, aren't they?*

Yes, as are vampires'.

Bummer. I was going to talk dirty to you.

Damn. I hate to miss that.

Maybe later. I could talk dirty to you mentally, she suggested boldly.

Very tempting, but it looks like you have some nibblers.

Vampires are taking the bait? she asked, staggering a bit to one side. *Already?*

Definitely. Two approach from your five and three more from your eight.

Ooh. I like this. No more guessing how many I'll face or trying to sneak a peek at them.

How did you live through six years of this?

I'm good at what I do.

Just don't get cocky.

I won't. Any sign of mercenaries?

Silence. *No. Nothing with my eyes. Nothing with the infrared. What about you? Any human auras lurking in odd places?*

She paused at a crosswalk and looked around as though trying to remember where she wanted to go. The vampires scattered like cockroaches, their auras leading the way.

No. No humans.

Good.

Half singing under her breath, she led the vamps away from the frat houses, past eating establishments that would have been packed with students only a couple of hours earlier, and toward the science buildings that would give them a little more privacy and be less likely to draw the attention of anyone out and about this late.

Adrenaline surged through her veins as she ducked into a darkened area she suspected was used for deliveries and paused. It was the closest thing to an alley nearby and would have to do. Reaching beneath her coat, she drew her borrowed shoto swords and spun around. "Hi, guys."

Those vamps who had already bent forward in a menacing crouch, intending to taunt and frighten her, frowned. Straightening, they looked at each other, then her.

She grinned. "I believe this is where I'm supposed to say: It's on."

Étienne appeared behind the vamps at the mouth of the pseudo-alley, swords drawn. "Actually," he countered. "it's not on. Did you forget we need to talk to them first?"

The vamps spun to face Étienne, drawing weapons they had thought they wouldn't need to slaughter a drunk sorority girl.

Krysta swore. "Yes, I did. I see now why that grumpy older guy didn't want to do this. It kinda ruins the flow of it all."

"What the hell?" one vamp asked, looking back and forth between them.

"An Immortal Guardian," one sneered, his eyes flashing a bright blue as they slid to Krysta. "And his mortal Second."

The others' eyes flared to life in a variety of colors. Some actually hissed liked movie vampires did.

Étienne raced right through their midst and planted himself in front of Krysta.

Damn it! She shifted to the side, far enough away not to hamper his swing.

"Kill them!" the first vampire snarled.

Étienne raised one of his swords and pointed it at them almost like a teacher singling out a student for behaving badly. "Gentlemen, I suggest you slow your roll." Over his shoulder, he murmured, "That's a saying, isn't it?"

It was kind of hard to be miffed at him when he made her want to laugh. "Yes." Was he trying to use modern slang to make himself seem younger to her after their little conversation?

He focused once more on the vampires. "We have some information that might interest you."

They responded with a lot of posturing and spewing of epithets.

"Human mercenaries are hunting you," Étienne went on

doggedly. "They want to capture you, torture you to learn about the virus and your abilities, then kill you."

"What kind of bullshit is that?" one blurted.

"It's bullshit is what it is," another answered.

So clever, that one.

"Yeah, since when do immortals want to help vampires?"

Étienne sighed. "Since any information the mercenaries gain from torturing *you* can be used against *us*. These humans are enemies of both of us. If we work together . . ."

Weapons still at the ready, Krysta glanced at him when he trailed off.

The vampires shifted and exchanged confused looks. At least those who weren't twitching with the need to attack.

"You know what?" Étienne said finally. "This is pointless. Every vampire here is so insane they're making my head hurt." He swung his swords with a flourish and met her gaze. "Now it's on."

He blurred, shooting forward with incredible speed. Blood sprayed as carotid arteries sprang leaks in the wake of his blades. Two vampires swung their weapons wildly, then sank to their knees, hands grasping their throats and trying futilely to staunch the flow of their life's blood. A third engaged Étienne, the battling duo blurring and zipping around like the Tazmanian Devil.

The two remaining vamps faced Krysta with evil smiles. Their orange auras streaked toward her a second before their forms leapt forward. She swung her blades, scoring hits that sparked snarls of fury. And retaliation.

She began a slow trek backward as she swung where their auras directed her. Her thigh stung as one of their blades cut through her clothing and hit flesh. Then her side. Her hip. Her swings and thrusts neither ceased nor slowed.

Something large flew over her head and hit the brick wall to her right hard enough to shower them with dust. The vampire Étienne fought?

One of her opponents slowed and stumbled, dropping the bowie he had swung wildly. Blood poured from his wrist and neck.

About freaking time! It usually didn't take her that long to find the arteries. She was off her game tonight.

The other vampire jerked backward, then hit the wall beside the other one.

Étienne was on him so fast she couldn't see exactly what he did. But when he stilled and stepped back, the blades of his swords dripped crimson liquid and the vamp began to shrivel up.

Breathing hard, Krysta lowered her weapons.

Étienne turned to her, eyes glowing a vibrant amber. Ruby droplets speckled his face and glistened on his clothing. "Are you all right?"

She nodded and smiled. "We rock!"

Some of the tension left his shoulders. Shaking his head, he wiped his blades on his coat and sheathed them. "Where are you hurt?"

"What makes you think I'm hurt?" She didn't want to admit it. If he knew she was injured every time she hunted, he might refuse to hunt with her again in an attempt to protect her and . . .

Well, she didn't know what would happen next. She'd like to think she would just go back to hunting on her own, but doubted Étienne or the elder immortals would let her.

That galled a little.

Or a lot.

"I can smell your blood," he said, closing the distance between them. "And you're favoring one side."

Thwarted again by his acute senses and attention to detail.

Since she couldn't refute it, she settled for making non-sensical grumbly noises as she wiped her own blades clean and sheathed them.

"Krysta."

"It's just a few cuts."

"Where?"

"My left thigh, my left side, and my right hip."

His jaw clenched. Leaning down, he swept her into his arms. Though he was careful not to touch any of her wounds, it still hurt.

"I can walk," she insisted between teeth gritted against the pain.

"You wouldn't be able to keep up."

The world around her blurred. A strong breeze whipped through her hair, tugging it across her face.

When everything came back into focus and her hair fell away, she discovered they stood on top of a building down the street.

"Wow. You weren't kidding when you said I couldn't keep up. What—?"

"I didn't want to take any chances. The mercenaries always seem to show themselves after the fight is over, as though they want to make sure they nab the immortal victor instead of the vampires."

Alarm rose. "Did you see any closing in?"

"No. Will you watch the battle scene for me while I inspect your wounds?" He gingerly lowered her to her feet. "Are you okay to stand?"

"Yes and yes. I really don't think the cuts are too deep. They just hurt. And stop looking like that."

"Like what?"

"Like I've suffered a mortal injury or something and you want to go back and kill the vampires again."

"Here." He handed her his infrared scope. "I *would* go back and kill the vampires again if I could. I don't like you getting hurt. I don't like you being in pain."

She raised the scope to her right eye and squeezed her left eye closed. The world appeared before her, normal black combined with weird shades of blue and purple and occasional splashes of yellow, orange, and red.

Étienne peeled her coat back and bent to check the wound at her waist. "What do you see? Any humans?"

"I see a guy driving past in a truck. A couple back near the frat—Jeeze! I think they're having sex! Euw! In the bushes? Who *does* that?"

Was that a laugh?

She opened her left eye and checked.

Yes, she had wrung a smile from him. Good.

She grunted when he prodded the cut. "That hurts, you know."

"It needs stitches."

"No, it doesn't. Just get me home. Sean will take care of it."

"Keep looking," he instructed and turned his attention to her thigh. "Good. They missed the artery."

She squinted through the scope again. "Yeah. What is it with vampires and hamstrings?"

"They're like lions trying to bring down a gazelle. They think to hobble you, then move in for the kill."

"Bastards."

"Yes."

She turned in a complete circle, eliciting more French swear words from Étienne, who was still trying to examine her wounds. "I'm not seeing anything. I don't think they came tonight."

He waited for her to settle, then checked out her hip. "This one needs stitches, too."

"Quit complaining."

He straightened and took the scope from her. "I'm not complaining. I'm expressing concern."

"Well, you're harshing my mellow. We defeated five vampires tonight. That's something to celebrate."

He raised the scope to his right eye and turned in a circle. "I think if they were here they would have come out of hiding by now."

"They certainly didn't dawdle the last time we encountered them."

"Wait here a moment. If you see anything, think a warning and I'll hear it."

"Where are you—?"

He vanished. Or moved so swiftly he seemed to. But his aura helped her trace his movements as he returned to the area in which they had fought.

Krysta raised the scope to her eye and looked around. No mercenaries.

Ooh. His aura looked really freaky through the scope as it streaked back toward her.

"Okay," he said, stopping before her. "Let's call it a night."

"What did you do?"

"Confiscated the vampires' weapons and tossed their clothing into the Dumpster."

"Oh."

"Let's head for the car."

She halted him when he bent to lift her into his arms. "I can walk, Étienne. Really. The wounds aren't that bad."

Brushing her hands aside, he lifted her into his arms anyway. "This is faster. *And*, if it will soothe your ego, you can tell yourself that I'm not doing this because I think your injuries have weakened you. I'm doing it because I was looking for an excuse to hold you."

"I can do that," she said, looping her arms around his neck. "Which one is it?"

"I'll let you decide."

"So, we're really going to do this?" she asked.

"Do what?"

"Hunt together?"

"That's the plan. At least for the time being."

Good. They made a great team. And the more time she spent with Étienne, the more time she *wanted* to spend with him.

Krysta combed her fingers through his thick locks. "Your hair is so soft."

He smiled as the world blurred.

Chapter 12

David reclined in his comfy chair, his feet propped on the edge of his desk, as he devoured the latest Stephen King novel.

Seth lounged in a chair on the other side of the desk, his large boots also gracing the scarred wooden surface as he studied his cell phone.

Outside, the sun was high in the sky, its rays filtering in and brightening the room naturally.

The house was quiet, save the occasional snore. Marcus and Ami were fast asleep. Bastien and Melanie were, too, having opted yet again to spend the day at David's so Melanie could be near Ami.

Roland and Sarah had surprised them all by choosing to spend the day there as well. Seth thought Roland was beginning to pick up on Marcus's tension. Roland may be antisocial, but he was fiercely loyal. And Marcus had been a good friend to him over the centuries.

Even Darnell slumbered.

Seth and David should be getting some rest as well. So many needed their help on a nightly basis that both often went days without sleep. But, when one's sense of hearing was as acute as theirs, quiet was hard to come by and could often only be found during times like this.

"I think our secret is out," Seth murmured.

David grunted and kept reading. A moment later he turned the page. "Which one?"

"I keep getting messages from immortals wanting to know why there are so many *gifted ones* in this area."

"Tell them it's something in the water."

"I did. They didn't buy it."

"Coincidence?"

"They didn't buy that either."

"Too smart for their own good."

"It doesn't take a lot of smarts. Word gets around. First Roland found a *gifted one*, then Bastien and Richart. They all think Marcus has found one, too."

David nodded, his eyes still on his coveted book. "This love thing is becoming an epidemic."

"And everyone wants to be infected."

"Can you blame them?"

Seth sighed. "No. Happily ever after, when you live as long as we do, sounds . . ."

"Phenomenal."

"Yes." He motioned to his phone. "You see? Another immortal requesting a transfer to North Carolina. They know something is up."

"How long do you think it will take them to connect the unusually high *gifted one* population to the presence of a network headquarters?"

"I don't know, but once they figure out we guide *gifted ones* to *all* areas that boast a network headquarters—"

"There will be hell to pay."

Seth nodded. "They'll think I'm playing matchmaker."

"*And* playing favorites."

"That's ridiculous."

"Exactly. Everyone knows I'm your favorite and yet I remain distressingly unattached."

Seth grinned. "Angling for me to set you up on a blind date?"

"Hell, no."

Laughing, Seth shook his head. "I don't blame you. My record as a matchmaker sucks."

"Bethany had a long, happy life."

"And Marcus was miserable for centuries."

"Marcus wouldn't have found Ami if you hadn't inadvertently denied him Bethany."

"You're giving me a headache."

David smiled.

Seth swore. "I have to go. Friedrich needs me."

David looked up from his book. "Be safe."

"As always."

Seth vanished.

Sean watched Krysta and Étienne arm themselves. Last night had been both informative and nerve wracking. He felt reasonably sure now that the immortals were on their side and truly *were* different from vampires. He was a little *less* sure that Étienne wasn't messing with Krysta's head.

The man was telepathic and clearly attracted to her. How easy would it be for him to manipulate her thoughts and plant an interest in himself?

Because she was clearly interested. Sean hadn't seen Krysta this captivated by a man since before she had taken up vampire hunting.

Even when she had returned home from their hunt wounded last night, she had been unable to drag her gaze away from the Frenchman.

She laughed at something Étienne said.

She seemed to laugh a lot around him, too. Though it worried him, Sean had to admit it was good to see her in such high spirits.

Absently he rubbed his hip, where it still ached from healing her.

Cam had patiently answered all of Sean's questions while they had waited for the hunting duo to return. He had encouraged Sean to get some rest, but Sean had been unwilling to turn in until he had seen for himself that Krysta was okay.

He had healed her wounds without complaint, grateful as usual that they weren't fatal. Her eyes had sparkled with excitement as she had recounted their battle with five vampires.

She laughed again.

She really was taken with Étienne. Sean could understand her being grateful to the man for saving her life, but . . . was she really considering pursuing something romantic with him?

Hell. He supposed he couldn't blame her. The life they had led for the past six—seven—years had been a lonely one. Krysta hadn't been willing to give up or even cut back on her vampire hunting in order to date. And he hadn't been able to date while he was watching her back and racing to her rescue every night. Even when he had lucked out and found a woman who hadn't minded the weird-ass hours or the emergency calls that had interrupted their dates, he had had difficulty concocting plausible explanations for the wounds that had opened on his body when he had healed Krysta's. So he had dated as little as Krysta.

He just wished Krysta would have fallen for Cam or one of the other Seconds instead of an immortal. That was a little hard to stomach.

Cam caught his eye. "You about ready?"

He nodded.

Krysta raised her eyebrows. "Ready for what?"

Sean straightened away from the doorjamb he had been propping up and entered. "Cam is taking me to network headquarters. I'm going to be working with Dr. Lipton tonight."

"She's the pretty brunet from the meeting, isn't she? The one married to Bastien?"

Étienne nodded. "She's as fierce a fighter as you are, but doesn't hunt. She's been too valuable in the lab, searching for a cure for the virus. She's the one who developed the antidote to the tranquilizer the mercenaries use against us." He met Sean's gaze as he slid one last dagger into the sheaths sewn into the lining of his coat. "She'll be able to answer all of your questions regarding the virus, immortals, and vampires. *Gifted ones*, too."

Sean nodded. He had a lot of questions.

"I have a few questions myself," Krysta said.

"I'll answer them while we hunt," Étienne promised.

He had been surprisingly amiable toward Sean, considering Sean had woken him yesterday by pressing a blade to his throat.

"She's your sister. You'd die to protect her. I understand that," Étienne had said.

Sean had doubted that until he had encountered Étienne's sister Lisette. According to Cam, Lisette's husband had been turned, but had hidden it from her until the insanity had kicked in. Then he had attacked her and transformed her against her will. Étienne and Richart had slain her husband and offered her their blood in an attempt to hide her condition from everyone else, not knowing that frequent exposure to the virus through bites would infect them as well. So for two hundred years, Lisette had been burdened with the knowledge that she had accidentally transformed her brothers.

And Étienne had never once held it against her, insisting he would have done nothing different had they known beforehand what it would cost him. Richart, too.

So Sean supposed they did have *that* in common. He

would give his life to save Krysta. Étienne would give his life to save Lisette . . . *and* Krysta, which made it damned hard for Sean to continue resisting her involvement with the immortal.

"All right," Cam said, drawing a set of keys from his back pocket and heading for the door. "We're out. Call me if you need me."

Étienne nodded.

Krysta waved with a smile.

The trip to the network took about forty-five minutes. Étienne lived way out in the boonies, distanced from towns and neighbors alike.

Sean studied the exterior of the building as Cam pulled into the parking lot occupied by more vehicles than Sean would've expected to see at this hour.

It was a little anticlimactic. Krysta had mentioned several times the power Chris Reordon, the leader of the East Coast division of the network, wielded. Sean would've thought the place would look a little more . . . remarkable.

Cam laughed as he shut off the engine and opened his door. "I know. Bland as hell, right?"

"Yeah." Sean exited the car.

"That was deliberate. Chris wanted something that wouldn't interest anyone who happened upon it because they took a wrong turn."

Then he had succeeded. Surrounded by thick evergreens on all sides, it had been built far from strip malls, business districts, and residential neighborhoods. The one-story concrete structure looked aged and worn and reminded him of a storage facility for a package delivery service.

"Is this the front or the back?" he asked as he followed Cam to a plain wooden door.

"Back. There really isn't much of a difference, though."

The plain wooden door wasn't so plain, Cam soon discovered. The inside was lined with steel and was as thick and heavy as the door of a bank vault. As Cam closed the door behind them, Sean found himself in a glass vestibule with a locked door and a view of a lobby.

Sean gave the glass an experimental rap with his knuckles. "I'm going to go out on a limb and guess this is bulletproof glass."

"The glass in the previous network headquarters building was bulletproof. *This* stuff will stop a fucking missile."

The lobby was a modern collection of grays that comprised a U-shaped arrangement of comfortable-looking chairs. Large Peace Lilies on side tables injected what otherwise would have been a somewhat cold room with warmth and color.

Half a dozen guards manned a granite-topped security desk opposite the locked door. A good twenty more stood sentry beside elevators behind the desk. Rather than wearing traditional security guard uniforms, they all bore the standard black hunting garb of a Second.

And they were very heavily armed.

Cam waited while one of the guards at the desk rose and approached the door. He then held up an ID card.

"Hey, Cam," the guard said, withdrawing some kind of laser scanner from a pocket on his belt.

"John. How's the evening been?"

"Nice and quiet." He scanned the card through the glass, then tucked away the scanner. "Clear," he said over his shoulder.

A buzz sounded.

Cam grabbed the door handle and opened the door.

"Who's your friend? Chris said you'd be bringing a visitor, but didn't go into detail."

"This is Sean Linz. Sean, John Wendleck."

They shook hands.

Sean followed Cam and John toward the elevators.

"Sean and his sister Krysta are vampire hunters," Cam mentioned.

John tilted his head to one side. "Don't we all pretty much qualify as vampire hunters?"

"Yes, but they've been doing it on their own with no knowledge of our existence for the past six years. And by doing it on their own, I mean actively seeking out vampires, luring them into traps, and killing them."

John's eyebrows flew up. "You've been hunting vampires on your own? Damn. That's ballsy."

Several of the other guards nodded their agreement as the trio circled the desk.

A pair of elevator doors opened.

John reclaimed his seat behind the desk.

Sean stepped inside the elevator with Cam and looked around. "This is a one-story building. What's the point of the elevator?"

Cam leaned forward and pressed a button marked S5. "There are five floors underground. We're going down to the fifth, the sublevel with the tightest security."

The doors slid closed.

"Why the tightest?"

"Vampires live there."

Sean stared at him. "Come again?"

"Dr. Lipton's office is on S5. Her lab is, too. She does all of her work down there and part of that includes working with two vampires who surrendered to the immortals."

"If they're vampires, why didn't the immortals just kill them?" Sean demanded. What the hell? Vampires were the enemy. They were monsters.

"First, you might want to watch what you say because the vampires can hear you," Cam cautioned. "Second, the madness hasn't taken them yet. They're good guys in a messed up situation and have asked for our help. Dr. Lipton is trying to do that. She's trying to find a cure or at least to find a way to prevent or slow the brain damage they suffer as the virus progresses."

"Are you saying vampires run around freely down here?"

"No, of course not."

A bell dinged. The doors slid open.

Sean's heart stopped.

Two vampires—one African American and one White—stood there, eyes glowing, fangs gleaming as their lips drew back into snarls.

"We do now," the African-American vamp growled.

Fear shot through Sean. He hadn't been allowed to bring any damned weapons!

The vampire threw back his head. "Bwah-ha-ha-ha-ha!"

The White vampire howled.

A tall, menacing figure garbed all in black suddenly appeared behind the vamps and popped them both on the back of the head.

"Ow!" they cried, grabbing their heads.

"Cut the crap," the immortal ordered.

Sean recognized him from the meeting, but couldn't remember his name.

"Aw, come on, Bastien," the African-American vampire complained. "We were just razzing the new guy."

"You're lucky the new guy isn't carrying. Get back to the lab."

The White vampire grumbled something and dashed away. The other vampire grinned at Sean and shrugged. "Things were getting boring around here. No hard feelings?"

Before Sean could answer, he, too, darted away.

Sean stepped off the elevator with Cam. Just outside, a dozen men stood at the ready, faces tense, fingers on the triggers of their automatic weapons.

"Relax," Bastien told Sean. "Those two are harmless."

Sean tilted his head in the direction of the guards. "If the vampires are harmless, why are these guys so tense?"

He smirked. "They aren't worried about the vampires. They're worried about me." He blurred, zipping down the hallway after the vamps.

Cam cleared his throat. "Would you like to meet Dr. Lipton now?"

"Um. Okay. Sure."

This shit was weird.

More guards lined the hallway.

They nodded as Cam and Sean passed, boots clomping on the industrial-grade linoleum floor.

"Is security always this tight?" Sean marveled.

"Only when Bastien visits."

A sardonic laugh floated through an open doorway coming up on their right.

Cam led the way inside what ended up being a large lab with every kind of medical testing equipment a doctor could wish for. The vampire practical jokers appeared to be doing everything they could to burn out the motors on two tread-mills placed side by side. A brunet in a lab coat leaned over a desk, writing something in a file while Bastien lounged in a chair nearby, admiring her.

"Dr. Lipton?" Cam said.

Straightening, she turned around. Her furrowed brow cleared as her face brightened with a smile. "Hi, Cam." Setting her pen down, she crossed to them and offered Sean her hand. "We weren't formally introduced last night. I'm Melanie. You're Sean, right?"

He smiled and shook her hand. "Yes."

"So nice to meet you." She motioned to the vampires. "Those two are Cliff and Stuart. Cliff's on the left," she said, indicating the grinning African American. "Stuart's on the right." Both vampires' legs moved so quickly that they blurred, while their upper bodies remained almost stationary. It was a bizarre effect. "And this is my husband Bastien," she finished.

Sean nodded to Bastien and offered his hand. "Nice to meet you."

Face darkening, Bastien rose. "What—are you fucking with me?"

Melanie's eyes widened. Reaching out, she patted Bastien's arm. "No, honey. I think he hasn't heard the rumors yet."

"What rumors?" Sean asked, wondering what was going on.

Bastien's face cleared. "Oh. Well. Good to meet you, too." He belatedly shook Sean's hand.

Cam rolled his eyes. "I'm out. Sean, you have my number. Call me when you're ready to leave and I'll come pick you up."

Sean thanked him, even though the fact that he couldn't come and go as he pleased grated. He had no idea what the network had done with his car, but he wasn't allowed to use it anymore because it could be traced. When he had suggested borrowing or renting a car, Chris had rejected the idea, saying, "I know it's an annoyance, but until we get to the bottom of this latest mercenary threat, we need to restrict your movements and ensure you have a guard with you at all times. It's for both your safety and ours."

Annoyance didn't quite cover it.

Cam left.

Sean looked at the vampires. "What exactly will this tell you? Are you testing their endurance?" he asked, curious to know what such activity would indicate.

Melanie snorted. "No. They're just fooling around. Cliff bet Stuart he could go faster on a treadmill."

The vampires grinned.

"Okay."

Bastien smiled. "They aren't allowed to leave the premises, so things can get pretty boring around here for them."

"They're really vampires and not immortals just messing with me?" Sean asked. The pair didn't seem at all crazy.

Bastien shook his head. "They're vampires. And, since you'll hear it sooner or later . . ."

Melanie shook her head violently and repeatedly drew her hand across her throat in a slicing motion. When she noticed Sean watching her, she smiled and pretended she was scratching her neck.

"Until a couple of years ago," Bastien continued, "I thought I was a vampire myself, raised an army of a hundred or so vampires, and waged war with the Immortal Guardians, intending to kill every last one of them."

Sean stared at him. No wonder the other immortals had seemed rather hostile toward Bastien at the meeting.

"Damn it, Bastien," Melanie complained. "We could have finally had someone on our side, but, nooooo. You had to go and open your mouth."

He shrugged. "May as well be honest. It sounds a lot less damaging coming from me." He looked at Sean again. "Oh, and I once killed an immortal."

Melanie hit him on the arm. "Stop talking!"

Sean laughed. As did the vampires.

She smiled sheepishly. "Sorry. He really is a good guy. But I'm having trouble convincing the others of that."

"Well, you won't be getting any grief from me," Sean assured her. When Bastien looked doubtful, Sean shrugged. "I'm new to this world and not invested in its past. As long as you don't screw with me or my sister, I'm fine with you."

Bastien raised his eyebrows. "I think I like you."

"Gay!" Stuart called breathlessly. A loud clunk sounded as the motor of his treadmill let out a burst of smoke and stopped turning. Still running at top speed, Stuart slammed into the front of the treadmill, bounced off, and hit the wall behind him hard enough to crack the Sheetrock.

Cliff burst into laughter and slowed to a halt.

Melanie sighed. "I told you not to break anything!"

Stuart groaned and picked himself up off the floor, staggering a little. "Laugh it up, asswipe," he told Cliff. "I won."

"Dude, I totally let you win because I knew that would happen."

"No, you didn't."

"Yes, I did. It happened to me the first time Dr. Lipton put me on a treadmill."

Melanie winced. "I still feel bad about that."

Cliff didn't seem to hold it against her.

Bastien smiled. "Cliff was a member of my army. Stuart is a new recruit."

This was not at all what Sean had expected.

Melanie smiled. "You look a little shell-shocked."

He watched Cliff taunt Stuart while Stuart brushed the dust off his clothes and shook it out of his hair. "I've never encountered sane vampires before."

"Well, hopefully our research will pay off and the era of psychotic vampires will end soon," she said.

"I'd love to hear about the work you're doing. I'm a medical student at Duke and Chris mentioned recruiting me. He said, if I did, we'd be working together and you'd mentor me."

She nodded. "Are you considering it?"

"Yes."

"Excellent!" Grinning, she started toward him.

Bastien scowled. "Hug him and I'll have to kill him."

She stopped and blew him a raspberry. "Spoilsport."

"A jealous spoilsport." Bastien drew her into his arms. "It's time for me to hunt."

"Okay. Do you have the antidote on you?"

"Yes."

She bussed his lips. "Be safe."

"Always." He claimed her lips in a kiss that lingered. "I almost forgot. I have a surprise for you." Crossing to a coat stand just inside the door, he removed a long, black coat. The interior was lined with as many weapons as Étienne's was.

Delving into an outer pocket, Bastien returned to Melanie and held out several small packages.

Melanie took one and turned it over. "No way! Organic chocolate turtles?"

He nodded and smiled.

Whooping with excitement, she jumped up and wrapped her arms around his neck and her legs around his waist for a tight hug.

Bastien laughed and hugged her back.

As soon as she dropped her feet to the floor, she tore into the first package and popped the whole candy into her mouth. Her eyes closed in ecstasy. "Oh man," she said around a mouthful of chocolate. "This is *so* good."

Sean raised his eyebrows.

Meeting his gaze, she covered her mouth and laughed.

Bastien shook his head with a smile and crossed his arms over his chest.

She chewed and swallowed. "I haven't been immortal that long and had to give up all of my favorite foods, so I've been craving them like crazy."

"Why did you have to give up all of your favorite foods?"

"Because none of them were organic. Our stupid sense of taste is just as heightened as our vision and our sense of smell. And, trust me when I say, foods that contain artificial flavoring and other synthetic chemicals do *not* taste the same as the real deal. As Bastien once warned me, vanilla and synthetic vanillin taste as different to us as turkey and tofurky do to you." She stuffed another chocolate turtle in her mouth and endeavored to speak around it. "Bastien's been looking for organic alternatives to some of my favorites and I *love* turtles."

Laughing, Bastien cupped her face in his hands and kissed her. "You are too adorable." He kissed her again, longer and deeper. "You taste good, too."

Her cheeks flushed as he released her.

Bastien nodded at Sean. "Have fun." He pointed to the vampires. "You two . . . behave. And leave Melanie's candy alone. She can kick your ass without a thought now."

Cliff and Stuart clicked their heels together and saluted.

Shaking his head, Bastien left.

Melanie wadded up the empty packages and tossed them into a wastebasket on the other side of the room.

"Nice," Sean praised with a smile.

"Thanks. I imagine you have some questions."

"About a hundred of them."

Smiling, she motioned to a couple of chairs over by a desk. "What would you like to know first?"

He waited for her to sit, then seated himself beside her. "Well, I've always wanted to know why I can heal with my hands."

She dropped the rest of the candy packages on the desk and leaned forward, her face lighting with interest. "You can heal with your hands?"

He nodded.

"That's wonderful. Two *gifted ones* who are descendants of a powerful healer just came to our attention recently, but neither can heal with their hands."

Cliff dragged a chair over to join them. "So, you can just lay hands on a wound and heal it?" He sat down. "That's so cool. I wish I could do that."

Stuart nodded as he pulled up another chair. "Me, too." Seating himself, he surreptitiously reached toward the candy on the desk.

"Touch it and die," Melanie warned without looking at him.

He snatched his hand back.

"Now," she said. "You can heal with your hands because your DNA is very unique. Every human has forty-six DNA memo groups that provide the blueprint for his or her existence."

"Okay," Sean said.

"*Gifted ones* have seven thousand."

"Awesome!" Stuart said. "I don't know what that means."

Sean wasn't sure he did either. "Why?"

She shook her head. "We aren't sure."

Fascinated by the information he proceeded to acquire, Sean spent the next several hours alone in a room, conversing with a beautiful immortal and two curious, genial vampires with a fondness for practical jokes.

It was the strangest night of his life.

Étienne smiled faintly. He and Krysta sat on the edge of Davis Library's roof at UNC Chapel Hill. It had taken some coaxing to get her to do it, and then to relax. Like many humans, she had a fear of heights.

It isn't so much a fear of heights, she had said, *as a fear of plunging to my death.*

I won't let you fall, he had vowed.

It meant a great deal to him that she had believed him, sitting down, then shakily scooting to the edge and dangling her legs over the side.

Tranquility embraced them, broken by a dog bark here, a cat yowl there, or the occasional vehicle passing on the street.

They had been hunting and training together for almost two weeks now while Sean studied with Dr. Lipton. Étienne had not enjoyed anything so much in decades.

Moments like this were his favorites.

Her shoulder pressed against his arm. Her scent enveloped him, mingling with the chicken sandwiches Cam had made them. Her mere presence provided a balm he hadn't realized he had needed. Calming. Comforting. Dispelling the emptiness inside him.

"I love hunting with you," she said, reaching for the bottle of tea on her other side.

His pulse leapt.

"I haven't eaten this much or this well since I lived with my parents," she continued with a wry smile.

He laughed. For a moment, he had thought—

Her eyes widened as alarm rippled across her moonlit features. "Oh, crap. My parents!"

"What about them?"

"What if the mercenaries go after them to get to me. Or to get to you *through* me?"

He waved a hand. "Chris took care of that when you and Sean moved in with me. Your parents are heavily guarded at all times."

"Really?" Frowning, she took another bite and chewed it thoughtfully. "I'm surprised they haven't called. What did they say about it? I haven't talked to them in almost three weeks. Mom has a knack for sensing when something is wrong and I didn't know what to say to her when she asked what was up."

"They don't know about the network guards. Chris's men are in stealth mode."

She took another bite.

He liked that she had a strong appetite. He didn't know why he enjoyed watching her eat so much, but he did. Perhaps because he knew she and Sean had had some lean times.

"No one has approached my parents? No mercenaries? No suspicious characters?"

"No one."

"Is that a good thing or a bad thing?"

"We don't know. None of us have encountered any mercenaries since they hit your house. We don't know if that means they're regrouping, or have given up, or what. We don't know who these mercenaries are, how large their PMC is, who leads them . . ."

"What's a PMC?"

"Private Military Company."

"Oh."

"If they're a small group, perhaps we did enough damage to make them rethink things. If they aren't, they're probably plotting something."

"Hmm."

More quiet, comfortable, soothing.

"This sandwich is *really* good."

He smiled. "I'm glad you like it."

"There are definite perks to hunting with you."

And there were perks to hunting with her. Like spending hours and hours together every night. Getting to brush up against her and steal kisses and—

Think about something else. Something guaranteed to keep you from getting turned on. "Your parents," he blurted.

Raising her eyebrows, she finished the last bite and tucked the empty tea bottle into their dinner bag. "What about them?"

"Which one of them is a *gifted one?*"

"Both."

"Really?" That was pretty rare in this century. "That must be why your gifts and your brother's are stronger than that of other *gifted ones* in your generation."

She nodded. "My mom can feel other people's emotions and my dad can sometimes see the future."

"Bastien can feel other people's emotions."

"The immortal everyone hates?"

"Yes."

"Sean likes him."

Étienne sighed. "Bastien has his moments."

Several minutes passed.

Krysta looked at her watch. "We still have a few hours of hunting left and nothing much is happening. You want to make out a little?"

He laughed in surprised delight. "You're a saucy wench, aren't you?"

"Hey, when I want something, I go for it."

His body hardened. "And you want me?"

"Yes." She studied him intently. "Your eyes are glowing."

"I want you, too."

A breeze ruffled her hair, bringing with it the scent of blood.

He swore. "But, yet again, it looks like it's time to go to work."

"What is it?"

"Vampires, heading this way from the north."

He stood, brushed the crumbs from his lap, then held his hand out to her.

She curled her small fingers around his and stood, hastily moving away from the roof's edge. "Thank you."

He brought her hand to his lips for a kiss.

She smiled. "You are so hot."

"Don't distract me, minx."

She laughed. "Are we going to do this your way or my way?"

They had alternated between using Krysta as bait and hunting Étienne-style, which pretty much just entailed patrolling this campus or that and pouncing on any vampires they found.

Both got the job done. Unfortunately, neither reduced the danger to Krysta. No matter how many vamps they fought or how the battles began, she ended up wounded and in need of her brother's healing hands. Both siblings seemed pleased, insisting she suffered far fewer wounds when she fought with Étienne. But it frustrated him that he couldn't prevent the injuries entirely.

Étienne breathed deeply, collecting and sorting through the scents riding the wind. Tilting his head slightly, he caught snippets of conversation.

"There could be as many as a dozen. Three are fresh from a kill and boasting of it to the others." He shook his head. "They relished every scream they elicited from their victim. Those three are beyond help. The others aren't as vocal, so we'll have to see if any are salvable enough to be swayed to our side."

She grimaced. "It seems so useless, asking them to join

us. Not one we've encountered so far has responded with anything other than disbelief and psychotic rage."

"I know. But Seth and David want us to keep trying."

"It still feels weird to take orders from someone else."

"You'll get used to it," he said. They all had. And it helped that the ones giving the orders were exceedingly wise and fair.

He refocused on the smells and sounds of the vampire troupe. "With numbers that large, herding them into an alley might be tricky, restricting our movements."

"True."

"Let's do this my way and just confront them head-on."

"Will that give you enough time to read their minds and gauge their levels of madness?"

"Not as much as using you as bait would. But I want you by my side when the battle begins so I can watch your back."

"Just don't endanger yourself by trying to keep an eye on me constantly, okay? I don't want you to get hurt."

He refused to make that promise. *Think your thoughts to me from this point on. They're getting close enough to hear us.*

Okay. And don't think I didn't notice that you failed to agree.

I said you could hunt with me. I didn't say you could tell me what to do or that I wouldn't watch over you in battle. He scooped her up into his arms.

Stubborn.

And you aren't?

She looped her arms around his neck.

Ready?

She nodded. *As I'll ever be.*

Bending his head, he touched his lips to hers. *Hold on tight.* Étienne stepped off the roof.

Her silky hair whipped his face as they dropped eight stories. He landed smoothly on the balls of his feet, the impact pulling her lips from his.

That is so cool.

Smiling, he lowered her feet to the grass. *Fun, too. I admit, when I was younger, I went through a phase in which I repeatedly tested the limits of my abilities by jumping off higher and higher buildings.*

She stepped back. *What happened?*

I found out it isn't fun to reach one's limits. He had broken a lot of bones that night. *And that doing stupid shit pisses Seth off.*

She smiled.

Silently, they wound their way up sidewalks and between buildings. Étienne used his senses to estimate the vampires' route, then decided to confront them where Bastien had once ended a bloody rampage: in the narrow parking alley—empty this time of night—between Peabody and Sitterson Hall.

Here they come, he warned.

Chapter 13

Krysta stood beside Étienne, nerves jumping. *Anything more from their thoughts?*

I think some of the group are fairly recently transformed. They're uncomfortable with the bloody trio's boasts.

You mean we might actually recruit some vampires tonight? Unbelievable. *Only* you *could make me recruit instead of kill.*

Actually only Seth could.

I'm not a Second, so I'm not officially part of the group yet. I'm doing this for you.

You're determined to distract me, aren't you?

Yes.

His lips twitched. *Why?*

Because I had an intriguingly racy dream about you this morning and have been distracted picturing you naked and imagining your hands on me ever since.

His eyes flashed amber.

Her pulse picked up. *Were you there? As* you, *I mean? You said you could do that.*

Unfortunately, no.

Disappointing. She had been sleeping in Lisette's room each night, but that dream had almost driven her to cross the hall. *Well, I only thought it fair that you share a little of the pain.*

He lowered his gaze to her lips. *So you were serious when you suggested we make out on the roof?*

Pretty much.

You do realize I'm now going to have to fight the vampires with a raging erection, right?

Her gaze dropped to his groin. Wow. He wasn't kidding.

No, I wasn't.

Oops. She must have been broadcasting again. *I thought you guys had tremendous control over your bodies. Can't you just . . . think it away?* What a waste. Damned vampires.

Lips twitching, he closed his eyes. *I'll try.*

Since his eyes were closed, she didn't bother to avert her own. That was quite a bulge. Even more impressive than the one he had sported in her dream as he had torn off her shirt and tongued her breasts.

Damn it! Close your mind to me!

Oh. Sorry. What was the opposite of sexy and seductive? What was so *not* sexy that, if she pictured it, it would be the equivalent of a bucket of ice water dousing him?

Hmm. Sean's nasty-ass meat loaf might do it.

Or the girl from *The Exorcist* projectile vomiting.

A skinny, saggy, one-hundred-year-old man dancing around naked.

He grimaced. *Where the hell did you see a one-hundred-year-old man naked?*

In a movie I really wish I hadn't watched.

Well, thank you. I guess. It worked.

She grinned.

What the hell was the brown and green lump you showed me first?

Sean's meat loaf.

He shuddered. *Okay, sober up. They're about to come around the corner.*

She could hear the vampires herself now. They weren't exactly trying to keep their movements or boasts unobtrusive. As Étienne had said, three of the vamps seemed to be doing most of the talking.

The group strutted into view.

Krysta did a quick head count and came up with eleven.

They halted at the sight of her and Étienne.

"Gentlemen," Étienne greeted them.

"Well, well, well," one vampire said, his glowing blue eyes fastening on Krysta. Blood soaked his shirt and pants down to the knees.

What the hell had he done to his victim?

Another stepped up beside him, a sleazy smile shaping his thin lips. "Looks like tonight's fun isn't over."

Étienne snapped his fingers. "Over here, gentlemen."

They frowned at him.

"Apparently it has escaped your notice that I'm an Immortal Guardian."

The eyes of all the vampires lit like lamps, glowing in varying shades of blue and green and amber. Almost as one, they drew weapons. Mostly bowie knives and machetes.

Krysta drew her shoto swords.

Étienne's weapons remained sheathed. "I have a proposition for you."

"I have a proposition for you, too," one of the other vamps sneered. "I propose we kick your ass."

"Yeah," another said. "An Immortal Guardian killed Mac and Keith."

"And Eddie."

Étienne shrugged. "I suppose it could have been me, but that's neither here nor there."

"Fu—"

"A new enemy has arisen. One that poses a threat to both vampires *and* immortals."

"Horseshit!"

"Humans are hunting us," Étienne continued, unperturbed by the swears and slurs and shifting movements of the vamps. "More specifically, *mercenaries* are hunting us. They want to catch one of us, dissect us, and use the virus for economic gain."

"Then I say we hand you over to them," the first vampire jeered.

"That would be monumentally stupid."

"*You're* stupid!" a vamp in the back shouted.

"Great comeback," Krysta muttered.

They turned their attention to her.

"Ah-ah-ah," Étienne reprimanded. "Over here."

They looked to him once more.

"As I was saying, turning me over to the mercenaries would be monumentally stupid. Whatever they learn about the virus and our physiology from dissecting *me* could be used against *you*. And vice versa. Which, by the way, is the only reason any of you are still standing."

"We're still standing because we outnumber you, jackwad."

"I'm two hundred years older than you. Two hundred years stronger than you. Were your numbers twice what they are now, I could still defeat you."

Really? Krysta asked mentally. That was damned impressive.

No. I'm bluffing. One of the elder immortals could, though.

More curses and denials and posturing. The blood-covered vamps and a few of the others were getting pretty amped up.

Krysta tightened her grip on the shoto swords, watching their auras carefully for any hint of impending attack.

"Though they're human," Étienne stubbornly persevered, "the mercenaries pose a serious threat. They've developed a new weapon to use against us. A tranquilizer—"

"Drugs don't work on us," a vamp snorted.

"This one does. It takes several darts to incapacitate an

immortal. But a single dart will drop one of *you* in your tracks instantly and land you on the dissection table."

Krysta nodded. "I've seen the darts in action. He isn't bullshitting you. These guys could take out every one of you without even getting near you."

"They're just fucking with us!" a bloody vamp snapped.

"No, we're not," Étienne said, never raising his voice. "We're proposing an alliance."

"Vampires working with immortals?" another scoffed. "My ass!"

Étienne raised an eyebrow. "Your ass will be tortured if you're caught. I suggest you work with us and—"

"Fuck this shit! Fuck him up!" the vamp with the saturated shirt shouted.

His orange aura shot toward Étienne a second before the vamp did. Half a dozen more did the same. The others darted toward Krysta.

She swung her swords, striking flesh as they closed in on her. Two fell back with howls of rage and pain. Then a third.

A blade cut across her hamstring.

Hissing in pain, she spun and sliced.

The vamp behind her bent forward, clutching his middle.

Yelps and hisses and gurgles of pain filled the night as Étienne tore into his opponents and Krysta continued to hold her own.

The tip of a blade pierced her side.

Gritting her teeth, Krysta swiveled and stabbed the vamp attacking on her left.

Pain exploded in her head.

She staggered. *Shit!* A vamp must have punched her. Her knees weakened as little sparkly bits of glitter flirted with her vision.

Brilliant purple and white swept in a circle around her, laying out all of the vampires swarming around her as he had once before.

Étienne paused in front of her, his face close to hers. "Are you all right?"

A vamp came at his back.

"Behind you!"

He spun around, swinging his sword, and swept the vampire's head from his body.

The vampire beside him gaped and lowered his weapon, wide eyes latching onto Étienne. "Oh, shit!" He took a step back, then jerked and danced as holes opened in his chest and blood sprayed.

Two more vampires fell, their torsos peppered with bullets.

Krysta jerked as a bullet pierced her shoulder. Another filled her arm with fire.

Her hand went numb. Her sword fell to the ground.

Swearing, Étienne dropped a katana and swept Krysta behind him, holding her there with one arm as he backed up against the nearest wall.

A dart pierced a vampire's neck. He collapsed to the ground, unconscious. Another vamp fell to a dart.

The remaining vampires froze, then raced for the opposite building, flattening themselves against the wall. There were only . . . five vampires left, those not killed by mercenaries having been taken out by Étienne or Krysta.

A vampire directly across from them stared at Étienne with wide eyes. "That shit was true?" he cried, voice high with fear. "What do we do?"

The others all waited in fearful silence.

Krysta, call Cam. Don't use names. The mercenaries may be listening.

She sheathed her other shoto sword and yanked out her cell phone. As soon as he answered, she whispered, "Mercenaries are attacking us!"

While she gave their location, Étienne ordered two vamps to cross the alley and join them.

They must have been too afraid to do anything but obey,

because they only hesitated a second before they streaked across and hit the wall beside them.

A flurry of bullets whizzed past, missing them and ricocheting off the pavement with little sprays of asphalt and dirt.

"Protect the woman," Étienne commanded.

"Are you fucking kidding me?" Krysta demanded shrilly, stuffing the phone back in her pocket.

I'm going to sweep around and come up behind the soldiers, he said.

You can't take them out alone!

I don't intend to.

Before Krysta could ask him what he meant, he continued. *The mercenaries are on foot.*

The vamps all gasped and gaped at Étienne.

Was he talking to them telepathically, too?

"Dude," the vampire beside her said, "how'd you do that?" A former Tar Heel hunting his old stomping grounds, according to his T-shirt.

It doesn't matter. As I said, the mercenaries are on foot and are closing in on us. The bulk of the group will strike from the east. The rest plan to circle around and attack us from the west, essentially boxing us in here.

"Let's just run," the second vamp hissed.

Let them live now and they will find you another night.

All of them swore.

Decide quickly, gentlemen, and don't say anything that will indicate your impending actions. They're listening.

The Tar Heel looked at his fellows and nodded.

One by one they all nodded back.

He turned to Étienne and gave him a thumbs-up.

Smart man. You stay here with André the Giant, he said, indicating the huge, hulking vamp on the Tar Heel's other side, *and guard the woman.*

I can't believe this shit, Krysta muttered to him.

Étienne glanced at her from the corner of his eye. *I've*

*read their thoughts. Any intention they had of harming you is
gone.* He nodded to the three vamps across the alley. *I'm
going to meet the larger group head-on. You three meet those
who are circling around to the south. Keep moving. They can't
tranq or shoot what they can't see. Stay between them if you
can and maybe you'll luck out and trick them into killing each
other. Go. Now.*

Étienne blurred and shot away.

When the three vamps hesitated, Tar Heel scowled and indicated with a furious wave that they should get their asses
moving.

They blurred and shot away, too.

Krysta, drew the tranquilizer gun Étienne had insisted she
carry. One dose, he had told her, would either kill a human or
sedate a vamp.

She eyed the vamps nervously.

They shifted from foot to foot, hands clenching and unclenching on their weapons, gazes shifting back and forth
from one end of the alley to the other.

Étienne had better be right about them.

Until he had met Krysta, Étienne had not felt real fear
in . . . almost two centuries. He had had some scary moments
in the first years following his transformation, but nothing
like this.

Krysta was wounded and bleeding and he had just en-
trusted her care to two vampires. He continued to monitor
those vampires' thoughts. But, if they changed their mind and
either attacked her or left her to fend for herself, he may not
be able to get back to her in time to save her.

The notion terrified him.

Sticking to the shadows, Étienne headed first for the
building from which he knew a mercenary was playing sniper

and guiding the others. He leapt up to the roof, not bothering to soften his landing.

The mercenary swung around. Eyes wide, he raised a tranquilizer gun. This was probably the bastard who had shot Krysta.

Étienne closed the distance between them and knocked the gun aside before the man could squeeze the trigger.

Wrapping one hand around the man's throat and lifting him onto his toes, Étienne drew a tranquilizer dart—one with a human dose—from one of his pockets. "You wanted me," he growled as the man fought his hold. "You got me."

He shoved the dart into the man's throat. The soldier had just enough time to realize what had happened and wet himself before he passed out.

Étienne dropped him and drew out his cell phone as he stepped off the roof.

"Oui?" Richart answered.

Étienne landed nimbly on the ground. "Mercenaries are attacking us at UNC," he said, whisper soft. "Meet me at the northeast corner of Chapman Hall."

Richart appeared a few feet away.

Étienne pocketed his phone and swiftly filled his brother in telepathically.

Drawing his weapons, Richart stared at him as they headed toward the larger group of mercenaries and came up behind them. *You left two vampires guarding Krysta? Are you out of your fucking mind?*

I hope not.

The mercenaries approached the entrance to the alley. Had they not all been edging forward with caution, they would have already reached it.

While Étienne dashed toward their front, blocking their entrance, Richart teleported directly into the middle of the group.

Étienne grinned as chaos erupted.

On the other side of Sitterson Hall, screams of pain split the night as the vampires went to work on the other group of mercenaries.

Étienne tore into the soldiers, trying to read the minds of those he killed or wounded. Most were so full of fear and hatred—almost as much hatred as he encountered in a vampire's mind—that he couldn't discern their leader's name or the name of their PMC.

Bullets and tranquilizer darts flew in every direction. When one hit Étienne, he administered the antidote without missing a beat. The soldiers began to panic as their numbers dwindled and started taking out each other with friendly fire as they swung their weapons in wide arcs, trying to hit anything that moved.

Étienne lost count of the mercenaries they fought and wondered how the hell Chris would clean up something this big on a college campus. They were damned lucky it was often deserted this late.

Three mercenaries broke for the alley.

Étienne started after them, then stopped and resumed fighting when he heard Krysta fire her tranquilizer gun.

He heard one of the three vamps he had sent after the other contingent fall to a tranquilizer dart. The other two started to freak out and considered bolting.

Hold it together, he ordered sternly, remembering Tanner—Bastien's Second—telling them that the vampires Bastien had led had all feared him. *Fall back into the alley so the others can help you, but do* not *let any of the soldiers harm the woman. Fail me in this or flee the battle and I will torture you myself when I hunt you down.*

He was actually a bit surprised when that snapped them out of it.

Several bullets slammed into his back.

Bastards. Étienne spun around and swung a sword at the shooter. No, *two* shooters.

Are you leaving any alive? Richart asked dryly.

Ummm . . .

Richart laughed.

Ah, hell. Krysta has run out of darts and is leaping into the fray in the alley.

Go to her. I have this.

Another quick head count yielded few enough soldiers left here that Étienne felt comfortable leaving his brother to face them alone. Because of his gift, Richart tended to fare far better than other young immortals when facing large numbers.

Étienne raced into the alley.

Half a dozen soldiers fought there.

All four vampires remained in perpetual motion as they darted in and out and around the men, delivering cuts and gashes and fatal wounds.

Krysta hung back, a sword in the hand of her uninjured arm, waiting for an opportunity.

The vamps parted. She darted in and swung, slicing through an arm wielding a tranquilizer gun, then jumped back as one of the vamps circled around again.

Damned if it didn't look like they were all working together. Krysta must be wondering if Hell had frozen over.

The last two soldiers gave up on following orders and trying to bring them down alive. Planting their backs to each other, they opened fire with their silencer-equipped automatic weapons. Once again, panic shot through Étienne.

Krysta.

The smaller of the two vamps he had left guarding her tackled her and took her to the ground, covering her body with his. The other three vamps and Étienne were hit with bullets as Étienne rushed forward and cleaved the soldiers' heads from their bodies.

Both dropped to the ground.

Stark silence engulfed them, broken only by the harsh breaths of Étienne and the vampires.

Richart appeared beside him. The vampire covering Krysta clambered to his feet. Krysta rose and, staring at the vamp in utter disbelief, sidled over to the d'Alençons.

Four vampires—bleeding from multiple wounds, standing side by side, hands still clutching weapons—faced them.

The silence stretched as all waited for action.

"Thank you," Krysta said to the one who had taken several bullets for her.

He nodded once, jaw clenching, hand not loosening its hold on his blade.

She glanced at Étienne. "Now what?"

"I don't know," he answered honestly. "I've never gotten this far before." Only Bastien had ever successfully recruited vampires.

Speaking of which . . .

He sheathed one of his weapons, drew out his phone again, and dialed.

"What?" Bastien answered.

"It's Étienne. I can't believe I'm saying this, but I have a situation and could use your help."

Bastien grunted. "I bet that hurt."

"Where are you?" Étienne asked, refusing to take the bait.

"In Melanie's office at the network."

"Richart is on his way."

He pocketed his phone and met his brother's gaze. "He's in Melanie's office."

Nodding, Richart vanished.

The vampires gasped.

"How does he do that?" the Tar Heel asked. According to his thoughts, his name was Jeremy. He seemed to be the most lucid of the group.

"Stick around and you'll find out." Étienne looked at the vamp on the far right, who was considering bolting. "Don't run. You won't get far and having to chase you will piss me off."

The vampire swallowed.

"Now, all four of you did me a solid," he went on, then looked to Krysta. "That's a saying, right?"

Though her pretty face was pinched with pain, she smiled. "Yes."

He returned his attention to the vamps. "All of you did me a solid, so you can relax and stop worrying about me attacking you."

Jeremy's shoulders loosened a bit. "What about Kenny?"

"The one felled by the tranquilizer dart?"

"Yes."

"I'm good with him, too." Satisfied that the vamps were in line, he carefully pulled Krysta into a hug. "Are you okay?"

She nodded, leaning into him. "Do you think Richart could take me home to Sean while you guys work out whatever it is you're going to do?"

He swore. "I should have had him do that first."

She shook her head. "I would have missed out on the hug."

One of the vamps—Ben, according to *his* thoughts— leaned toward another and whispered, "Is it me or does this look like it's about to turn into a chick flick?"

Krysta laughed, then grunted in pain.

Étienne put just enough distance between them to peel off her coat.

She growled at the agony it caused.

"I'm sorry. I want to make sure you aren't losing too much blood." The bullet that had struck her arm had thankfully missed her brachial artery. The wound in her shoulder still bled sluggishly, but didn't look too bad.

Draping her coat over her shoulders, he drew her into his arms again.

Richart reappeared with Bastien at his side.

The vamps tensed and eyed the two anxiously.

Bastien's eyebrows rose. "I'll be damned. He wasn't bull-shitting me."

"Richart," Étienne said, "would you take Krysta to my place so her brother can heal her?"

"Of course."

Releasing her, Étienne touched a finger to Krysta's chin and tilted her head back so he could lower his lips to hers for a soft kiss.

"Chick flick," Ben whispered in a singsong voice.

Krysta smiled. "That one's a keeper."

Shaking his head, Étienne stepped back.

Richart touched her shoulder and whisked the two away.

Bastien sighed. "When Richart returns, have him take you, too."

Étienne opened his mouth to protest. They had quite a mess to clean up.

Bastien held up a hand. "Don't worry. I've got this." He glanced at their vampire audience. "And a cleanup crew is on the way to take care of the rest, most likely with Reordon to oversee them. So do it. Everyone here can see that you want to be with her." He raised his eyebrows at the vamps.

They nodded.

"It's totally obvious," Jeremy said.

"So obvious," Ben agreed.

Étienne sighed. He really did want to be with her, so he would trust Bastien this time.

Jeremy shifted. "Who's the new guy?"

"Someone with whom I thought you might feel more comfortable," Étienne said. "Sebastien Newcombe."

They stared, then exchanged amazed looks.

"Sebastien as in Bastien?" Jeremy asked. "*The* Bastien, who raised and led an army of vampires in war against the immortals?"

"Yes," Bastien responded. "But I don't like to brag."

Étienne sighed and motioned to the vamps. "Bastien, meet our new recruits."

The vampires all relaxed. Apparently, they were new

enough that they didn't consider him Bastien the Deceiver as the crazier ones did.

"There's a fifth around the corner there. He was tranqed while helping us hold off the mercenaries," Étienne added.

"I'm Jeremy," Tar Heel proclaimed eagerly.

Bastien smiled and offered his hand. "Good to meet you." He shook hands with the other vamps next, the action requiring each of them to sheath their weapons.

The man knew how to handle vampires.

Richart returned. "Sean's healing her."

"Thank you." *Would you be okay wrangling Bastien and the vampires by yourself?* he asked mentally.

Of course. I used to hunt with him, remember?

Right. Étienne had forgotten.

A familiar passenger van full of network guards sped down the street and turned into the alley. A low rumbling told the immortals a bus full of cleaners followed more slowly.

Once more, the calvary had arrived.

Good timing, too. Cam must have lit a fire under their asses to get them here so fast.

Network guards approached, armed and alert, Chris at their forefront.

"The mercenaries are all either dead or down," Étienne informed them. "There's one on the roof there." He pointed. "The rest are on the ground." He motioned to their vampire audience. "These wise vampires have agreed to join us. Bastien will aid you with them. Richart will fill you in on the rest when he returns."

"Where's he going?" Chris asked, issuing orders to his men with hand signals.

"Krysta was shot twice and is at my home, being healed by Sean. Richart is going to take me to her, then return to offer his assistance, along with an accounting."

"Okay."

Étienne hesitated. "Really? You aren't going to bitch and moan about me not sticking around?"

"No. I've seen how you guys are with your girlfriends."

Étienne didn't bother to deny it this time. Hell, he *wanted* Krysta to be his girlfriend.

"Go ahead and take off. I'll handle things here."

Étienne frowned. "Don't forget to check them for tracking devices."

"I won't." Chris left to inspect the damage.

"Ready?" Richart asked.

He nodded.

Richart touched his shoulder. UNC's campus dissolved into Étienne's living room.

"Where is she?" Étienne asked.

"In Lisette's room," Richart said. "You need blood first."

A thud sounded downstairs. Krysta cried out.

Étienne raced for his sister's bedroom and barreled through the open doorway.

Sean was on the floor beside the bed, Krysta and Cam kneeling beside him.

Krysta looked up when Étienne entered, tears in her eyes. "He collapsed after healing me."

Étienne nudged Cam aside and lifted Sean onto the bed. Blood stained Sean's shirt on his shoulder. Étienne tore the neck of Sean's T-shirt and pulled it down to confirm Krysta's wounds had opened on him. *All* of them by the looks of it.

"He's never collapsed before," she said on a sob. "Is he dead?"

Étienne shook his head. "He's alive." But he had expended all of his energy to heal her and, as a mortal, may now be incapable of healing himself. Étienne turned to Richart as he entered. "Get Roland."

Richart grimaced and drew out his phone. "I'll call Seth first. Roland tries to kill me whenever I teleport to his home."

"Still?"

He nodded. "I wouldn't be here if I weren't so good at dodging flying daggers." He dialed and held the phone to his ear.

Étienne took Krysta's hand and drew her up against his side. "He'll be okay."

She shook her head, tears spilling over her lashes. "He warned me so many times that I might kill him."

Étienne wrapped both arms around her trembling form. "He isn't gong to die, Krysta."

"Maybe not *this* time, but . . ."

Perhaps she finally realized Sean was right.

The sounds of battle came over Richart's line, carrying to Étienne's sensitive ears.

"Yes?"

"Seth. Richart. Are you busy?"

"One moment." The clang of metal striking metal reached them, accompanied by howls of pain. *Many* howls of pain. Then silence. "Not right now, no. What do you need?"

Étienne fought a smile.

"Sean collapsed after healing Krysta. Could you—?"

Seth appeared beside Richart, pocketing his phone. "Let me guess. Roland still hurls daggers at you whenever you teleport to his home."

"Yes."

"I'm going to have to talk to him about that."

Richart looked at Étienne. "I'm going to head back to UNC."

He nodded.

Richart vanished.

Seth approached the other side of the bed. "So. What happened?"

Krysta sniffed. "He was just finishing up healing the worst of my—"

"Not that," Seth interrupted, resting a hand on Sean's chest. "How were you injured?" His hand began to glow.

Chapter 14

Krysta stared.

Sean's pale face rapidly regained color.

Seth removed his hand.

"That's . . . that's it?" she asked incredulously. It had only lasted seconds and Seth didn't show any signs of fatigue at all.

"Yes," he answered simply.

Unsure whether to believe him, she leaned down and pulled up Sean's shirt. No wounds marred his skin where hers had opened on his flesh. No bullet wounds. No gashes. No bruises. Only dried blood. "That's amazing."

I told you he was powerful, Étienne said.

I know, but . . . damn. "Why isn't he waking up?" she asked.

Even though Seth had healed him, Sean didn't stir.

"He expended all of his energy to heal you. He needs rest, so I commanded him to do so."

"Uh-huh. And, despite the whole unconscious thing, he's obeying you?"

"It wasn't that kind of command. You might say I forced

sleep upon him." Seth crossed his arms over his chest. "One more time. What happened?"

Krysta and Étienne took turns telling him what had happened.

The powerful leader of the Immortal Guardians did not seem pleased.

"First," he said, "you two need to abandon your doubts and insecurities and just get together already. You're so perfect for each other that you're finishing each other's sentences."

Krysta looked at Étienne, who seemed as taken aback as she felt. "Really?"

"We finish each other's sentences?" Étienne asked.

She hadn't realized it either.

"Yes. Second, you left two vampires guarding Krysta?"

Étienne nodded. "It was a risk I had to take. Their thoughts indicated they could be trusted to at least do that much. They were scared shitless and looked to me to get them out of there alive."

Krysta held up an index finger. "I personally didn't think I needed a guard."

"You did," Seth said in a tone that brooked no argument. "Have Chris outfit you with a pair of Glock 18s with thirty-round clips like Lisette. Guns may not be your weapon of choice for taking out vampires, but they *are* good for holding off humans. You also should consider, once more, serving as a Second until this new mercenary threat has been extinguished."

"No, thank you."

He raised an imperious eyebrow. "You can see vampires coming and know their movements before they make them. But the auras of humans offer you no such warning, do they?"

"No," she muttered, reluctant to admit it.

"I know you don't like to hear it, but you *are* a liability, Krysta. Étienne already has to divide his attention between fighting *and* reading the minds of as many opponents as he can. Keeping an eye or ear out for you, too, distracts him even more. He could have been hurt far more seriously than he was tonight as a result."

Her stomach sank as she turned to Étienne. "You were hurt?" Krysta gave him a quick once-over, but there was no way to know how much of the blood painting him was his. And his coat had already sported several bullet holes before the night had begun because he had neither replaced nor mended it after his last encounter with mercenaries. "Where? What happened?"

He glared at Seth. "I'm fine."

Seth shook his head, strolled around, and placed a hand on Étienne's chest. That hand began to glow as he healed Étienne's wounds. "He was shot multiple times by the mercenaries and suffered a few deep gashes at the hands of the vampires before they decided to join forces with you."

She hadn't known. She hadn't even guessed. How many of those injuries had he incurred while he was looking out for her? While he was distracted, listening to ensure the vampires hadn't either turned on her or abandoned her?

"Don't," Étienne said.

"Don't what?" She looked from him to Sean, lying so still on the bed.

"Krysta," Étienne said.

All she could do was stare at him, feeling sick inside.

From the corner of her eye, she saw Cam look back and forth between them and clear his throat. "I, uh, I'm going to go see what the word is on the vamps you recruited tonight." He backed out of the room.

Seth's hand ceased glowing as he dropped it from Étienne's chest. "And I am going to go see if you left any mercenaries alive."

"I did."

"Then I have some minds to read. Hopefully, when I'm

finished, we will know who we are dealing with and how they learned about our existence so we can end this."

He vanished.

When Étienne walked toward her, Krysta held up a hand to keep him at bay.

Étienne took that hand and carried her palm to his lips for a kiss. "Don't."

"You already said that."

"You're still doing it."

"Doing what?"

"Beating yourself up. You were injured, too, you know."

"But that wasn't your fault," she said, throat thick.

"Wasn't it? How long did we walk and watch that campus? The mercenaries were likely there the whole time. But I forgot to use the damned infrared scope to check shadows too dark for my eyes to pierce."

"Because I distracted you."

"Because I'm accustomed to not needing it, to depending upon my own enhanced vision. Had I been more thorough, I would have known they were there, summoned aid, and captured them all alive without you suffering a single injury."

"My being shot wasn't your fault."

"And *my* being shot wasn't yours."

"Sean collapsing was."

"Sean knows his limits."

"And I pushed him to those limits. You aren't going to make me feel better about any of this."

Étienne sighed. "Fine. Then make *me* feel better about it." Tugging her hand, he brought her close and wrapped his arms around her.

Krysta leaned into him, locking her arms around his waist.

"I should be angry at you, but not for any of the reasons you think," he muttered, resting his cheek on her head.

"Why?"

"You actually made me understand Bastien," he grumbled.

"How so?" she asked, tired, lost.

"Bastien is not my favorite person. Despite what I learned about him recently, I have not been able to abandon my dislike for him entirely because he killed a friend of mine two hundred years ago. But there was a night—before I met you—when he thought the woman he loved had been killed and went berserk in the true sense of the word. He painted UNC red with blood and was coated with it himself by the time I came upon him. I thought he had gone mad. He was, for all intents and purposes, gone, wanting only to kill and punish. And, tonight, when I saw those bullets strike you, I wanted the same. I knew exactly how he felt." His arms tightened around her. "I wanted to kill every mercenary, then kill every vampire for distracting me so much that I didn't hear the damned mercenaries' approach until it was too late. But I couldn't. I had to think of the fucking greater good," he said with such disgust that she found a laugh. "I had to take some of them alive."

"And you did."

"They'd better damn well yield some information."

She hoped so. Those bastards had tried to kill her. Again.

The two of them stood that way for Krysta didn't know how long. A minute passed. Ten? Twenty? She couldn't tell and didn't really care.

"I don't know what to do," she whispered, unable to calm her thoughts.

Leaning back, he gazed down at her.

His handsome face wavered as moisture welled in her eyes. When a tear slipped over her lashes and trailed down one cheek, he brushed it away with his thumb.

She shook her head. "This is all I've known, Étienne, all I've done, for six years."

"You never told me what sparked your vampire-hunting career. Not all of it anyway."

"I was a student at UNC," she began, reluctant to revive

those memories. "My fiancé and I were walking back to the dorm one night—"

"You were engaged?" he interrupted.

Was that jealousy sharpening his tone?

She nodded. "Michael and his family moved into a house down the street when we were both in the ninth grade. We hit it off from the start, became best friends, and"—she shrugged—"fell in love. We dated throughout high school and intended to marry as soon as we finished college." It all seemed so long ago. Another life. Another *her*. She had been so young and naïve and innocent then. Michael had been, too. Looking back, it sometimes felt as though decades had passed since that last night they had been together instead of a mere half dozen years.

Were Michael alive today, she doubted he would even recognize the hardened warrior she had become.

"Anyway, Michael and I were walking back to the dorm when two vampires attacked us. They tortured Michael. And made me watch." It had been agonizing. And was still agonizing to recall. She doubted any amount of time would alter that or lessen the impact his screams of pain had had on her, though her grief had finally dulled. "Then one bit me and I lost consciousness, I think from blood loss. I don't know what happened after that, why they let me live. But I never forgot their faces or what they were."

"I'm surprised you remember it."

"I don't think the chemical that you told me is released when vampires or immortals bite someone works on me." Apparently it acted like GHB and made victims more pliable. It also affected their memories, which explained why none of the victims she had spoken with had had any recollection of being attacked.

"Did you tell anyone?"

"The policeman who took my report at the hospital. He said I had been rufied and was confusing things. He didn't believe the vampires were real." Her gaze strayed to the bed. "Sean believed me, but told me I'd be committed if I didn't stop pushing it."

"So you decided to hunt them down yourself."

"Yes. Hunting and destroying vampires is all that has driven me for years. How can I give that up?"

"You don't have to."

"Yes, I do. I can't keep hurting the people I care about. I have to stop."

"Sean is going to be fine, Krysta."

She took a chance and met his gaze. "I wasn't just talking about Sean."

He stilled.

"Twice now Seth has warned me I'm a liability. By stubbornly insisting on hunting, I'm endangering you."

"I don't care about that. I'm immortal. I can take it." He cupped her face in both hands and studied her intently. "Are you saying you care about me?"

Krysta didn't think she had ever felt so vulnerable in her life. Not emotionally anyway.

"Never mind," he said with a gentle smile. "You don't have to answer that."

Hell. She was too tired and heartsick to lie or evade. "I think I'm falling in love with you," she confessed.

He sucked in a sharp breath. His eyes flashed bright amber.

Étienne thought his heart would burst from his chest. "What?" The jealousy that had infiltrated him as she had spoken of Michael fled.

She bit her lip. "Don't make me say it again."

"Why?'

"Because it scares the hell out of me."

He stroked her lovely face with his thumbs. "It scares me, too."

"Why would it scare you? You've probably been with hundreds of women and had dozens of relationships."

He shook his head. "There have been fewer than you think. And I didn't love any of them. I fell for *you* the first night I saw you fight vampires."

She swallowed. "No, you didn't."

"Then why was I so relieved to learn you and Sean were brother and sister, rather than lovers?"

"Really?"

"Yes. I'm over two hundred years old, Krysta, and have never been so drawn to a woman before, so consumed by thoughts of her or longings for her. I'm falling in love for the first time in my long existence. It's rather . . . daunting." Confessing it was even more so.

Reaching up, she pressed her palm to his cheek.

He turned into her touch, nuzzling her soft skin.

"What are we going to do about it?" she asked softly.

"I know what I *want* to do about it," he said.

"What?"

"This." Dipping his head, he brushed his lips against hers.

Étienne hadn't lied. He had never longed so much for a woman, her company, her touch . . . and that longing magnified a hundredfold when Krysta parted her lips and drew her tongue across his lower lip.

Flames licked his veins as he deepened the kiss, stroking her tongue with his own, eliciting a feminine moan. And, oh, what that moan did to him.

He tightened his hold, pressed her as close to him as he could get her, his body burning at every contact point.

Rising onto her toes, she locked her arms around his neck. His pulse raced as she combed her fingers through his hair and clenched them, giving a light tug, even as she rubbed her hips against his erection.

Oh, yeah.

A throaty laugh escaped her.

"What?" Urging her back against the wall, he slid one hand down over her tempting ass and ground her against him. Damn, she felt good.

"You project your thoughts when you're turned on," she purred.

He smiled. "So do you."

Obeying one of those thoughts, which mirrored his own desires, he found one of her breasts with his free hand. Small and firm, it fit perfectly in the palm of his hand, just as he had known it would. He teased her nipple, hard beneath her shirt and sports bra. Stroked it. Pinched it.

She moaned and strained closer, her heart pounding so hard he could feel it in his own chest. *More.*

He lowered his fingers to the hem of her shirt, slipped his hand beneath it and smoothed it up her warm, satiny skin. Squeezing beneath her tight sports bra, he again palmed her breast.

She gasped. Releasing his hair, she lowered one hand to his chest.

At first, he thought she meant to stop him. She covered his hand with hers over her bra, squeezed. Then, she moved on, forging a burning path down his stomach to cup his heavy erection.

He groaned and thrust against her.

Smiling against his lips, she drew her hand back.

Étienne's heart damned near stopped when she slid one leg up his and hooked it over his hip, opening herself to him. Urged on by her thoughts and her delicious body, he rocked against her.

Both moaned this time, loving it, needing it, equally frustrated by the cloth that separated them.

Trailing his lips across her cheek, he licked and kissed

his way down to the soft skin at the base of her neck. "Wrap both legs around me," he whispered.

Krysta's already racing heart went wild at the hoarse request. Without hesitating, she jumped up and wrapped her other leg around his hips.

A breeze whipped her as their surroundings blurred. Then she found herself in another bedroom. Very masculine. Very posh. Very neat for the bedroom of a longtime bachelor.

She met Étienne's glowing gaze.

"I want to make love to you," he stated boldly.

She swallowed hard and nodded. She wanted it, too.

"Call me crazy," he added, "but I didn't want to do it in front of your brother."

Her eyes widened. "Oh, crap." She had been crawling all over Étienne with Sean lying in bed just a few feet away. "How did you make me forget about him?"

He shook his head and strolled toward the bed, every movement creating lip-biting friction between their bodies. "I would have forgotten myself if my hearing weren't acute enough to pick up his breathing and heartbeat."

He stopped beside the bed.

Krysta lowered her legs to the floor and stood for a moment, staring up at him, her body tingling and aching for his touch.

"You can change your mind," he murmured, so damned sweet and understanding it only made her want him more.

She shook her head. "I want this." Again, she reached up and stroked his face, "I want *you*."

For a moment, he looked so hungry for her she thought he might pounce.

Then a teasing gleam entered his luminous eyes. "Want to see a neat trick?"

Raising her eyebrows, she smiled. "Okay."

He blurred. She felt a tug.

In a blink, they were both naked, clothing and weapons scattered around their feet.

He laughed. "I've never seen you so wide-eyed."

"That is *awesome!*" she praised.

Grinning, he picked her up and tossed her onto the bed.

Krysta shrieked with delight as he dove after her.

"Shoes on or off?" he asked.

She laughed when she realized they both still wore their boots. "Off."

Sitting up, he quickly doffed his own, then turned his attention to hers.

She liked this playful side of him. Liked the feel of his large, warm hands grasping her calf as he removed first one shoe, then the other.

His gaze roved her body, splayed out before him like a banquet, scorching her and making her squirm with the need to feel all of that hard, muscled flesh against her.

And, just like that, all levity was shoved aside by lust.

He peeled a sock off, kissed her ankle, lowered her foot to one side of him. Peeling the second sock off, he kissed that ankle and lowered her foot to the other side of him. He smoothed his hands up her calves, up her thighs, his thumbs coming *so* close to the heart of her.

Damn, she wanted him.

He growled, exciting her even more. "Now *you're* the one projecting."

Her breath caught as he rose above her and settled his big, warm body between her thighs.

Étienne wanted Krysta so badly he nearly shook with it as he palmed one of her breasts.

Lowering his head, he drew the hard tip of her other breast into his mouth, loving the feel of her writhing beneath him. His fangs descended, as they often did when he experienced strong emotion, but he was careful not to let them pierce her soft skin.

"Are you hearing my thoughts?" she asked, her small hands exploring his back and hips.

"Yes." They fired his need as much as her touch did.

"Then you know what I want," she gasped, burying her hands in his hair as he teased her nipple with his tongue.

Fast and hard.

The thought came through loud and clear.

Reaching down between them, he found her already wet and eager for his touch, arching up when his fingers found her clit.

Now, she insisted. *Please, Étienne. I want you now.*

Hell, yeah.

Positioning his cock at her entrance, he met her gaze and slowly pressed forward. An inch. Then another. And another. Slowly stretching her. Savoring the feel of her.

She groaned. "You're killing me."

He winked, struggling to maintain his tenuous hold on control. "But what a way to go."

She laughed.

He plunged inside to the hilt.

Both gasped.

She was so warm and wet and *tight*.

"Am I hurting you?" he asked.

Krysta shook her head, catching the concern in his eyes as he gazed down at her. She hadn't been with anyone in a long time and Étienne was big, but . . . "You feel so good," she breathed.

He withdrew, almost leaving her entirely, then thrust again. Hard.

"Oh, yeah." She slid her hands down that wide, muscled back and over his ass as he thrust again. "Yessss."

He thrust again, sending sparks of pleasure dancing through her.

"Again," she urged, wanting more, *needing* more.

And he gave her what she wanted.

"You are so fucking beautiful," he murmured, taking her lips in a passionate kiss. "The things I want to do to you . . ."

"Tell me," she panted, pleasure mounting.

He did. In explicit detail. Making blood rush to her face and her body burn hotter as he explored her flesh with his hands and that wicked mouth, continuing those long, deep thrusts until an orgasm ripped through her, stealing her breath and wringing a cry from her lips.

As her body continued to ripple with sensation, he stiffened above her and cried out with his own. Breathing hard, he closed his eyes and lowered his forehead to hers, those strong arms keeping the bulk of his weight off of her.

Her own chest rose and fell so fast one would think she had just run a marathon. Heart still pounding, peace sifting through her, Krysta was content to just lie quietly and enjoy the moment.

Her hands didn't quite get the message, though. She couldn't resist the need to slowly slide them up and down his back, loving the feel of all of that strength above her.

At last he raised his head. The amber glow in the eyes that met hers had lessened, allowing some of the brown to seep through.

He stroked her hair, both his touch and his expression tender. "Okay?"

She didn't know if he was asking if she was okay physically—it *had* been a long time and he hadn't exactly been gentle, giving her exactly what she had wanted—or if she was okay emotionally. But the answer to both was, "More than okay."

He smiled and delivered a gentle kiss that stole her heart. Then he dipped his head and kissed her shoulder, where she had been shot.

Rolling them to their sides, he settled his head close to hers on the pillow.

His brow furrowed. "No lingering pain from your injuries?"

"No." Which made her realize . . .

"What?" he asked, recognizing her unease.

She bit her lip. "Is it weird that we didn't wash the blood off first?" Both had been wounded. And, though their wounds had been healed, smudges of dried blood remained where bullets and blades had marked them.

"No," he responded, the lack of concern in his voice a relief. "The blood is ours and we're both so accustomed to seeing it that it means little to us. *And*, on my part at least, I wanted you so badly that I could think of nothing else."

She smiled. "Me, too."

A teasing glint once more entered his light brown eyes. "*If*, however, it troubles you, I think there is only one thing we must do."

"What's that?" she asked with false gravity.

"Head in there . . ." he pointed to a door across the room that opened onto a bathroom.

"Okay."

"Immerse ourselves in the cleansing waters of a whirlpool bath . . ."

"I'm liking it so far."

"Bathe every inch of each other's body . . ."

"*Really* liking it."

"Then make love again, giving me a chance to do some of those things I mentioned wanting to do to you."

Her pulse jumped. "Go get the water running," she encouraged him in a throaty voice she barely recognized as her own.

Grinning, he stole a kiss, then leapt naked from the bed, giving her an eyeful of aroused immortal male as he headed into the bathroom.

Smiling, Krysta scooted off the bed and followed.

Seth felt his fury rise as he examined the unconscious mercenaries. There were eight of them being held in one of the holding rooms designed for vampires at network headquarters. All were chained together and lay on cots that had been hastily erected. Not to make the men more comfortable, he suspected, but so he wouldn't have to kneel down to read their minds if touching them became necessary.

Two of the mercenaries were brain-damaged. The immortals were still having trouble determining how hard they could hit humans without killing them or rendering them useless.

He rested his palm on the forehead of a third, then a fourth, a fifth, his anger mounting.

He turned to face his companions.

Chris, Bastien, and Melanie all took a cautious step backward.

Bastien wrapped a protective arm around Melanie's shoulders.

Seth drew in a deep breath and let some of the rage drain out of him. "There's nothing."

Bastien frowned. "Did Richart and Étienne hit them too hard?"

"A couple of them. But those who are merely unconscious yield no information that can aid us. They don't know who their commander is. They don't know the name of his operation. And they don't know where it is located."

Chris swore. "How the hell is that possible?"

"Each one of them was recruited from another PMC, except for that one. He's an army veteran. Chris, I'd like to see if we can't win him over to our side. He seems like a good man. He's just been misled."

Chris nodded.

"All are single—no families—and were approached by a man who claimed he worked for an elite Private Military Company that regularly received government contracts. He told them he had a highly secretive mission that involved homeland security."

"Was he bullshitting?" Chris asked.

"We won't know for sure until we confront their commander. Once they consented, he sedated them and took them to the compound from which they operate. They travel to and from it either blindfolded or in windowless transport vehicles. They don't know where it is. And they don't know who *he* is. He gave them a code name."

Bastien frowned. "Are they stupid? How can they just go gunning for people based on something someone they can't even identify told them?"

"They aren't stupid. Just gullible. Mostly. Those three there would shoot their own grandmother for a paycheck. And they were offered a *big* paycheck."

"How big?" Melanie asked.

"The equivalent of a Second's salary."

Chris whistled. "So whoever these guys are, they're very well funded."

"Which makes them even more dangerous," Seth finished for him. More money meant more resources.

Bastien released Melanie and strolled forward to scowl down at the men. "So there's nothing?"

"Nothing."

"Did you see the face of the man who recruited them?"

"Yes. I don't recognize him."

"Shit."

"Exactly."

Bastien combed his fingers through his long hair. "If *these* men know nothing, we have no reason to believe any of the *others* will tell us anything."

"Precisely."

Quiet filled the room as brows furrowed.

They had been operating on the assumption that, if they could capture one of the mercenaries, Seth could learn the whereabouts of the group and they could swoop in and kill them.

And they *did* intend to kill them this time. *All* of them.

Chris's face suddenly brightened. "Tracking devices."

Seth tilted his head to one side. "What?"

"Their minds may not be able to tell us where their base is, but their bodies can. We do to them what they did to us. Plant tracking devices on them and let them lead us home."

Seth met Bastien's gaze. "That's not a bad idea."

Bastien nodded. "They think we're monsters. I doubt they would credit us with the forethought it would take to turn the tables on them."

Melanie didn't look convinced. "What if they're more paranoid than that? What if they check the men with metal detectors the way Chris checked these and the vampires you brought in?"

Bastien shrugged. "Plant the devices on their weapons. I'm sure they disarm before they're scanned. *If* they're scanned."

Chris smiled. "You devious bastard. That would work."

Bastien raised an eyebrow. "Is it doable?"

"Hell, yes. You saw how small the one the mercenaries used was. My tech guys can duplicate that and make it magnetic," Chris said. "Would you and the other immortals be able to plant them on the weapons without them knowing?"

"To quote you, *Hell, yes.*"

Seth nodded. It was a solid plan. And it was good to see these two working together and leaving past animosities behind them. He clapped Bastien on the back and looked to Chris. "Put your men on it immediately and distribute the devices to all of the immortals in the area when you have enough. Their Seconds, too."

"I'm on it. What do you want me to do with these guys?"

"Hold them for now. Preferably elsewhere so their complaints and shouting, once they awaken, won't disturb the vampires."

Chris nodded. "When Bastien started talking about re-cruiting vampires, I bought an abandoned missile silo and outfitted it with all of the trappings of a vampire's prison in case the shit hit the fan. Do you want me to transfer them there?"

Once more, Chris had thought of everything. He was a damned good man to have on their side. "Sounds perfect. We'll decide what to do with them after we discover who their commander is. Keep the veteran comfortable, though. The others are in it for the money. He's in it to protect his country." And he likely would be the only one Seth would let live . . . *if* the man joined them.

"And the vamps?" Chris asked.

"I'll see to them next."

Bastien took a step forward. "They seem sincere in their desire to side with us against the mercenaries." He wanted so badly to help vampires, having seen firsthand so many fight the madness that infects them.

Seth looked to Chris. "Would adding new apartments be a problem?"

Chris glanced at Bastien. "This far underground, it would be a bit of a challenge, but it's possible." He met Seth's gaze. "I'm more concerned about security. If you give all of them the okay, we'll have seven vampires living here amongst the human employees. We've given Cliff and Stuart more leeway lately and let them move around more freely on this floor. We can't do that with seven vamps. Not unless you start assigning immortals to serve as guards. Two vampires against three dozen human guards armed with automatic weapons and tranquilizer guns won't win. Seven might."

Seth corrected him. "Three dozen guards and one immortal. Melanie is very strong. As strong as Roland despite her youth."

Chris swore. "I keep forgetting she's immortal now."

"And Bastien lingers here most nights."

Bastien caught Seth's gaze and tapped his temple. *Can you hear me?*

Yes.

Would you take the four of us somewhere private for a moment? Somewhere the vamps can't hear us.

Seth teleported them to Chris's home and used telekinesis to flick on the lights.

Giving their surroundings a hasty inspection, Melanie wrinkled her nose.

Bastien took in the piles of clothes, stacks of papers, discarded pizza boxes, and assorted other crap that cluttered the living room floor and furniture and frowned. "Where the hell are we?"

"My home," Chris said, glaring at Seth, "and don't say a word."

Bastien wisely held his tongue. "Look, the whole purpose of recruiting vampires is to get them to help us spread the word and get *other* vampires to avoid the mercenaries. Or help us fight as they did tonight, if it comes to that. They can't do that cooped up at the network."

Seth agreed. "What do you propose?"

"I think we should see if Melanie can find a way to surgically implant tracking devices on the vampires, so we can turn them loose every night."

Melanie regarded him with surprise.

"Richart can teleport them to my old lair each evening, so they won't be able to disclose the location of the network. They can then roam where they will and get the word out to other vampires. When they return to my lair before dawn, Richart can then bring them back."

Chris arched a brow. "And we'll just go on faith that they aren't preying upon innocents while they're *roaming where they will* and *getting the word out?*"

"We can reduce the chances of that by keeping them supplied with blood at the network and having Lisette or Étienne read their thoughts nightly or weekly, however you want to do it. I'll hunt while the vamps are out and about. And, when they're not, I'll serve as guard at the network. At least while Melanie is working."

Chris gaped at him. "*You* serve as guard? Are you shitting me?"

Bastien shrugged. "It would allow me to spend more time with Melanie. Cliff and Stuart like me being around. The new vamps will likely be more comfortable with me around. It's a win-win situation."

"Yeah," Chris said, "except most of the emergencies we've had at the network in recent years—which spawned *many* injuries and a hell of a lot of damage to the property—were instigated by *you*."

"So?"

Chris just pointed at Bastien and looked at Seth.

Seth shrugged. "Bastien is with Melanie now. He has a vested interest in keeping things calm and safe around there. And, if he gets out of hand himself, Melanie will kick his ass."

Melanie smiled.

Bastien grinned. "She's strong enough to do it, too."

Chris shook his head. "You are so fucking weird. Fine. Seth, if you want the new vampires to live at the network with the others, I'll begin construction on the apartments as soon as you give me the go-ahead."

"Go ahead."

"Done. What about Bastien's desire to let the vamps roam North Carolina freely?"

"Let's wait on that, give the vamps some time to settle in, and see if Melanie will be able to make the tracking devices work."

She bit her lip. "The challenge will be finding a way to keep the virus from expelling the devices the way it does bullets and other foreign objects . . . *without* the aid of the tranquilizer, that is. We know the tranquilizer slows down the healing process, and could probably help, but the vamps will need their wits if they're going to be mingling with other vampires."

"And they can't know about them," Chris added, "or they'll just dig them out."

"I'll bury the memory of them," Seth said.

Bastien spoke up. "If she *can* make it work, I'd like to take Cliff and Stuart hunting with me while the other vampires are out spreading the word."

Chris stared at him. "Hunting? You want vampires to help you hunt and destroy other vampires?"

"Yes."

"In violent, bloody battles, armed with weapons."

"Yes. Both Cliff and Stuart have proven their loyalty to us."

The two vamps had indeed proven their loyalty, but . . . "Cliff has been infected long enough to suffer the consequences," Seth reminded him gently. He didn't need to see the MRIs to know the damage had begun.

"I know. But he's holding it together," Bastien insisted. "And I think he'll hold it together a little longer if he can get some fresh air and exercise. He's been cooped up at the network too long without reprieve."

Bastien loved Cliff like a brother. A quick look into his thoughts told Seth Bastien wanted the young vampire to experience a last taste of freedom before the madness claimed him. And Seth, after his own attempts to help the young vampire, held the same desire. Cliff had proven to be incredibly strong and fierce in his determination to hold off the madness. It was going to break Bastien's heart when he finally lost the battle. Melanie's, too.

"If Cliff broke and made a run for it, do you think you could catch him?" Seth asked.

"Yes." And the dread in Bastien's face and voice told them all without words that he would do what had to be done when he caught him, just as he had with Vince.

Melanie took his hand.

"Very well," Seth decreed. "Cliff has always been loyal to you, Sebastien. You need not wait and can begin taking *him* hunting with you now. Stuart and the others, however, will have to wait for the tracking devices."

"Thank you."

The fact that Chris made no objection confirmed that even *he* had a soft spot for Cliff.

"Excellent. I'll meet with the vampires now."

"May I accompany you?" Bastien asked.

Seth grinned as Chris's mouth fell open once more. "Melanie has been a good influence on you."

Bastien grimaced and swore. "I'm doing it again, aren't I?"

"What?"

"Being nice," he said with much disgust.

Melanie smiled.

Seth laughed. "Yes." He teleported them back to the holding room with the mercenaries. "Shall we?" He could have just popped them into the room with the vampires, but knew the network guards liked to keep track of their movements for safety's sake.

Bastien kissed Melanie, then led Seth out into the hallway and to the holding room next door.

Melanie returned to her office while Chris headed for the elevators.

A guard standing in front of the vampires' holding room took a security card from his pocket.

Seth shook his head and waved a hand in front of the lock. A thunk sounded. Opening the heavy door, he stepped inside, Bastien right on his heels.

A thought closed the door behind them.

Five vampires stood shoulder to shoulder, eyes wide with trepidation, heavy titanium chains weighing down their right arms and anchoring them to the walls.

Seth said nothing as he scanned their minds.

The virus had not progressed far in these. The brain

damage was minimal. They must have all been turned during the past year.

"Good evening, gentlemen. I'm Seth, leader of the Immortal Guardians."

They exchanged nervous looks.

One wearing a Tar Heels T-shirt swallowed. "Are you the one they call the Day Walker?"

"Yes."

"Why do they call you that?" another asked.

Seth glanced at Bastien, who clapped a hand to his forehead. "Because I can walk in daylight," he explained.

"Ohhhhhhh."

Okay, so he wasn't the smartest kid Seth had encountered. At least he wasn't manic.

Chapter 15

"You aren't sleeping," Étienne commented.

He lay on his back, Krysta's lovely naked body cuddled up against his side in bed.

"I'm procrastinating," she said, drawing circles on his chest with her fingers.

"About sleeping?"

"No. There's something I want to ask you and I'm not sure how you're going to react."

"I don't know that I like the sound of that," he admitted. Tentative was not a word he would ordinarily use to describe her.

She sat up, the covers falling to her waist, and swiveled to face him.

Étienne's gaze instantly dropped to her breasts.

She began to speak earnestly, but—for the life of him—Étienne didn't know what she was saying.

He held up a hand.

She quieted.

He raised his eyes. "If there's something you wish to discuss, you're going to have to cover up. I can't concentrate with your beautiful breasts in my face, tempting me to touch and taste them."

She dragged the covers up and tucked them under her

arms, her lips forming a small smile. "What breasts? I'm built like a ten-year-old boy."

"The hell you are. I love your breasts. They're perfect. And, if you doubt that . . ." He motioned to the sheet tenting over his erection.

She smiled and licked her lips. "Ooh. Nice."

His breath caught as she reached for him.

Stopping inches away, she drew her hand back. "No. Not now. I really do need to talk to you."

Damn.

"But hold that thought."

He could do that. "What's troubling you?" He took her hand and began to toy with her fingers. Did she regret making love with him?

"The same thing that troubled me before," she answered. "With the mercenary threat combining with the increased vampire population, I can't continue to hunt the way I have been. I'm putting too many people I care about in danger."

And he was one of those people. Étienne still couldn't believe it. "Krysta, I told you. You aren't—"

"Let me finish."

"As you wish."

"There's an obvious solution. One that will keep me from putting you in danger and from harming Sean when he heals my wounds."

"Okay." Had she decided to follow Seth's advice and become a Second? As much as Étienne wished to keep her safe, he would miss hunting with her each night.

"I want you to transform me," she blurted, then held her breath.

Étienne stared, convinced he had heard her wrong. "I'm sorry. What?"

"I want you to transform me."

His heart began to thud against his ribs. His hand

tightened on hers. He sat up, the motion drawing them closer. "Krysta . . ."

"Just hear me out," she said anxiously.

"Only weeks ago you thought I was a vampire and were contemplating killing me."

"I wasn't. I mean, I *did* think you were a vampire, but I already knew I couldn't kill you. You're freaking irresistible and you know it."

"True," he said, just to goad her.

Smiling, she shoved him in the shoulder with her free hand. He laughed.

"I hear what you're saying." Her face grew solemn. "But I know now that you're immortal. That you're just like me, only infected with a virus. I know you won't go crazy. I know you don't prey upon innocents. I know how the virus works. Sean has spent every night with Dr. Lipton and explained everything to me in excruciating detail. I just think this is the best solution. The *only* solution." She tightened her hold on his hand, her face earnest. "If you transformed me and made me immortal, I could keep hunting and hold my own better against vampires. And I would heal without Sean's help if mercenaries shot me."

The thought of her being shot made him lose his erection. He hated the idea of her getting hurt.

"Sean would be safe. *You* would be safe, knowing I could take care of myself—"

"If you think I would stop worrying about you if you were immortal, you are mistaken."

"But you would worry about me less, right? Because a bullet wound or two or four wouldn't kill me or endanger my life."

Yes, damn it.

"Right?" she pressed.

"Yes," he conceded.

"Then . . . what do you think? Will you do it?"

He hesitated. "I just don't want you to rush into anything. I know seeing Sean collapse shook you, but there are other healers among us to whom you could go when—"

"I can't keep depending on someone else to patch me up. I want to be able to heal on my own. Like you and the other Immortal Guardians. I want to be able to continue hunting vampires. I want to be able to help you defeat your enemies."

"They've tried to kill you three times. They're your enemies as well."

"I know. And I'm vulnerable, facing them as I am. I want to be strong like you. I don't want to have to settle. I don't want to have to stop hunting and become a Second."

"Seconds fight in battles, too. I've lost more than one in the past to vampires' blades."

"But they don't actively hunt."

No, they didn't.

Étienne studied her. He wanted to be objective here, to look out for her best interests instead of going with his own. Did *he* want her to transform? Absolutely. They had made no promises to each other yet, but they had each admitted they were falling in love and . . .

He couldn't deny that an eternity spent hunting alongside Krysta sounded blissful. An eternity laughing with her and teasing her. Making love with her.

But those were all *his* wishes.

This was a decision which, once acted upon, was irreversible.

"Let me read your thoughts," he requested.

She frowned. "What?"

"Let me read your thoughts. All of them, not just those you send me. I need to know you really have considered this thoroughly and have no doubts. No reservations. That this isn't a knee-jerk reaction to Sean collapsing."

She hesitated.

"Seth will insist on doing the same before he renders his decision."

"We have to ask his permission?"

"Yes."

"Why?"

"He's our leader. That's how it's done."

She didn't look too pleased.

"You'll have to answer to Seth if you transform, Krysta. You'll have to obey the rules like the rest of us. *And* his orders."

"Well . . . I kinda already am, so . . ."

He arched a brow.

"Okay. I won't lie. It'll be hard. I've been doing my own thing for years. But you did say he's the wisest among you."

"He is."

"That will make it a little easier."

"So? Your thoughts?"

She bit her lip. "I'm not hesitating because I have doubts. I'm hesitating because there are things up there that I'm not sure I'm ready for you to see."

He supposed he would feel the same way. But Étienne wouldn't approach Seth with the request until he was sure she wasn't merely panicking and grasping at straws after seeing her brother collapse, pale as death, after healing her. Or panicking over having to give up hunting. Or just plain panicking. She could have been killed tonight. Again.

"Fine," she said, thrusting her chin forward. "Read my thoughts."

As soon as he sensed she had let down her guard, Étienne explored her thoughts. There *was* guilt and concern for Sean. Guilt and concern for *him*. Conviction that transforming was the best course of action for her. A lot of lust for him. And . . .

His pulse began to pound in his ears.

Love.

Krysta loved him.

After learning she'd been engaged, Étienne had feared her heart would always belong to Michael, but . . .

She really did love him. *Him.* Étienne.

She was afraid to believe it, because it had happened so fast. But she loved *being* with him. Hunting. Talking. Laughing and teasing. Making love. Watching television. Sharing a sandwich. Even just sitting quietly on this campus or that, their shoulders and thighs touching as the night breeze caressed them.

And he felt the same. Étienne hadn't realized *he* could fall in love so quickly, but living with her these past two weeks and spending so much time together . . .

He couldn't get enough of her and was astounded that she felt the same way.

Dipping his head, he took her lips in a long, passionate kiss.

She drew back. "Damn it! I didn't want you to see that!"

"See what?"

"How I feel about you! That's why you kissed me, isn't it?"

"Yes."

She covered her face with her hands and spoke something so jumbled into them that he couldn't decipher it.

"Krysta, sweetheart." He pried her hands away from her pink face. "I feel the same way."

"You do?" she asked uncertainly.

"Yes."

"But it's too soon."

"I know it feels that way. But it's not like we're dating and only see each other a couple of nights a week. We've been together constantly since you and Sean moved in, only parting to sleep." He smiled. "And there were times we didn't even do that."

At last, he managed to coax a faint smile from her. "True."

She sighed. "You didn't see anything else up there that would embarrass me, did you?"

He winked. "I saw some very interesting fantasies you've been fabricating around me."

"Of course you did," she acknowledged dryly.

"Would you by any chance care to explore a couple? No, make that *a few*. We have all day."

She raised her eyebrows. "Really?"

"Unless you aren't ready—"

"I'm ready." She shook her head. "Wait. We're getting distracted again. Are you going to transform me?"

"I will take the request to Seth and, if he gives his permission . . ."

She leaned forward.

"Yes, I'll transform you."

Grinning, she threw her arms around his neck and hugged him close, those tantalizing breasts pressed to his bare chest. "Thank you."

He slid his hands up and down her back, loving the feel of her soft, soft skin. "There *is* one thing though . . ."

"Crap." Releasing him, she plopped back onto her heels. "What?"

"Younger immortals are always weaker than older immortals."

"That's what Sean said."

"Sarah isn't. She was turned only two or three years ago and should be weaker than I. Instead, she's as strong as her husband, Roland, who turned her."

"Isn't he like a thousand years old?"

"Close to it, yes. We don't know if she's so strong because of his age or because he's a healer. But you might consider having Roland turn you."

She scrunched up her face. "I'd rather you do it."

"You won't be linked to him emotionally afterward, if that's your fear," he assured her.

"Euw. I didn't even think of that."

"You would be stronger than me," he said, even as he wondered how he would talk Roland into doing it.

"If you turned me, would I be as strong as you or weaker than you?" she asked.

"I don't know. If the age of the immortal and not his gift is the determining factor, then you would have the same strength I possess, I would imagine. Perhaps slightly less."

"I'm good with that."

"Don't be so hasty, Krysta. Being stronger would be an advantage. The stronger you are, the safer you are in battles against mercenaries and vampires. You'll move faster. You'll heal faster. You'll have a greater tolerance for the sun."

"I want *you* to transform me."

He took her hand. "Just think about it."

"I don't have to. If I spent a month mulling it over, I would come to the same conclusion. If Seth says I can be transformed, I want *you* to be the one to do it," she insisted.

And he *wanted* to be the one to do it. But he wanted her to be safe even more. "Okay. Then mull this over. When we first met, I came to your rescue each time you were in over your head. *And*," he continued when she started to protest, "you *were* in over your head. Even *you* know you would have been killed coming up against the numbers of vampires you did if I hadn't jumped into the fray and aided you."

She frowned. "I know. It's just galling to admit it."

"Well, if Roland transformed you, our positions could very well reverse. *You* could be the one coming to *my* rescue when things got rough, because you would be stronger than I am."

She tilted her head to one side. "Okay, I won't lie. That does sound good."

"Then you'll consider it?"

She sighed. "I guess."

"Don't think that I don't want to transform you myself.

Because I do. I just want you to be safe and don't want my selfish desires to impede that."

"Okay." She still seemed disappointed.

Reaching up, he brushed her hair back from her face. "Why is it so important to you that *I* transform you?"

"Sean told me how it's done and . . ." She squeezed his hand. "If someone else's blood is going to flow through my body, I want it to be yours."

His hand tightened around her fragile fingers as his body went rock hard. "Would you think me strange if I told you that turns me on?"

She smiled. "A little bit, but I don't mind."

Grinning, he yanked her into his arms and fell backward onto the sheets.

She laughed as her hair fell down around them in a silky curtain, closing them off from the rest of the world.

"You're the most incredible woman I've ever met," he murmured.

"I find that hard to believe. You've lived for two hundred years." And she wasn't fishing for compliments. She really didn't seem to understand her own worth, how unique and exceptional she was.

"It's true," he vowed. "Sometimes I fear this might all be a wonderful dream from which I will soon awaken."

She kissed his stubbled chin. "If it is, I don't want to wake up."

He hugged her close. "I've been lonely for so long, Krysta," he admitted.

"I have, too," she said softly.

"I've waited two hundred years for you."

"I hope I can live up to your expectations," she murmured, brow furrowing.

He shook his head. "You've already surpassed the fantasies and expectations I compiled over the decades and centuries."

She smirked. "You don't want much, do you? Just a skinny girl to aggravate you every once in a while and put your life in danger?"

"You don't aggravate me, you entertain me. Endangering my life keeps me on my toes. And I don't know why you have issues with your body. The only issue I have with it is that it's clothed far too often."

Laughing, she wrinkled her nose. "I was mocked throughout high school for being flat-chested and spent four years watching every male except my fiancé, who was just my boyfriend back then, drool over all the girls with big boobs. So it's hard not to be self-conscious." Her face lit with an *Ah-ha!* expression. "Hey! When I'm transformed, will the virus make me beautiful like Sarah, Lisette, Melanie, and Jenna?"

"You already *are* beautiful," he declared. He loved the way she looked.

She pouted. "It won't change my appearance?"

"No. If you were older, the virus would reverse the damage aging had wrought and make you young again."

She smiled. "Jenna seems very excited about her gray hair having turned brown again."

He grinned. "Yes, she is."

"But it won't change my shape?"

He shook his head. "If you were emaciated, the virus would rebuild the muscle mass you had lost, heal the damage done, and render you a healthy weight once more. If you were obese, the virus would swiftly burn through your fat stores—"

"Let me guess. Heal the damage done?"

"Yes, and render you a healthy weight. Since you're neither, there should be no noticeable difference."

"So . . . no big boobs?"

"No big boobs. Not that you need them."

She grimaced. "It just would have been nice to have an

hourglass figure that wasn't achieved by wearing a stiff, uncomfortable push-up bra."

"I prefer *no* bra to a push-up bra, at least around me," he mentioned.

"You are so easy to please," she said with a smile, wiggling from side to side atop him in a way that sent shocks of pleasure darting through him.

His voice deepened. "And you please me endlessly."

Her look turned flirtatious. "You know, the rest of me may not be too much to brag about, but I *do* happen to have a lovely mouth." Lowering her lips to his chest, she tongued his nipple and delivered a love bite.

He hissed in a breath, pulse leaping. "Yes, you do."

She moved to the other nipple and repeated the gestures. "A very talented mouth."

Mmmm. "Do tell."

She sent him a provocative smile. "You sound doubtful."

Étienne was surprised he could make any sound at all beyond a moan as she slid down his body, her satin skin teasing his cock, and kissed his belly.

"Perhaps a demonstration is in order?" she suggested innocently, dipping her tongue into his navel.

He nodded. "A demonstration. Yes, please."

With a sultry laugh, she curled her fingers around the base of his shaft and gave the tip straining toward her a long lick.

Étienne groaned and buried his hands in her hair, fire igniting his blood as she circled him with her tongue, then drew him into her warm, wet, admittedly talented mouth.

Krysta hummed as a litany of French poured forth from Étienne's lips. He was beautiful, muscles rippling, head arching back, face flushing with pleasure. Pleasure that soon swept through *her* as she continued to tease and torment him with her lips and tongue and fingers. She was so wet. She could almost feel him inside her, thrusting deep.

Étienne suddenly released her hair and grabbed her arms. Dragging her up, he rolled her beneath him and plunged inside her.

Crying out, Krysta clamped her hands on his ass and drew him in deep, urging him on as he began to move, thrusting and withdrawing, rocking against her, hitting all the right spots.

"Like it?" he growled in her ear as he slid a hand to her breast and pinched her sensitive nipple.

She nodded, too breathless to speak. *Yes.*

"Want more?"

Again she nodded. *Hell, yes.*

He withdrew, rearing back onto his knees.

She opened her mouth to protest and gasped as, instead, he flipped her over onto her hands and knees, then plunged into her again, taking her from behind.

Oh, yeah!

A low laugh vibrated her back as he buried his lips in her hair, seeking and finding the base of her neck as he fondled her breasts with one hand and slid the other down over her stomach to delve into the curls beneath and stroke her clit.

Krysta never would have described herself as being noisy in bed until that moment. Sounds of pleasure emerged with every breath, every thrust, until a climax ripped through her, her body clenching and unclenching around his.

Étienne's grip tightened almost to the point of pain as he found his own release.

The two collapsed onto the sheets. Krysta barely had time to acknowledge just how heavy all of that muscle was before he rolled them to their sides and spooned around her.

Several minutes passed as they regained their breath. Little aftershocks of pleasure continued to dart through her. She didn't think she had ever had such an intense orgasm.

"And I didn't even get to show you how talented *my* mouth is," he murmured into her hair.

She smiled. "Next time."

Étienne felt a twinge of nerves as he dialed Seth's number.

"Yes?" Seth answered on the second ring. Once more, his voice was accompanied by the sounds of battle.

"It's Étienne. Are you busy?"

"A bit. What's up?"

Étienne glanced at Krysta, who stared back with furrowed brow as she bit her lower lip. "I wanted to talk to you about something."

"Go ahead."

A scream of pain rent the air in the background.

"Are you sure this isn't a bad time?"

"Hold on. Friedrich, *haben Sie diese?*"

"*Ja.*"

"*Ich werde bald wiederkommen.*" Seth appeared beside Étienne, a bloody katana in one hand. He nodded a greeting to Krysta. "What's up?"

Étienne pocketed his phone. "Krysta would like to be transformed."

"Okay."

Étienne waited for him to say more.

The silence stretched as Seth stared at him expectantly.

"That's it?" Étienne asked. "Just . . . okay?"

"Yes. Anything else?"

More silence.

Étienne met Krysta's confused gaze, then looked at Seth. "I don't get it."

Seth arched a brow. "What's not to get? She wants to be transformed and I have no objection to it."

"Oh. I guess I just thought that there was more to it than that. That you would want to read her mind or something."

"Normally, I *would* read her mind to ensure this was what she truly wanted rather than a hasty decision or that she wasn't being pressured into it. But I actually saw this coming."

"What?"

Krysta took a step forward. "What do you mean?"

"Occasionally I get glimpses of the future. Krysta becoming immortal was one of those glimpses, which is why I felt no guilt when I urged her in that direction by repeatedly pointing out that—because she's mortal—she's a liability."

Krysta frowned. "I've really come to hate that word."

Seth shrugged. "Did it help you reach your decision more quickly?"

"Yes," she grumbled, "but I still don't like it."

He smiled. "Ahhhh. She already sounds like an immortal."

Étienne laughed. "We're all a pain in your ass, aren't we?"

"Just so. Now, if you will forgive me, I need to return to the battle before Friedrich is overrun." He bowed. "Welcome to the family, Krysta. If you have any questions about the transformation, what will happen or how long it will take, I'm sure Dr. Lipton would be happy to answer them for you."

"Thank you," she said.

Étienne offered Seth his hand. "Yes. Thank you."

Seth shook his hand and clapped him on the back, then vanished.

Étienne met Krysta's gaze. "Looks like we have the go-ahead."

She nodded. "I expected there to be more to it, too. I thought we'd have to plead our case or something."

"Seth is an enigma."

She tilted her head to one side. "Are you sure he's an immortal?"

"Yes. Why?"

"His aura is different."

"How so?"

Her gaze roved him. "Your aura is a combination of purple and white that swirls and mingles, but never blends."

"Really? Is that different from vampires' auras?"

She nodded. "Vampires' auras are orange. Human auras vary according to health and mood. Auras of immortals and vampires don't."

"So how is Seth's different?"

"There's no purple. It's just pure white. Almost *blindingly* white. It's actually quite beautiful."

Étienne frowned. "All immortals have purple in their auras except for Seth?"

"Yes."

He pondered that a moment. He had never questioned it before. Seth had gifts like all of them. His eyes glowed when he was gripped by strong emotion like theirs did. He had fangs . . . didn't he?

Now that he thought about it, Étienne couldn't recall ever having seen any on the eldest immortal. "Does David's aura contain purple?"

"Yes, but only a sliver. I thought he was like Seth at first, then saw the purple."

"Perhaps it's just an age thing."

"I suppose so," she conceded. "Roland has more white in his aura than you and Richart do."

He relaxed. "That's it, then. And, speaking of Roland, would you like me to go ahead and give him a call?"

"Yes, please." She crossed to him and leaned into his side. "I still wish it could be you."

He kissed her tempting lips. "Me, too."

His call went straight to voice mail. "Roland, it's Étienne. Give me a call when you receive this." He started to put his phone away, then paused. "Let me try Sarah. Those two are rarely apart. Maybe Roland is just being his usual antisocial self and not answering because he doesn't want to talk to anyone." He dialed Sarah's number.

"Hello?"

"Sarah?"

"Yes?"

"Hi. It's Étienne."

"Hi," she said, with what sounded like false enthusiasm. "How's it going?"

"Good. I'm trying to reach Roland. Is he there?"

"Um . . . no. He's . . ." She lowered her voice to a whisper. "He's avoiding you."

"I can hear you," Roland said in the background.

"Damn it!"

Étienne frowned. "Why is he avoiding me?"

"He's thinks you're going to ask him to transform Krysta."

"I *am* going to ask him to transform Krysta."

Roland's voice came over the phone. "Not going to happen."

The line went dead.

Swearing, Étienne dialed her number again.

"Hello?" Sarah answered innocently, as though she didn't know who was calling.

"Put him on," Étienne said.

Roland let loose a stream of epithets in the background.

"I'm . . . not going to repeat that," Sarah said.

"You don't have to," Étienne told her. "Look, I know he's antisocial, but—"

"It isn't just that," she said, lowering her voice.

"Then what?"

"He found out that . . ."

"What?" he prodded.

She sighed. "The guys on theimmortalguardians.com website are calling him The Transformer. Like the robots."

More foul epithets from Roland. "I will *not* be disrespected!"

"I'm sure they don't mean it as an insult," Étienne lied.

Roland wasn't a favorite amongst immortals because of his . . . personality and his tendency to terrorize any Seconds sent to serve him, so any gossip that concerned him on the website tended to be unflattering.

"Yes, they do," she said. "I'm as furious as he is. Roland should be applauded for helping those he transformed, myself included, and the guys on the net are all being dicks about it."

Étienne's eyebrows flew up as Roland burst into laughter in the background.

"What?" Sarah demanded. "I can't curse? It pisses me off."

"I understand," Étienne said, wondering how he could spin this and change Roland's mind. "But I don't think Krysta should have to—"

"I'm not doing it," Roland insisted. "Three is my limit."

"But—"

Rustling sounded.

"Roland," Sarah warned, her voice fading, "don't you dare smash my—"

The line went dead.

Étienne tucked his phone away. "Roland isn't terribly enthusiastic about the idea."

Stepping back, Krysta smiled and shrugged. "Then it'll be you after all. Good."

"Give me one more chance to win him over. Everyone has been sticking pretty close to David's when they aren't hunting. We can go by there later and see if I can't change his mind."

"Okay, but I don't think you're going to have any luck. Everyone I talk to says Roland is as stubborn as a mule."

"And they're right. But Seth and David will be there and might urge him along."

"If you say so."

"Maybe I'll buy Sarah a new phone as a peace offering," he mused.

"What happened to her old one?"

"I'm pretty sure Roland just destroyed it."

"Yeah. Good luck changing his mind."

"Come on, Roland," Étienne urged. "Do it for *me*."

Leaning against the bar that separated David's dining room and kitchen, Roland crossed his arms over his chest. "And I owe you what?"

Richart, Jenna, Lisette, Tracy, Sheldon, and Cam formed a horseshoe around them. Ethan, Edward, Yuri, Stanislov, and their four Seconds stood just behind them and watched over their shoulders.

Étienne swore silently. "Then do it for Krysta."

"And I owe *her* what?"

Patience fraying, Étienne gestured to Jenna and Richart. "You turned Jenna for Richart."

"I turned Jenna because she's my descendant."

Cam looked at Jenna and Richart. "Is *that* why Richart keeps calling you Gramps?"

Roland glared daggers at Richart.

"How do you know Krysta isn't your descendant?" Étienne asked. It was a stretch, but . . .

"Because I keep track of them," Roland responded.

Sarah stood sentinel beside her husband and frowned at their audience. "You see? I told you he has a big heart. He's been watching over them all this time."

"Keeping track isn't the same as watching over them," Roland murmured.

Sarah elbowed him. "Give me my moment, honey. I'm defending you."

He smiled.

"Roland," Étienne said, "you must understand my position. I want Krysta to be as strong as possible so she'll be as safe as possible."

"I'm an Immortal Guardian," Roland said, unmoved. "I hunt and destroy vampires. I am *not* a transformer."

A few snickers sounded.

Étienne growled in frustration and dragged his hands through his hair.

Marcus smiled and shook his head as he looked at the immortals around him. "I told you not to fuck with him. What if *you're* the next one who falls in love with a *gifted one?* Wouldn't you want *him* to transform her, as Étienne does, so she would be stronger and safer? You all just screwed yourselves for a laugh."

That sobered them up. As many immortals as there had been falling in love lately, it wasn't out of the realm of possibility.

"I'll do it," Sarah said.

Roland's head snapped around. "What?"

She shrugged. "I'll do it. I'm as strong and as fast as you are."

"Awesome!" Sheldon exclaimed, drawing everyone's gaze. "Chick-on-chick action!"

Cam popped him on the back of the head.

Étienne rolled his eyes and returned his attention to Sarah. "I appreciate the offer, but you aren't a healer."

"Oh. Right. I was thinking of the strength part and forgot it might be because he's a powerful healer."

Seth and David entered from the kitchen, carrying huge platters of baked cornish hens and filling the room with a mouthwateringly delicious aroma.

Étienne abandoned trying to convince Roland and turned to Seth. "Couldn't *you* transform her, Seth?"

"No." He placed the platter on the ever-growing dining table and turned to face them. "Nor can David."

David nodded as he did the same.

"Why?"

"We're older and more powerful than all of you," Seth

reminded him. "We don't know which of those factors—age or being a powerful healer—causes immortals turned by Roland to be stronger than expected. However, since David and I possess both, chances are excellent that Krysta would be as strong and as powerful as we are if one of us transformed her."

Sarah arched an eyebrow. "So? What's wrong with that?"

Jenna crossed her arms over her chest and nodded, chin rising.

"Don't even go there," Seth said. "It isn't a misogynistic thing. I don't know a single immortal male who isn't drawn to strong women."

"Yourself included?" Sarah asked.

"Of course."

"You hear that, ladies?" she said, a speculative gleam entering her eyes. "We need to find Seth a good, strong woman."

The women responded with amusing enthusiasm.

"Do you like your women tall or short?"

"Slender or full-figured?"

"She'll have to be a *gifted one*, so she can be transformed."

"Or an immortal. There are other female immortals, aren't there?"

"I'm sure there are."

"Hey, I bet we could get Chris to give us a list of them."

"Or maybe we could ask around on the website. Is there a *Personals* section on the website? We could post a *single and looking for* ad for him."

Seth turned a little green and looked to their husbands. "Um . . . a little help?"

The men raised their hands in a *What can we do? It's out of our hands* gesture.

"Anyway," Seth hurried to interrupt them. "We can't have a youngster running around with the power we wield. I know we make it look easy, but David and I have had thousands of years to accustom ourselves to it and learn control."

Étienne sighed. So much for Krysta being as strong as possible. He met her gaze and found excitement rather than disappointment there.

"Looks like it's going to be you," she said with a grin, adding several tiny hand claps. "Yay!"

He laughed and shook his head. "I'll let you choose the time and place."

"Actually," David spoke up, "you should do it here, where I can be available to assist you."

Sarah nodded. "He helped me when I transformed. I don't remember much about it beyond being submerged in a bathtub full of ice and water with Roland and seeing David leaning over me, but I know he helped me."

Krysta bit her lip. "How bad does this whole transformation thing get?"

Sarah came forward and stood next to her. "I'll tell you all about it after dinner."

"Thank you."

The front door opened. Bastien, Melanie, and Sean entered.

Étienne took Krysta's hand. "You really aren't disappointed?"

She shook her head and squeezed his hand. "You know why I wanted it to be you."

He did. And recalling it made him hard again, so he hurriedly escorted her to the table, where everyone gathered around to enjoy the sumptuous meal Seth and David had miraculously found time to prepare.

Chapter 16

As the meal drew to a close, Seth looked around the table. "Seconds, and Sean, I'd like you to leave us for a few moments. Please adjourn to the training room. You'll find a selection of desserts and refreshments awaiting you. Spar. Gorge. Gossip. Do whatever makes you happy. We'll let you know when our business here is concluded."

Surprised looks were exchanged all around. Immortals visually consulted each other and found no answers as the Seconds rose, pushed their chairs close to the table, and headed for the hallway without comment.

Ami rose.

Seth touched her arm. "I'd like you to stay, sweetheart."

Swallowing hard, she retook her seat.

Marcus wrapped an arm around her shoulders and drew her close.

Jenna cleared her throat. "I'm not sure what I should do here. I'm immortal, but I don't hunt vampires yet, so . . . should I leave or stay?"

"Please, stay," David said. "Your input will be particularly important in the matter we wish to discuss."

Her eyebrows shot up. "Really?" She glanced at Richart, who shrugged.

"Krysta," Seth added. "You'll be immortal within the week, so you may stay as well."

"Darnell, you stay, too," David continued.

Darnell nodded, then called to the others, "Close the doors to the basement and the training room so we won't have to listen to Sheldon get his ass kicked."

"Oh, ha ha," Sheldon said, his voice dripping with sarcasm. "Wait. You meant in a sparring session, right?"

Cam nudged him along.

Étienne wondered what the hell was going on. Seth had never done this before. Seconds were *always* privy to the business of immortals. They needed to be aware of every threat in order to better serve and protect them. What could Seth not want them to know?

The door to the basement closed. Boots tromped down stairs. The door to the training room closed.

"What do you think is going on?" he heard Sheldon ask.

"They can hear you, genius," Cam reminded him.

"Oh. Right."

Richart sighed and rolled his eyes.

Soon conversation began to flow below. Movies. Books. The latest goings-on at the network.

Here at the table no one spoke.

The tension rose. All present, like Étienne, believed an ax was about to fall.

At last, Seth spoke. "A situation has arisen. Something unprecedented. Something that has left even David and I uncertain how to proceed."

Roland shifted slightly. "I thought you two had seen and done it all."

"So did we. What we discuss here will remain between those seated at this table. Do not share this with your Seconds or with any other mortal members of the network. Torture will not extract this information from immortals. It *will*, however, draw it from most mortals. Considering the many enemies we have faced in the last few years, we cannot take that risk."

All nodded.

What the hell was Seth going to tell them?

"I've misled you. I did it intentionally for the reason I just disclosed. I have kept from you a secret that was not my own to share and intended to keep it from you longer, but circumstances have eliminated any further hope of maintaining silence."

Roland leaned forward. "Any secret you share with us will be guarded with our lives. Should anyone here betray you, I will take care of him or her myself."

The pledge may have surprised everyone present, but none doubted the veracity of it. Roland may be antisocial and grumble, but he could be ruthless when defending a loved one and was a man any warrior would feel fortunate to have guarding his back.

"Thank you."

A faint thumping began to distract Étienne. It took him a moment to realize it was the heel of Ami's boot striking the floor as her knee bobbed up and down.

She stilled as everyone looked at her. "I'm sorry. I'm nervous."

Marcus glared daggers at everyone.

Hell. This was going to be big, wasn't it?

"As you know, Ami was a primary target of Emrys, who gained knowledge of her association with us through Montrose Keegan, then passed that knowledge along to Donald and Nelson."

All nodded.

"Because mercenaries who may be linked to Donald and Nelson's group have risen against us, I feel compelled to explain why it is more important than ever that we keep Ami out of their hands."

It *was* unusual to order immortals to risk their lives to

protect Seconds instead of the other way around. Immortals were very rare in the greater scheme of things, so the loss of even one had great impact.

Richart frowned. "Why did they want her so badly before? Did they find out she's a *gifted one?*"

Seth leaned forward. "Ami is not a *gifted one*. She's an extraterrestrial."

Étienne stared at him blankly.

And he wasn't the only one.

"She's from another planet," Seth clarified.

Dead silence.

Ami nibbled her lower lip. Marcus . . . was preparing to kill them all by the looks of his darkening features.

"That is so cool," Krysta said, daring to speak first.

Étienne glanced over and found her staring at Ami with a combination of awe and delight.

"What planet are you from?" she asked.

Across from Ami, Sarah nodded. "Are you from Jupiter? Because I've always wanted to know what's at the center of that big-ass storm."

Some of the anxiety left Ami's face, replaced by a tentative smile. "No, I'm from a planet called Lasara in another solar system. But I can tell you what's in the storm on Jupiter."

Seth held up a hand. "Let's save that for later."

Roland leaned forward. "Are there others from your world here?" His gaze remained on Marcus, though he spoke to Ami.

If either immortal were telepathic, Étienne would swear the two were silently communicating.

Then again, they *had* known each other for eight hundred years. Speech may no longer be necessary.

Ami shook her head. "No."

"*Will* there be others?"

"No."

Étienne felt Krysta tug his hand and listened to her thoughts.

She's all alone? Do you think she crashed?

I don't know.

A slew of questions leapt from lips all around the table.

David cleared his throat. "Your questions can wait. And, if Ami isn't comfortable answering them, I trust none of you will press her."

In other words, leave her the hell alone. Message received. Ami wasn't comfortable discussing her origins. Not surprising, considering she had been tortured by the humans who had captured her. Or, at least, he assumed Emrys and his men had captured her.

That also explained why they had pretty much dissected her, taking advantage of her regenerative capabilities to learn everything they could about her alien race, the bastards.

"There's more," Seth said, face somber.

More?

Everyone gave him their full attention.

"Ami is pregnant."

Several immortals gasped.

Sarah's face lit up. "Oh, my gosh! Congratulations!" She started to jump up, intending to run around the table and embrace the couple, but Roland stopped her.

Étienne peeked at her thoughts and caught her confusion, then her understanding.

Krysta squeezed his hand. *Is this as bad as I think it is?*

Yes. He felt for Marcus. No wonder he had been so tense lately.

They don't know how the virus will affect the baby?

Right.

Or what will happen with the whole human and alien DNA combining thing?

Gifted one *and alien DNA. Yes.*

"Jenna," Melanie said. "You're the only immortal we know

of who has ever had a baby, so I would appreciate your input as I guide Ami through her pregnancy."

Jenna nodded. "Of course. I don't know how much help I'll be though."

Bastien spoke up. "Did you cramp when you were pregnant?"

"Yes. Throughout most of the pregnancy."

"How severe were the cramps?" he pressed.

She thought for a moment. "They were like mild menstrual cramps. In fact, for the first two weeks I was pregnant, I kept thinking I was about to get my period and didn't realize I was pregnant. So they were more annoying than painful. Nothing that would make me reach for pain relievers or anything." She grimaced and glanced around the table. "I'm sorry. Is that too much information?"

"No." Bastien turned to Melanie and raised his eyebrows.

She smiled. "I know. I know. You're brilliant." Bastien brilliant? Must be an inside joke. "Thank you, Jenna."

Nodding, Jenna turned to Ami. "Congratulations, Ami. How bad is the nausea?"

Ami grimaced. "Pretty bad."

"I'm surprised you made it through dinner."

"I almost didn't. The smell of most food tends to make me gag."

Jenna nodded. "I was the same way. I threw up half a dozen times a day sometimes in my early weeks."

Some of Marcus's tension eased. "That's normal?"

"Sure. It—"

"Is Ami infected with the virus?" Roland interrupted.

Marcus met his gaze once more. "No."

Melanie shook her head. "I've found no trace of it in her blood."

"If she *were* infected," Roland asked, "would she turn immortal or vampire?"

"We have no way of knowing," Seth answered.

Somber stares all around. So she couldn't be transformed.

"If you're worrying about me growing old, dying, and leaving Marcus alone in a few decades . . ." Ami began.

Yes, they were. Marcus had come very close to the edge after losing a woman he had loved for eight centuries. Like Étienne, everyone present feared what losing Ami would do to him.

"Then don't," she continued. "My race is very long-lived. It will take me centuries just to get my first gray hair."

Their time together would still be finite, but at least they would have centuries rather than decades.

"Ami and the baby are both doing well," Seth announced. *Thus far* went unspoken. "I trust you understand now why I want Ami to be protected at all costs?"

Everyone nodded. This *was* unprecedented. Étienne didn't remember ever having heard of an immortal female giving birth *or* an immortal male fathering a child with a mortal. And he *would* have heard it if it had happened.

"Then you also understand why she will not be aiding us in tracking down the mercenaries this time."

"Of course," Roland voiced, and glared at everyone else until they nodded or said the same.

Antisocial, but loyal. Roland was going to be protective as hell of that baby once it was born.

If it was born.

Étienne silently prayed that all would be well with Ami's pregnancy and that she would give birth to a healthy babe. She had suffered tremendously at the hands of Emrys and his doctors. He hated to think of her suffering more.

Seth thanked them for their discretion and for forgiving his deception. (It had been Seth who had told them all Ami was a *gifted one*.) He then wished them all happy hunting.

Every immortal present, save Seth and David, hugged Marcus and Ami and congratulated them before seeking out their Seconds.

Étienne hugged Ami, then Marcus, slapping him on the back.

Krysta smiled down at Ami. "Are you having any weird cravings? Can we pick something up for you while we're out hunting?"

Étienne's chest swelled with what he could no longer deny was love for her.

Ami smiled and shook her head. "I've really been having a hard time keeping anything down. Anything but lollipops, that is. They seem to be the only sweets I can tolerate."

"Lollipops it is," Krysta promised with a smile.

Étienne and Krysta moved away as Jenna hugged Ami and started to chat her up.

"When do you want me to transform you?" he asked as they sought out Cam to let him know they were leaving.

"Tonight?" she asked hopefully.

He nodded. "Let's let David know before we leave."

A few minutes later, calling good hunting to those within, Étienne and Krysta stepped out into the night. As they crossed to his car, Étienne glimpsed Roland and Marcus within the shadows of the forest that surrounded the drive.

Roland dragged Marcus into a rough hug.

Marcus's hands clenched into fists on Roland's back, knuckles showing white. His mind was full of what-ifs. And all were terrifying.

Roland's mind was full of the same, along with a heavy dose of concern for his friend and . . . guilt. Roland was keeping something from him.

Étienne frowned. Who the hell was Zach? And what did he have to do with Ami and Lisette?

"Where do you want to hunt tonight?" Krysta asked, unaware that they weren't alone.

Étienne hastily looked away from the duo before Roland could catch him staring. Opening the car door, he waited for Krysta to slide inside. "Let's try UNCG." Lisette had been hunting there of late.

"Okay. Let's pick up Ami's lollipops on the way so we won't forget."

"Sure." He closed the door. Strolling around to the driver's side, he glanced at the forest and discovered the elder immortals were gone.

They only encountered three vampires that night. All were insane. So all were destroyed.

Étienne was unharmed in the brief battle. Krysta barely earned a scratch. Yet they both bore their fair share of bloodstains when they returned to David's home and claimed what Étienne called a quiet room in the basement.

"What's a quiet room?" she asked, checking it out.

"A room that has been so thoroughly soundproofed that the other immortals in the house won't be able to hear anything that transpires within it."

Good to know.

"So. How are we going to do this?" Krysta asked, beginning to feel a bit anxious now that the time of her transformation was at hand. Guilty, too, because she hadn't told Sean of their plans for fear he would spend hours trying to talk her out of it.

"Let's wash the blood and sweat off first," Étienne suggested and peeled off his coat.

"Sounds good to me." Krysta removed her own coat.

Minutes passed as they disarmed.

She grinned and shook her head as the pile of weapons they stacked on the nearby love seat grew. "We're quite a pair, aren't we?"

He winked. "Perfect for each other."

She agreed wholeheartedly.

Her breath caught as he drew his shirt over his head.

All that muscle . . .

His long fingers dropped to the zipper of his pants.

Krysta hurriedly yanked her own shirt over her head so she wouldn't miss anything.

He slid the zipper down. Tucking his thumbs in the waistband, he peeled off the pants *and* his boxers and kicked them aside.

Her heart beat faster.

He was already hard.

"Waiting for anything in particular?" he asked innocently.

Grinning, she pulled her sports bra off and let it fall to the floor. "Have I mentioned how much I love it when your eyes glow?"

"No," he murmured, his luminous amber gaze devouring her as she unfastened her pants and slid them down to her ankles, along with her bikini panties. "Damn, you tempt me."

Good. Because she couldn't wait to feel him inside her again.

Groaning, he closed his eyes for a moment, then turned and strode into the bathroom.

As she followed him, she heard the faucet give a faint squeak. Steam poured from the shower as she entered the sleek room.

Immortal Guardians must have a thing for bathrooms, because this one, like those in Étienne's home, was as gorgeous as a millionaire's spa.

Tugging the elastic band from the end of her braid, she untwined her hair and finger-combed it while she admired Étienne's gorgeous form.

He held his hand out to her.

Smiling in anticipation, she took it and stepped into the granite-tiled shower more than big enough for two.

Steam encapsulated and caressed them as he slid the glass door closed. Drawing her up against him, Étienne stepped back into the fountain of water and let it flow over them like hands.

Krysta touched his shoulders, drew her fingers down his slick chest as he tilted his head back.

Water turned his hair into a sleek, black cap, straight and soft and shiny against his handsome face. Reversing their positions, he settled his hands low on her spine.

Krysta arched her back and reached up to run her fingers through her hair as the warm water swiftly saturated it.

Étienne pressed his hips into hers, sliding his hard cock between her parted thighs and sending shocks of pleasure through her.

Her breath caught. She lowered her chin and met his gaze. "You're so beautiful, Krysta."

Abandoning her hair, she gripped his biceps. "So are you."

He leaned closer.

Anticipation rose as she focused on his lips.

He drew back, a bar of soap and two washcloths in his hand.

Had he just been reaching past her?

"Tease," she grumbled as he stepped back, breaking all contact.

He laughed. But that glowing gaze continued to roam her as he lathered up one of the cloths and handed it to her.

Krysta took it and began to vigorously scrub one arm, removing splotches of blood as she watched him lather up the other cloth and return the soap to the dish behind her.

"Slower," he instructed, voice silky smooth.

She paused.

Étienne kept his eyes on Krysta, focusing on her exquisite, expressive face as he drew his soapy cloth down one arm in long, leisurely strokes, then up again.

Hunger flared in her gaze as she watched the motion, then mimicked it herself, slowing her movements to sensual strokes.

He smiled, hard and aching and loving the suspense, loving having to wait, loving making *her* wait, knowing how explosive it would be when they finally joined.

He drew the cloth down over his other arm.

Krysta did the same.

He slid it down his side, over his hip and down one leg.

Krysta continued to follow his lead, her gaze frequently skipping to the erection that strained toward her.

Up one leg, then down the other. Then back up the leg and his other side. He slid the cloth over his chest, dragging the material over his nipples and imagining it was her hands.

Krysta did the same, gasping and biting her lip.

He dropped his cloth. She dropped hers and took a step toward him.

Étienne shook his head. "Not yet."

She stopped and stared as he slid his soapy hands over his chest. Then she cupped her breasts in soapy hands and squeezed them with a moan.

His pulse raced. For a moment he forgot to move.

Her hips shifted restlessly as she continued to fondle her breasts, stroking, squeezing, and pinching the hard, pink tips. Then she slid one hand down her flat stomach.

Étienne slid a hand down his own.

Her fingers brushed the dark thatch of hair at the juncture of her thighs.

His fingers brushed his.

She widened her stance.

His body caught fire.

She slid those delicate fingers between her legs and moaned again as she stroked the nub hidden there.

Étienne fisted his cock, heart pounding against his ribs as he drew his hand down the long length and squeezed the sensitive tip.

She eased back a step. Water struck the back of her neck and sluiced down over her shoulders, rinsing the soap away and making her skin gleam as she continued to squeeze and massage one breast while stroking herself between her legs.

She rubbed and circled and pinched her clit, breath coming quick, as her eyes met his. Her hand slid lower. Arching against her palm, she thrust two fingers inside her warm, wet sheath.

His hand tightened on his cock.

"This is where I want you," Krysta whispered, withdrawing her fingers, then thrusting them inside again, imagining it was him.

Étienne's eyes flashed an even brighter amber.

"Only you," she murmured, need rising. "So long and hard and thick."

Muttering something in French, he blurred.

Krysta heard the shower door open, became weightless, then found herself in bed on her back in seconds. Étienne loomed over her, no longer soapy. Muscles bunching, he settled himself between her thighs, then thrust inside her.

Pure pleasure.

Krysta cried out as he buried himself deep, then withdrew and thrust again. And again. And again. Reaching down, she grabbed his ass and urged him on, arching up against him, moaning with every breath.

He cupped the breast she had neglected in one large hand, squeezing and caressing and doing all of the things she had been imagining when she had touched herself.

"I need you," he growled.

I need you, too, she thought, so breathless she couldn't speak.

Fire burned through her. She arched against him. Over and over. So good.

His lips teased the sensitive skin of her neck.

Do it, she urged him.

He reached down between their bodies, sought the source of her pleasure.

An orgasm ripped through her, wringing a cry from her lips as her muscles tightened and her body clenched around his cock.

Pain followed as his fangs pierced her neck.

Krysta's hands clenched, her nails digging into his flesh.

I'm sorry, he thought.

She forced herself to loosen her hold and tried to relax into it. *It's okay.*

He continued to move inside her with slow thrusts. His fingers went to work once more, stroking her clit and sending sparks of renewed pleasure dancing through her.

Her breath caught.

Yeah. That helped.

He thrust harder, squeezed her breast.

That helped *a lot.*

She felt him smile against her.

The pain continued. But he fed the pleasure, building it until she was once more thrusting and straining against him.

Another orgasm swept through her.

Cold began to seep in. As did weariness.

As darkness closed in, she thought she heard him say, *I love you.*

Krysta woke to the feeling of being watched. Frowning, she opened her eyes, then jumped when she found Étienne lying inches away, staring at her intently.

"Don't do that!" she said, heart racing. "You startled me."

"I'm sorry. I didn't mean to. It took you longer to regain consciousness than I expected and I was worried."

"Oh."

She lay there for a moment, taking stock of things. "I don't feel any different."

Smiling, he brushed her hair, still damp from their shower, back from her face. "You will."

He wasn't kidding. Within hours she felt like she had a really bad case of the flu. Nausea. Vomiting. (Étienne was a little miffed when she wouldn't let him hold her hair for her, but she did *not* want him to watch her puke. Gross.) Fever. The worst headache she had ever had in her life.

For someone who hadn't been sick himself in over two centuries, Étienne was surprisingly helpful. He brought her hand-squeezed orange juice mixed with club soda to settle her stomach. Crackers and salty pita chips, too. He kept her supplied with ice packs for her head and a wide selection of DVDs to keep her entertained while the virus raged through her.

He told her stories of his youth. Stories of his immortality.

He even admitted that he and his twin had once wagered over which one of them could go the longest without sex.

"No sex at all?" she asked, fever making it feel like flames were pouring from her eyes.

He nodded. "No sex. No pleasuring oneself. Nothing but cold showers. It was the longest thirty-two years of my life."

"Thirty-two years!"

He nodded, his smile wry.

"Who won?"

"Neither. It was a draw. Lisette found out why we had been so pissy, as she put it, and told us to cut the crap and get laid or she'd tell Seth it was distracting us when we hunted."

She smiled. "What would Seth have done?"

He laughed. "Honestly, I have no idea."

The room began to spin. Her stomach turned over.

She closed her eyes and hoped it would calm. The whole vomiting thing was getting old.

"Krysta."

Had Étienne just said her name? She tried to pry her eyelids open, but couldn't.

Krysta, darling, please wake up.

Wake up? She wasn't asleep. She had just closed her eyes for a second.

Cold needles pricked her skin. Pain pierced her. Everywhere.

Screaming, Krysta finally managed to open her eyes and found herself in a bathtub full of ice and water with Étienne at her back.

Étienne ignored the cold stinging his skin and locked his arms around Krysta, holding her tight as she fought to get out of the tub.

Melanie and David emptied more bags of ice into the water.

Tears threatened as Étienne subdued Krysta. Tears of relief. He had thought he had lost her. He had been talking to her, telling her about that stupid bet, and she had lost consciousness.

There had been no dreams or thought. Her breathing had become shallow.

David had sensed his panic and come to check on her. Melanie had followed. The alarm that had crossed her face when she had taken Krysta's temperature had scared the hell out of him.

Krysta's struggles slowed. Her breath came in pained pants.

Étienne could regulate his body temperature enough to warm her, but that would defeat the purpose. *I'm sorry.*

She didn't think an answer to him. Étienne wasn't even sure she was lucid.

Then one of her hands—shaking violently—rose, clasped one of the arms he had clamped around her, and gave it a light squeeze.

Eyes burning, he dipped his head and buried his face in her hair.

* * *

"Could I just say again that this is awesome?" Krysta asked as they strolled, hand in hand, through UNC's campus in Chapel Hill.

Étienne laughed. "Which part?"

"All of it. Being so strong and fast. Being able to see so much. I can't believe I can walk around in the dark without a flashlight now."

Grinning, he shook his head. She had been immortal for a couple of weeks now and had made the adjustment beautifully. She wasn't even squeamish about infusing herself with blood, though he suspected that would have been vastly different if she actually had to *drink* it.

"I can hear *everything*," she marveled. "Which can be kinda creepy. I've never paid much attention to wildlife, so I don't know what animals are making the sounds I keep hearing and I'm hearing a *lot* of sounds. And the smells . . . So many! Good *and* bad."

"It's heady, isn't it?" he asked.

"It really is." She leaned into him and sent him a flirtatious look. "You smell very good, by the way."

"As do you."

"Those vampires," she said, "on the other hand, do *not* smell good. They smell like . . . old blood or rancid meat or something."

"Excellent." He had caught their scent only seconds before she had. "How many are there?"

Her nostrils flared as she drew in a deep breath. "Four."

"How far away?"

"That one's harder." She bit her lip. "A mile?"

"Almost two."

She swore. "I'm still having a hard time judging distance."

"It will become easier as you grow more accustomed to your heightened senses. The vamps are also traveling quickly, so that can throw you off."

"Oh."

"Sounds like they're headed for Keenan Stadium. Let's see if we can't keep them from tearing it up for shits and giggles. That's a saying, right?"

She laughed. "You can ease up on the slang now. We're together."

He grimaced. "I just don't want you to think I'm too old for you."

"I don't. And, if I ever had—which I didn't—one night in bed with you would have convinced me otherwise."

"Minx. Don't arouse me before a fight."

"Why not? It might distract the vampires."

He laughed. "I guess it would. Let's go."

Holding her hand, he sped toward UNC's football stadium. Halfway there, he stopped short, jerking Krysta to a halt, too.

"Ow," she complained, rubbing her shoulder. "Maybe we shouldn't hold hands when we run at preternatural speeds."

"Forgive me," he said absently, senses on high alert. He raised her hand to his lips. *Do you smell that? Answer me with a thought.*

She sniffed the air. Her brow furrowed. *Is that . . . gun oil?*

Yes. Let's head up to the roof. He motioned to the building beside them. Since she hadn't had much experience with jumping yet, he lifted her into his arms and nimbly leapt up onto the roof.

I really want to learn how to do that, she said as he lowered her feet to the asphalt.

Étienne pulled the infrared scope from his pocket and raised it to his right eye.

Is it mercenaries? she asked, scanning the darkened campus with her sharp brown eyes.

It took him a moment to confirm it. *Yes. Even with the scope they're hard as hell to locate. There are two in the bushes there.* He pointed. *Two more on that roof nearly hidden by the air-conditioning unit. Another on that one. More on the ground. They must be wearing that camouflage netting I've seen hunters wear. Without the scope, I can't differentiate them from the foliage.*

Wow. These guys are determined. How many are there?

I don't know if I'm seeing them all. There don't seem to be nearly as many as the last time. Maybe a dozen.

He drew her over into the shadows beside the air-conditioning unit and handed her the scope. *I don't think they've spotted us yet.*

So, what's the plan? she asked as she peered through it. *What are we supposed to do with them? Wait. What's that clicking noise?*

Shh. He listened. Counted the clicks until they stopped. *What time is it?*

She consulted her watch. *3:00 AM.*

They must have been ordered to check in at the top of every hour. They were clicking their walkies to give a head count and let their leader know they're still in position and that all is well.

How many clicks were there?

A dozen.

Why do you think there are so few?

I don't know, and we've run out of time to speculate. The vamps are almost here and we can't let the mercenaries get them.

What do you want to do?

He needed to read the minds of the soldiers before he killed them to ensure none possessed any information. The current assumption was that they wouldn't. But he wasn't comfortable with letting the opportunity go by. And then there were the tracking devices he and Krysta both carried. *You take care of the vampires.*

Her eyebrows flew up. *Really? You trust me to do it by myself?*

You could handle those boys with your hands tied behind your back, he said proudly.

Don't you want to read their minds first to see if any are worth recruiting?

They aren't. They're broadcasting as loudly as a bloody boom mobile and I'm getting nothing but depravity. Go get 'em, Tiger.

Are you trying to use slang again or is that a new pet name for me?

Both? I thought, as a warrior, you might want something more fierce than sweetheart.

Rising up onto her toes, she brushed his lips with hers. *I like sweetheart.*

And I love you. Go do your thing.

She drew her swords and grinned. *Will do.*

There's just one more thing . . .

Chapter 17

Krysta confronted the vampires in the shadows where trees and buildings blocked the view of the mercenaries on the rooftops. Only one mercenary lurked nearby, tucked in the bushes several yards away.

Étienne wasn't kidding about the camouflage. If he hadn't told her the mercenary was there, then shown her with the scope, she wouldn't have known it. Even his scent had been dampened so much that it was nearly undetectable.

The vampires stopped short when she halted in front of them.

Yeah. These guys weren't right. Their eyes were glowing and she hadn't even confronted them. Their longish hair was unkempt and greasy. Their clothing looked and smelled as though it hadn't been changed in days and carried the odors of multiple blood types. Their breath alone could kill a person.

Gross. She did *not* want to know what—or whom—they had been eating.

Breathing through her mouth, she watched them take in her presence, her weapons. They presented an interesting contrast. Two of them constantly fidgeted and twitched. The other two stood deathly still, like twisted mannequins.

The last was a little creepy.

Don't underestimate the still ones. They'll be as fast as the others, Étienne spoke in her head.

You just do what you have to do and leave these clowns to me, she ordered.

They didn't ask if she was an Immortal Guardian. They just attacked.

Krysta began to swing her swords. Her new speed, coupled with her ability to see their auras and anticipate their actions, made it seem as though they moved in slow motion. She struck with such unerring accuracy that they didn't have a chance.

Don't get cocky, Étienne warned.

I think you've said that before.

She killed them all with an ease that astonished her, earning only the most superficial of wounds herself.

The mercenary there in the bushes will try to tranq you now, Étienne warned. *Act swiftly.*

Sheathing her weapons, she raced toward the bushes in a zigzag pattern.

Sure enough, a damned dart shot past her, nearly nicking her ear.

Reaching through the foliage, she knocked the tranq gun from the mercenary's hands, seemingly by accident, and yanked him out into the open.

He was younger than she had expected. Sean's age. Maybe less. For some reason she had thought he would be older. Face rough-hewn and hard. Skin lined and leathery from too many hours in the sun.

This guy's skin was smooth and clean-shaven.

Eyes wide, he reached for the tactical knife on his belt.

Krysta knocked it from his grasp and, clutching the front of his shirt with one hand, yanked him close. So close the automatic rifle hooked to the strap around his neck was forced to the side and back, out of reach.

"Run," she ordered, calling upon all of her high school drama class lessons to present a facade of fear.

"What?" he asked as he pried at her hand.

"Run!" She unobtrusively planted a tracking device on his rifle, then grasped his shirt with both hands and shook. "While you still have a chance. He's coming. He'll kill you!"

"You're one of them!" he spat, unable to break her hold.

"I was turned against my will." She wished she could squeeze out a few tears, but wasn't that good an actress. "I—"

"What are you doing?" Étienne demanded behind her.

The mercenary's fear magnified as he looked over her shoulder.

Krysta released her hold on the mercenary and moved to his side.

When he gripped his rifle, she stayed him. "Don't. You'll just piss him off. Run!"

"What the hell are you doing?" Étienne demanded. *Remember what I told you. Give it your all. He has to think it's real.* He charged toward her.

Heart stopping with dread, Krysta drew back her fist and swung with all of her preternatural might. Pain shot up her arm as her fist hit his jaw.

Étienne, with all of the flair of a stuntman in a freaking action-adventure blow-'em-up movie, flew backward and struck the wall of the building behind him with a grunt, then collapsed to the ground.

"Go!" she shouted at the mercenary, who gaped first at Étienne and then at Krysta.

He reached for the walkie on his shoulder.

She shook her head. "They're all dead. I heard him kill them. It's why he left me to fend for myself with those monsters who attacked me."

He tried the walkie anyway and got nothing, his panic palpable.

Étienne rose with a groan, eyes glowing with what the

mercenary no doubt took for promised retribution, but Krysta suspected was actually . . .

Was that desire?

She grabbed the mercenary by the shoulder and gave him a shove to get him moving.

Whatever it was, she didn't want to have to hit Étienne again. Her hand was throbbing and she didn't like hurting him. "Go, damn it!" she cried. "Run!"

"Come with me," he said, shocking the hell out of her.

Either she was a better actress than she had thought or he wanted to score points with his superiors by *capturing* an immortal.

Shaking her head, she looked at Étienne. "He'll catch me. He *always* catches me. And he'll torture you for helping me." She added a hitch to her breath and was pleased at how close to a sob it sounded. "Just go."

He did.

As the mercenary's feet pounded the pavement, Étienne stalked toward her. *Hold your breath and tense your neck muscles.*

She didn't ask why, just did it.

Étienne wrapped the fingers of one hand around her throat and lifted her off her feet just as the mercenary's footsteps slowed and he turned to look back.

Krysta wrapped her hands around Étienne's wrist and kicked her feet, pretending to fight even as she used her new strength to push herself up and ease the pressure on her neck.

Étienne wrapped an arm around her and shot off into the night. The hold on her neck became a caress. Krysta took several deep breaths as the campus swept past. Étienne jumped. The ground fell away and she found herself on the roof of . . .

Actually Krysta didn't know the name of this building. But they were still on campus and could see the mercenary in the distance.

Étienne set her down, drew out his phone, and dialed.

"Reordon," Chris answered.

It was so odd to be able to hear both sides of the conversation without the phone being on speaker.

"It's Étienne. We tagged a mercenary at UNC Chapel Hill. He's fleeing the campus, heading south on foot. I need a cleanup crew to come collect the eleven dead or unconscious mercenaries he left behind."

He hung up before Chris could say anything, pocketed the phone, and yanked Krysta into his arms. "I'm sorry. I had to make it look real. I didn't hurt you, did I?"

"No. It was just uncomfortable for a second."

His arms tightened as he swore in French. (She was beginning to recognize some words now.)

"What about you?" she asked to distract him. "Am I wrong, or did my knocking the crap out of you turn you on?"

Leaning back, he summoned a sheepish smile and pressed his hips against hers to let her feel his arousal. "You weren't wrong."

"Really? Are you into the rough stuff?" She had never thought of trying that kind of thing herself.

"I didn't think so," he said with a baffled shake of his head, "But you were"—his glowing eyes grew brighter— "magnificent."

"Hmm. Is this . . . something you want to explore? Sexually?" She wasn't sure how that would work. She knew without trying it that hurting Étienne wouldn't turn her on. And she sure as hell didn't want *him* to hurt *her*. Pain tended to piss her off.

"Not really," he said. "I just adore your strength and seeing you in action aroused me." He hesitated. "I'd try anything you asked me to, though. In bed or out of it. I want you to be happy."

She smiled and shook her head. "Let's leave the pain on the battlefield."

"Agreed." He dipped his head and kissed her.

Her pulse leapt.

As he teased her lips with his tongue, she palmed his erection. "Want to do something about this while we wait for the cleanup crew to arrive?" *She* sure as hell did. She didn't know if it was the adrenaline still coursing through her veins or just knowing that he wanted her, but she was already wet for him, her body tingling and desperate for his touch.

"That depends," he whispered against her lips, leaning into her. "How do you feel about making love in front of an audience?"

"That's not my thing either," she admitted. She had never been an exhibitionist.

A throat cleared. "Then you might want to step away from my brother," Richart drawled behind them, "so I won't get an eyeful."

Krysta yanked her hand away so fast you'd think Étienne's crotch had caught fire.

Spinning around, she found Richart standing there with one eyebrow raised.

"What are *you* doing here?" she asked, face heating.

"Étienne summoned me while he was dealing with the mercenaries."

Krysta glanced back at Étienne. "My, aren't *you* the multi-tasker."

"Forgive me. I forgot I called him as soon as you hit me." *And turned me on. You managed to scatter my thoughts quite efficiently.*

She could understand that. The desire he had sparked in *her* had made her forget about the mercenaries he had left strewn who-knew-where. She smiled. "Okay. You're forgiven." Particularly since Richart's sudden presence had doused her lust as efficiently as a fire hose.

Étienne raised the scope and looked around. "Krysta, would you keep an eye out for more mercenaries while

Richart and I gather together the dead and unconscious soldiers?"

"Sure." She took the scope.

He brushed a kiss across her lips, then motioned for his brother to follow him over the edge of the building.

Krysta raised the scope to her right eye and turned in a slow circle, searching the campus in all directions.

If you get bored, Étienne suddenly spoke in her head, *feel free to talk dirty to me. Richart can't hear you.*

She smiled and did just that.

Sitting on his haunches, Zach took in the melee below. UNC Greensboro's campus was quiet and deserted save the immortal warrior who battled five vampires down on the ground.

A rare smile lifted his lips.

She was magnificent, remaining in constant motion, swinging her blades with merciless intent.

The vampires Lisette fought had long since lost their grasp on sanity. Zach searched their thoughts easily, and the things they wanted to do to her sickened him.

A vamp got in a lucky strike.

Blood formed a glistening streak across the back of her long coat.

Zach rose and curled his hands into fists, an unfamiliar feeling sweeping over him.

The lucky striker went down and began to shrivel up. His friends trod upon him in slavering urgency.

Again she struck a killing blow. Another vampire fell.

A noise distracted Zach. Then a scent.

He searched the darkened campus with eyes that needed no infrared scope to pierce the deepest shadows.

Human males with automatic weapons closed in on Lisette's location.

Mercenaries.

He hadn't expected this. He had merely wanted, for reasons he couldn't discern, to see her in action. He hadn't wanted to see her captured.

The hours he had spent watching Seth and his little super-heroes, coupled with the hours he had spent eavesdropping at David's house, had revealed what these men would likely do to her if they caught her.

The last vampire fell. Breathing hard, she cleaned her blade on the shirt of one of the fallen vamps and sheathed her weapons.

The humans took their positions.

A dart struck her in her pale, vulnerable neck.

Wincing, she reached up to identify the source of the sharp pain. Alarm crossed her pretty face as she staggered. She pulled something that looked like a fat, white pen from her pocket and stabbed herself in the thigh with it.

The mercenaries closed in, forming a circle around her.

Lisette dropped the pen and straightened.

A tense moment passed. Then another.

Zach took a step forward.

Moving so fast she blurred, Lisette drew her Glock 18s and raced toward the building on her left.

Muffled gunfire erupted as she leapt up a couple of stories, pushed off the side of the building and landed on the roof of the building across from it.

The soldiers scattered as she sprayed them with bullets from above. Four went down as holes opened on their torsos.

She jerked, bullets tearing through her slender body as the mercenaries scored hits of their own, but didn't cease firing or run away.

Zach clenched his teeth.

She couldn't win. She *wouldn't* win.

And she lacked the time to call her brothers for aid.

She backed up and crouched down. Ejecting the long clips from her weapons, she drew two more from a pocket of her coat and shoved them into place.

Zach had never handled a gun before and admired her smooth, sure movements.

Staying out of sight of the men below, she headed for the opposite side of the building and leapt to the ground.

The mercenary group divided into thirds. One third remained in place. The rest divided in half and began to circle the building on both sides.

Shit!

Lisette sped into the open, crossing to the next building, and sprayed the soldiers with bullets.

They jerked and fell to the ground, only getting off a few shots of their own.

Maybe he had been too hasty. Maybe she *would* actually come out the victor.

No sooner had the thought struck than a dozen more mercenaries entered the fray.

Lisette raced directly into their midst, wreaking havoc, breaking necks, cutting throats, and taking more bullets and tranquilizer darts.

The darts didn't worry him. He had heard the immortals say the antidote prevented further exposure to the sedative from affecting them. But the bullet wounds . . .

Instead of healing, they continued to bleed, a symptom of the weakness infiltrating her and spreading within as she continued to lose blood.

His heart pounded. His breath shortened.

She was slowing down. Still fighting. Still slaying. But slowing down. Suffering more wounds.

The soldiers tightened ranks, again boldly encircling her.

He sensed no fear in her, only a determination to take out as many as she could before she breathed her last breath.

Well, fuck that.

Knowing the step he was about to take would forever alter his future, Zach released his wings and took to the air.

Panting, gritting her teeth against the pain, Lisette swung her shoto sword at the soldier in front of her and sliced open his chest.

How many were there? It seemed as though every time she slew one, two more took his place.

And she was weakening, moving almost as slowly as a human, losing the edge immortal speed and strength had given her.

A breeze coaxed some of her hair from its braid.

She felt a presence behind her.

The mercenaries all gasped and stumbled backward, looking over her shoulder.

Lisette spun around . . . and gaped.

It was him. The elder immortal she, Roland, and Sarah had interrogated.

Zach.

Facing away from her, he wore only low-riding dark leather pants similar to the ones he had sported when she had abducted him. His wings were stretched wide, their tips brushing the walls of nearby buildings.

More than one of the mercenaries crossed themselves.

Zach waved a hand.

The mercenaries dropped their weapons to the ground with a clatter.

Lisette glanced behind her.

Yes. Those had dropped their weapons, too.

Dizziness assailed her.

She staggered, barely managing to remain on her feet. She had lost count of the number of times she had been shot.

Darkness threatened.

She couldn't think, didn't know what was happening.

Was Zach working with the mercenaries?

She stared at the back of his head, at his windblown, longish, raven hair.

"You," he said, pointing at a soldier.

The mercenary stepped forward.

The elder immortal made a motion with his hand and closed it into a fist. The other mercenaries all collapsed to the ground, sightless eyes wide as they drew their last breaths.

Those beautiful wings folded in against Zach's back.

He turned to face her.

Lisette tilted her head way back to look up at him. He was well over a foot taller than she was and she stood at five foot six.

"The tracking device," he said, his glowing golden eyes locking on hers.

"W-what?" she rasped.

He held out a large hand, palm up. "The tracking device you're supposed to plant on him. Give it to me."

She dropped one of her beloved shoto swords and fumbled with the outer pocket that contained the tiny tracking device Chris had given her. Her fingers wouldn't cooperate. She couldn't even get the pocket open and it wasn't buttoned.

Zach gently brushed her hand aside and tucked his own hand in the pocket. When he withdrew it, the tracking device was carefully pinched between his thumb and forefinger.

He waved the mercenary over.

The soldier approached robotically and waited patiently while the immortal picked up one of the discarded M16s, then attached the device to it.

Lisette wanted to protest when he handed the man the weapon, but couldn't find enough breath for it.

"You saw neither of us tonight. Vampires attacked your squad and only you survived," Zach said.

The mercenary nodded, then turned and jogged away.

Zach swiveled to face her.

"M-mind control?" she managed to ask.

He nodded.

She tried to ask about the others, but could only motion to them.

"Ruptured aneurysms. I've never altered the health of a human before and am actually surprised it worked."

She nodded. Her knees buckled.

Zach caught her before she could hit the ground. "Easy," he said, his voice soft and deep. Kneeling, he laid her on the ground with her upper body cradled in his lap.

Moonlight formed a halo around his head as she stared up at him, struggling for breath.

The bullets had done a lot of damage. She knew that, rather than kill her, excessive damage would send her into a sort of stasis not unlike the hibernation of a water bear. But she had never done that before and couldn't help but fear the prospect as she felt her heart rate slow. And slow some more.

He rested a hand on her chest.

At first she thought he was feeling her up and forgot everything else in a few seconds' shock. Then she realized his thumb rested upon her collarbone and his fingers weren't splayed enough to reach her breasts.

His hand heated, warm and comforting. A tingling feeling engulfed her, part pleasure and part pain, beginning in her chest and sweeping down her arms to her fingers, down her torso to her thighs, calves, and toes. Misshapen bullets emerged from her flesh. Bleeding ceased. Wounds closed. Bones shattered by bullets fused themselves back together.

Her collapsed lung reinflated. Her breathing grew easier. The pain receded, then vanished entirely.

He removed his hand from her chest, curling it into a loose fist, then rubbing his thumb against his fingers as though touching her had made *him* tingle.

She sat up, but didn't move away. Just to double check, she pulled the neckline of her sticky shirt away from her body and peered down through it at her bare chest and bra-encased breasts. No wounds. Only dried blood.

She let the material fall back against her and stared up at him, too tired to attempt to stand yet. He had healed her wounds, but severe blood loss still rendered her weak.

A shiver shook her.

He unfurled his beautiful wings and cupped them around her like a tent, keeping the breeze at bay.

"Who *are* you?" she asked when she could find her voice. "Really?"

"Zach," he said simply.

"That only tells me your name, not who you are."

He shrugged. "Seth calls me Cousin."

"You're Seth's cousin?" *Merde*. He really *was* an elder. She had never heard of any immortal other than David being so close to their leader in age. Or who may actually be able to match his power.

And that had been quite a power display, killing the mercenaries without even touching them.

"Why have I never heard of you?" she asked. "Why don't you ever come inside when you visit David's? Why do you keep your presence a secret?"

"Neither Seth nor David would want me there."

"Why? Did you have a falling-out?"

He seemed to weigh his words. "Seth and I chose different paths when we were still young men and disagreed with each other's choices."

David would have, of course, taken Seth's side. He and Seth were like brothers.

"Are you enemies?" She was pretty sure she would have heard about it if this man had been actively trying to kill Seth or wage war with him.

"No."

Just no. Nothing more.

She had a feeling she wasn't going to get anything more specific than that, but tried anyway. "So, you're immortal, but don't lead the life of an Immortal Guardian? You don't hunt vampires or have a Second?"

"Correct."

"Until tonight."

"Technically, I let *you* slay the vampires, then took care of the mercenaries when you faltered."

And saved her life. Had he not stepped in when he did, the mercenaries would have captured her. "So you intervened where, in the past, you would not have."

He hesitated. "Yes."

"Why?"

He clenched and unclenched his jaw. "I couldn't let them take you."

"Why?"

His brow furrowed. "I don't know."

If she didn't need blood so badly just then, she was sure her heart would have begun to beat faster.

Had he veered from his chosen path for *her?*

"You need blood," he pointed out.

She nodded, a shock of excitement darting through her at the idea of leaning into him, pressing against that wide, muscled, bare chest, and touching her lips to his neck.

"I can't give you mine," he said, his deep voice full of . . . regret?

"Okay." What the hell was she doing? Was she *attracted* to

him? A man who had freely admitted he was at odds with Seth, the wisest man she knew and to whom she owed her life and allegiance?

Snapping out of it, she fumbled with her coat, seeking the right pocket and—fingers tangling in a couple of holes—managed to draw out her cell phone.

Or what was left of it. A bullet had forged a hole through it on its way to her liver.

Wonderful.

"May I borrow your phone?" she asked. "I need to call my Second." Tracy could take care of notifying Chris that a cleanup crew was needed and have Richart bring Lisette some much-needed blood.

"I don't carry a phone."

Okay. Plan B.

She looked at the lifeless mercenary bodies around them. Tucking them away, out of sight, seemed a monumental task as low on energy and strength as she was right now. And when her energy was low, her telepathic range diminished greatly.

Étienne? she called. Perhaps he and Krysta were hunting nearby.

Nothing. *Étienne! I need you.*

Still nothing.

Richart? She had an even smaller chance of contacting Richart because he couldn't send his reply telepathically. He could only think it and hope she would pick up on it.

"I can take you where you need to go," Zach said, his eyes never leaving her.

She shook her head. "I can't leave these bodies here. I need to contact the network and have them come clean things up, hide what happened from the humans."

He sighed. "If I were a different man, I'd say you owe me one."

One what? And shouldn't being in this powerful immortal's debt alarm her? "For killing the mercenaries and saving me?"

"No, for this." He closed his eyes.

He was so handsome. Straight nose. Strong, shadowed jaw. Ebony brows over eyes so dark a brown they were almost black . . . when they weren't glowing golden. Just like Seth's.

He opened those eyes and met hers. "Help is on the way."

"It is?"

"Can you sit by yourself?"

She hadn't even realized he had been supporting her with an arm behind her back.

"Yes." She sat up straighter.

Withdrawing his arm, he rose and backed away.

"Thank you," she said, sensing he wouldn't stay until help arrived.

He nodded. Bending his knees, he leapt up into the air and brought those powerful wings down, shooting into the sky like a missile and disappearing from sight.

Lisette didn't know what to think. Of him. Of what he had done.

Seth appeared several yards away, his back to her. "What?" he growled. "I don't appreciate being summoned so . . ." He trailed off.

Lisette felt as anxious facing Seth now as she had the first time she had realized just how much power he wielded.

Would he view her interaction with Zach as a betrayal?

He took in the dead mercenaries and turned around. "Lisette!" In a heartbeat, he knelt beside her and touched her shoulder. "Are you all right?"

She nodded. "Just weak. I've lost a lot of blood."

A couple of humans strolled in their direction, not yet in sight of the carnage.

Seth waved a hand in their direction, mentally guiding them

away. "I was summoned here by another," he said, studying her closely.

She swallowed. "Zach was here."

No visible reaction. "Did he hurt you?"

"No. He saved me."

A long pause followed, during which she fought the urge to squirm.

Was he reading her thoughts, surfing through them and replaying what had happened?

He drew out his phone and dialed. "Chris? Seth. Send a cleanup crew to UNCG. A couple of dozen mercenaries attacked Lisette and are dead. One fled bearing a tracking device."

He had definitely read her thoughts. Lisette just hoped he hadn't noticed the fascination and, yes, attraction she felt for the other elder.

"They did? Excellent. Keep me posted." He pocketed his phone. "Étienne and Krysta also engaged mercenaries tonight, over at UNC Chapel Hill, and succeeded in planting a tracking device on one. Chris is already tracking him."

"Good."

"Can you hold out until the cleanup crew arrives, or shall I take you home or to David's for blood now?"

"I can wait." For blood. She couldn't wait for a verdict on her encounter with Zach. "Are you angry?" she asked tentatively.

"With you? No."

"With Zach?"

"I haven't decided."

"Who is he, Seth?"

He looked at the bodies around them again. "I'm not sure anymore."

"He said he's your cousin," she pressed.

"Did he?"

A human approached, accompanied by staticky walkie-talkie speech.

Lisette's heart skipped. More mercenaries?

Seth covered her hand with his. "Campus security." He looked in the direction from which the sounds came.

The human's footsteps stopped, then carried him away.

Disturbed's "Down With the Sickness" swelled from Seth's pocket. Retrieving his phone, he answered, "Yes?" He met Lisette's gaze and smiled. "Word travels fast. Yes, she's here. She's fine. Her phone was just destroyed." He held out the phone. "It's Tracy." *Don't mention Zach.*

Lisette took the phone, aware that Seth had neither confirmed nor denied that Zach was his cousin.

"Two mercenaries tagged," he murmured as she assured Tracy she was fine and glossed over what had happened, leaving out Zach. "It's been an interesting night."

Once the immortals and Seconds staying at David's had bedded down for the day, Seth and David retreated to David's study.

Seth told him what had happened with Zach and Lisette.

David's brow furrowed. "He *helped* her?"

Seth nodded, still unsure what to make of it.

"How did he kill the mercenaries? I didn't think he carried a weapon."

"He told Lisette he gave them all ruptured aneurysms."

"That takes both power and precision."

"He must be practicing."

"On whom? And why?"

"I don't know."

Perhaps when Seth had warned Zach months ago that the Others couldn't best him because Seth had been exercising and growing his powers, it had struck a nerve.

"How did he even know Lisette was in trouble?" David asked.

"I suspect he was following her."

"Why would he do that?"

"She, Roland, and Sarah captured him a couple of weeks ago and interrogated him."

David's eyebrows nearly met his hairline. "I assume he *let* them."

"Yes."

"Why?"

"I don't know. Not yet."

"What did they ask him?"

"He's been seeing Ami. They wanted to know why."

David's face filled with pure menace. "By *seeing* her . . ."

"He's been meeting with her on your roof."

Utter disbelief mingled with the menace. "How did I not sense his presence?"

Seth shook his head. "He's learned to mask it in some way. I didn't even sense it myself. Had I not read Lisette's thoughts, I would not have known anything about it."

Judging by his expression, the idea that Zach could come and go without their knowledge unsettled David as much as it did Seth.

"Apparently," Seth went on, "Ami *can* detect his presence and joins him up on the roof whenever he pulls gargoyle duty up there."

"In her condition?" David said with disapproval.

Seth snorted. "She's as sure-footed as a cat and has exhibited no dizziness thus far. I don't think we have any worries there."

David grunted. "So he can mask his presence, but not his energy signature."

"Yes."

"What is Ami's interest in him?"

"I don't know," Seth admitted. He seemed to be saying that a lot lately. "I think that's the biggest puzzle of all."

David frowned. "You don't think it's romantic, do you?"

"No. Ami sees no one but Marcus in that light."

"I agree." David pondered the mystery for some time. "Perhaps he reminds her of you."

Seth grimaced. "I hope not."

The sound of a car turning onto the long drive caught his ear. He looked toward the front of the house the same time David did.

A window rolled down so the driver could lean out and punch in the security code.

The music of Miles Davis floated to their ears.

"Chris," they said in unison.

Reordon always played Miles when he was stressed.

The car seemed to crawl up the lane so slowly Seth thought Chris could have walked and reached the house faster. The engine stopped. His car door opened and closed.

"Does Chris ever sleep?" David asked as they followed his progress up the walk and through the front door.

"Not much. Not enough. But he refuses to delegate."

Footsteps approached from the hallway.

"You ever been to his place?" Seth asked.

David nodded. "Looked like a typhoon hit it."

"Come on, guys," Chris complained, entering. "I'm right here."

"We know," they said.

He dropped a briefcase on the floor and flopped down in the chair next to Seth, across the desk from David.

"How did the tracking go?" Seth asked.

"Very well." He opened the briefcase, drew out a folded piece of paper, then leaned forward and spread a map out on the desk. "Both mercenaries headed for the same rendezvous point here." He pointed to an area on the outskirts of Chapel

Hill. "They remained there until daybreak, presumably to ensure they weren't followed by immortals or vampires, then headed *here* on wheels they must have stashed somewhere because they moved much more quickly." He pointed to an isolated area between Mebane and Saxapahaw. "Again, they waited, then were probably taken blindfolded by someone they met there—if the mercenaries stayed true to what they did before—to what I believe is the PMC's base here near Burlington."

He reached into his bag again and drew out an iPad. "Here's a satellite image of the area," he said, bringing it up for them.

Seth set the tablet on the desk so David could examine it, too, and leaned forward. "Did one of your new contacts send you this?"

"No. I'm leery of risking their involvement."

Seth hesitated to say anything. Chris still labored under the ass-load of guilt piled on his shoulders after discovering that his former contacts *and* their spouses and children, had all been either tortured to death or shot execution style by the last mercenary group they had fought in an attempt to extract information and send a message. But one of the things that made Chris indispensable to the Immortal Guardians was his ability to recruit contacts in very high places. Contacts who had been invaluable in the past. "Chris—"

"I know. I'll get there. I will. If I thought lives depended on it now, I would risk it in a heartbeat," he said.

"Then where did you get this?" Seth tapped the satellite image of a building surrounded by forest.

"This is a map I got off the Internet. You can get satellite images of just about any place on the net by typing in the address or GPS coordinates, but the images are often out of date."

"I don't know anything about that," Seth murmured. "I don't have time to explore crap on the Internet."

David nodded. "And I'd rather read a good book when I find a few free minutes."

"Admit it," Chris said. "You're both just a couple of old farts who are technologically challenged."

"True."

"Admitted without shame."

Chris smiled and shook his head. "You can zoom out or in by pressing these buttons."

David pressed the zoom out minus sign a couple of times and studied the area. "So this is probably out of date? The mercenaries could have expanded the structure or added security features?"

"Yes. This looks pretty generic, so I think you can pretty much bet on it. If they transport the mercenaries blindfolded and in windowless vehicles, I'm pretty damned sure they're going to have every kind of security and surveillance feature they can afford."

Seth caught David's gaze. "Shall we go have a look?"

"I'm game."

Chris slumped farther down in his chair. "I'll wait here until you get back. Give me a call if you get into trouble."

"Go lie down," David urged him, rising.

Chris shook his head, eyelids heavy. "I'm good here."

"You said it yourself," Seth pressed. "We're a couple of old farts, not youngsters."

"Several thousand years your senior," David added.

"So you don't have to baby us," Seth finished.

"To quote Sheldon and Melanie: Says you."

The elders laughed and shook their heads. Striding from the room, they headed down the hallway, out the front door, and into bright afternoon sunlight.

"Teleport or fly?" Seth offered.

David closed his eyes and turned his face up to the sun. "Fly."

That had been his choice as well. Flying was a real stress reliever.

The shadows they cast on the brick path morphed into that of large vultures as he and David shifted form and took to the sky.

Chapter 18

North Carolina was a beautiful state. The area above which Seth and David soared boasted rolling hills and meadows, corn fields, hay fields, and forest. Rivers and streams wended through the countryside like arteries, feeding numerous lakes and ponds. Wildlife abounded. And the two eldest immortals were not the only "carrion birds" surfing the breeze.

A vulture that shared their glossy black wings joined them, searching the ground below to see what had caught their attention and regarding them curiously.

Inwardly, Seth smiled.

I needed this, David said.

I did, too.

The trip did not take long by air. Soon the land beneath them began to mimic the satellite image Chris had shown them. There were differences, as he had warned. Fewer trees, thanks to logging and a new housing development under construction that was still in the skeletal stage. The mercenaries probably wouldn't like that. They wouldn't want neighbors so close to their home base.

That must be it, he said as the thick trees beyond parted, revealing a building that looked quite different from the one in the dated satellite image.

The mercenaries had doubled its width, but the different-colored roofs—old and new—allowed Seth to discern the original structure. The flowering trees in front of it had been removed, leaving a large open area and a small parking lot. Two large hangars rested like small football stadiums nearby. Barracks that reminded him of those their previous mercenary enemy had employed formed rows between the main building and the hangars. A nice collection of Black Hawk helicopters rested on helipads beside the hangars, in which Seth glimpsed armored personnel carriers and Humvees.

All was surrounded by a twenty-foot fence woven throughout and topped with razor wire.

As with the other PMC encampment, one road led in and out and required inspection by guards armed with automatic weapons.

Déjà vu, David uttered.

Seth agreed. It was all very similar to Emrys's base, to which Donald and Nelson had been frequent visitors.

Do you think all mercenary bases look like this? David asked.

I know little about them, Seth confessed.

Each building bore surveillance cameras. The main building bore two different-colored bricks where Seth guessed they had replaced windows with walls. The front door was steel.

More soldiers, bearing automatic weapons, walked the grounds and the perimeter.

I'm getting a bad feeling, David said.

So was Seth. The feeling that they had indeed screwed up and missed something. The similarities were too numerous. This base was too reminiscent of the other. Coupled with the knowledge that these men had acquired the tranquilizer, Seth could only conclude that—

We must have missed something, David announced grimly.

Yes.

Do you think it's Donald and Nelson?

Their memories were wiped, so if it is them, they're operating on whatever information the hard drive or whatever gadget we missed contained.

Which could be a little or a lot.

Their feathered companion swung away just as a scent reached Seth.

You smell that? he asked.

Death.

They banked, circling around to follow the vulture to its feast.

"Are those vultures?" he heard a guard down below ask.

"Yeah. I told you the body was too close. If the wind changes it's gonna smell like shit."

The vulture led them to the body of a mercenary who had been shot in the head.

Seth and David joined the bird in circling above it.

Do you think it's one of the men Lisette, Étienne, and Krysta tagged? David asked.

I'm not sure. Why kill only one of them?

And, if they killed him because they found the tracking device, why are they still here? Why aren't they all bugging out?

Let's widen our circles so we can fly over without raising suspicion and pick their brains. Perhaps they're busy designing a trap if they think we know where they are.

Reading the minds of the guards from this distance was a challenge, simply because maintaining this form already took a lot of concentration, but both elders could do it.

You weren't exaggerating, David said. Had they been in their usual forms, Seth knew David would be shaking his head. *They know almost nothing about the outfit that employs them.*

Most don't care because it pays so well.

I'm not hearing anything about traps. No anticipation of our arrival.

Nor any mention of the tracking devices.

They seem to regard the slain one as a betrayer, yet can't say why.

They were told he had betrayed them, but not how.

A couple more vultures joined them, circling the carcass below.

I'm going to read the minds of the men in the hangars and the barracks, Seth said. *You take the men in the main building.*

It was a time-consuming task. Holding these forms for extended lengths sapped their energy, but neither complained. What they learned here could save lives.

By the time they finished, half a dozen vultures were picking the dead soldier's bones clean.

I got nothing, David said at length. *None are aware of any plans to capture us. No one has been warned about or knows anything about the tracking devices. And, while they're all speculating and coming up with their own ideas, none know why the dead soldier was deemed a traitor.*

Apparently only the commander of the army knows why and he isn't here.

And, of course, they don't know where he is. This is ridiculous, David said with irritation he rarely exhibited. *There is a point at which gullibility ceases and stupidity begins.*

I know. They passed that point as soon as they saw their first paycheck and, because they assume that everything they are doing is legal and at the behest of some government contract, they have no problem with the killing.

Money has made them imbeciles!

They were imbeciles before that. The money just gave them a chance to confirm it. How are you holding up? Generally the only time David's mellow temperament succumbed to irritation or anger was when he was in pain. They had been out in the strong midday sun for a few hours now while expending large amounts of energy to retain the forms of vultures. While Seth was weary, David was probably really feeling it by now.

I could use some blood, he admitted reluctantly.

We aren't going to learn any more here today. Let's head home.

The fact that David didn't protest told Seth the pain was substantial. He should have asked David to shift forms and wait on the ground in the shade at least an hour ago.

Five miles beyond the fence, Seth banked toward the ground.

David followed without question.

Seth shifted just above the grass and landed on his feet.

David did the same, but stumbled.

Seth braced him until he could get his balance, then drew him into the shade of a nearby tree and placed his hand on David's chest, absorbing his pain. "Forgive me. I lost track of time."

"I didn't. We needed the information."

When David sighed with relief and nodded, Seth removed his hand and clapped him on the shoulder, teleporting them home.

"You seem nervous," Krysta said, eyeing Étienne with some concern. The only other time she had seen him this nervous was when he had been about to ask Seth if she could be transformed.

Even facing multiple vampires and mercenaries didn't make him nervous. So what was up?

The two continued to arm themselves for the night's hunt while she awaited his response. Cam was training with Sean in the home gym down in the basement.

Sean hadn't been as pissed as she had thought he would be

when she had transformed. He actually had seemed relieved that she would now be much safer when hunting.

Étienne cleared his throat and opened his mouth. Let it hang open. Closed it and turned back to the cabinet in which he kept his many daggers.

"Oh, come on. It can't be that bad," she coaxed. "Can it?"

He gave her a quick glance from the corner of his eye. "Do you have enough daggers?"

"Just tell me what it is!" she blurted, then clamped her lips shut. "I'm sorry. It's just that imagining whatever catastrophe might make *you* nervous is beginning to make *me* nervous."

"It isn't a catastrophe," he muttered. "Or wasn't. I seem to be making it one. Cam warned me I would, damn him for being right."

She pursed her lips.

Crossing to him, she took the dagger from his hand, slipped it into its sheath and turned him to face her. "What's wrong, sweetie?"

He smiled. "Have I mentioned how much I like it when you call me that?"

She smiled. "Yes. So, what's up?"

He leaned back against the cabinet and crossed his arms over his chest. "I talked to Chris earlier. He mentioned assigning you your own Second now that you're immortal and said he has a couple of houses in mind for you and Sean to choose from."

"Oh." Her stomach sank. She had thought . . .

Well, she *hadn't* thought. Not about this.

When she and Sean had first moved in, living with Étienne and Cam had been a temporary arrangement. She had even mentioned staying in a hotel. But then she had gotten to know Étienne and fallen hard for him. They had made love and admitted their feelings for each other. He had transformed her and helped her adjust to her new condition. They had spent nights hunting together and days . . .

She hadn't slept in "her" bedroom in weeks. She spent the days with him in his. The subject of moving out had just never come up.

"I don't want you to go," he said.

Relief left her buoyant. "I don't either. I mean, we never talked about it and I don't want to push you into anything you aren't ready for—"

"I love you, Krysta." He straightened and took her hands. "I don't think I could sleep without you beside me. I don't *want* to sleep without you beside me. And I want you to be right there with me every evening when I wake up."

"Me, too."

He pulled her into his arms and claimed her lips in a kiss that seemed to carry with it everything she felt herself: relief, excitement, lust, love . . .

"Too bad we have that meeting tonight," he said, trailing heated kisses down her neck.

Her pulse leapt. "We're both immortal now. Can't immortals have quickies?"

He laughed. "Immortals give quickies a whole new meaning. But . . ." He drew his hands up her sides and brushed her breasts with his thumbs. "I like to savor you."

"That disappoints me and excites me all at the same time."

He brushed her lips with his once more. "So you'll stay with me? You'll live here with me?"

"Yes." Happily.

"How would you feel if I told you that I'm an old-fashioned guy—"

"I already knew that."

"—and wish to marry you and spend the rest of eternity as your husband?"

She stopped breathing. "You want to marry me?" Marriage was big for immortals. For them, *'til death do us part* could mean hundreds, even thousands, of years.

"More than anything," he vowed, the sincerity in his voice unmistakeable.

Krysta threw her arms around his neck and squeezed him tight.

"Is that a yes?" he asked, sliding his arms around her and burying his face in her hair.

"Yes. A very enthusiastic yes!"

He hugged her close and said with some regret, "I wanted more time to woo you."

She grinned. "To what me?"

He popped her lightly on the butt. "Stop mocking me."

She laughed. "I can't help it. It's fun."

Straightening, he brushed her hair back from her forehead and cupped her face in his large hands. "I wanted to spend months courting you properly. I *planned* to spend months courting you properly once we'd quashed this latest threat. But Chris kept mentioning the damned house . . ."

"Étienne, you *have* been courting me."

"No, I haven't. All we've done since we met is train and fight vampires and mercenaries."

"Sweetie, I'm not a flowers and chocolates kind of gal," she said, leaning into him. "Well, maybe the chocolate."

"I was going to say."

She laughed. He had seen her put away a *lot* of chocolate. "I don't need flowers. I don't need jewelry. I don't need . . . whatever other frilly things men give the women they're dating." She hadn't dated anyone long-term since Michael and couldn't remember what men usually brought their girlfriends. "I need weapons. And you have given me some *beautiful* weapons."

She no longer carried Lisette's weapons. Étienne had, over the weeks, gifted her with her own personal arsenal. Shoto swords. Katanas. Daggers. Throwing stars. Glock 18s. Sigs. Her very own uncomfortable rubbery suit to wear if she had to venture into daylight.

"We've talked for hours," she said. "We've laughed and flirted and teased." She nipped his chin. "Seduced."

"You're very good at that," he said, voice deepening.

"Which one?"

He began to move from side to side, the two of them swaying to slow, nonexistent music. "All of them."

She smiled. "You see? We're even dancing."

"Is that what this is? I was just enjoying the feel of you against me."

She shrugged. "That's what we called it at my high school prom." And she was loving the feel of his hard body pressed to hers.

"Dancing was very different in my day."

"Would you teach me?"

"I would love to."

A throat cleared.

Cam and Sean stood in the doorway.

Cam raised his eyebrows. "Should I call and tell them you'll be late for the meeting?"

Smiling, Étienne shook his head. "No. And you were wrong. It wasn't a catastrophe."

Krysta grinned. "We're engaged."

Sean's face brightened. Striding forward, he hugged her and shook Étienne's hand. "Congratulations."

Cam did the opposite, hugging Étienne and shaking Krysta's hand.

"Listen," Sean said, "while we're talking about the future . . ."

"I hope you'll stay with us," Étienne said, then looked to Krysta.

She nodded. "Absolutely." Unlike many siblings she knew, they rarely fought. And, since Cam already lived with them, it wasn't as if Sean would be intruding upon their privacy or anything.

Sean tucked his hands in his pockets, a nervous gesture

she hadn't seen him make in a long time. "Actually, I've come to a decision."

She didn't like the sound of that, nor the somber look on his face. Had he changed his mind about working for the network? He had seemed very happy working with Dr. Lipton these last few weeks.

"Étienne," Sean said, "I would like you to transform me."

Krysta's jaw hit the floor. "What?"

Sean held up his hands. "Now, hear me out—"

"That would be awesome!" she practically shouted.

Sean blinked. "What?"

Jumping up and down, she tugged on Étienne's arm. "You have to do it! That would be so cool! You have to do it! You have to do it!"

Étienne hesitated. He didn't want to disappoint Krysta or squash her excitement, especially after she had just *made his existence* by agreeing to be his wife, but . . . "Are you sure?" he asked Sean.

"I'm sure. If you doubt me, read my mind."

Étienne did and found, to his relief, absolute certainty.

"I'm as proficient with weapons as Krysta is," Sean said, "so I wouldn't require a lot of training."

Krysta nodded. "He's good. He really is."

Étienne smiled. She was like a child trying to convince a parent to buy her that one special toy she wanted for Christmas. "What about medical school?"

Krysta sobered. "Oh. Crap. I forgot about that."

"I didn't," Sean said. "Since I'll be able to do *everything* faster, including read, I can finish my studies in record time under Dr. Lipton's instruction. She has already agreed to oversee my education and I can serve my residency at network headquarters."

Étienne was impressed. "Sounds like you've considered everything."

"I have. When I'm not studying, I'll be able to hunt instead of having to sit on the sidelines as I have for the last six years." His thoughts revealed just how much that had bothered him. "I'll be able to heal—Krysta or anyone else who needs it—without risking my life. And I could potentially live forever."

With everything that had been happening in recent years, the enemies who had risen up against them, the Immortal Guardians could use another healer in the area. "As long as Seth grants his approval, I'll do it."

Squealing, Krysta threw her arms around Étienne and hugged him tight, then hugged her brother.

Cam clapped Sean on the back. "Congratulations."

"Thanks."

"So . . . you're okay with what will happen when Étienne bites you?"

Sean nodded. "Dr. Lipton told me what to expect and I saw what Krysta went through with the illness, so yeah."

Face solemn, Cam shook his head. "I wasn't talking about the illness. I was talking about the other thing."

What other thing? Étienne asked him silently. *What are you doing?*

Just having a little fun with him. Play along.

"What other thing?" Sean asked, smile fading.

Cam lowered his voice conspiratorially. "You know. The intense sexual bond it will forge between you two."

Étienne was looking at Krysta when Cam made the absurd claim and nearly burst into laughter. Lightning fast, her eyes widened, she flashed all of her teeth in a grin, then sobered just as Sean turned a stricken gaze upon her.

She nodded solemnly. "It's true."

You are so bad, he told her.

Don't make me laugh! This is hilarious! Look at his face!

"Dr. Lipton didn't say anything about a sexual bond," Sean said, the picture of unease.

Krysta shrugged. "She was probably too embarrassed. You're about to become her student. I doubt she wanted you to know she was overcome with lust for Roland and tore his clothes off when he bit her. Especially since she and Bastien were already a couple then," she lied with silent glee.

Cam nodded. "You've seen the movies. Being bitten is always . . . incredibly erotic."

Krysta nodded. "Orgasmic."

Sean swallowed. "Umm . . . Okay. Wait." He actually began to sweat.

Krysta burst out laughing.

Unable to keep a straight face any longer, Étienne did, too. Then Cam.

Realizing he'd been punked, Sean swore and gave Cam a hard shove. "You asshole!"

Cam staggered. "You should have seen your face!"

"Uncool, man." He turned to Krysta. "And you!" Locking an arm around her neck, he drew her down and ruffled the hell out of her hair.

She laughed all the while, letting him do it even though she was strong enough to toss Sean through the roof if she wanted to.

When he released her, Sean smiled wryly up at Étienne. "So you'll transform me?"

"With Seth's permission, yes."

"And there won't be anything sexual?"

"No."

Krysta shook her head, still smiling. "The bite actually hurts like hell. You won't be having any warm and fuzzy feelings for him. Trust me."

"Good." He narrowed his eyes and shook his head. "You guys are so wrong."

"I wanna be a cowboy," a man began to sing to an eighties beat. "And you can be my cowgirl."

Scowling, Étienne glanced around, then realized it was his cell phone. Damn it. He really needed to figure out who kept changing his . . . ringtone. He looked at Cam, whose mirth was unmistakable. "You?" he demanded incredulously. Cam was as staid and stolid as they came.

Or he had been until five minutes ago.

Laughing, Cam shrugged.

"You've been my Second for seven years now and haven't once cracked a joke until tonight."

"Because you were always so somber," Cam said. "I thought you were a stick in the mud like the last immortal I served. Damn, Petrus was boring. I practically begged Chris for a transfer, then you ended up being the same. But you started loosening up after you encountered Krysta." He shrugged. "So I did, too."

Étienne narrowed his eyes. "Remind me to kick your ass later." He answered the call. "Yes?"

"It's me," Lisette said. "I just talked to Chris. We're striking the mercenaries' compound tonight. Come loaded for bear."

Krysta sat at David's dining room table, Étienne on one side of her, Sean on the other, and marveled over how dramatically her life had changed. Two months ago, she and Sean had been struggling to make ends meet and risking their lives every night as they tackled the vampire threat on their own. Exhausted. Lonely. Their futures uncertain.

Tonight she was immortal, even stronger and faster than the vampires she hunted. She fought alongside a powerful immortal warrior she loved and who had asked her to marry him earlier this evening with charming uncertainty. Her brother, still studying medicine, would soon be immortal himself and free of the threat of death if he had to heal her. And the three of them sat at a table, surrounded by more than a dozen other immortals and their Seconds, all of whom would fight to the death if necessary to defend each other *and* her like family.

Yes, the task before them—besieging the mercenary compound—was daunting and made her stomach flutter with nerves. But the future was bright. And, for the first time in years, Krysta was happy.

At least, that was, until she glanced down the table and found Roland staring at her. Again. He had been watching her and studying her ever since she had arrived and it was seriously starting to aggravate her.

Seth and Chris had not yet arrived. Everyone else chatted and joked and wondered aloud if this battle would be as volatile as the last big battle with mercenaries had been.

Krysta hoped not. Étienne had told her about it and about the attack that had inspired it. And it had sounded like something out of a freaking Michael Bay movie.

Beneath the table, Étienne took her hand and rested their entwined fingers on his thigh.

They had decided not to tell anyone they were engaged tonight, since—

Across the table, Lisette sucked in a breath. "You're engaged?"

All conversation stopped as heads whipped around and gazes honed in on her and Étienne.

Krysta stared back, eyes wide.

Crap. She must have been reading my thoughts. "I—"

"Yes," Étienne announced.

Lisette whooped and circled the table so fast she blurred, drawing Krysta into a hug, then squeezing the stuffing out of her brother. "I'm so happy for the two of you."

Richart rose and approached more slowly with a broad grin. He, too, hugged them both, as did Jenna.

When Sheldon rose and tried to hug Krysta, Étienne shoved him aside with a roll of his eyes.

Congratulations and well wishes abounded.

Even the quiet giant, David, sitting at the head of the table on the other side of Sean, wished them happiness and expressed his pleasure over the union.

All retook their seats.

And still Roland stared.

"Okay," Krysta said when she couldn't take it any longer. "*Why* do you keep staring at me?"

Étienne glanced down at her, then followed her gaze to Roland. "He's staring at you?"

"Yes, ever since we arrived."

Étienne frowned. "If you're still pissed because I asked you to transform her—"

"That isn't it. I was trying to recall where we had first met."

"You and me?" Krysta asked with a frown of her own. "Here at David's place the night the mercenaries tore up my house."

Roland shook his head. "No. We met before that. I just couldn't remember where until a few moments ago."

"I'm pretty sure I would remember it if I had met you before."

"Not if you had just been bitten by a vampire."

Her blood chilled. She had only been bitten by a vampire once . . . the night she and Michael had been attacked. "You were there?"

"Yes. I'm the reason the vampires didn't kill you. I intervened when the scent of blood led me to you."

She gripped Étienne's hand like a lifeline. "No. I remember the attack. The chemical—whatever it is—that affects memory when humans are bitten doesn't affect me. The vampires grabbed us, dragged us away from campus, tortured Michael, and fed on me. Then I blacked out from blood loss."

Roland shook his head. "Vampires don't leave witnesses.

Particularly female witnesses. Did you never wonder why they let you live?"

She had. Every day.

Why had they let *her* live and killed Michael?

That single question had spawned a nearly suffocating guilt that had never left her.

"Yes," she said. "But, I don't remember you being there."

David leaned forward, drawing her gaze. "Do you *want* to remember? All of it?"

All these years she had thought she *had* remembered it. "Yes."

He reached past Sean and touched the tip of his middle finger to her temple.

Nothing happened at first. Then images flooded her mind. Memories buried by either the concussion the vamps had given her in their initial attack or the drug the vamp's bite had released into her system.

A drug against which she had believed she was impervious.

She saw it all at lightning speed. Strolling hand in hand with Michael. The vampires confronting them and dragging them away. The pleasure they took in cutting and biting and torturing Michael while they made her watch. One of the vamps turning his attention on her and thrusting his fangs into her throat. Then . . .

Roland arrived, striking with a ferocity that was as frightening as the vampires, his white and purple aura contrasting with the bright orange of theirs. He tore the vampires apart, as vicious as an animal, then turned to her. The vampire feeding from her bolted. Krysta let her gaze stray to Michael, saw his chest rising and falling in pained pants.

Roland took out his phone and called for a cleanup, then started after the vampire.

Krysta caught his pant leg as he passed, clutching it with a hand that shook. "P-Please."

He knelt beside her, brushed her hair back with gentle fingers.

"H-help him," she begged, looking at Michael, too weak to point. "S-save him."

Roland shook his head, his strong face full of compassion. "I'm sorry," he said softly. "One of them tried to turn him. If he lives, he will become a monster like them. Dying is far more merciful."

Darkness threatened.

David withdrew his touch.

Krysta stared at Roland through eyes full of moisture. "You *were* there."

He nodded. "I arrived too late to save him. He had been infected on too large a scale and, as a human, would have turned vampire. Had he lived, he would have long since lost his sanity by now."

She blinked, knowing he spoke the truth. Tears trailed down her cheeks.

Beside her, Étienne released her hand and wrapped a comforting arm around her.

"Thank you for saving me," she said.

He dipped his head in acknowledgment and looked from her to Étienne. "I am doubly glad now that I was able to do so."

The front door opened and Chris entered, the strap of a bulging soft leather briefcase looped over one shoulder. Securing the door behind him, he headed for the table and took one of the two unclaimed chairs, leaving the chair at the opposite end of the table from David empty.

Greetings flowed around the room as Darnell took out his phone and dialed, but the call went to Seth's voice mail.

He met David's gaze as he put away the phone.

David turned his head to one side, as though listening, and closed his eyes. "Seth."

Everyone exchanged glances.

"Yes." David opened his eyes and faced them. "He shall be here shortly."

Sheldon stared. "Where is he?"

"Anchorage."

"Alaska?"

"Yes."

"And he could hear you?"

"Yes."

Lisette met Étienne and Richart's gazes. "That's amazing. I have to at least be in the same state to hear my brothers."

Krysta looked up at Étienne as he nodded.

David shrugged. "I'm older. It requires a great deal of power."

"That's awesome," Sheldon said. "Can you contact *any* immortal that way?"

"Yes."

"Would you tell Oscar in California that I want the hundred bucks he owes me? He isn't answering his phone."

David stared at him.

Sheldon swallowed. "You aren't telling him, are you?"

"No."

Krysta's tears dried as amusement sifted through her.

Seth appeared just inside the front door, katanas in hand, his face and clothing blood-splattered. "One moment," he told them, then vanished.

Krysta heard a faucet turn on down in the basement. Rustling. The water shut off.

Seth reappeared, face and hands clean, fresh clothing adorning his tall form, weapons sheathed. He took his seat. "Sean," he said, "I understand you wish to be transformed."

Every eye turned to Sean. "Yes, sir."

"You have my permission. Étienne may transform you at any time of your choosing *after* tonight."

"Thank you."

"Tonight I would like you to remain here and offer what

aid you can in the infirmary in case any of the wounded come here instead of going to the network. A staff is already on hand, ready to be of service, and have been informed of your ability."

"I'll do whatever I can to help."

"Do *not* push yourself too far healing or you may not live long enough to be transformed."

"Yes, sir."

"Chris?"

Chris rose and, opening his briefcase, began to hand out file folders. "Seth and David inspected the compound this afternoon. These are the schematics they drew. Since the tracking devices could be discovered at any moment, we need to strike tonight."

Étienne took the folder offered to him. "How do you know they haven't already been discovered?"

"My men have been surveilling the place all day. There has been no increase in activity. Although we do believe the commander arrived just before sunset with two other men. The mercenaries all saluted him and treated him with deference and respect."

Krysta took a folder, feeling a sense of pride that she was now one of them and treated as such. Even Sean was given a folder.

Chris handed David one and rounded the table.

Marcus took a folder. "Do you know who the commander is yet?"

"No. My men had to keep their distance to avoid compromising their mission and couldn't get a good look at his face."

Krysta studied the map. A large main building. Two hangars that shielded who knew what. Helicopters.

Marcus scowled. "This is nearly identical to the last compound we conquered."

Seth leaned back in his chair. "Yes, it is. There's no

denying anymore that there is a connection. We just don't know what it is."

Ami bit her lip and met Seth's gaze, worry shadowing her pretty green eyes.

Seth spoke softly to her. "Ami, I want you to sit this battle out. Stay here with Darnell and help him coordinate the other Seconds. And help Sean with the wounded if you can."

Ami looked up at Marcus and nodded. "All right."

"Jenna," Seth added. "I'd like you to remain here, too. You haven't completed your training and aren't prepared to face the opposition you would if you accompanied us."

Beside Richart, Jenna nodded. "If you find yourself in need of an extra pair of hands . . ."

He smiled. "Richart or I will come for you."

David leaned forward and clasped his hands on the table. "Since it worked well for us before, we're going to employ the same strategy we used the last time. The immortals will strike first, catching them off guard and clearing a path. Then the Seconds and network guards will sweep in behind us."

Chris nodded. "I have Black Hawks, two Sisu XA-180 armored personnel carriers, and two Humvees full of men standing by a few miles from the compound. The Seconds here will accompany me to the rendezvous point in a van."

"A majority of the mercenaries will likely be in the main structure," Seth said. "David, Roland, Sarah, Marcus, Lisette, and I will tackle that. Bastien, Melanie, Étienne, and Krysta, take the barracks. Richart, Ethan, and Edward, handle the guards on the grounds, but beware of land mines and other traps. Yuri and Stanislov, take the hangers."

Chris held up a finger. "Once more I'd like to request that you keep the vehicles intact, if possible, so that we can use them ourselves in the future."

Yuri and Stanislov both sighed with disappointment.

"You are forever spoiling our fun, Reordon," Stanislov complained.

Seth smiled. "Immortals, make sure you have several doses of the antidote on you stowed in different pockets, so if a bullet destroys one you will have another available."

"Elder immortals," David said, "Keep an eye on the younger immortals and lend them assistance when needed. Sarah and Melanie, because you possess the speed and strength of elder immortals, I include you in that category."

The two women nodded.

Melanie winked at Bastien. "I get to keep my eye on you."

He grinned. "You always do. My *ass*, that is."

"Because your ass is hot."

"I know."

Roland sighed loudly.

Chuckles erupted.

"Any questions?" Seth asked.

No one spoke.

"Okay. Let's book."

Krysta rose and started to follow the others toward the door.

Sean caught her elbow and pulled her into a hug. "Be careful."

"You, too. Like Seth said, don't overdo it."

"I won't."

She saw Sarah tug on Roland's hand as they walked past. "Why couldn't *we* have had siblings like that?"

"I don't know. We got screwed."

Sean laughed.

Smiling, Krysta took Étienne's hand and followed the others out into the night.

Chapter 19

Krysta stood with Étienne and her immortal brethren (it felt so weird to think of them that way) in the shadows of tall, fragrant evergreens. The moon was new, something that should work to their advantage. Unless the compound bore ultrabright stadium lights, there should be plenty of shadows from which immortals could strike.

Étienne tightened his grip on her hand. *Keep your mind open to me.*

You look nervous, she said, peering up at him. She was a little nervous herself. *Are you planning to propose to me again?* she teased.

He smiled. *Not if your answer will change.*

Krysta shook her head. *It will always be yes.*

He stole a quick kiss.

Feel better? she asked.

Yes.

You were worrying about me getting hurt, weren't you?

You know me well.

She liked to think she did. *We've fought mercenaries and won before.*

There were far fewer to fight and you still ended up getting shot.

I'm immortal now. Bullets won't kill me.

But they hurt like hell and, as I've said before, I don't like seeing you hurt.

I am so in love with you, she professed.

I love you, too, he said, eyes acquiring an amber glow.

I know. Don't let that distract you tonight. I don't want you worrying about me. I can kick ass like the rest of them.

He raised her hand and pressed a kiss to her knuckles. *As you wish.*

You're totally lying and are going to worry about me anyway, aren't you?

Again, you know me well.

Seth appeared in their midst. *Chris and the Seconds are in place. Time to go to work.*

Stay sharp, David advised.

All nodded and drew their weapons.

Seth and David vanished. Krysta thought at first that they had teleported, then realized as sounds of their flight reached her ears that they were just so freaking fast that they had only appeared to.

Roland, Sarah, and Marcus shot off after them.

Melanie and Bastien followed.

Richart teleported.

Krysta, Étienne, and Lisette raced forward.

Ethan, Edward, Yuri, and Stanislov brought up the rear.

Anxiety filled Étienne as they whipped through the trees, feet barely touching the ground, making no sound that would alert the guards to their approach.

Krysta was a fantastic fighter and lacked nothing in the confidence department. But she wouldn't be fighting vampires this time. Her ability to see auras would not aid her as they did with vampires and . . .

He just wasn't sure how she would react to killing humans.

We're at war, she thought, *and lives are at stake. Immortal. Vampire. Gifted one. And human, if these people succeed in creating their army of supersoldiers. I'll feel the same way killing them as I would if I were in the army fighting to defend my country.*

How did you do that? he asked, nonplussed.

Do what?

Read my thoughts?

You were . . . what is it you call it? . . . projecting or broadcasting them.

Big-time, Lisette added.

And still he worried.

An explosion rocked the night.

The forest they navigated parted and a twenty-foot fence entwined with razor wire loomed.

Étienne leaped it easily and held his breath until he saw Krysta do the same.

An alarm sounded, *wonk wonk wonking* at deafening decibels.

Gunfire erupted as guards swung around to face the threat and fired blindly at the blurred figures racing through the yard.

Several soldiers cried out as Richart, Ethan, and Edward went to work eradicating them.

Bullets whizzed past and filled the air like swarms of mosquitoes. Étienne dodged as many as he could as he and Krysta followed Bastien and Melanie to the wooden structures beside the main building.

Étienne didn't know how Seth and David had gained entrance to the main building, but the brick facade looked as though a wrecking ball had hit it several times.

Screams rent the air. The scent of blood thickened on the breeze.

Étienne saw crimson liquid spurt from Krysta's shoulder and clenched his teeth.

I'm fine, she said. *Stop worrying about me.*

Easier said than done.

Ahead of him, Bastien swore foully as Melanie burst through the door of one of the barracks without waiting for him.

Étienne headed into another, Krysta right on his heels.

Merde. This must be one the damned day guards used because the fucker was full. Men in T-shirts and boxer shorts were already leaping out of bed and grabbing weapons, having been given a few seconds' warning by the damned alarm that continued to blare outside.

Étienne never slowed. Swinging his katanas, he barreled through them like the bulls of Pamplona. Howls of pain ensued.

At the opposite end of the room, he stopped and spun around.

Krysta remained in constant motion, zigzagging from side to side as she cut down the soldiers and herded those still standing toward Étienne's deadly blades.

Two more bullets hit her. Pain erupted in her side and her thigh.

Gritting her teeth, she powered forward, glad she had chosen to wield katanas tonight rather than the shorter shoto swords. The longer blades worked well against humans with guns and seemed to scare hell out of them at the same time.

The humans' auras took on a dark, muddied red as anger and fear seized them.

Krysta wished their auras would warn her when and where they intended to shoot, because those damned bullets stung!

She was *so* glad Étienne had transformed her. Had he not done so, she would be down on the floor, bleeding to death.

Étienne started working his way back toward her.

The scent of fear mingled with the strengthening odors of blood and death.

A tranquilizer dart whipped past, narrowly missing her ear. Crap!

She singled out the shooter and . . .

Oh. She had meant to knock the weapon from his hand with a katana, but overextended herself and severed his hand.

Screaming, the soldier gripped his wrist and sank to the floor.

A bullet struck her in the shoulder.

She faltered.

Krysta! Étienne shouted mentally.

Right. She swung at the next soldier. And the next. And the next. Stepping over bodies as she methodically made her way toward Étienne.

Something stung her neck like a bee . . . and the world went black.

Étienne took out two soldiers with one swing and glanced through the shifting bodies that still fought to check on Krysta.

A dart hit her in the neck.

Her knees instantly buckled and she hit the floor hard.

"Krysta!"

One tranquilizer dart shouldn't have felled her like that. It should have only made her woozy. And he didn't see any other darts sticking out of her.

Krysta!

She didn't move. Didn't respond to his shout. Just lay there like a corpse.

Étienne? Lisette said. *What is it?*

Krysta's down!

He plowed through the soldiers, cutting as he went.

How could there still be so many?

Melanie burst through the door, zipped over, and knelt beside Krysta.

Either she had heard his mental shout or Lisette had told her Krysta needed help.

Étienne kept one eye on them as he battled the damned mercenaries.

Melanie yanked out the dart. "Listen to my thoughts," she called over the racket. *Can you hear me?* she asked as she pressed two fingers to Krysta's neck.

Yes. Something's wrong. She was just hit with the one dart. She lost consciousness instantly.

Okay. Don't panic. She's alive.

That relieved him a little. Seeing Krysta drop like that had scared the hell out of him.

Melanie delved into a pocket, withdrew an autoinjector full of the antidote, flipped the lid, and jammed it against Krysta's neck.

Nothing happened.

Bullets peppered Étienne's chest.

Focus! David rebuked him. He and Seth must be listening in and monitoring the situation.

Étienne impaled the shooter. Dropping a sword, he grabbed the man's automatic weapon and opened fire on the soldiers rushing toward Melanie and Krysta, still swinging his other sword at the soldiers closest to him.

More bodies sank to the floor.

Krysta's eyelids fluttered, then lifted.

"Can you hear me?" Melanie asked her, leaning in close to draw eye contact and to be heard over the alarm and screams and sounds of battle.

Krysta nodded. Even from where he was, Étienne could see how sluggishly she responded.

"Can you move?"

Her hands twitched. Her feet, too. Slowly, she dragged her arms closer to her body. "Weak," she whispered.

Melanie delved into her pocket again and took out another autoinjector.

Wait, Étienne said. He remembered Richart telling him Melanie had freaked out when Bastien had tested the antidote on himself because it was so strong it could kill an elephant. She had feared it might make his heart beat so fast that it would merely flutter instead of beating and cease pumping blood through his body.

Melanie ignored him, jamming the pen into Krysta's arm.

Krysta gasped. Eyes widening, she jackknifed into a seated position, chest rising and falling with rapid breaths.

"Are you okay?" Melanie asked, taking her by the wrist.

Krysta nodded. "My heart is racing."

"Any chest pain?"

"No."

"Difficulty breathing?"

"I'm breathing kind of fast, but . . . I think I'm okay."

"Let me know immediately if that changes for the worse."

Krysta nodded and scrambled to her feet, picking up the swords she had dropped.

Melanie caught Étienne's gaze. *Tell the others the mercenaries have upped the dose. One dart will fell them so swiftly they won't have time to use the antidote. Any immortal felled should be given the antidote twice.* "You're sure you're okay?" she asked Krysta.

Nodding, Krysta leaped into the fray again, a big grin lighting her face. "I'm fine. Thank you!"

Melanie darted out the door.

Seth warned the others before Étienne had a chance.

Étienne jerked his head to the side just in time to avoid a dart.

Moments later, the last mercenary fell and Étienne raced forward to yank Krysta into his arms.

"I'm okay," she muttered into his shirt.

He could feel how swiftly her chest rose and fell, heard her racing heart, and wasn't so sure about that. "You're practically panting."

"What can I say? You turn me on," she retorted.

"Don't joke about this!" he snapped, tightening his hold on her.

"I'm sorry," she said and leaned back. "I'm okay. Really. I think double the antidote is a little too strong, but I don't feel like I'm dying or anything."

"Forgive me. I didn't mean to snap."

"I know, honey. I really am okay. I actually feel . . . *great*." And damned near danced in place, seeming unable to remain still. "Really juiced. Like I could . . . I don't know . . . take out a helicopter or something." Laughing, she tugged him toward the door. "Come on. Let's go. We still have lots of ass to kick."

Étienne steadied her when she nearly tripped over a body in her haste, then followed her outside.

Bastien and Melanie raced past toward the third and last barracks.

"We've got the last one," Bastien called and plunged inside, Melanie right behind him.

Richart appeared in front of Étienne and gave Krysta a quick once-over. "Are you all right?" he asked, face full of concern.

"I'm awesome!" she declared with worrisome enthusiasm.

Richart cast Étienne a dubious glance.

"You heard Seth?" Etienne asked.

His brother nodded. "Stay safe." He vanished.

You, too, Étienne thought.

Ethan and Edward, along with Richart, steadily reduced the numbers of the guards outside.

All hell had broken loose in the hangars, judging by the sounds of it, so Yuri and Stanislov appeared to have things under control there.

Or not.

Three mercenaries fled one hangar and scrambled into a

helicopter. The blades began to rotate as the engine hummed to life.

Krysta gave Étienne a huge grin, her face lighting with excitement. "I'm doing it!" she blurted, sheathing her swords and drawing two daggers.

"What?"

"I'm taking out that helicopter!" Whooping, she dashed away.

"Wait!" He took off after Krysta. *Melanie!*

Yes?

Can a double dose of the antidote cause erratic behavior?

That's definitely a possibility. It's a stimulant and frighteningly strong. Why?

The helicopter lifted off the ground.

Krysta picked up speed, running damned near as fast as an elder.

Because I think Krysta has lost her damned mind!

The helicopter began to move away, strafing the yard with machine gun fire.

Krysta veered toward a Humvee, jumped onto the hood and, without slowing, leaped into the air.

Étienne nearly dropped dead of a fucking heart attack as he watched her fly through the air and dive through a side door, tackling one of the door gunners.

Fuck!

Jumping onto the Humvee, he leaped after her.

The helicopter wobbled and began to spin away.

Étienne brushed the landing gear with his fingers and latched on, pulling himself up and through a side door.

One door gunner was dead. A second soldier fell out the other side. The pilot . . .

Krysta buried a dagger in his heart as he spun toward her with a 9mm.

The helicopter tilted and spun as the pilot abandoned the controls and slumped over dead.

"Now what?" Étienne demanded incredulously as she turned a triumphant smile on him. *He* sure as hell couldn't fly this thing. And they couldn't jump without being caught in the rotors.

Her face fell. "Oh, shit. I didn't think of that."

Seth!

The ground rushed toward them.

Seth appeared in the helicopter and promptly bumped his head. "Ah! Shit!" Reaching out with both hands, he grabbed their shoulders.

Étienne breathed a sigh of relief when they teleported to the tarmac in front of one of the hangars.

Fire reached toward the sky as the helicopter crashed and exploded. Pieces of the rotor blades tore off and shot through the night, taking out several more mercenaries for them.

"You!" Seth said, pointing an authoritative finger at Krysta. "Calm the fuck down!"

Eyes wide, she nodded hastily. "I'm sorry. I don't know what—"

"It's the drug. I know. Étienne, keep her in check." He vanished.

Krysta stared up at Étienne, eyes wide. "I can't believe I just did that. I'm so sorry. Are you hurt? You aren't hurt, are you?"

"I'm fine. You just scared the hell out of me."

"I'm sorry," she said again. She hadn't thought. Energy had poured through her, demanding an immediate outlet. She had seen the helicopter and . . .

She hadn't thought. She had just acted.

"Are you okay?" he asked, grabbing one of her Glocks and firing over her shoulder at some threat behind her.

"Yes."

"No chest pains?"

"No. My breathing is even beginning to slow." And rational thought was returning.

He nodded.

"I really am sorry," she said. They could have died in that helicopter. One of the rotor blades could have decapitated them when it crashed. Or they could have burned to death in the fire.

Could fire kill immortals?

"It's all right. Let's go help Yuri and Stanislov—"

Eyes rolling back in his head, he dropped to the pavement.

"Étienne!"

A dart stuck out of his shoulder.

Looking past him, she jerked to the side to avoid a dart aimed at her, then flung a dagger at the mercenary aiming his tranquilizer gun at them.

It sank to the hilt in the man's chest, felling him as quickly as the dart had dropped Étienne.

Kneeling, Krysta rolled Étienne onto his back and drew out two autoinjectors with shaking fingers. "Étienne?" She flipped the lids open and jabbed them into his neck.

A few seconds later he gasped. Eyes flying open, he sat up so swiftly he rammed his head into hers.

"Ow! Shit, your head is hard!" she complained, rubbing her throbbing forehead.

"What happened?"

"Seriously, you didn't feel that?"

"Feel what?"

"Never mind. You were tranqed. Are you okay?"

"I'm good." His chest rose and fell with rapid breaths. "I'm great!" He leapt to his feet, a wide smile splitting his blood-painted face. "Let's go kick some ass!"

Krysta scrambled to her feet as he sped into the nearest hangar. "Wait!"

Something exploded inside.

"Oh, crap." She took off after him.

* * *

As Seth swung his katanas with deadly precision, he heard David laugh on the other side of the building.

Seth smiled wryly, confusing his opponents. *I think we may have a new problem on our hands.*

It would seem so.

Have you been hit with a dart yet?

No. Strike that. Yes.

Do you need me?

No. It's a great deal stronger than the darts used against us in the past. I had to use the antidote.

Two doses?

No. One sufficed for me. The young ones must be more susceptible.

The closer Seth came to the back of the building, the thicker the soldiers grew. They were definitely protecting something.

Or someone.

A dart hit him in the chest.

Seth yanked it out.

Another hit him in the neck.

Again he yanked it out and cursed the damned hallway that allowed so little maneuvering. All the humans had to do was fire blindly in his direction and sooner or later they'd hit him.

He worried anew about David.

I'm fine.

Warn me if you need to use another dose of the antidote. If it juiced David up as it had Krysta and Étienne . . .

Hell, with his power, there was no telling what havoc he could wreak.

David laughed. *Don't worry. I won't risk it. And shouldn't have to. I've nearly eliminated all of the soldiers over here.*

Any sign of the commander?

No. And the soldiers' minds are too chaotic and plentiful to read.

I suspect I'm on his trail.

Bullets continually peppered Seth's large form.

The soldiers' panic multiplied as they watched with wide eyes as every bullet that pierced him, within seconds, reemerged from his body and fell to the floor at his feet.

"What the hell *are* you?" one shouted.

The childish "wouldn't *you* like to know" taunt floated through his head, wringing another smile from him.

A smile that seemed to terrify the soldiers even more.

A mercenary ducked out of a doorway farther down and aimed a shoulder-fire missile at him. "Fire in the hole!"

The remaining soldiers all hit the ground as fire and smoke accompanied the missile's launch.

Seth waved a hand, directed the missile up through the ceiling, the roof, and detonated it in the night sky.

The soldier gaped.

Seth arched a brow. "Care to try again?"

The soldier swallowed as his comrades regained their feet.

"That's what I thought. Now why don't you show me what—or whom—you're hiding?"

Weapons raised and resumed fire.

Through the hole in the roof, Seth saw Chris's Black Hawk helicopters swoop past. A rumbling sound, wafting through the gaping maw he and David had left in the front of the building, told him the armored personnel carriers and Humvees full of network guards had also arrived.

Enough. He needed to end this, if he could, before the humans fully entered the fray.

Ignoring the injuries constantly opening on his flesh, he cut down the remaining soldiers and eyed the door they had been defending.

Waving a hand, he slid the bodies away from it and took a step toward it.

Wait, David said.

Seth paused.

David streaked up the hallway and stopped beside him. "The building's clear. Roland, Sarah, Marcus, and Lisette took out everyone in the basement levels and are outside lending aid wherever it's needed, so whoever is behind this door is all that's left."

There was an electronic palm pad with keys requiring a code to open the door. Seth waved a hand. Sparks shot from the gadget and a loud clunk sounded. He pushed the door inward.

Automatic gunfire resounded as bullets bombarded him.

Three men, wielding the weapons, backed away to the far side of the room.

Seth recognized two of them.

Donald and Nelson, David said, yanking the weapons from their hands with a thought and flinging them out of reach.

Nelson drew a grenade from his pocket, pulled the pin, and threw it.

David again used telekinesis to send it out into the hallway and up through the hole in the roof Seth had created with the missile.

Show-off, Seth remonstrated as it exploded. *Hold them still while I find out what we missed.*

The men froze, the only movements David allowed them the rising and falling of their chests and the blinking of their eyes.

Seth delved into their minds. Was it a hard drive? A laptop? A hidden backup server? An e-mail? What had they missed? How had Donald and Nelson rediscovered vampires and immortals and begun the hunt anew?

When Seth found the answer, shock seized him.

"What is it?" David asked, brow crinkling with concern.

"It isn't possible," he whispered.

"What isn't?"

Seth met his gaze. "Their memories have been restored."

David stared at him, the same disbelief Seth felt writing itself upon his face. "That's not possible."

"It shouldn't be. We buried them ourselves." So deeply the memories could never have surfaced again on their own. Nor with drugs. Nor with hypnosis. Not even manifested in dreams.

"Humans lack the ability to accomplish such a task on their own," David said.

"Yes." Rage began to simmer within him.

"Such could only be accomplished . . ."

"With the help of an immortal," Seth finished for him, speaking the unimaginable.

Had one of their own turned against them?

David looked at the mercenaries in question. "Can you see who did it?"

The mercenaries' faces contorted with pain as Seth ruthlessly tore through their memories.

"No."

"We can't let them live."

Seth agreed. They had only let the mercenaries live before because their PMC was elite enough that Chris had feared the deaths of both men might draw too much scrutiny. But they had no choice now. No human with any memory of this operation could be allowed to live.

Seth stopped the men's hearts.

David let them fall to the floor.

An immortal had aided the enemy.

The building around them began to tremble as Seth's control slipped, succumbing to the fury and, yes, hurt, swelling within him.

A clap of thunder split the night. Then another. Cracks opened in the walls. Sheetrock fell from the ceiling.

David reached out and rested a hand on Seth's shoulder.

They stared at each other.

Calm seeped into him from David's touch, dampening some of the fury.

Seth took several deep breaths.

The building stilled.

Utter silence reigned outside for several long minutes.

Gradually, work and conversation resumed.

David shook his head. *How could any immortal betray you like this?*

Betray us, Seth corrected, feeling sick. *Whoever it is has betrayed us all, put us all in danger.*

After you helped him adjust to his new way of life and did a thousand other things to improve his existence and foster happiness and contentment.

Or her.

David looked as ill as Seth felt.

Boots struck linoleum, carrying someone up the hallway toward them.

They faced the doorway just as Chris stopped in it, garbed in black and carrying an automatic weapon. "Everything okay?" he asked tentatively. Only *he* would have the balls to approach them now.

Seth nodded as David dropped his hand.

Wise man that he was, Chris said nothing of the thunder and tremors that had resulted from Seth's slip. "All is secure. The compound is ours and we've already begun the cleanup." As his gaze strayed to the three dead men, he swore. "So it *was* them. How the hell did they regain the information? What did we miss?"

"Nothing," Seth said, unable to tell him yet that they had been betrayed by one of their own.

Chris scowled. "What do you—?"

"Later," David said with a shake of his head.

Chris looked from David to Seth and gave a slow nod. "Sure." The walkie on his shoulder squawked. Chris mumbled something into it as he left and retraced his steps up the hallway.

Silent, Seth and David followed and stepped through the hole in the front of the building.

The air outside was heavy with the scents of smoke and death. The helicopter Krysta had crashed still burned. Network guards carted bodies to the hangars. More walked the fence and manned the gated entryway. The immortals . . .

The immortals clustered together about twenty yards away, smiling and laughing as Krysta recounted Étienne's antics in the hangar. Some partook of the blood Chris had brought them. None were sorely wounded. All gave the appearance of being relaxed and pleased with the victory they had achieved.

Normally, Seth would join them, slapping backs and congratulating them on a job well done.

Tonight, however . . .

Tonight he knew that one of them had betrayed him.

How could any of them be working against us? David murmured mentally.

I don't know, Seth said, already dreading the punishment he would have to deliver.

Chapter 20

The next day, Seth stood outside Lisette's home, procrastinating.

The sun clung to the center of the sky, no clouds creeping past to obscure its light. Birds twittered. Squirrels scuttled about in the detritus, looking for goodies.

No sounds of movement came from within the two-story domicile. If he listened closely, he could hear a single slow heartbeat and the soft sounds of somnolent breath.

Still, Seth hesitated.

He and David had agreed that only a telepath could have aided Donald and Nelson. Bastien was empathic. He could feel and manipulate other people's emotions, but he couldn't manipulate their thoughts.

Étienne and Lisette were the only telepaths in North Carolina. And there were none in surrounding states. Any telepaths farther away would've had to have been teleported in, and a quick examination of Richart's thoughts had confirmed that he hadn't teleported any immortals into the area without mentioning it.

Seth had just left Étienne's home. He had dropped by on the pretense of checking on them both to ensure neither had suffered any lasting effects of the double dose of stimulant.

They hadn't, thankfully.

While Krysta had apologized again for the helicopter debacle, Seth had smiled and nodded and examined every nook and cranny of Étienne's mind, relieved to find nothing more incriminating than some interesting sexual fantasies he intended to pursue with Krysta.

Which left Seth standing outside Lisette's home, already dreading what he would find in her thoughts. As well as the punishment he would have to deliver when he confirmed she was the deceiver.

Although he would never admit it to anyone other than David, who knew without having to be told, Seth had a soft spot for Lisette. Female Immortal Guardians were exceedingly rare. Most female *gifted ones* suffered torturous deaths at the hands of vampires before they could complete their transformations. So those, like Lisette, who survived were treasured.

And Seth understood well the burden of guilt beneath which Lisette existed. He understood *her*, or so he had thought. Being deceived by her in such a blatant, heinous way was a blow from which he didn't think he would ever recover. He could neither forgive nor forget it.

Nor would he try to.

Hardening his heart, he rang the bell.

Lisette answered the door herself, wearing a pretty pink camisole nightgown and robe. Staying in the shadows, she squinted against the bright afternoon sunlight. "Hi, Seth."

"Lisette." He stepped inside and waited while she closed the door. "Where's Tracy?"

"Shopping, I think." She yawned and combed her fingers through her mussed hair. He hadn't seen it unconfined by a braid in years and hadn't realized it now fell in thick waves to her hips.

"I'm sorry I woke you."

She offered him a sweet smile that broke his heart and led him into the living room. "Don't worry about it. Are you hungry? Would you like me to make you a sandwich or something?"

"No, thank you."

She sank down on the sofa and motioned to the chair across from it. "What's going on? Is David's place too crowded today? You're welcome to stay here, if it is."

"No." He watched her draw her long, slender legs up and tuck them under her robe. "I sensed there was something you wished to tell me."

And there it was. The unease he had expected to see cross her features when she had first opened the door to him.

While she bit her lip and hesitated, he told himself to get on with it and delved into her thoughts.

"Not tell you," she said slowly, oblivious to his presence in her mind, "so much as *ask* you."

"Very well."

"We all know how powerful you are," she began. "And it's been sort of an unspoken rule not to ask you about . . . all the things you can do."

She had surprisingly strong mental barriers for an immortal her age, but they only slowed him down for a moment or two.

"David wasn't exactly thrilled when we found out he could shape-shift," she mentioned.

Seth grunted. "He knew there were those who would want to turn it into a parlor trick to be exercised upon request."

She sent him a wry smile. "I'm sure Richart has had a hard time keeping Sheldon from asking for an exhibition."

Damn it, he wasn't finding *anything* about Donald and Nelson in her memories.

"What did you want to ask me?" he pressed.

"I feel like I know better now what you're capable of

and . . . I just wondered . . . When we face large numbers of vampires like we did when Bastien raised his army or large numbers of mercenaries like we did last night . . ."

"Yes?"

"Why don't you just do what Zach did and give them all aneurysms or heart attacks or something? Why engage in battle at all? Why let us fight and risk our lives when you can kill them all with a thought?"

He stared at her. "Son of a bitch." *Zach*. No wonder the only guilt he could find in her thoughts was that which she continued to nourish over transforming Richart and Étienne. She hadn't betrayed him. Étienne hadn't betrayed him. *None* of his beloved Immortal Guardians had betrayed him.

Zach had betrayed him.

Sort of.

They weren't exactly close and . . .

Actually, he wouldn't even consider Zach a friend. Not until recently, when Zach had come to him in South Korea, seeming different. Changed. He had actually *aided* Seth that night. Seth had taken it as a good sign and had thought . . .

He held onto his temper enough to keep Lisette's home from shaking, but was helpless to stop the clap of thunder that rumbled outside as outrage rose.

Lisette's eyes widened. "I'm sorry. I shouldn't have asked. It's none of my business and I—"

Fucking Zach. Seth had suspected that the numbness was wearing off and he had been right. But that was the *only* thing about which he had been right.

When Seth had discovered Zach's *meetings* with Ami, he had hoped they might be beneficial. But Zach hadn't been drawn to Ami's goodness. He hadn't been spending hours on end, perched atop David's roof because he was curious about the relationships of those beneath it.

He had been collecting information to give Donald and Nelson.

"I'll kill him," Seth growled furiously.

"Kill whom?" Lisette asked, lowering her feet to the floor and sitting up straight.

"Not important," Seth lied and forced the fury down. He rose and headed for the door. "I must go."

Lisette hurried after him. "Seth, I'm sorry. I didn't mean to upset you."

He stopped short and turned around. "You didn't. To answer your question, there is a delicate balance that must be maintained in this world."

"I don't—"

"Vampires have an unfair advantage when they prey upon innocent, unsuspecting humans. The humans can't compete with their speed and strength. We hunt vampires to correct that imbalance. When we fight humans ourselves and battle the mercenaries, there *must* be a balance to it. We have speed and strength. They have deadly weapons. If I exercised my powers to their full extent and killed all of the humans with a thought, we would become the equivalent of the hunter sitting up in the hunting blind, firing upon the defenseless deer that grazed below. The balance would be lost. And the consequences would be apocalyptic."

She chewed her lower lip. "I don't know what you mean about the consequences, but I see your point about maintaining a balance."

He reached for the doorknob, but didn't turn it. "Lisette," he said, pausing to face her once more.

"Yes?" she asked, her pretty face troubled.

"You have labored long beneath the guilt of transforming your brothers."

She looked away, unhappy with the change of subject, ever unwilling to discuss it.

"But both Richart and Étienne have now found happiness. It is time for you to let go and allow yourself to seek your own."

Her slender throat moved with a swallow. "I don't know how to," she whispered.

He shook his head. At himself, not at her. "Nor do I."

Making sure no sunlight would touch her, he opened the door and slipped outside.

Krysta stood beside her brother, the two siblings staring into the large bathroom mirror. "It's weird, isn't it?" she asked.

Their reflections gazed back, eyes glowing a vibrant amber.

Sean nodded. "Beyond weird."

She grinned, flashing a very fine pair of gleaming fangs, inspiring Sean to do the same.

"Did you ever think you would see this?" he asked, snarling and making monster faces.

"No. I *feared* I would see this. My worst nightmare was that things would get out of control one night while I was out hunting and we would both end up being turned." She crossed her glowing eyes and made a goofy face.

Sean laughed.

"What about you?" she asked curiously.

He shrugged. "Honestly, that first year you hunted vampires, when I envisioned the future, I thought I would be dead by now."

Sobering, she turned to him. "I'm sorry, Sean. For all of the pain I've caused you over the years. For risking your life so many times in my pursuit of . . . justice or revenge. I don't know anymore which motivated me."

"And I'm sorry for secretly resenting not being the one who went out every night and did the hunting."

"Well, you'll get to hunt now. Has Chris found you a Second?"

He nodded. "He said there are three at network headquarters who just completed their training."

"Three? So you get to have your pick?"

"Apparently so. He wants me to go over there tomorrow night and meet with them, hang out for a while, see which one I feel the most comfortable with."

"Are you sure you don't want to stay here with us? Cam can serve as your Second, too." Not that she had asked him.

"Cam's already pulling double duty as *your* Second. And, honestly, it's time I had a place of my own."

She wrinkled her nose. "I guess I can understand that. How do you feel about having a stranger move in with you?"

Living with Cam had taken some getting used to when she and Sean had moved in. Étienne, on the other hand, had been a comfortable fit from day one.

Sean shrugged. "If we're going to live together, I assume we won't be strangers for long." He gave her a boyish smile. "Did I mention that one of my potential Seconds is a woman?"

Her interest spiked. "Really? Is she cute?"

He rolled his eyes. "I don't know. I haven't seen her. Chris said she's been ready to serve as a Second for a while now, but he's had a hard time placing her."

She frowned. "Is she difficult? Because the last thing you need after living with *me* all this time is to be stuck with a bitchy woman."

He laughed. "You aren't bitchy. You're stubborn."

"I'll second that," Étienne said from their bedroom down the hall. Apparently he had been following their conversation.

Krysta blew him a raspberry, then grinned when he chuckled.

"She isn't difficult," Sean said. "Male immortals just don't like having female Seconds because they're old-fashioned and can't bear the idea of a woman dying while protecting them."

"How do *you* feel about that?"

"I'm good with it," he said, straight-faced, then laughed when she hit him. "Just kidding. I don't like the idea either, but Chris thought that—after living with *you* for the past six years—I might be more amenable to fighting alongside a woman. *And*, since I'm a healer . . ."

"You can heal any wounds she incurs on your behalf. Cool. I say go for it. Especially if she's hot."

"You're incorrigible."

Not really. She just wanted him to find the same happiness she had.

Étienne appeared in the doorway. "How do I look?"

Krysta froze. *Holy crap.*

She had only ever seen him naked, in sweatpants, or in his hunting clothes. This . . .

She gave him a long, leisurely look from his neatly combed hair to his feet, encased in shiny shoes that probably cost more than a semester of Sean's college tuition had.

His tall, broad-shouldered form was beautifully garbed in a black three-piece suit with silver pin stripes. A bright white shirt stood out starkly against his naturally tan, clean-shaven jaw. As she stared, he lifted his chin a bit and reached up to adjust a black and silver tie.

Daaaaaamn, he looked good.

"You're drooling," Sean drawled.

She nodded, never taking her gaze from Étienne. "Daaaaaamn, you look good."

He grinned. "I do?"

"*Really* good. Like . . . edible good. In fact, Sean, if you wouldn't mind giving us a few minutes alone . . ."

Étienne's brown eyes flashed amber.

Sean sighed. "No offense, but this is one of the reasons I want my own place."

She smiled, still drinking in her fiancé. "You look *hot*."

"That's a good thing, right?"

"It is for me," she professed, looking him up and down again.

"I'm not overdressed, am I?"

Probably, but she wasn't going to say anything. She wanted to spend the rest of the night, as Sean said, drooling over him. She'd just go put on something dressy herself to even things out.

"No. I haven't changed yet. I'll be ready in a couple of minutes." As she moved to squeeze past him in the doorway, she rose onto her toes, looped her arms around his neck, and took his lips in a long, passionate, I-wish-I-could-strip-you-naked-and-have-my-way-with-you-right-here-right-now kiss.

He groaned when she pulled away.

"I mussed your hair," she murmured and left him gazing after her with glowing eyes full of desire.

And adorably mussed hair.

Forty minutes later, his hair was once more tamed, she was squeezed into a little black dress and heels, and Sean wore slacks and a dress shirt. Together, the three strode up the sidewalk in front of a modest middle-class home parked on a nice-sized plot of land in the country outside of Carrboro.

When they reached the front porch, she turned to smile up at Étienne and did a double take. "Everything okay?"

"Yes," he said, fidgeting inside his suit jacket and smoothing a lapel. "Why?"

"Your eyes are glowing."

"They are?"

"Yes."

"Oh. Okay." He closed his eyes, drew in a deep breath and let it out slowly. His lids lifted. "What about now?"

"Still glowing."

He swore, then closed his eyes again. Breathed deeply.

Sean caught her eye and raised his brows.

Krysta shrugged. No bulge strained against the front of
Étienne's slacks, so it wasn't lust.

He opened his eyes. "What about now?"

"Still glowing."

Again he swore and repeated the process.

"Sweetie, you aren't nervous, are you?"

"Of course not."

On the other side of him, Sean mouthed, "Yes, he is."

This time, when Étienne's lids lifted, they revealed warm
brown eyes bereft of the glow. "Now?"

"You're good."

He nodded. "Thank you."

She rang the doorbell.

Footsteps approached from inside. The locks turned. The
door swung open.

Krysta donned a bright smile. "Hi, Mom!"

Wings spread, Zach rode the breeze, swooping and twirling
as he raced the motorcycle eating up the asphalt below.

The slender figure guiding it nearly scraped her knee on
the pavement as she leaned into a curve, taking it far too fast.
Her long, midnight braid flapped and danced in the wind,
bouncing off the sheathed shoto swords strapped to her back.

Garbed all in black, she wasn't wearing her long coat
tonight and, no doubt, would have generated a great deal of
attention if any other drivers on the road could keep up with
her long enough to notice the multitude of weapons she bore.

Slowing, she turned onto David's drive and stopped before
the security gate.

Zach's gaze lingered on her long legs, outlined nicely
by fitted cargo pants, as she straddled the bike and typed
in the code.

When the gate swung open, she shot forward once more.
Zach swept his wings down, propelling himself forward

and following her progress through breaks in the trees that formed a canopy between them.

Completely distracted, he nearly crashed into a large owl. Feathers flew as the owl panicked. Talons threatened. Zach banked, reversed, dodged, and lost sight of Lisette. By the time he caught up with her, she had stowed her helmet away and was striding up the walk to David's front door.

He waited until she entered, then spread his wings and gently floated down to the rooftop.

A heavy weight slammed into his middle, knocking the breath from him, breaking several ribs, and lifting him from the roof.

North Carolina vanished, replaced by icy tundra being swept clean by a blizzard.

Zach grunted in pain as his back slammed down into a glacial surface as hard as stone. Several bones in the wings he hadn't had time to retract broke, snapping like twigs. Ice pellets peppered him, stinging like needles and abrading skin left bare save his usual leather pants.

Squinting against the white, he focused on the figure kneeling above him, face dark with fury, eyes glowing gold.

Seth.

"What—?"

"Did you think I wouldn't know?" Seth bellowed over the howling winds. "Did you think I wouldn't figure it out?" His large hand closed around Zach's throat and held him down.

Zach tried to teleport and couldn't. Seth must be doing something to block or hamper his gifts.

"I warned you," Seth said. "I warned you I've been exercising and growing my powers while you and the Others sat on your asses. Did you think I lied?"

When Zach opened his mouth to respond, Seth lifted him and slammed him against the ice again, breaking more bones in Zach's wings.

"Just tell me why!"

"Why what?" Zach growled as agony overwhelmed him.

Lightning streaked through the sky and struck the glacier a few yards away.

He had never seen Seth so enraged.

"Don't fuck with me! Why did you restore Donald and Nelson's memories? Why did you help the mercenaries prey upon my Immortal Guardians?"

Zach shook his head, unable to speak past the fingers clutching his throat.

Roaring, Seth rose to his feet and waved an arm in a circle.

The wind ceased blowing. The snow it had been carrying fluttered down to the ground, settling upon Zach and decorating his eyelashes as silence engulfed them.

Shit. Seth could control the weather?

Zach started to rise, but found he couldn't.

Seth held him in place telekinetically, his power a frightening and tangible force. "Only you or an Immortal Guardian could have done it. And my immortals wouldn't betray me. Just tell me *why* you did it."

Zach shook his head. "Your problem, Seth," he gasped, "has always been . . . that you think yourself . . . invulnerable. Is it . . . so hard for you to believe . . . that one of your precious . . . Immortal Guardians might have betrayed you?"

"You deny it was you?"

"I deny nothing," he snarled, his own fury now matching Seth's.

"So be it."

The blizzard resumed, wind whipping Seth's long hair.

So quickly he appeared to vanish for a moment, Seth drew a dagger and—kneeling—plunged the blade into Zach's chest an inch from his heart.

Pain shrieked through him.

Seth leaned in close and turned the blade, heightening Zach's suffering. "Listen closely, Cousin. This is but a tiny fraction of the power I wield. Betray me again, endanger my

Immortal Guardian family again, and I *will* destroy you. If the Others don't like it and choose to confront me, they will meet the same fate."

He rose while Zach struggled for breath.

"Stay away from Ami. Stay away from Lisette. Stay away from *all* of us." He shook his head, his face full of scorn as his glowing gaze raked Zach. "What a fucking disappointment."

He vanished.

The pressure holding Zach in place fell away.

Raising a shaking hand, Zach grasped the handle of the dagger and slowly pulled it from his chest.

It fell to the ground, staining the ice red.

He tried to teleport and found he couldn't. Seth had done something to drain his powers.

Gritting his teeth, he sat up with a growl of agony and dragged his wings with him.

A shiver shook him.

He glanced around at the frozen landscape.

No structure or shelter in sight.

For the next several hours, until his broken wings healed enough to carry him home, Zach's only company would be the anger festering inside him.

That and the satisfaction of knowing he *wasn't* the one who had betrayed Seth.

Apparently, somewhere out there, an Immortal Guardian was plotting to take down his or her *illustrious* leader.

Étienne stared at Krysta's mother and felt warmth fill him, easing some of his anxiety.

Opening the door wide, she waved them inside.

She was smaller than her daughter, standing no taller than five feet. Same slender build with slightly wider hips conservatively clothed in a floral-print dress. Shoulder-length, brown hair streaked with gray framed a friendly face that was the spitting image of Krysta's, only hers bore faint laugh lines.

"Honey!" she called over her shoulder, "they're here!" She hugged Krysta and Sean as a man, who was at least as tall as Étienne, joined them.

He, too, bore an athletic build, garbed in slacks and a dress shirt with the sleeves rolled back. His black hair was cut short and showed gray at the temples. His expression was welcoming.

Smiling, he waited for his wife to get her hugs in, then claimed his own.

Krysta gave him a hearty embrace, then stepped back and took Étienne's hand. "Mom, Dad, this is Étienne d'Alençon. Étienne, these are my parents, Evelyn and Martin Linz."

Her mother smiled up at him. "Call me Evie."

When she offered her hand, he took it and brought it to his lips. "A pleasure to meet you, Evie." He offered his hand to Krysta's father. "And you as well, Mr. Linz."

"Call me Martin. Nice to meet you, Étienne."

Étienne's mind went blank. Two hundred plus years old and he found himself tongue-tied in the face of his fiancée's parents.

Not surprising. He hadn't formally courted a woman since his transformation.

Evie grinned up at her husband. "He reminds me of you, honey. So handsome."

Heat stole up his neck.

Krysta's eyes widened. "Are you blushing?"

"No," he denied swiftly, sparking laughs.

Evie motioned for them to continue through the living room and into the den. "Come in and make yourself comfortable. Dinner will be ready in a few minutes."

Martin smiled. "Can I get you something to drink, Étienne?"

"Yes, please. Whatever you're having."

Krysta raised her brows. *It won't relax you. Alcohol has no affect on us*, she reminded him as Martin crossed to a small bar in one corner and poured them both a Scotch.

I thought refusing would seem odd, Étienne said. *And I want to appear as human as possible.*

"Krysta, do you want anything?" Martin asked.

"No, thanks, Dad."

"Sean?"

"No, thanks."

Martin returned and handed Étienne a glass.

Étienne ignored the urge to down it in one gulp and, instead, sipped it slowly.

Martin sipped his own, moving to stand beside his wife. "So. Should we assume by your presence here tonight that it's all over?" he asked them.

Étienne looked at Krysta, not knowing what he meant.

She seemed just as confused. "All what?"

He motioned to the front of the house. "Whatever inspired you to station guards around the property."

Étienne froze.

Krysta gaped. "You knew about that?"

They nodded.

"How?"

"Honey," Evie said gently, "you know I have strong empathic abilities. I could sense them out there."

Merde. How were they going to explain that?

"I can't tell you how hard it was," Evie added, "for me to refrain from taking them some sandwiches or soda or something to help them through the long, boring hours, but they didn't seem to want us to know they were there."

"Uh-huh," Krysta muttered, apparently as at a loss as Étienne.

"So? What happened?"

Krysta swallowed audibly. "There was . . . a . . . uh . . ."

"Stalker," Étienne blurted. "Krysta acquired an Internet

stalker who lost his head over her beauty and cleverness and we feared he might harm you in his desire to get to her."

Krysta sent him a relieved smile, then nodded somberly.

Sean pursed his lips and watched his parents.

Martin looked down at Evie. "I like him. He thinks fast on his feet."

She nodded.

They knew he was bullshitting?

Hoping Krysta wouldn't kick his ass later, Étienne did what he had sworn he wouldn't do tonight and read her parents' minds. He had intended to let them get to know him the regular way without peeking into their thoughts and using whatever he found there to manipulate them into liking him. But he needed to know what it was they thought they knew.

Evie proved to be as difficult to read as her daughter. But Martin . . .

Étienne sucked in a breath.

"What?" Krysta asked.

"They know."

"Know what?"

"Everything."

"About us? What, are you reading their minds?"

"Yes."

She turned to her mother. "You know we're engaged?"

Evie's eyes widened. "You're engaged?" Squealing, she yanked Krysta into a hug and jumped up and down. "My baby's engaged! Congratulations! We just thought you were lovers."

Sean laughed.

Étienne kept his eyes on their father.

Martin knew everything. He knew Krysta had spent the last six years hunting vampires, something she thought she had successfully kept from them. He knew Sean had helped her. He knew Étienne had saved her ass. More than once. He knew they had been battling soldiers. And he knew Étienne was immortal.

Sort of. He thought Étienne was a "good vampire."

Evie released her daughter and hugged Étienne.

Surprised, he wrapped his arms around her and gingerly hugged her back.

"Congratulations," she said.

"Thank you." He met Martin's gaze. "I wanted to seek your permission before I asked her, but circumstances were such that I could not," he admitted. And, damn it, his accent had just gotten thicker and his speech had reverted to the more formal tones of his youth.

Krysta eyed him curiously. "Everything okay?"

Hell, no.

Her mother backed away, face still bright with a grin.

"Krysta," Étienne asked (casually he hoped), "what did you say your parents' gifts were?"

"My mother is empathic and my dad is precognitive."

"He can see the future?"

"Yes. Why?"

"Because he has been seeing yours quite clearly for some time now."

She looked at Martin. "What do you mean?"

"They know you've been hunting vampires."

Her parents nodded.

Krysta shook her head. "No, they don't. No way."

Sean cleared his throat. "Um . . . Krysta . . . Étienne just said they know you've been hunting vampires and they didn't flinch or frown or make a cuckoo sign with their fingers. They nodded. I think that pretty much confirms it."

Krysta kept shaking her head. "No. They would've stopped me."

Her mother shrugged. "Why do you think we refused to pay your and Sean's college tuition?"

"You didn't refuse to pay it. You *couldn't* pay it. You lost everything when the stock market tanked in 2008."

Evie waved a hand in a pshaw gesture. "Martin saw that coming from a mile away, as well as the value it would regain over the next few years. We're actually quite wealthy now. But we knew the only way we could reduce the time you spent risking your life hunting vampires was to ensure that you had to work as many hours as possible to cover rent and help Sean pay his tuition after you dropped out your junior year."

Martin nodded. "I didn't foresee Michael's death, baby. I'm sorry." He met Étienne's gaze. "But I did foresee Étienne and how happy he would make you." He smiled at Krysta. "If we had come up with a way to keep you from hunting vampires, you never would have met him. So we settled for doing what we could to limit your hours, so to speak."

"You know I'm immortal," Étienne asked, hardly able to believe it, "and still approve of our impending marriage?"

"Yes," he responded simply.

Evie nodded. "So?" She turned to Krysta and Sean and rubbed her hands together with anticipation. "Let's see 'em."

Krysta and Sean exchanged a glance.

"See what?" Krysta asked.

"Your fangs."

The siblings looked equally astonished.

"You know about that, too?" Sean asked.

She nodded. "I've been trying to get a glimpse of them ever since you arrived."

"You're not upset?" Krysta asked.

"That we don't have to worry about our children ever getting sick or dying? That you'll be young and healthy forever? No."

Martin nodded. "Or that you'll both spend eternity with someone you love? Someone who makes you happy?"

"No," Evie said again.

"Hell, no," Martin seconded.

"Wait," Sean said. "Are you saying I'm going to marry an immortal, too?"

"Yes," Martin stated with confidence.

"Who is she?"

He shrugged. "I don't know. I've never seen her outside of the visions."

Evie leaned toward her children and waggled her eyebrows. "So? What are you waiting for? Flash me some fangs."

Krysta and Sean exchanged another glance, then peeled their lips back from their gums, let their fangs descend, and snarled.

Evie clapped, her eyes bright with excitement.

Smiling, Martin again offered his hand to Étienne. "Welcome to the family."

Étienne shook it, not needing precognition to know he would enjoy being part of it.

Krysta caught his eye and winked as she continued to growl and ham it up for her mother. *I love you.*

He smiled. *I love you, too.*

"Ooh! Marty, look!" Evie said with excitement. "Her eyes are glowing! Isn't she pretty?"

Étienne laughed as Krysta rolled her glowing eyes.

Don't miss the next
Immortal Guardians novel by
Dianne Duvall,
coming in October 2014!

And catch up on the previous
books in the series . . .

Darkness Dawns

Once, Sarah Bingham's biggest challenge was making her students pay attention in class. Now, after rescuing a wounded stranger, she's landed in the middle of a battle between corrupt vampires and powerful immortals who also need blood to survive. Roland Warbrook is the most compelling man Sarah has ever laid hands on. But his desire for her is mingled with a hunger he can barely control . . .

In his nine centuries of immortal existence, no woman has tempted Roland as much as Sarah. But asking her to love him is impossible—when it means forfeiting the world she's always known, and the life he would do anything to protect . . .

> "These dark, kick-ass guardians
> can protect me any day!"
> —Alexandra Ivy

Night Reigns

Ami isn't much for trusting strangers. She has a hard time trusting anyone. But she's no coward, and she's no pushover in the protection department either. So when she comes across a mysterious warrior taking on eight deranged vampires on his own, she doesn't hesitate to save his bacon. Of course, that was before she realized what one little rescue would get her into . . .

Marcus Grayden has been an Immortal protector of humanity for eight hundred years, and he's not interested in backup. From the moment Ami arrives in his life, he can't deny that she's strong, smart, and extremely skilled at watching his back. But she's also destroying his protective solitude and stirring desires he can't bear to awaken. After all, whatever her secrets—how can she defeat death itself?

"A thrilling and chilling new paranormal series.
Fantastic!"
—*Romantic Times*

"Whizzing along at light speed . . .
this sophomore effort sizzles."
—*Publishers Weekly*

Phantom Shadows

Dr. Melanie Lipton is no stranger to the supernatural. She knows immortals better than they know themselves, right down to their stubborn little genes. So although a handsome rogue immortal seems suspicious to her colleagues, Sebastien Newcombe intrigues Melanie. His history is checkered, his scars are impressive, and his ideas are daring. But it's not his ideas that have Melanie fighting off surges of desire . . .

Bastien is used to being the bad guy. In fact, he can't remember the last time he had an ally he could trust. But Melanie is different—and under her calm, professional exterior he senses a passion beyond anything in his centuries of experience. Giving in to temptation is out of the question—he can't put her in danger. But she isn't asking him . . .